THE NEW LIFE

The New Life

Tom Crewe

Chatto & Windus
LONDON

1 3 5 7 9 10 8 6 4 2

Chatto & Windus, an imprint of Vintage, is part of the Penguin Random House group of companies whose addresses can be found at global.penguinrandomhouse.com

Penguin
Random House
UK

First published by Chatto & Windus in 2023

penguin.co.uk/vintage

A CIP catalogue record for this book is available from the British Library

HB ISBN 9781784744694
TPB ISBN 9781784744700

Typeset in 12/18pt Minion Pro by Jouve (UK), Milton Keynes
Printed and bound in Great Britain by Clays Ltd, Elcograf S.p.A.

The authorised representative in the EEA is Penguin Random House Ireland, Morrison Chambers, 32 Nassau Street, Dublin D02 YH68

Penguin Random House is committed to a sustainable future for our business, our readers and our planet. This book is made from Forest Stewardship Council® certified paper.

MIX
Paper from
responsible sources
FSC
www.fsc.org
FSC® C018179

For John and Deborah, my parents
and for Angela Baker (1942–2013), in fulfilment of a promise

Life aroused curiosity . . . It was an epoch of experiment, with 'some achievement and some remorse.

Holbrook Jackson, The 1890s

Part One
June–August 1894

I

He was close enough to smell the hairs on the back of the man's neck. They almost tickled him, and he tried to rear his head, but found that he was wedged too tightly. There were too many bodies pressed heavily around him; he was slotted into a pattern of hats, shoulders, elbows, knees, feet. He could not move his head even an inch. His gaze had been slotted too, broken off at the edges: he could see nothing but the back of this man's head, the white margin of his collar, the span of his shoulders. He was close enough to smell the pomade, streaks of it shining dully at the man's nape; clingings of eau de cologne, a tang of salt. The suit the man was wearing was blue-and-grey check. The white collar bit slightly into his skin, fringed by small whitish hairs. His ears were pink where they curved at the top. His hat – John could see barely higher than the brim – was dark brown, with a band in a lighter shade. His hair was brown too, darker where the pomade was daubed. It had recently been cut: a line traced where the barber had shaped it.

John could not move his head. His arms were trapped at his sides; there were bodies pressing from right and left, from behind, in front. He flexed his fingers – they brushed coats, dresses, satchels, canes, umbrellas. The train carriage rattled in its frame, thudded on the track, underground. The lights wavered, trembling on the cheekbone of the man in front. John hadn't noticed that, hadn't noticed he could see the angle of the man's jaw and the jut of his cheekbone. There was the hint of a moustache. Blackness rushed past the windows. The floor roared beneath his feet.

He was hard. The man had changed position, or John had. Perhaps it was only a jolt of the train. But someone had changed their position. The man's jacket scratched at John's stomach – he felt it as an itch – and his buttocks brushed against John's crotch, once, twice, another time. John was hard. It was far too hot in the train, far too crowded. The man came closer, still just within the realm of accident, his buttocks now pressed against John's crotch. John's erection was cramped flat against his body. The man and he were so close it was cocooned between them. Surely he could feel it? A high, vanishing feeling travelled up from John's groin, tingling in his fingertips and at his temples. He could not get away, could not turn his head, could only smell the hairs on the back of the man's neck, see the neat line of his collar, the redness on the tops of his ears, could only feel himself hard, harder than before, as though his body were concentrating itself, straining in that one spot. Surely he could feel it? John felt panicked; sweat collected in his armpits. He dreaded the man succeeding in pivoting about, skewering the other passengers with his elbows, shouting something, the carriage turning its eyes, a gap opening round his telltale shame. And yet he knew that he did not want it to stop, that he could not escape the grip of this terrible excitement.

The man began to move. At first John was not certain, he thought again that it might be the jolting of the train. He had been willing the hardness away, counting from a hundred in his head, breathing slowly through his teeth, when he felt the slightest movement, as though the man were pushing back against his erection, as though he were gently tilting against it, rising and falling on his toes. John's first sensation was a rush of dread, followed quickly by a rush of something else, that same high, vanishing feeling running through his fingers and up to his temples. He had no control. He was crowded on all sides – he was fixed at the centre of a mass of bodies, his entire consciousness constricted, committed to this small circle of subtle movement. This man's buttocks, pressed so tightly against him it almost hurt, moving up and down. A bead of sweat, released from his armpit, ran quickly and coldly down his side. He tried to look about him, at the other passengers, but could not: instead he gazed frantically, surrenderingly, at the man's collar, the redness on his ears. Was that a smile, creeping to the edge of the moustache? And still it went on, unmistakable now, the rising and falling, the pressure, almost painful, moving up the length of him, to the tip and down again. He breathed heavily through his nose, breathed heavily onto the man's neck. He wished he could move his arms, that he could move anything at all: that his whole being were not bent so terrifyingly on this sensation, this experience, that he could for a moment place himself outside it. He breathed heavily again, saw how his breath flattened the whitish hairs on the back of the man's neck. His face hurt. He felt a strange pressure under his ears. He swallowed, took another breath. Pomade and eau de cologne, cigarette smoke, salt. Up and down, the pressure dragged painfully to the tip, down again. He was sinking under it. He could barely breathe.

The train slowed. They were coming to a stop. He gasped onto the man's neck. He longed for escape, for it to be over. Up and down, up and down, pleasure lancing through his body. The light changed; he saw over the man's shoulder the brighter lights of a platform. He tried to step backwards, could not, yet. He heard the doors being opened, heard the aggravated noise of the platform, waited for the pressure to ease, for movement in the carriage, for people to depart. He longed to turn his head. But more people were pouring in, more darkness, black pressure: umbrellas, canes, satchels, dresses, coats. He and the man were forced even closer than before; he could feel the full warmth of the man's body, the climbing curve of his back, the shoulders braced against his. And his lips were nudged onto the man's neck; he felt the hairs on his lips, tasted the pomade and the eau de cologne. The man was still tilting against him; they were moving together now, in a slow, crushed dance, rising and falling in time.

The train pushed off, the lights quivered. It was unbearably hot. He felt faint-headed, almost in pain. And then he felt the man's hand, a hand, unbuttoning him, felt the slight opening, an access of air, his erection pressing forward to fill it. Panic, a terrible excitement. And then the man's hand, a hand, wriggling into the gap, struggling into it; he felt the wait of seconds to be unbearable as the hand fought through the stiffness of the tweed, found the second opening in his drawers. And then it was in, the hand, was closing round it. His eyes were closed by fear; the man's neck was slippery beneath his lips. The carriage rattled in its frame, the lights shot darts behind his eyelids. The hand closed round it, he felt each finger find its place, begin to pull the flesh tight, to release, to guide it down into some sort of tenderness, to draw it tight again. He could barely breathe. He felt stretched tight, stretched beyond endurance. His body ached. Up and down, up and down. Fingers spanned the length of him, pulled tight, pulled faster. His hands were suddenly free, he had them on the man's hips, was reaching up into the damp warmth inside his jacket, feeling his ribs beneath his shirt. Then down, fumbling with his buttons, cupping the swell of his cock. His hand was in the man's trousers, the cock warm in his hand, he rubbed the head with his thumb. It was happening so fast now, up and down, faster and faster. Rising in him, through his fingertips, up to his neck, under his ears, at his temples. He was gasping. The man's neck was wet beneath his lips.

It was like the pumping of blood from a split vein, a deep wound. He was woken by the violence of it, helplessly halfway. He squeezed his eyes shut. Air seeped past his gritted teeth and escaped at the corners of his mouth. He lay still a long moment, waiting for his nightshirt to be weighted onto his leg, for the slime to settle on his skin and begin to trickle. He was far too hot – his legs were slick with sweat, wet behind the kneecaps. Catherine was asleep, her face composed against the pillow. He peeled back the coverlet and swung his legs over the side, spreading his toes on the floorboards. The mess on the front of his shirt seemed almost to gleam; he could see one large patch, and other, smaller ones, a succession of smears. He pinched the fabric to hold it away from him and then with his other hand pulled the shirt forward from the back, over his head – this was the method he had developed after too many times pulling it up over his face, dragging the mess into his beard – and sat naked on the bed. His cock, struggling to keep its shape, drifted drunkenly between his thighs, sticky at the tip. He held it a moment, letting it cool between his fingers. The darkness in the room was filmy, as if the small amount of light leaking through the curtains was slowly percolating it. His body was luminous; his legs and arms, even his shrinking, sluggish cock, had a greeny Renaissance sheen, like some dying Christ. He felt obvious, transparent, sacrificial, sat naked on the bed. His head hurt; his eyes were sore. Emissions exhausted him.

It must be early in the morning. Too early for the servants, who might otherwise be heard scuttling on the corridor. He looked at his nightshirt, puddled on the floor, and thought again of them having to wash it, stiff and yellow, starched with their master's seed, four or five days a week. A succession of pungent patches, smears. He could hardly bring himself to look at Susan, who he knew collected the dirty things. If they talked about it downstairs, it was possible only that they chuckled over Mr and Mrs Addington's honeymooning still, but he felt sure that they would be able to tell the difference between marital possession, even excessively practised, and incontinence. Servants knew more of these things as a rule, and he remembered hearing that Susan had older brothers. Did she think of them as she handled this forty-nine-year-old infant's underthings? Ask herself whether they too, her handsome brothers, were victims to shaming impulse? Perhaps it satisfied her to decide they were not.

It was especially bad now. He blamed the heat, which inflamed him. He had not masturbated yet, but he could not go on very much longer without doing so. It was something he did only in his greatest extremity, pleasurably – pointless to deny it – but furtively, furiously, fearful of discovery by Catherine or one of the children (particularly when they had actually been children, forever stumbling into his study) or a servant, a pretty Susan backing into the room with arms full of fresh linen, to find sir hunched over himself, softly gibbering. And yet he would still do it, in extremity, discounting even the cost to his health.

How to define extremity? The greatest extremity? Lust, not as quickened heartbeat or lurch into dizzy possibility, but as lagging sickness, a lethargy. Lust as slow poisoning. Lust as a winter coat worn in summer, never to be taken off. Lust as a net, cast wide, flashing silver, impossible to pull in. Lust as a thousand twitching, tightening strings, sensitive to every breeze. Lust as a stinking, secret itch. Lust carried leadenly in the day, dragged to bed. Lust at four in the morning, spent chokingly into a nightshirt. Lust as a liquid mess, dragged into your beard, drying into tendrils, the smell trapped in your nostrils.

It was lust that used to drive him to sleep with his wife, nervously mounting her as one would an unfamiliar horse, sensitive to every tremor and shifting movement, rucking up her nightdress and shuddering into her. He had tried to bury his lust in her, to stake it and walk away. This was what he had been urged to do. It was on doctor's orders that he had married her. But they had agreed, after their second daughter was born, to stop. Years passed, and he was ready to split his head, and had crawled onto her again. There was another pregnancy. And so they had ended – ended it – with three girls, a family. And still he yearned, wanted, itched.

A sound stood out in the darkness. The clop-clap of hooves. He gently levered himself off the bed and walked to the far window, parting the curtain with a finger and putting his eye to the gap. A cart passed on the far side of the street, the horse kicking up dust, the driver with his cap pulled down against a band of sunlight. He followed its progress as far as he could, and then turned back into the room, briefly blinded by dazzling, dancing dark. There was a basin in the corner of the room, filled the night before. He dabbed a sponge and cleaned himself, wiping away the last oozings and scrubbing at the stuck-down hairs on his thighs. Another cart went past the house in the other direction and the curtain shifted in its wake, driving an avenue of light briefly across the floor. He towelled himself and squeezed out the sponge. At the same time he realised Catherine was awake, pulling herself up by her elbows, her face a shade of dark above the white of her nightdress, the collapsed bed linen.

'What is it?' There was sleep in her voice. She was a sound sleeper – normally he could wash and dress without her ever knowing he'd woken prematurely.

'A spill.' This was their word for it: a soft, married word, evoking nothing of its violence, the stuff that was wrenched from him. He moved towards the bed as he spoke, placing a hand over his privates when he saw a small reflex of anxiety quiver her face. 'I am going to get dressed.'

'It is early, John.'

'I won't sleep.' He picked up his nightshirt and turned away, conscious of presenting her with his back and buttocks, the shadow of his testes, feeling alien to himself. Not sure whether she was still watching, he took his dressing gown from its hook and put it on. Then he let himself out, stepping softly across the corridor – still no sound of

9

servants – and into his dressing room. He lit the lamp, picked out a suit, and was half-dressed when he found himself becoming hard again. Without hesitating, he unbuttoned his trousers, tugged his cock through the gap, and began to pump it with savage determination, groaning as he spewed into a handkerchief.

Ten minutes later, John Addington, fixing his hat on his head, stepped out into the clean June sunshine and began to walk, accompanied only by the shreds and tatters of his dream.

II

Henry Ellis was standing at the window in his wedding suit. He had been fretting his tie when he first noticed her, stalled further up the street in much the same posture as now: legs planted far apart, hands splayed on thighs, head hanging loosely between them, brown hair tumbling into the dust. While he was watching she had roused herself, lifting her skirt loosely in one hand and starting forward as though wading through water, taking long steps over the cracks of sunlight opened up on the road. And then she had stopped here, in the shade beneath his window, and dropped her head again – he could see the rise and fall of her breathing. Her skirt was stretched around her, a pitched tent.

It was early and the morning maintained an unsullied stillness. The cracks of sunlight were broadening into crevasses. His tie was still undone. Edith would be awake. There was a cup of coffee going cold somewhere. The woman tried to stand up, struggling under an invisible weight; she buckled, effortfully righted herself, her fingers searching against air, then staggered in a wide, ludicrous circle as though noosed. Her knees gave way; she collapsed into an ugly curtsey, stumbled, flailed, and fell across the kerb on the opposite side.

From his position at the window it was hard to judge how much it might have hurt – the fall had been soundless and so weightless, a mime. She did not get up. He looked intently, at the upturned soles and rubbed heels of her boots, the undersides of the toes edged by sunlight, the rest of her in shadow; at the skirt flattened under her, puffed at the back, her hair fallen over her face. Her breathing wasn't visible now, but he could not believe she was dead. Dead drunk, poor wretch. He began to fiddle with his tie, knotting it with nervous fingers. She still hadn't got up. He could be outside in a minute; less if he didn't lock the door first. His flat was on the second floor, he usually took the stairs two steps at a time. He finished with his knotting. His stomach made a draining sound. What if she were to vomit, or be bloody from her fall? He was in his wedding suit. He could change, but it had taken him an hour to get ready, and she might need to be taken to a hospital, in which case he would miss the wedding altogether.

He put his forehead to the glass, peered. The knot of his tie pressed hard at his throat and the window wetted his head. The sunlight had crept up her boots a fraction. He looked down the street both ways, seeing no one. The windows of the house opposite, in whose shade she mostly lay, were curtained against her. He consulted his watch. He reasoned: a fall like that could not kill a woman, no matter how inebriated. She had not struck her head, as far as he had been able to tell. Perhaps she'd cracked a rib on the kerb. That would explain her taking some minutes to collect her breath, fearful of movement. She would not die of it. Probably she did not even feel it yet. Likely she was just sleeping. During his medical training, he had seen women like her in their homes, in a screaming, hurling frenzy – he had been called out by neighbours, a frightened husband on more than one occasion – only to watch them sink abruptly into unconsciousness, a silence so irrevocable they might have been dead.

Satisfied, he turned back into the flat, found his cold coffee and sipped it wincingly, looked in the mirror and smoothed his beard. He revisited his tie, brushed his hat and his boots. He thought about eating something and decided against it, used the closet, dismissed the urge to take up his book. Finally the sound of traffic in the street drove him back to the window – half-expecting a hospital van, he saw instead a departing cart and an empty, sunny spot where the woman had been. Checking his watch again, he put on his boots and left the flat. Outside he looked left and right, crossed the street and stooped to examine the kerb. There was no blood, only a small piece of jewellery trapping light, so cheap it resembled a fragment of painted eggshell. He picked it up and slipped it in his trouser pocket before setting off in the direction of the register office, feeling conspicuous in his suit, walking quickly to avoid the notice of his neighbours.

The register office was a tall, wide building, made taller and wider by the flight of steps leading up to it. When Henry arrived, Edith was leaning against a pillar, washed in bright sunshine, eyes closed, her hat held in front of her waist and her head tilted back. She was wearing an outfit he'd seen before, a neat grey skirt and jacket; a gold brooch appeared to be her only concession to the occasion. Nearby was his best man, Jack Relph, taller even than Henry, wearing the same green velvet jacket as always. He was talking animatedly with the only other guest, Edith's friend Mary.

'That is freedom you can feel on your face,' Henry called to Edith from the bottom of the steps.

'Will it ever come again? I am savouring it.' She spoke loudly but only opened her eyes afterwards, slowly, as though they had been pressed tightly shut by the sun. 'Hello, dear boy.'

She came down to him and he stopped a few steps short of her, making them momentarily the same height. She leaned forward perilously, throwing both arms round his neck and kissing him on the cheek.

'You look wonderfully yourself,' he said, taking her by the shoulders and passing her back onto her step. He was pleased she hadn't made any special efforts – her dark hair was combed the same way, back from her forehead to form a sort of crest; her complexion was as fresh as ever, and her eyes – how could they have been different? and yet he was pleased – contained their usual grey gleam.

'And you look very fine.' She tugged playfully at his lapel. 'A new suit! Is it horribly uncomfortable?'

'Horribly. Freedom lost for freedom gained.' He smiled, but felt again and all at once his discomfort – the tightness of his trousers, the pinching tie, the itch of his hat on his brow. The sun lay heavily on his shoulders. Nearby, a volley of pigeons fired into the air. He looked back at the street, at the clattering traffic and the people slowing their walk to try and spy an emerging or entering couple, and felt a keen desire to move inside. He glanced at his watch.

'I hope it wasn't expensive,' Edith said. 'And yes, we'd better.'

As they turned, Jack jogged down eagerly, clapped Henry on the shoulder and exclaimed over the suit. Mary reached and kissed him on the cheek; she'd only ever shaken his hand before and he felt grateful to her. All four of them were briefly occupying different levels and heights, casting broken, blended shadows down the steps.

They went in – the entrance hall dark and cool, muffled and municipal-smelling – stated their business and were directed down an even darker corridor. Edith had taken Henry's arm and with her small tight grip seemed to communicate some of her confidence in the rightness of what they were doing. He drew her close, attempting to do the same. The registrar met them outside his room and explained their various responsibilities. Henry looked not at him but at Edith, who was following every word, nodding vigorously like a child who has accepted the explanation long before it has ended.

Listening, he was reminded of the great weight they were willingly taking onto their backs, to be carried out into the sunshine. It was curious, at last, to think of Edith being linked to him by anything other than her own free will, that they would have an identity beyond the one they had chosen for themselves: in records, rolls, shopkeepers' books, contracts, certificates; reduced to paper and ink, births and deaths. But he felt proud too – proud, he supposed, in the way of most men on their wedding day – that this woman, with her grey eyes and crest of dark hair, in a neat skirt and jacket with a gold brooch, had chosen him, judged him worthy. And even though he knew how little looks had to do with it, he could not help being – as he supposed most men were – more than usually aware of himself, of his physical self, presented to the woman beside him, but also to the registrar, to Jack and Mary, to the passers-by who would stop to watch when they came outside: here I am, a man, with my height, my long arms and slender fingers, my long face and high forehead, my black beard; this woman will know me, see me from all angles, see beneath this too-tight suit, touch my skin where you cannot. It was a heady feeling, and surprising, because truthfully he was not like most men on their wedding day. He and Edith were going much further together, taking on the usual forms only to show how they might be stretched to fit new purposes. He watched Edith nodding along and saw how excited she was. He was excited too.

The room was large, with a window at the back looking onto a garden shaded from the sun, a strip of cornflower sky above it. The ceremony took a long time; he was so concentrated on answering at the right moments and with the right words that each separate delay was intolerable. His voice wavered and he could not look the registrar in the eye, choosing instead to focus on a section of gold picture frame to the right of his head. Edith answered clearly and happily, seeming to gather the deeper, secret implications of the registrar's words into her smile, conveying them in the turn of her head from one man to the other. Henry's hands twitched for the security of hers and he reached for them the moment they were pronounced husband and wife; at the same time she moved forward for a kiss and he had to bend quickly to meet it. When he looked up he saw Jack and Mary standing in their seats, greyish and indistinct in the light of the window, their applause resounding in the large dim room like the beating of wings.

Afterwards they went to a café for breakfast. Entering, coming up against its warm, moist air, its yielding wall of chatter and whistling kettles and clinking cutlery, was like being prodded sharply awake, reality pushing in. Henry felt shy again in his suit, folding himself into his seat and draping a napkin over his shirtfront, that odd sensation of pride already dribbling away.

They were served coffee and toast. He'd worried about what sorts of topics might be appropriate to the occasion, but apparently no one else had. Mary and Edith were discussing the Society; Jack wanted to know about the essay he'd just written. Later the conversation flowed back into one channel: Edith was describing her next project, a lecture series on the modern woman, which she would deliver as Mrs Henry Ellis. The lectures would cover relations between the sexes; love and marriage; work and family-raising.

'It's only been an hour,' laughed Jack, showing his enormous, tooth-filled smile. It stretched almost to the lobes of his ears, which sat stiffly on the sides of his head like the folded wings of a bat.

'The bookings are for November. That will be nearly six months.' Edith's mouth set firmly. 'And anyhow it is a matter of argument, of stating clear principles.'

'What about children? You can't know the first thing about bringing up children.' Jack looked over at Henry with another smile. The words, in his deep lazy voice, seemed to loll out of his mouth.

'Experience can come later,' Edith said, also looking at Henry, 'when the suppositions are good.'

'It's not as if Edith hasn't read a great deal,' added Mary. She was pale, paler than usual, beneath her pile of red hair.

'I bow to you,' Jack said.

'So you should. I know her best.'

Jack's eyebrows darted.

'I don't understand children,' Henry said. 'I should like to understand children better.'

'Of course,' Edith said, fixedly spreading butter on her toast.

Henry took his hands out from his pockets, in one of which he had been absently rubbing the broken piece of jewellery. He stretched his fingers on the table and hooked his feet behind the legs of his chair. 'The first time my father took me away to sea on his ship – I was seven, or I was when we set off – there was a cat, that the men kept on board. A tortoiseshell cat. They all petted it and threw scraps and so on. It used to walk along the rail of the ship, like on a wall or a fence. Sea legs, I remember my father saying. One morning I was up very early – I enjoyed reading on deck when there was still hardly anyone around – and the cat was walking along the side. And I went over and pushed it into the sea.'

There was a gasp. 'What happened?'

'I only looked for a moment. I went back to my book. It wasn't saved.'

Edith was looking at him warily, as if he might be about to say or do something else unexpected. 'Why did you?'

'I don't know. I have never regretted anything more in my life.'

They parted outside. Jack offered to walk Mary home, leaving Henry and Edith standing in a wedge of shade on the pavement.

'Is Mary all right?' he asked.

Edith smiled. 'Yes, she's all right.'

They went over their plans for the next morning – the time of their train, where they would meet, what they should bring – not because they hadn't already, but because they needed something to say. He felt unmoored, as if the two of them had floated out to some glassy point beyond reach or rescue, even as people continued to walk past and the café burbled behind. He took hold of Edith's hand.

'Goodbye, dear boy.'

'Goodbye, Mrs Ellis.'

She laughed, corkscrewing her body away. Then she was serious again. 'Does it feel strange to you?'

'It's strange to think of it being done, and everything –' he gestured vaguely towards the café – 'being the same.'

'It won't always. And it is different for us, already.'

'Are you sure, already?'

'You are wearing a new suit. That is change enough for any day.'

He laughed. 'The New Life.'

'The New Life.' She let go of his hand. 'I will see you tomorrow at ten o'clock.'

'You will.'

She smiled up at him. 'Don't kill any cats.'

He laughed again, opened his arms wide: 'The New Life!'

She turned, laughing too, and began to walk away, raising her small hand in its glove. 'Goodbye, Mr Ellis.'

'Goodbye, Mrs Ellis.'

He watched her go, bowed against the sunlight, and revelled in his great luck.

III

It was a bright, warm day, the warmth as yet more suggestion than reality, the clear early-morning air feeling veined by it, as though it were heating up in the running, like water in a faucet. It was an effect of the sunshine; everything was softly gazed at, not yet pinioned, borne down on – the shadows seemed depthless, accidental variants of the same easy light. Trees stirred awake. The occasional passers-by, magnified in their isolation, walked less urgently, demanding less of life.

These streets would be clogged with traffic within the hour. John had hated traffic as a child: the thickened, tense aliveness of it, the horses stamping and shirking, shit dropping between their legs, the drivers shouting across at each other, discreetly spitting, wrenching the reins in sudden gusts of desperate activity; all those people trapped barely above ground, jammed up against crates and animals and bits of furniture. Almost his only memory of his mother was of sitting with her in their carriage, about a year before she died. She had been wearing a pink dress; he could not have been older than three. The driver briefly lost control of the horses coming down a hill. The carriage had begun to lurch and pitch; he remembered a feeling of weightlessness, his stomach jumping, as if they were taking flight from the road, or were about to drop beneath it. And her grip, dreadfully tight on his shoulder. But that was all. Everything else – her face, the sound of her voice – was lost entirely, preserved only as a sort of mental impress, the sense of his once having seen it, heard it, tangible and intangible as an unremembered dream. He only ever thought about her in the summer, though she'd died in November. The summer months were when he and his father used to visit her grave. For years he was too short to look over the railings behind which she was kept, so he had looked between them, the iron cool in his hands, at the grass as it gathered and leaned over the tablet, at the water that collected thinly in the letters of her name. He had always been very conscious of his father watching him, and worried about how he should appear. As long as he kept his face empty of expression, he could look only at the grass and the water and his father seemed satisfied. Now Dr Addington lay in the same grave, and John was watched closely still.

When he reached Hyde Park, the walks were quiet, though there was a stream of men heading for the Serpentine, bags banging silently against their thighs or rolled under their arms. John slackened his pace, falling a little behind them; it did not do to look too eager. Besides, this way had its compensations. He let his eyes range over the men ahead of him, rapidly alighting on differences, distinctions, but also dwelling on the constantly surprising, reassuring – surprising and reassuring for the same reason, for the pleasures they vouchsafed – similarities: the twist of hair on a nape; the way loose collars sometimes showed a glimpse of naked shoulders; the way trousers encircled a waist, brought out its beauty, like a bracelet on a woman's wrist; the way these men walked, unselfconsciously, slouching a little, their bodies tipping from side to side, foot to foot, sometimes with a childish little jump in their step.

Another thing – as he neared the water, his whole person enlarging as with a gulp of clear mountain air – was the way they sat, scattered over the grass: the spread or arch of their legs and all that begging space between, the way they hugged and gripped themselves, the coiled energy in the poses. And – as he moved a little way off, sitting down against a tree and opening a book as his defence – the way they undressed: the rough, careless way they pulled off their shirts, dragging them over their heads, sometimes bending so that the shirt slid right off onto the ground, the knobs of the spine prominent under the skin; the practised, unthinking way they unfastened their trousers, tugged them down, often while gazing out across the water or up into the trees; how they stepped out of their drawers, if they had them, like out of a bath, carefully, raising their knees high. How they stood, in their nakedness, that very first moment – what they did with their hands, sometimes so free as to run them through their hair, or place them on their hips, while they spied where the shore was emptiest. And their cocks: delicate, caressable things, so simple in the daylight, making no claim. The way they nodded and rubbed against the slouching, jostling testes as the men walked down to the water.

'Poem' was Whitman's word for a man's cock: 'This poem drooping shy and unseen that I always carry, and that all men carry.' John wondered how Whitman described to himself the tremor in a man's buttocks as he stepped down towards water, their heart-seizing paleness.

He could not live without these early mornings by the river in the park, the two hours allotted for swimming. To sit here, as he did now, to watch the men arrive, claim their small patch, put down their bags, undress, walk down to the water; most of all to see them return to dry land, clumsy as they staggered onto the shore, the water pouring off them, running in rivulets through their hair, through the hair on their legs, budding on the ends of their cocks, all of them shining in the light, as if light were the very thing they had bathed in, something sticking and clinging, was to come as close as he dared to his ideal. It was how he imagined Greece in the time of Plato. The dance of light, the sound of water; men in the company of men, nakedness carelessly worn; everything natural, pure; the clean pleasures of the body. He sometimes looked at these men, in these shining minutes snatched before they went away to their work, at their physiques moulded and stamped by labour, and saw in them another kind of life.

The grass beneath him was nicely damp. It must have just been cut – bits of it were sticking to his trousers and hands. He had never swum here, though he'd been sorely tempted; he could not, in the end, imagine undressing, leaving the land behind. A young man was crouching naked at the edge and cupping water to his face, slapping it on his chest and shoulders. His testes hung like a bunch of soft fuzzed fruit. John watched as he straightened, waded in, the water finally coming up to the top part of his buttocks, and then dived, surfacing a moment later, shaking his head, scattering pearls.

Three weeks ago, John had gone down to Cambridge, where his old friend Mark Ludding was professor of philosophy. The two of them had walked and talked, in their usual way. And then, after taking tea in Mark's study at Newnham, where Mark's wife Louisa was mistress, John had produced a copy of his *A Problem in Greek Ethics*, privately printed, passing it in its wrapping over the cups still standing on the desk. It was something remarkable – he was not being immodest in thinking so, or not only. The book was an account of Greek love. Of love between men, love of men, as it was practised in and celebrated by Hellas. John had been brave before in what he had written, however guardedly – about the nature of the passions in Greek poetry; about the fact (his discovery) that many of Michelangelo's sonnets were addressed to his friend Tommaso; about the manly love hymned by Whitman. He had certainly paid for it in sneers, jibes, implications. But he had never been so brave, so direct as this.

Before giving the book to Mark, he had pondered how much to say about its contents; at first he thought of saying nothing, but then began to fear that in his ignorance Mark might mention it to Louisa, or leave it somewhere in plain sight. So he found the words in the memory of their friendship.

'It is on an impossible subject,' he said.

'Impossible?' And then Mark's face cleared in understanding, only to darken again. The book, partly unwrapped, looked very small in his large hands, with their long fingernails. His beard, so grey now, reached down to touch it. 'You are going too far with me, Johnny,' he said.

'I know I am. But with whom else am I to go?'

'You do not have to go anywhere at all.' He clicked his tongue. His nails rapped on the cover. 'If I must read it, I will.' And then he placed the book in a drawer, pushed it shut. They arranged that Mark and Louisa would come to London for dinner in three weeks' time. Tomorrow. Mark had sent no word since.

John watched another man go down to the water, disappear under it, break the brilliant surface. His erection ached. The seat of his trousers was damp and sticking uncomfortably to his skin. The sun was stronger, the river leaching ever more of it into itself, so that the bobbing heads and shoulders had become almost indistinguishable, dark shapes on the diamond-cut water. There were fewer of them now. The grass was largely cleared of the mounds of caps, shirts, boots, trousers and drawers that had covered it. A trail of men led back towards the gate, where, if he concentrated, John could hear the dull chorus of traffic striking up. A man arrived, undressed with furious haste, and raced down to the water, throwing himself into it, arms looped over his head. He surfaced noisily, rubbing under his arms, sinking himself again, and then swam a few noisy strokes before returning to the shore, charging up it, towelling himself with determined energy, his glistening body shaking perceptibly. Finally, the tired clothes were pulled up and over. There was a poem in this, John thought. In this rapid transmutation from one thing, one century, to another, and then back again.

He watched the man depart, nimbling through the gold and green dapple. Then, once he could do so decently, he stood, putting away the book he had brought and brushing himself down, picking off individual stubs of grass. He turned onto the path, feeling, as always, relieved, but also wound to too high a pitch. His senses were pricked. The sunshine was harder and hotter.

A young man was at his side. John heard him only at the last moment – the onrush of his breathing.

'My name's Frank.'

He had clearly been in the water. His blond hair was dark and heavy with it, there was water beaded along his short moustache. His shirt was clinging to him in transparent patches. But John didn't recognise him; hadn't noticed him undress. Which dark shape had he been? Regret pierced him, even as he stood stock-still and fumbled for a response.

'Can I help you?'

'It's a lovely day,' the man said smilingly, rubbing the back of his neck. There was London in his accent, dragging on every word.

'It is.' John smiled back, and started to walk on toward the gate, as though this had been merely an exchange of pleasantries. He had been stopped before, never as many times as in his worst imaginings – only twice, in fact. Both times he had extricated himself quickly, almost run away, his head light and his pulse skipping. Neither time had the man been as beautiful as this.

Frank walked with him, stopping as he did. 'I saw you watching. No, no—'

John had taken fright, set off again. He felt the man's hand on his shoulder. The grip was gentle. He turned back, swallowing panic, looking into the beautiful face. 'No, no,' Frank repeated, something pained in his blue eyes. There was still water sheltering amid the hairs

24

on his chest, visible at the opening of his shirt. 'I saw you watching, nothing wrong with it. A lovely day. I only thought you might need a friend, keep you company.'

'That's kind,' John said. He felt his strength returning with the absurdity of his response. Perhaps the man was only slow. Perhaps it was funny. He disbelieved these thoughts as soon as he had them.

'Is it?' Frank smiled again; such a beautiful smile, the teeth a bright line under his moustache. 'It doesn't feel that way to me. Though I do believe in kindness, sir. That is something I believe in. There's precious little of it.'

People were walking past where they were islanded in the middle of the path. A dog hesitated over and dismissed John's ankles. Frank seemed completely at his ease. John looked round, to reassure himself that the world was carrying on, that it remained to be got back to. 'Well, thank you for the thought,' he brought out. He looked at Frank as if for permission to leave. There was no answering movement in his face, which had become thoughtful.

'Well shall we?'

'Shall we what?' The fear came back. Not the same fear exactly. He said it almost in a pant.

'Be friends.'

John looked away at the three children scattering that moment around them, the mother lightly laughing an apology. It was as if this man in front of him were an invisible door and he was paused on the threshold.

'There's no hurry,' Frank began again. 'I'm sure you've things to be getting on with. I'm not idle myself, but you must be a busy man. Wait a moment – here's my address.' And he passed John a neatly folded piece of paper, taken from his pocket. He fixed John's eye. 'It's not kindness though, sir. I don't know exactly what it is, when you make a friend. But I don't think it's kindness.'

The paper was warm in John's hand. 'Well, thank you again,' he said. He hated himself for saying this – felt that it wasn't interesting enough, that this man would not be interested by it. But Frank was already stepping away.

'Goodbye, sir. My reading's good, if you choose to write. You should have no worry on that account.'

'I won't.' John found himself smiling.

'Well then. What a nice thing this is. And on a day like today.' Frank pointed up to the sky with a grin. 'I almost fancy another dip. Goodbye for now.'

'Goodbye, Frank.'

As soon as he came out with it, he wondered at it: the use of the man's name. As though they really were friends, as though what had just taken place could be blithely counted among the haphazard happenings of a day. Frank seemed to appreciate it. He grinned again, doing a strange little jump, his arms pressed to his sides.

'Goodbye!'

And then he spun round and pretended to swim away along the path, bringing his arms up and over in alternating strokes, head bowed, cutting through the air. He didn't look back to see whether John was laughing.

IV

Henry woke the morning after his wedding a virgin still. While he washed at his basin, the light held behind the curtains falling onto his feet, he considered and then sheered away from the possibility that he might not be a virgin tomorrow. It threw a shadow across the simplicity of yesterday.

His sexual innocence was not of the stupid kind, the savourless, parched fruit of ignorance. He was not ignorant about or indifferent to the subject. In fact, Henry was unusually interested in issues relating to sex, which he took to be the central problem of life. This perception he traced first to Australia, where he had lived between the ages of seventeen and nineteen, serving, by strange fortune, as headmaster of a little school at Kanga Creek, a nothing town thrown like a pebble into the vast emptiness of New South Wales. It was on account of his father, a sea captain, that he was there: he had joined him on another of his voyages, but had grown shy of him, of the people on board the ship, of travel, and asked to be let off at Sydney, where he might find some work. It seemed very brave to him now – he had soon regretted it. Mr Tillnott, the Englishman who'd preceded Henry as headmaster of the school, had a daughter, Marie. It was of course irregular, to be seventeen years old and replacing in his post a man old enough to have a daughter of about the same age, but such things seemed, if not sensible, then possible, in that hugger-mugger place. Mr Tillnott had resigned his position on account of a falling-out with the authorities, but maintained a keen interest in an educational establishment so promisingly begun and invited Henry to visit him at his house every Sunday, where from a low sofa, sunburned, bald (where he was especially burned), and eloquent, he would denounce his rivals in the town, criticise the maladministration of the colony, as well as of the British government, and offer Henry advice as to how the school should be run in spite of these obstacles, emphasising the great opportunity he had been given, and the high trust he had received.

This was very dull, but Henry was so lonely, both at the school – it was in fact a single room under a shingled roof – and in his wooden cabin, that he passionately looked forward to walking to the house on a Sunday afternoon, to hanging up his hat in the hall, to being waited on by the servants, and to sitting in a halfway comfortable chair, nodding when Mr Tillnott's sentences required it. Being bored by a familiar Englishness was a great comfort to him, when at all other times he felt so terribly proximate to disaster – in the hot, dusty schoolroom, challenged by rows of vacant, dirty faces; alone in his hot, dusty cabin; abroad in the wide empty hostile spaces of the colony, where one could so easily lose the thread of civilisation. Being bored, Henry decided, *was* civilisation.

But boredom was not Marie Tillnott's friend, except perhaps as it served as a tutor for action. Her interest in Henry, evident to him once he had appeared at the house several times, was unnerving. She was not attractive: over-plump, with a bad complexion and features too much like her father's. But her interest gradually acquired a distinct appeal. It licked into existence a self-consciousness in him. He saw himself, for the first time, as the object of a woman's desire. Marie Tillnott was no longer Marie Tillnott. She was a symbol of sex, beckoning something forth. And – though he did not see this clearly until years afterwards – he was indubitably a symbol for her. For there was no romance. No hint of a courtship. No great politeness or attention paid. It was as if a flag had been run up to signal all this unnecessary, for the first message that Marie secretly passed to him assumed everything already. Henry read it with amazement and relief. She said only that she wanted them to undress and lie naked on their separate beds at four o'clock the following afternoon, thinking of each other. Nothing more. He could not guess what it had cost her, to write out her desire so plainly. He never did know.

He sent back a note of one line, agreeing, and the next day undressed in his cabin. It was summer and the cabin was stiflingly hot, so that it was a blessing to take off his clothes. He drew his curtains, but the daylight was so strong it formed a second frame at each window, where dust motes rolled and fell, rolled and fell. The room was scarcely darker. He stretched out on the bed as his watch struck four. His whole body was warm. Birds chirruped outside. He was hard. He lay there and tried to think of Marie, naked in her own room, but found, again, that what was exciting him was himself. His body, the substantial fact of it, his ticking heartbeat. The fact of his erection, pulling there at the centre of him. He looked at the blue vein that stood out on its side. His foreskin had rolled back and the head had a shine on it like silk. He looked at his chest, hairless but manly, its shape something a woman might try to discern beneath a shirt; observed his nipples, his thighs and legs and tall feet. He closed his eyes and followed the colours twisting under the lids, felt his body pulse, his erection pull. The air swelled with heat. Sweat ran down over his ribs. He rubbed the damp inside of his crotch and the back of his scrotum and smelled the dark sweat on his fingertips. He felt wondrously alive, like a marvellous secret kept and discovered by himself. And then after half an hour he got up and dressed again.

When he met Marie the next Sunday, there was a change. This thing, sex, flowed between them. It was present even during that afternoon's conversation with Mr Tillnott, like a rippling reflection thrown upon the wall. Afterwards, Marie passed him another note, asking that they repeat their arrangement. For a further two months, it continued. Each time, Henry lay down for half an hour with his erection; examined his body, breathed, familiarised himself with the push and pull of his blood. Finally, on the tenth week – he did not remember any particular reason, unless he had simply reached the limit of his resistance – he began to touch his cock lingeringly, tenderly; grasped it, felt its hardness, hesitated, tugged the skin, shuddered, tugged again, surrendered to a rhythm, shut his eyes. The spatter landed all the way up on his face, which had never happened before. He was shocked by it. The sour-sweet smell rushed. He had to wipe the mess off his face with his forearm – it was clinging to his eyebrows, strung over his nose. He felt immediately that everything had been spoiled. That sex, that vague, potent atmosphere, had condensed into one selfish, self-harming act – that he had sullied Marie Tillnott and the trust she had placed in him. That his body, too, had been sullied. When he received her next note, with its time and date, he wrote back a refusal. Marie did not reply. They still saw each other every Sunday, but the rippling, shimmering thing was gone, only a shade, a stain of it remaining.

Outside on the street, the other side of the globe and the other side of his life, some children were shouting. Staring into his basin, bringing handfuls of water to his face, an English sun warming his feet, Henry heard running, a jiggle of high-pitched words, and then quiet, broken shortly afterwards by the sound of wheels. He went back to his bed and lay down on the coverlet. He looked at himself: his chest, with its small hoarding of hair; his length of stomach; his puckered cock; his thighs and knees and tall feet, standing up on their heels, the toes serried like watchmen. He was fully conscious, now, of the error he had made then. And he had never forgotten those moments of time abandoned to his physical self, or forgotten that Marie Tillnott had enjoyed them too. That sense of himself, as a marvellous secret, persisted. It proved that sex was inherent human potential, an instinct existing independently in each person, women as well as men. His error had been to miscarry it – not by masturbation, though that was a waste of strength – but by surrendering to shame. He had seen this quite quickly, seen that the sex instinct might be a great engine for happiness, if only it could be liberated from shame. At first he hadn't known what to do with this thought. While he was still in Australia he began to read beyond the English and French literature that had filled his luggage. He purchased medical textbooks and sensed, as if through his fingertips as they turned the pages, the power of science to expose the truths of human nature. In his cabin at Kanga Creek he became enthusiastic about the future. His Christian faith boiled away in the heat of his reading, leaving almost unnoticeably, bit by bit, but he discovered something similar in his identification of a role for himself in the time to come. His determination to realise this role was the life spring concealed behind his shyness, the motive that, in his own mind, excused it – indeed had come to justify it, as a necessary shield against distraction.

When he returned to London – this was 1881 – he decided he would train as a doctor, and started the next year. His training took him into the homes of the poor. He saw how poverty by its unceasing pressure warped the relationships between the sexes. He met women whose bodies had been wracked by repeated pregnancies, their lives stretched so thin you could see right through to their end; saw the children, stunted and paled by their surroundings, bending to bad prospects. His reading expanded to cover this new ground. He became concerned with the provision of education, with the creation of instruments for public health; with birth control, the illegitimacy and divorce laws. He spied the problem of sex somewhere beneath them all, like a great rock whose scale and shape was forever obscured by the waves crashing and spraying against it. He tried to imagine the sea becalmed, the rock standing clear and comprehended.

His reading strained against his temperament and, while he was still a medical student, carried him into the company of others. The Society of the New Life held meetings every other week at a house leased on Doughty Street; several members lived there on communal principles (Henry once arrived early, to find one of the men brushing the step). There was usually a lecture, and a discussion to follow, and some kind of vote. Henry did not speak in meetings – nearly ten years later, it still did not occur to him to do so, even when he was frustrated or inspired and words bubbled on his tongue. He sometimes spoke them at home afterwards, pacing about his sitting room, great rushing sentences sweeping one after the other, his hands dug like trowels into his trouser pockets. Or he braced himself at his desk to write them out, more carefully and insistently, tightening and paring his argument, excising and starting over. He had a sheaf of notes like these, state-ments that detonated on the page without obvious cause, resounded without answer. But in meetings he did not speak. Only sat at the back of the room with its smell of well-trodden carpet and stacked Blue Books, sometimes whole rows between him and the rest of the group, one long leg crossed over the other, his head often as not propped on his curled fist, eyes fixed on his balanced foot, flexing his toes so that they showed in outline under the flagging leather. Listening and not speaking, arguments silently constructing themselves in his head. On municipalisation, nationalisation, mutualisation; criminal law or employment law, rational dress or vegetarianism. Like this, ideas worked their way under his skin, until they became part of his whole response to the world, tingling under the surface of everything, flar-ing like fever when he encountered some prejudice, some small

Comhairle Contae
Átha Cliath Theas
South Dublin County Council

Le Dea-Mhéin With Compliments

Comhairle Contae Átha Cliath Theas,
Halla an Chontae, Tamhlacht,
Baile Átha Cliath 24, D24YNN5

South Dublin County Council,
County Hall, Tallaght,
Dublin 24, D24YNN5

Fón - Tel: +353 1 414 9000
Rphost - Email: info@sdublincoco.ie
Idirlíon - Web: athcliaththeas.ie - sdcc.ie

Lean muid ar - Follow us on
Facebook, Twitter, YouTube
deisighdoshráid.ie - fixyourstreet.ie

Housing Customer Centre Opening

As part of our ongoing Customer Services and Digital Transformation Strategy, the new **Housing Customer Centre** will officially open on Wednesday, 12th July. The Customer Services desks in County Hall, Tallaght & Clondalkin will be closed from this date forward.

Access to the Housing Customer Centre will be by appointment only, to request a meeting, contact us on **01-4149000.**

Housing Services are easily accessible, 24/7 through our Housing Online Portal. **Scan the QR Code** to find out more, or visit: **www.sdcc.ie/en/ services/housing**

WWW.SDCC.IE

Comhairle Contae
Átha Cliath Theas
South Dublin County Council

How to make a Housing Maintenance Repair Request On-line

Tenants of South Dublin County Council should log their maintenance request through **Housing Online**. If you haven't already done so, you can register at Housing Online to set up your account by scanning the **QR code** or by visiting **https://hol.sdublincoco.ie**

If your request for works is an emergency, for example, sparking fuse board, or relates to works for a communal area please contact us by telephone on **01 414 9393**, our opening hours are **Monday to Thursday 9.00am to 5.00pm, Friday 9.00am to 4.30pm.**

Please make sure that you have your rent account number ready when you call us, as you may be asked to provide it for verification purposes.

Please note only telephone calls in relation to emergency works, communal areas, requests from older tenants, JAM Card holders or persons who require assistance will be taken during office hours. All other requests for maintenance works must be now logged online through Housing Online.

If there is a potential risk to human life or significant risk to the property, outside of office opening hours, you can call the emergency line **Out of Hours service**, after 5.00pm or at the weekend/bank holidays on **01 457 4907.**

backwardness that made the world seem vast and intractable in its stupidity. Except, even then, he would be choked by shyness in the face of it; would go home and pace the sitting room.

At least he no longer felt that he was failing anyone. He did not need to speak once he discovered that he could write. The New Life wanted champions. Old ideas needed to be taken down from their pedestals, handled, brought to the light and declared excellent fakes, or not even. Practical, material reforms must be proposed, but so must a moral regeneration. A new economy entailed a new ethics. Henry, like his fellows in the Society, recognised the sham nature of the oppositions – individual–society, man–woman, town–nature, work–leisure, production–consumption – which they had been brought up to believe immutable. 'Solidarity *and* personality' was their mantra. Socialism was not the enemy of individualism, but its greatest friend: only when embedded in society can true individualism take root and flourish, when each soul is nurtured and free to find fulfilment.

After a year as a member of the Society, Henry had started to send out essays on advanced literary and scientific subjects. The first to be published, in no less a place than the *Westminster Review*, was an appreciation of Thomas Hardy, and Henry received a letter from the author himself, declaring it 'a remarkable paper, in many ways'. The editor at the *Review* asked if Henry would write on other books, and soon they were coming in great quantities to his mother's house in Croydon (where at that time he still lived), stacking up on a table in his room, the publishers' slips fluttering like leaves if a breeze was let in. Other commissions arrived from other places, and more books. He was soon working harder on his writing than on his degree, which took two years longer than expected to finish, eight years in total. It was the foundation for his present career, dependent on literature for his existence.

But the New Life also had to be lived, under the skin – that was most important of all. Simplicity was an item of their creed. Members of the Society liberated themselves from the trappings of convention, of fashion; they lived plainly and without hypocrisy, refusing servants and petty purchases. (On his income, Henry found this all very easy.) They took walks, organised outside the city, to root them in nature. A group of them – ten or twenty – would step down from the train into a new quality of light, their collective purpose suddenly baggy and ill-fitting, but finding that it no longer mattered once they were away, cutting across fields, climbing stiles, following the unravelling of rivers. Perhaps it was simply difficult to continue sitting in hard judgement of the world when it seemed to look so kindly on them, the clamour of London – the permanent sense there of being overlooked, overhung, beetling under buildings, spires, omnibuses – giving way so easily and generously to the calm open spread of countryside, beauty without claim or consequence.

It was on one of these trips that Henry had first spoken to Edith, almost two years ago. She had joined the Society a few months before. He had seen her at meetings, noticed her comings and goings and the people she seemed to know, but became properly conscious of her only that morning as they boarded the train, her small, compact figure rising in front of him on the step: the hair pinned so that only a wisp emerged from beneath her hat; the ruffed shoulders of her nettle-coloured jacket; the absence of scent. He heard her voice – could not help hearing it, seeing as she did not pause, carrying on speaking to the man in front as she reached up to take his hand. A voice with decision in it, clinching, clipped, concentrated, but with the potential to skid on its own hard surface, as it did then, the man saying something and her responding with bright laughter which filled the corridor as they all found their compartments. Henry did not see any more of her after that; and when they got off at High Wycombe he watched her stride away, still with the same man, her voice subdued but not dissolved in the general chatter. He followed some way behind, talking sparingly with a few others.

It was late September and the fields were a dark, saturated green; the atmosphere damp and expectant; the trees gingery, gold-tipped. He had a habit on these walks of stopping to explore any churches they passed, and when after about an hour he spotted one set back from the footpath he took leave of his companions and went through the gate. The church was plain, pale grey, with fifteenth-century features. He studied the wearied graves a while and then went inside, enjoying as usual the slight resistance given by the door, the first chill breath of age-tasting air. It appeared to be empty. He was craning up at the organ when he sensed movement behind him and recognised Edith examining some tablets on the wall to the right of the altar, her small nettle-coloured figure muted in the quietened light, resembling a solitary weed grown up through the flagstones. He turned back to the organ and tried to resume his concentration but couldn't, hearing footsteps and unable to tell if she was coming closer. Relenting, he looked and saw that in fact she had barely moved – there were dozens of tablets on the wall, and she was reading each one. Curious himself now, he walked tentatively down the nave towards her, letting his hand trail over the ends of the pews, their rounded peaks and scrolls.

She regarded him without surprise as he approached. Her voice came out, clipped and precise. 'I'm glad it isn't just me here – it's too nice.'

'It is.'

There was a pause while they took in the tablets, most of them from the last century.

'Sometimes,' Edith said, 'in churches, I wonder when I got so sure of things. No more sure than these poor souls, obviously.' She gave a short laugh. 'But sure differently. And yet that doesn't make us hesitate. We're as confident as they were.'

'Not so confident, I don't think. We look for more proofs. We admit heresies. That is, actually, all we do. Admit the heresies that are backed by proofs.'

'You are being too sure – it is Mr Ellis, isn't it? I have read some of your essays. You are being too sure. We also take our leaps of faith, as we must. We cannot have proofs for everything – some we have to make for ourselves.'

'On good suppositions.'

'On good suppositions, yes. You are trained in medicine, I think?'

'I am. I do not practise.'

'Why not?'

'It was never my intention. Which is why I do not like to use the title.'

'Then why did you train?'

'I was interested. There were things I wished to know – I wished to have a scientific mind.'

'And do you have one?'

'More than I would have otherwise.'

She smiled, looked back at the tablets. 'I was not convinced you could speak, Mr Ellis, only write.'

'Oh, I can speak, when I must.' He smiled back sheepishly – he felt it to be sheepish, but she was still looking away and didn't see it.

'Not in meetings,' she said.

'Afterwards, sometimes.'

'Not to me.'

'We hadn't met.'

'We met just now. See how easy it was?'

'Yes, I do see.' He could not tell with her, to what extent she was teasing him. And then he thought that perhaps she wasn't at all. 'You did not give me your name,' he ventured.

'Edith Vills. It is very nice to meet you, Mr Ellis.'

She put out her hand and he shook it. There was another pause while they went on reading. Henry noticed two tablets for missionaries who'd died in India.

'Do you enjoy the meetings?' she said. 'You don't look as though you do. And yet you've never missed one that I know of.'

'I do enjoy them.' He searched for something else to say.

She seemed to follow this struggle as it showed on his face. 'Well, that's a relief. I have felt quite sorry for you in your back corner – though, reading you, I have not worried for your principles. You make our case very well.'

'Thank you.'

'I also write. A novel, which has had some sale. And I am beginning to lecture.'

'I'm sorry not to have known of it. I shall look out your book.'

'It is called *A Woman's Journey*. I do not make great claims for it, only for the novelty of its treatment of its themes. It would shock these good people, I think. All to their betterment. Have you seen over on this side?'

They passed by the altar, Henry stopping to examine the pulpit while Edith pointed out its eccentricities. She would be a good lecturer, he thought, allowing himself to be directed by her eye, her run of clear sentences, with their ticklish undertow of humour.

Close by the pulpit was the entrance to the belfry, and they peered in at the bell rope, hanging thickly like an animal. Edith walked in and looked up, tipping her head back, the rope shifting round her, coming to lurk over her shoulder. Her eyes creased: 'Not a great deal to see.' Her voice had the effort of looking in it, an amount of strain, as though it had travelled up to the top of the tower and down again. She came out, and Henry took her place, with the air of this having been agreed between them. It was darker inside than in the rest of the church and the perfume of old stone was stronger. He pushed the rope away from him slightly, feeling it drift heavily back into the gap between his shoulder blades, and squinted up. The wide-open mouth and throat of the bell loomed at the top, lodged in shadow, its uvula just visible in the weak light entering the slit windows. He could smell the outside now, and hear it: the lonely chatter of birds in the trees. He stayed looking for a moment, then dropped his head; Edith was watching him through the doorway, a slightly amused expression on her face.

'There's a story—'

He only recovered her broken-off words later, digging futilely in his memory, searching for mitigating factors. For at that exact moment he decided to pull down hard on the bell rope. Once. Twice. Thrice. An access of childishness, perhaps, escaping from a forgotten, tamped-down part of himself. Or shyness, for once seeking its solution in sound. Or something else, in the moment, in the way she was watching him, the expression on her face, some odd instinct that told him to pull it all down about his head. The noise wasn't what he'd expected. Not mellow – an effect of distance and technique, he realised, belatedly – but harsh, a violent, swallowing racket as formless as pounding London traffic, but intensified, exaggerated, filling the ears to the painful exclusion of all else. Edith was frozen by it: he saw her over the great wall of sound, even as he was still pulling with both hands on the rope, almost sinking onto his haunches with the effort. Her face tight with surprise, her mouth still open on the words she was speaking, or unable to close on them, arms straight down by her sides, fingers pointed; rooted to the flagstones, a hardscrabble weed clinging grimly in the wrenching storm.

It seemed interminable. He stopped pulling and clamped his hands over his ears, but stayed standing where he was, frozen too, as if the ringing of the bell had suspended time rather than moved it on. They stared at each other for what seemed like minutes. What was left at the end was a humming; Henry's ears, when he took his hands away, were filled with it. It was tangible on his skin, as if the air were swarming with insects, blundering past on their tiny wings – visible, in the way Edith's face had become slightly blurred, impeded somehow. His head was full of recriminations, humming too.

Edith swallowed. Her arms loosened at her sides, one hand touched the buttons on her jacket. 'How old are you, Mr Ellis?' she came out with, finally.

'Thirty.' His voice wavered hatefully.

'As much as that.' There was a fierceness in her eye as she said it, something triumphant, some pleasure taken in her hardness. He felt numbed by his own stupidity, awed by it, rising all around him. 'I should be going after the others,' she said, 'though perhaps they've all come running. To your summons.' There was, he thought later, a lapse here, a small opening: a smile twitched very discernibly at the corners of her mouth. But then she marched away, down the nave and out, leaving him still standing in the belfry with his humiliation and the sounds of the birds, the rope hanging mockingly at his back.

It was correct, his feeling about that smile, even though Edith did not speak to him again that day, leaving him to tramp dejectedly through the fields, the countryside that had seemed so welcoming in its expansiveness now conspiring to emphasise his insignificance, the full wide stretch of his idiocy. When he got home, he stared into the mirror, whispering poisonous accusations against himself.

At the next meeting of the Society he avoided looking in her direction, putting his head on his hand and examining his boots, but she walked over unexpectedly at the end as he was pulling on his coat, his arm trapped in a kink in the sleeve.

'So much for your escape act, Mr Ellis. Or is this just the tease?'

He forced his arm through and reached up to wrench his collar into position. 'It was the tease. As you can see, I am now escaped.'

'Congratulations.'

He laughed, anxiously. He was reminded of school, where

conversations had so often seemed to possess a further dimension, which he could detect but never access. There was the same flailing for entrance now. 'Did you enjoy the lecture?' he said. And then, seeing a change in her face: 'Did you find it interesting? Did you agree?'

The lecture had been about the need for national food safety standards. The lecturer was a Mr Rogers, a small man from Leeds in a brown suit. He had spoken, Henry thought, most intelligently on the subject, which had the potential to be dull listening but had instead gripped from the outset. There were several insights which Henry planned to communicate to his notebooks when he got back to his flat in Brixton.

'I'm not sure anyone could have *enjoyed* it,' Edith replied. 'And to call it interesting would be to bring into question the category. But I agreed, yes, with every word.'

Henry took a breath. 'Well, it was sensible stuff.' His gaze began sliding off her face, seeking out some activity at the front of the room.

Her voice hooked it back. 'I have read a few more of your essays, Mr Ellis, since we last saw each other. I wanted to see you again, in that light.'

He winced. 'Yes, I see.'

'I find that we agree on almost every essential.'

'Yes?'

'Perhaps we could dine together.'

'Now?'

'Why not? You sometimes have a drink with the gentlemen. Unless you must get back to your desk. That I could forgive.'

She really was quite ingenuous, standing there in her hat and gloves, so small and yet so clear-cut, so *present* against everything. He could not think even to hesitate. 'No, no, I'm quite free,' he said. And, though he could see already that she was: 'Are you ready to leave?'

And so it had begun, again. But what was it, this once-got-into-never-got-out-of habit? Of eating together, walking together, sitting together, writing to one another, exchanging every thought, every thought being redeemed in the exchange? Certainly it did not feel like a courtship. Henry soon became aware that he was not attracted to Edith that way. He could not say exactly why, for, though short, she was good-looking, fresh-complexioned, well-dressed in the way he appreciated, in her loose dresses, wide skirts, her blouses and wide-lapelled jackets. He liked her grey eyes. Perhaps it had to do with the lack of encouragement from her side, for she gave no hint of wanting anything more from their friendship. But then, at the beginning, how could they have wanted more? They had found in each other something neither had found in quite the same way with anyone else. Which was understanding – not in the easy sense of agreement, but in the greater and deeper sense of responsiveness. The first time they ate together, after the lecture on food standards, in a small restaurant run by Italians, he told her about his time in Australia. Edith's first question hadn't been about the journey or the landscape or the people or how he'd managed and wasn't he lonely; instead – he could still see her face, looking calmly over the top of a glistering green candle – she had simply asked, 'What did you read?' Which was the only really important question, and the only one he felt properly equipped to answer.

There were many other examples of this sort. And he had found himself able to enter into the complexities of Edith's life. She was an orphan, albeit in a moral rather than a technical sense. Her mother died when she was twelve and her father had married again, to a woman who did not even attempt to understand her, inflicting the proprieties with deadly enthusiasm, crushing her in corsets, suffocating her with invitations, calls. Her father would not hear her appeals, so she had made her escape from Upper Norwood aged twenty-five, finding work as an amanuensis to a Mrs Percy, who was producing a pamphlet on the operation of the Housing Acts (this explained Edith's distaste for statistics). She had written her novel in her free evenings, in six months of concentrated activity. It was published around the same time as Mrs Percy's pamphlet, and received considerably more attention (Henry realised, later, that he had in fact heard of it). With her earnings Edith had taken her own rooms near Holborn, in the same building as a second cousin. She had already been following the Society of the New Life's proceedings for several months, and, armed with new confidence, began attending its meetings – when Henry had first seen her, and she him.

Henry read Edith's novel shortly after their first meal together. It was about a young woman reared captive to convention, who gradually emancipates herself from orthodox religion, from the expectations placed on her sex and from the justifications of a society she comes to see as hidebound and unjust. At the end, the woman breaks off her engagement with a well-meaning but ultimately timid and unimaginative young man, and finds satisfaction in freer relations with men and women committed to new ways of living. After finishing it, Henry wrote Edith a letter:

Dear Edith,

I have just finished reading A Woman's Journey. It has energy and decision: qualities I associate mainly with you. And it will do more good, I think, than any other work which may be pressed in greater numbers into the hands of young women (and young men!) this year or in years to come. I felt compelled to write this short note to the author only moments after reaching the final lines, so fulsome was my admiration.

Yours very sincerely,
Your friend,
Henry Ellis

It seemed to him one of the most unguarded responses he had ever made to a work of art, or to a person, for that matter. She replied:

Dear Henry,

Your letter is the kindest and also the most precious I have had about my book. Precious because I know that you understand what it cost me, and because the Journey is one that you have mapped yourself. We must make it together, and clear the path for others to follow.

Yours very truly,

Edith Vills

This exchange initiated a deepening in their relationship. And the note on which Edith ended her letter soon sounded as the dominant one. They recommended each other books and articles; they read each other's writing, giving detailed responses, fearless criticism. They felt themselves, with ever-increasing surety, to be partners in a shared attempt to make the New Life possible, to show it to be possible. It was inevitable therefore that marriage should have come into their minds.

Henry and Edith agreed that sex – for this was how they coolly referred to it – should be viewed clearly, stripped of every pretty, dingy accrual of secrecy, laid out cleanly as a healthy human impulse. But this way of thinking had cultivated in them a view of marriage that no longer had sex at its heart. The predominant influence of sex in the decision of most people to marry was a social fact, no matter how avidly concealed behind vows and frills and fancy lace. Throughout history the sexual impulse had been directed 'safely' into unsound, ill-considered marriages; frequently, it later surged and broke its banks, with miserable results. To think rationally about sex – to liberate it from the marital bond as conventionally understood – was also to escape its power of dictation, to rescue marriage for higher purposes. Henry and Edith's marriage was intended to stamp a pattern on their lives, a brand, with the known existence of the other, even when not immediately present or seen, acting as a constant reminder of all that might be done, a spur to activity. Always, breathing between them, over no matter what distance, softly back and forth, would be their shared interest in one another, their curiosity about what the other was doing, their understanding and concern. Marriage would be a brand, but also an atmosphere, a mesh of fine feeling, strung beneath and between them – an invisible support, bearing them up, but also a sieve, separating and shaking out the worst aspects of self.

The existence of these higher purposes meant that it was of no great import whether Henry and Edith were physically drawn to each other, and that they needn't live together, or needn't live together all of the time. It also followed that they were both free to develop other friendships. More than a year after their first meeting, Edith had told Henry that her most intimate relations were with women. She'd had close women friends since school; Mary was one of the closest. It was with them, she said, that she felt easiest. She gave Henry to understand that this was why she was not romantic with him, and yet he was not disappointed or insulted – rather, he was flattered. No other man, she told him, had succeeded in making a true connection with her; she thought no other man ever would. So their bond was unique in this respect too.

Henry, speaking for his part, did not disclaim an interest in the opposite sex, but admitted that his feelings for Edith were not passionate. There was some embarrassment in this, in stating that it was her personally, rather than women in general, who did not especially attract him, but Edith did not appear to feel any. She was right not to, of course. They had made a union more serious and sustained than that which existed between many of the married couples they knew. It was a prototype for changed relations between men and women, uncorrupted by sexual expectation.

And yet, for all that, their relationship had developed a physical aspect: they would sometimes lightly kiss, or lie in each other's lap to read. When marriage came into their minds, so, unavoidably, did its great implication. Edith was a virgin too. They sometimes talked of having children. Consummation was never ruled out and yet it wasn't agreed on either. It tended to slither out of their conversations as quickly as it entered them – to grab its tail and drag it back to the centre of things seemed to Henry indelicate, or, rather, insistent, in a primeval sort of way. So they had pushed on with their plans, this anxiety slithering after them.

It followed Henry now as he got up from the bed, dressed, and packed for his honeymoon. It sat down hungrily with him to breakfast, watched intently as he drank his tea, tickling his heart till it began to flutter. He and Edith had decided not to spend their wedding night together mainly out of practical considerations: neither of them had a bed big enough for two. But there was only one bed at the cottage they had taken in Norfolk. Obviously, Henry had never spent the night with a woman before, never been undressed in front of one. The idea of a week of it made him – yes, excited, as well as everything else.

His virginity had not needed to wait for marriage to be resolved. Its persistence reflected some bias in himself. He had been aware, at least since his experience with Marie Tillnott and probably before, that he did not need to lock his body with a woman's to obtain gratification. That he did not especially want to. A different prospect angled before his eyes when he thought about a woman, and yet this desire was not communicable – shame stopped his mouth. His innocence, then, had been kept not willingly, but not unwillingly either. Only it was surely impossible to keep it any longer – he saw this with a brisk advent of certainty – unthinkable, even. He was married, he was about to honeymoon; to preserve his innocence would be like booking a passage to America, putting all his worldly possessions on board, and then stepping back onto the quay as the ship set off. It was not that he looked forward with any great zest to the act: it was more that he was ready, achingly so, to have performed it. It was the afterward – attained manhood, definite experience – that excited him.

He cleared the table. The small, shabby room was full of careless sunlight, gambolling dust motes. It was with his new-found certainty that Henry tidied round, trying to anticipate the expanded self that would return. He found, to his surprise, that his confidence remained even when he thought more about Edith's own attitude. He was sure, somehow, that she would feel as he did. They had been daring in marrying; they would be daring still. His bag, when he picked it up, felt portentous. The clothes shifting inside had a soft fleshy weight.

The walk to Brixton station was quiet – he thought briefly of that drunk woman yesterday – but his train was delayed. He was late arriving at Liverpool Street, and had to run to meet Edith, his bag getting under his knees, the handle chafing his palm. Edith was wearing something cream-coloured and her face was strained under her hat.

'Quick,' she said, turning in the direction of the platform, 'we will have to be quick.'

The whistle of the train seared over their heads as they ran, like an incitement, hastening them to the marriage bed.

V

The tablecloth was warm under their hands. The knives and forks when they picked them up were warm, the light travelling in little eddies along the handles, urged into quick winks. The glass doors at the end of John and Catherine's dining room looked out onto the garden, but they had also folded back the partition so that the early-evening light could enter through the drawing-room window on the other side.

'I only wish you were able to take a degree,' Mark Ludding was saying to John's youngest daughter, Janet. 'It's no small thing that you will be with us at all, but that would make the difference.'

'I don't think I'll mind,' Janet replied.

'You will,' Mark's wife Louisa said. 'You think you won't because just now you're only pleased to be going. But you will, once you've done the work.' She brought a piece of ham to her mouth where it hovered a moment. 'You will find yourself grown quite full of your rights. Students always are, and the women have proved no different.'

'Perhaps I will, then.' Janet looked amused. 'I didn't mean that I wouldn't prefer a degree to a certificate. Anyone would, I imagine. And one hears of the women doing so well, coming first in their year and so on, which must make it worse. Not that I would, but—'

'You might,' Catherine said.

'I don't think so, Mother.'

'You might,' John said. He liked to support his wife in small ways. He was too agitated, anyhow, to think about what was being said.

'Yes, yes, all right,' Janet said. 'I will come top of my year and then I will be extremely angry at not being allowed to claim a degree, being very full of my rights. I look forward to meeting this Janet in three years' time. She is most impressive. I am a little frightened of her.'

'So you should be.' Louisa nodded. 'She would eat you for breakfast, were she here.'

'Is there any chance of reform, before she finishes?' Catherine asked.

Mark, chewing, raised his eyebrows articulately; he always had to draw his chair a little way back from the table, so that his beard didn't sit in his food. His wife watched him patiently. Finally, he swallowed. 'They can't hold out for ever. All the jokes have been made.' There was a note of exasperation in his voice. 'It is on the plane of argument now. And we have the better of them there.'

'Not that that is a guarantee of anything at all,' Louisa broke in. 'The world is too full of old fools, Cambridge especially.' She folded some salad under her fork. 'Actually, Oxford is worse.'

'The old fools have a lot to answer for. Johnny has always believed that.' Mark looked over at him.

Catherine looked over too. 'Oh, Johnny has never been patient.'

John grimaced at them. Mark and Catherine always talked to him this way. Or rather, talked about him, over him, between themselves. In the first years of their marriage he had worried that Catherine was over-friendly with Mark. She had seemed to strain for his approval whenever they met, heightening herself in myriad small ways; no one but John would have noticed the subtle differences, but that did not make them any less real. He had been nervous of Mark responding to it, despite what he knew of his friend – nervous for Catherine, who normally kept her feelings carefully in check, and nervous for himself, of the strange compound of feelings it might produce, of jealousy and relief and despair. But of course Mark hadn't responded, and Catherine eventually sensed in him the same lack as in her husband. As if in compensation, the two of them had chosen to make their shared knowledge and understanding of John the source and justification of their intimacy.

He had grown to miss that earlier version of his wife. Tonight she was wearing a mauve satin dress with a high lace collar; it looked well on her, deepening and darkening as she turned in the light. He had not seen it previously and wondered who it was being worn for. Not him, or Mark, or Janet; he supposed it was for Louisa, whom Catherine found intimidating.

Their plates were taken away. He had willed himself through the meal and felt a little sick for having eaten it. All evening he had been watching Mark for a sign. There had been none, unless the reference to old fools was meant to count. He couldn't begin to think about Janet going to Cambridge. The arguments of his book, *A Problem in Greek Ethics*, were running through his mind; certain phrases appearing in capitals like on an advertisement. He was scared all over again to think of Mark having read these; to realise that they now existed in someone else's head. And, mixed with this, there was since yesterday morning something else: that piece of folded paper he had locked in his desk, with an address written on it. He felt this too as a danger, another secret not bounded within himself. It was as impossible to undo that meeting in the park, to recover whatever that man had taken from it, as it was to make Mark un-read his book. He thought about Frank swimming away down the path and not looking back.

When dessert was brought out, he nearly rebelled. He'd forgotten about dessert. It was impossible to live like this, hemmed in by etiquette, by rules operating invisibly in your own home. The pudding sagged on his plate. Mark was tucking in, the cream catching in his beard. He'd always eaten like this, with the placid greed of an intellectual. It was cruel, John thought, for him to be behaving in this way, as though the book he had given him, and its contents, could so easily be accommodated within the old routines. He would have preferred him to be cold, obviously disturbed.

'What are you working on now, Johnny?' Mark asked, scraping a residue from his plate.

'You mean, now he has finished with whatever he was working on before,' Catherine said. 'I presume your question means he has finished it. We have been told nothing about it.'

'I think of writing an autobiography,' John said. This was true, though he had no intention of acting on it. He said it to see what Mark's reaction would be.

Catherine looked startled. There was a line across her forehead. 'What would you say?'

'What anyone says.'

She looked over to Mark for support.

'You are much too young, Johnny,' Mark said. 'We need to be able to see you in the round.'

'You would wait for my death?'

'No, not so long as that. Though we cannot be certain that death would be the end of your development.'

'As you know, I do not foresee any such further development. But I take your point. I would not want to presume on the public's interest. And yet, there is nothing to prevent me from beginning now, for my own advantage. I should like to understand myself.'

'You are not so very hard to understand, Johnny,' Catherine said.

'It does not seem that way to me,' he said, 'and I am in a position to know.'

'You have always overestimated your difference.'

'Have I?'

'You have.'

There was a silence. John murmured thanks to Lewis, as he removed his plate.

'You didn't eat your dessert,' Janet said to him.

'Cook overestimated me.'

'We'll leave you,' Catherine said, rising. Louisa and Janet rose with her. Catherine paused on the border of the drawing room and gestured to the partition doors folded away at the sides. 'Shall we shut you in?' She looked forbidding.

'No, thank you. We'll go into the garden.'

Mark accepted coffee from Lewis, but John waved his away, opening the glass doors. Steps led up to the lawn. It was warm still. The sunlight was lying quietly in the flower beds and had draped itself over the wall. The sky was whitening, a few pink ribbons of cloud left over from the day. The grass had been mown and the borders trimmed; severed stems bled their scent into the air. They stopped in the middle of the lawn; Mark slightly hunched, holding his cup and saucer close to his lips.

'Are you frightened, Mark? Of my memoirs?'

'I'm not afraid of any reference to myself, if that is what you mean.'

'It isn't what I mean.'

'Catherine was worried.'

'She has no reason to be.'

'Are you sure?' Mark said. 'I don't know what to think about you, Johnny. You've always been more reckless than either of us would have you. This book you've written—' He paused and sipped his drink, peering down at the bottom of the garden. The fronds of his beard were waving in the breeze. He had the habit of letting his mouth fall open a little, wide enough to admit a finger; his tongue was visible to John now, furred by the coffee.

'Please say it,' John said. 'I've been driven nearly wild by waiting.'

Mark sighed. 'It's a miracle of argument. I have no doubt of that. Your case is sound; the evidence is sound. But the tone, Johnny. The conclusion! You can't ever publish it.'

John felt a sort of numbness steal over his face. He had always considered the book unpublishable. Yet, confronted with it like this, he found the idea appalling. He was unexpectedly angry; it was anger that was setting like a mask on his face. 'I don't see the harm. Perhaps if the tone were adjusted. But I don't see the harm in stating facts. It is historical.'

'But who will benefit from it? Is it useful, for the public to know? Your career would be ruined. Catherine, your daughters, would not escape the stain. You have trodden this line before, with great difficulty, if you remember, and that was as nothing compared with this.'

'Old fools. You will not let them have their way about women's education.'

'It is different. The benefit in that case is so much greater, obviously so. And there is no question of the law.'

'What am I, Mark? Would there be no benefit to me?' John looked at him directly. They had lowered their voices, but this only had the effect of putting pressure on their words, which came out compact and hard-edged. 'And what are you? You are not so oblivious as to think there are only two of us. Is the law beyond scrutiny? It is a rotten, filthy law. That is the stain. The point of my conclusion, which you single out for scandal, is that there is a benefit, as you call it, in a proper comprehension of the past. The knowledge that what we punish with hard labour – a crime for which men used to hang in our fathers' time – was once praised, understood, practised, by the very men whose thought we teach our sons, whose heroics we pride ourselves on matching, whose marbles we line up for our edification; may that knowledge not do some useful work in the world? How can it not?'

'It may—'

'So!'

'It may, but I do not think it will. People would say what they have always said: here we pass over something regrettable; on this point we cannot follow the Greeks. You know how frequently I feel myself unadapted to this universe, Johnny, as you feel yourself to be. However, we have our ties. We are both married men, with positions of value in the world.'

'I do not feel that my position has value. I will not speak for you. I feel myself a fraud. I have grown sick on middle-class propriety. I am dying of it.'

'You exaggerate.'

'I do not!' Anger briefly throttled John's tongue. 'I do not. I am a married man only because I was told to be. I have tried to be a husband; I suppose I am not a bad one. I love my wife and my children. But Catherine is not happy. Neither of us ever has been. I have been disnatured. It is as simple and as terrible as that. No man should live his whole life in opposition to his nature – not when that nature is hymned by Plato. I will not suffer any longer, I have decided. That is what this book taught me in the writing. Perhaps it is why I felt compelled to write it. I had hoped you would agree with me.'

'You told me yourself it was an impossible subject,' Mark said.

'That was our old code.'

'It expressed a truth.'

'I have stopped believing in it,' John said. 'I am tired of codes. Yesterday I met a man in the park. He spoke to me. He said he wished us to be friends.'

'Johnny, don't be a fool. That is a code. Did he ask for anything?'

'Only that.'

'He will entrap you.'

'Perhaps. Perhaps that's it. But I am almost minded to take the risk.

It is another effect of this law you are so keen on, that friendship may turn out to contain its opposite. And yet, I have begun to think that even the simulacra of friendship may have more truth than my life as I have lived it.'

'You don't believe that.'

'I do. I have dreams, Mark. Every night. I am exhausted by them. I cannot go on.'

'There is no other way.'

'What of Whitman? Does he not point a way?'

'Whitman is vague. You cannot presume on his meaning. Besides, he was only a man, like the rest of us.'

John bit back on his reply, let his thoughts turn onto another track. His heart pattered against his chest. The light had changed. The sun had departed the flower beds, slipped backwards over the wall. 'When you sit down with your mediums,' he said, 'what do the spirits say?'

Mark drank from his cup, his eyes glossy and black above the porcelain. His tongue slid abruptly along his upper lip, lifting the hairs. 'They have messages mainly, for the living. They are asked questions. They are not always clear in their meaning.'

'So they do not soliloquise? Do not take up your afternoon? Spill all their secrets? List their regrets?'

Mark smiled ruefully. 'I have never experienced it. You know I am yet to be totally convinced.'

'Not one of them ever recognises their wife and asks, "What are *you* doing here?"'

'No.'

'It is that more than anything that makes me doubt it,' John said. 'I don't mean about wives, exactly. It does not tally with my sense of human experience.'

'I have never forgotten you saying that you believe in utter blankness after death. That this was a great relief.'

'Yes.'

It was growing dark. John examined Mark in the pinched light: his fine eyebrows, the unlined forehead, hair still clinging to black. It was hard to remember the face behind that awful grey beard of his. He was sheltering his cup and saucer close against his body. I frighten him, John realised. He looked towards the house, which had been lit up. Through the doors into the dining room the three women could be seen against the light. He looked back at Mark: 'Do you remember those first poems of mine?'

Thirty years ago, when they were at Oxford, he had shown Mark a sheaf of poems, which he kept in a small locked chest. He used to write them before he went to bed, committing feelings to words, like guilty prayers. After reading them, Mark had insisted on their being destroyed. He made John see the foolishness of what he'd done; the danger to his health and all his prospects if he continued to indulge himself. One Saturday afternoon they walked out into the country together, finding a lonely bridge. Without hesitation John dropped the chest over into the bright, heedless water. He'd felt, briefly in that moment, as though he were returning to life.

'I believed you were right,' he said now. 'I wonder which of us you were protecting?'

Mark threw the silt of his coffee over the flowers. 'It was you, Johnny,' he said, in a tired voice. 'It is always you.'

VI

Henry and Edith were in north Norfolk, on the second day of their honeymoon. Arriving the day before in the heat of the early afternoon, they had thrown down their bags in the hallway of the rented cottage and gone out walking across the salt marshes, on the banked, coiling paths Edith likened to the leavings of giant sandworms. They both exulted in the place. The landscape was so flat, a tint of green, yellow, brown printed under a great rectangle of sky, that the trees and houses in the distance seemed only a smudge on the fine line of the horizon; the fields of reeds fanning round them made tidal sounds in the wind, premonitions of the sea. After a mile or two they had taken off their boots, turned orange by the dust, and descended onto the mud flats in bare feet. They sank in up to their shins, the black mud sucking and squeezing, and walked stork-like to the shoreline, washing their legs in an inlet where a small dog was hopping madly, before climbing back onto the path and sitting on a grassy promontory stalled in its rush to the sea. They talked a little, and read their books, and went down to the water, and then walked back to the cottage, stopping for a glass of beer at the inn along the way. They made a small supper, their elbows arguing in the cramped kitchen, and afterwards worked companionably in the sitting room. When it got late, they went to bed. It was, almost, the kind of day they could have had at any other time, in the time before they were married.

So was today. Henry was lying in his shirtsleeves in the garden correcting the proofs of an article he'd written on Whitman. It was a beautiful morning and he had to squint at his pages, against which the intruding blades of grass seemed positively to shine green. He felt tickled by the heat, or the grass; it was a comfortable discomfort, lazily endured. A large tree whispered over the low wall in the warm wind, its branches reaching to touch the stone and then racing away again. Edith was working at the desk in the sitting room – when he looked over his shoulder he could just make her out through the window, her features partly obliterated by great streaks of sunlight, smears of sky and tree on the glass. But he was looking at his proof page, where was printed:

Whitman has made the most earnest, thorough and successful attempts of modern times to bring the Greek spirit into art. The Greek spirit is the simple, natural, beautiful interpretation of the life of the artist's own age and people under his own sky, as shown especially in the human body. 'If the body were not the soul,' he asks, 'what is the soul?' This is Whitman's naturalism; it is the re-assertion of the Greek attitude on a new and larger foundation. Morality is thus the normal activity of a healthy nature, not the product either of tradition or of rationalism.

He reread this paragraph, wondered about replacing 'larger' with 'grander' and then decided against it. Behind him he heard a sound. He rolled onto his hip and turned his head to see Edith pushing out the top window, her small white hand stealing into the sunshine, fixing the latch and withdrawing as she sat back down, safely obscure again behind the streaked glass with the restless leaves reflected in it. There was something in the brisk purposefulness of the gesture, in the fact that she hadn't even looked over, that pleased him. It was one of the things their marriage was intended for: the perpetuation of this sort of oblivious together-working.

Still, there was a twinge under his contentment, reminding, like a splinter he couldn't work out. It was only as they went upstairs last night that the scale of the silence they had constructed together on the subject of consummation finally became apparent, nearly crushed him with its awful weight and totality. There was the room, with its chest of drawers and wardrobe, into which Edith began placing the things from her case, the mystery going out of them, their intimate connection with her body and personality exposed as a sort of deceit. The bed, on which she periodically perched, was menacingly white. He stood there uncertainly, watching, until he was seized by the realisation that he should do the same, hanging up his few shirts and his jacket, folding his spare trousers and his underwear into the drawer she had left for him. Once this was done Edith looked up from where she was sitting on the edge of the bed, and he saw for the first time a tremor of uncertainty on her face. She looked as though she were nerving herself for a jump.

'Do you think we should undress together?' she said. 'There's downstairs.'

For a moment he struggled to see the angle of her concern. Then he understood that what was at stake was their vaunted openness, their insistence on the simple beauty of the body, threatened now by the supple shynesses and proprieties of their youth, into which he too felt an overwhelming urge to retreat. 'I think we should,' he said, fear and excitement constricting his voice.

'Yes, all right,' she replied, not quite holding his eye, beginning concentratedly to loosen her cream-coloured cravat and unbutton her blouse; beginning to undo the effect she had made that morning once he was capable of seeing her properly, seated in their compartment as the train began to crawl, the view through the window still showing the security of the station. When she had looked at him, still breathless from their run, her face flushed, and said, 'Here we start, Henry.'

He turned from her now, not thinking this dishonest, and slowly removed his boots and socks. He wound his watch. He could hear Edith behind him, tutting over something, and then the soft rushing of cloth lifted and allowed to fall. He glanced over to catch her still seated on the bed, her nightdress bunched around her waist; in the seconds before she tugged it down over her legs he saw the plumped cushion of hair, some of it copper in the light from the lamp. She looked back at him, and he knew that he had misused his time: she had nothing to do now but watch him. It seemed impossible to talk: the atmosphere was too heavy with their responsibility to their past selves, the man and woman who had sat fully clothed in brightly lit rooms and bandied around the word 'sex'. Edith pushed herself backwards on her palms to the head of the bed and got under the bedclothes. The shadows in the room peeled back a little as the lamp shone out without obstacle.

Henry unbuttoned his shirt and took it off. Edith was leaning against the pillows, observing him frankly, somewhat boyish. The light played over the keys of his ribs and he scratched the hair on his chest before fiddling with his trousers. As he stepped out of them, stooping to pull a leg over a heel, he staggered and put a hand out to the wall to steady himself, feeling at that moment more exposed than ever before in his life. But when he stood up in his drawers, Edith's eyes still on him, the ripple of a smile on her face, he felt himself going helplessly, unexpectedly hard. This experience, standing at the foot of the bed in the silence of the lamplit room, his member ratcheting upwards in small hiccups, with Edith watching him, perhaps watching *it* – its notations in the fabric of his underwear – was unlike anything he had ever imagined for himself, even in Australia, in that lonely cabin at

Kanga Creek. His eyes met Edith's over the white expanse of bed. Words retreated. There was nothing for it. He seized at the strings to loosen them and pushed his drawers down, his erection bending and springing. He could not look at Edith now – he reached for his night-shirt and pulled it over his head, feeling it catch ludicrously at the front, and advanced to his side of the bed, lowering and collapsing himself into it, stretching out his legs under the cover. His face was hot but the rest of him felt preternaturally cold, so that he rubbed his feet together fiercely.

'Shall I put out the lamp?' Edith said.

The embrace of darkness was welcome, almost warm. He breathed into it, adapting to the unfamiliar dimensions of the bed, the answering weight of a body close by. He could not bring himself to shift to face her, but could see her hands, dark like his, laid over the white cover. His erection, pitched against his shirt, invested Edith's every breath with significance; he could not believe it existed in such proximity to her, to a woman, could not bear now for something not to happen to it.

'Edith.' It came out in a parched gasp, so that he cleared his throat and repeated it: 'Edith.' He had the idea of the word being swallowed up by the darkness, disappearing into it like food into a child's mouth.

She did not answer. He did not want her to. She rolled onto her side; her right hand reached across – he shivered as it passed over him – took his, and brought it between her legs. Their joined hands travelled under her nightdress into the space between, grazed by hair; then her hand was guiding his fingers into an enveloping warmth, wet. Her fingertips were on his knuckles, pushing; he let himself be directed, pushed, until he picked up the rhythm. Her breath was close on his cheeks. He was breathing heavily too, as though they were exhausting each other.

'Now.' She said it urgently, on an outward breath, rolling onto her back.

Henry moved with her, barely conscious of his actions, compelled by something other than himself. He found he was still hard and got himself onto his knees at her side. He remembered they hadn't kissed and leaned over where he thought he could see her mouth, finding instead the side of her nose. She didn't appear to notice, putting a hand on his ribs and lifting her legs, shifting him so that he was in front of her. Still feeling strangely like a spectator of his own behaviour, Henry gathered up his shirt around his waist and then, thinking better of it, dragged it over his head, casting it off into the darkness.

He could see Edith a little better, the shape of her defined by the hazy grey of her nightdress. But she suddenly seemed quiet, passive, tense with waiting: he realised they had reached the limits of her knowledge. His senses pinching into alarm, the air picking at his nakedness, he nudged her nightdress up over her stomach, soft beneath his fingers, wanting but not daring to reveal her breasts. He shuffled forward on his knees, the sheet bunching under them and making him clumsy, and leaned into the gap between her legs, bracing his arms at either side of her head. Her face was under his now, but she looked past him, over his shoulder; her eyes closed and opened, she was breathing very quietly through her nose. He didn't know what to do; his cock was almost flat on top of her, her hair tickling it, and his arms were already beginning to hurt. It was ridiculous, to have attended births, to be able to name constituent parts, but to be so ignorant of technique, so unmanned by the dark. He hesitated to discern her body with his hands. 'Open your legs,' he whispered, hoping it would become obvious. She did, wider, and he backed away a little, pulling himself onto his elbows, feeling panicked as she turned her chin up to him. He pushed forward hopefully from his hips, felt his cock skim over her inner thigh, into a mesh of hair. The contact was so thrilling that he wasn't immediately embarrassed. He tried again, adjusting his position, and this time felt himself within the ambit of that surrendering warmth – though he seemed to travel somewhere across or above it. Edith lay prone beneath him, eyes glittering in the dark. Sweat prickled at the beginning of his buttocks; his arms ached. Heat was spreading up over his back, across his shoulders. He went once more, thrusting it forward like an unwanted offering, the sheet slipping treacherously under his knees: again it was misdirected. In response Edith shifted, slightly, as if in sleep, though he could see her expression in the speckled dark, the crease of worry in it, a sort of fixed concern – and his panic seemed to slow, to coagulate in his mind: no thought, no action could form in it. The heat washed rapidly along the full length of him and he felt his cock slacken, dip and drop, stagger into softness.

It happened with such instantaneousness that this too seemed some inevitable working out of physiological destiny, a further, ultimate abnegation of control. He remained staked on his elbows, wishing himself out of his body. It took a moment for Edith to realise what had happened. She pushed down her nightdress like a shutter. A hand spread on his chest. 'Dear boy,' she said.

The sun was seeping into him. His eyes were closed and he was lying on his back, a finger pinned to the right page in his Whitman proofs. All he could hear was the tree's whispering, the rustle and scrape of its returns and retractions. He and Edith had not yet made reference to last night – the sunlight already pouring into the room when they woke had seemed to question the reality of what had taken place in the darkness. And their nightclothes had all the warm, safe sleepiness of childhood on them. Would the coming of the evening make it unavoidable again? He felt ill-served – by his body, by his understanding, by Whitman even. For he did not want to go back to the bed, to the dark. Old certainties rode rampant in his mind, coldly trampling the newer:

he would never perform the act, it was not in his nature; what was in his nature was not communicable, it narrowed to him alone.

And yet, still it was wonderful, to feel the heat of the sun pushing idly through his senses, to think of Edith working in the sitting room, behind the glass. They were married. In some way, perhaps, the worst of the anxiety had lifted. They had faced experience together. Edith did not seem angry or concerned. He thought of the way her hand had stolen out into the sunlight. Marriage brought with it the possibility of permanence, permanent possibility. The tree rustled and scraped in the bright world beyond his eyelids.

He must have fallen asleep. For Edith was above him; a blackish shape knocking its head against the sky. And behind this shape another. He brought a hand to shadow his eyes.

'Call this work, Henry Ellis?'

He sat up, hot and oddly dizzy, his proofs sliding off his chest and sprawling in his lap.

Edith smiled down at him. As did the woman standing behind her.

'Henry, this is Miss Britell. She lives a little over yonder and stopped by to say hello.'

'Very nice to meet you, Miss Britell.'

'And you, Mr Ellis.'

Edith looked between them happily: Henry still squinting up from the grass, Miss Britell in an extraordinary green dress, covered with printed sunflowers. 'I thought we might go for a walk,' she said.

VII

The approaching meeting with Frank clung to the back of his throat like an impending illness. He could not help testing it, as with small coughs and touchings of the glands, and so it was that he had looked again at Frank's reply, taking it out of the locked drawer in his study.

Dear John,

It is nice to know your name, I couldn't make my mind up what it would be. Could you come Thursday evening at seven? If you were to meet me here, we could go on to another place I know.

Yours ever,

Frank Feaver

It was five o'clock. A day like all the others this month, starting bright and transparent before turning heavy and golden. John was wearing his lightest summer suit, but had spent the day sweating softly into it. Catherine and Janet were out visiting. The house was large and empty. He felt the heat sitting in it, along the corridors and in the rooms, like dirty bathwater. After putting the letter away again he stared out the window, down at the yellowish tongue of lawn protruding from the bottom of the house. Some lines in an admirable article he'd read this morning had struck him: '*Whitman is reasserting the Greek attitude on a new and grander foundation. Morality is thus the normal activity of a healthy nature.*' What did it mean, that someone somewhere thought the way he did?

He rang the bell. When Susan arrived, she had a rash on her neck, shaped like a spill of milk. Seeing him notice it, she said, 'It's the heat, sir. They just burn up and go away again the minute I cool down.'

'Heat rash.'

'Yes, sir.'

'There's no need for overwork. Not in this weather, with only me here.'

'No, sir.' She put her hands together in front of her apron and looked at him expectantly.

He paused, giving himself a chance to change his mind. 'Susan, I have a question for you.'

'Of course, sir.'

'Your brothers. Do you ever buy them presents?'

Surprise butted with relief on her face. 'Yes, sir. Birthdays and Christmas. There's only two of them, so it's not much.'

'And what do they like? What do you like to buy them?'

'Sometimes I make things, sir – gloves and mufflers for Christmas, usually. Socks Jim can never have enough of, even married. Small things. Things for their smokes. Pouches. Last year I got a cigarette case for William. He was pleased with that.'

'Was he?'

'Oh yes, sir. I had his name done on it.'

'You're a kind sister.'

She smiled hesitantly. 'Yes, sir. They say so.'

'Thank you, Susan. Would you have Lewis fetch a cab?'

*

The sun smacked him on the back of the neck and marched him down the steps, to where the horse dazzled with sweat. He gave Frank's address in Holborn, asking that they stop at a jeweller's on the way. In the seat it was even hotter, strong-smelling: leather, wafts of animal and driver. When they set off he put his hat in his lap and hunched forward, craving the breeze. The street shrank on itself and the hungry city claimed them. He felt brave, foolhardy, slightly unreal, hunched forward into the breeze. An odd sensation of being outside himself, frightened and admiring at the same time.

He bought a brass-plated cigarette case at the jeweller's. For the rest of the journey he turned it over inside a handkerchief, careful not to smudge it, seeing bits of the city shiver on its surface. Shortly after six they halted at a house halfway down John Street, built on a corner. The sky was fierce and it remained violently hot, but the sun was lower, glaring on the upper windows. John stood on the pavement. The house was the smallest and dirtiest on the street, a short narrow step fronting a door without a portico. It seemed beaten back by the temperature, a decrepit, unloved relative of its neighbour, against which it leaned exhaustedly. Net curtains, curling slightly, hung in the bottom window. He supposed the house must be divided into rooms.

Feeling all the irresistible strangeness of the situation, he approached the door, which abruptly opened away from his knock, a thickset youngish man rearing up in front of him, a newspaper trapped under his arm.

'Here for books?'

'No. For Mr Feaver.'

'He's on the first floor.' It seemed to John the man looked at him with curiosity. 'Well, we have books, if you're interested. I can't show you now as I'm going out, and my wife's out too, as it happens. But if you ever come again.'

'Thank you.'

'No trouble. Here you are.' He retreated into the dimness of the corridor and pressed himself against the wall, waving John in. The brims of their hats bumped as John came past. The man turned back to tip his with a large hand. 'He's upstairs, as I say. Good evening.'

The door shut and the dimness became a darkness until John's eyes began to approximate, making out a door on the right and a staircase. He walked to the stairs and stopped at the bottom step, his hand on the banister, excitement seeding in his stomach. Mark and his coffee cup whirled through his mind. He started to climb, hearing a door close. He was midway when Frank appeared on the landing, foreshortened, all trousers and boots.

'I saw you from my window,' Frank said. 'Then I heard Mr Higgs open the door and thought he might be showing you his books, and I didn't want to come down till he'd done. I thought it would be strange, the three of us.' As he spoke he came rapidly down the stairs, until they were two steps apart.

John looked up at Frank's face in the half-light. He might murder me, raced the thought. He could be my ruin.

Frank put a hand on his shoulder, coming down another step. 'Let's get out into the sunshine, shall we? What a day it's been! A scorcher.'

Outside, Frank took a left down Northington Street, then right, then left again, talking all the time. John watched his teeth, appearing and disappearing beneath the moustache, guarding the wet pink tongue. His blond hair was dark and coiled with sweat around the temples. He was beautiful, more beautiful than John remembered. At his side he felt large and unwieldy, cumbersome – like an old dog trying to run at the heels of a young master. 'It's just this way,' Frank was saying. 'Just somewhere to quench a thirst. I sometimes have a drink with Mr Higgs there. I half-wondered if it wasn't where he was going when he came out, but he turned the other way. You were lucky not to have to sift through all those books – he's hard to stop once he gets going. Then again, you were lucky to be asked in. He's careful. Must've liked the look of you.' He flashed a grin and John almost staggered under it.

'What books does he sell?' he managed.

'Political mostly. Hot stuff, is what I gather. And he's got a little magazine he's in charge of. Free-thinking.'

'Have you read any of his books?'

'After a fashion. Some of them I had a hand in.'

'Writing?' Unimagined possibilities populated in John's mind.

Frank laughed. 'No. I'm a compositor, I set the type. I work for Mr Owen, he's a publisher – he's the one who tipped me off about the lodgings. Mr Higgs is one of his customers. Here we are.'

They stopped in front of a tavern, the King of Prussia. The entrance slouched under the upper half of the building, vainly supported by flower baskets. There was a group of men laughing loudly by the door, haloed by smoke, their drinks lined up on the windowsill.

'Will this do?' Frank suddenly looked anxious.

'Of course.'

'Good.' He appeared relieved. 'I'm parched.'

Frank ordered two glasses of beer, without asking what John wanted. He had a tab. The woman behind the bar spoke loudly as she took down the glasses and pulled the drinks, half to them and half to herself, so accustomed to the sound of her own voice that it had begun to accompany her everywhere.

They sat at a small table, Frank on a padded seat, John in a chair with his back to the bar. The light through the window was tawny; it warmed the brown of Frank's jacket. They both drank their beer, Frank letting a sliver of foam sit for a moment in his moustache before he licked it away. John held the taste before swallowing, the liquid running into the dry parts of his mouth, warm and sour. He passed a hand over the moisture in his beard before drinking again, watching Frank over the rim of his glass. He thought he might be twenty years younger.

'You haven't said anything about my street,' Frank said, smiling.

'It's very nice,' John said, thinking of what he could add.

'I mean the name.' Frank continued the smile, dunking it briefly back into his glass.

John hesitated, then laughed. 'John Street. Do you know, it hadn't occurred to me?'

'It's the first thing I thought. It's always seemed strange to me, for a street, and then there you are. It suits you better.' He took another draw at his beer. 'John Addington. It's a nice name.'

'You don't know it?' Vanity pressed him to ask, even as it increased the risk.

'Know it?'

'I've written books.'

'You're a famous man!'

'No. Only in a small way, for those with particular interests.' He wanted immediately to change the subject, but at the same time liked the look on Frank's face.

'What do you write about?'

'I have written about the Greek poets, and about the Renaissance in Italy. I've translated Michelangelo's poetry from the Italian.'

'The Italian. You're a clever man.' Frank finished his drink, tipping back his head, stubble on his neck. 'I could tell. Shall we have another? You'll have to get it down you faster.'

He got up and went back to the bar. John obediently gulped at his drink. 'Do you like your work?' he asked, when Frank came back.

Frank lifted his eyes from the glass. 'Don't know any other kind. It was my father's trade, and his father's. I like the look of words, putting them together. You have to concentrate. Have to stand around a lot too. You never get the ink off – look.' He held up his hands, and John could see the bluish tinge of his fingertips. He had an impulse to touch them, to see whether it would transfer.

'Was your father a writer?' Frank asked.

'He was a physician. Do you work with yours?'

'Died two years ago. We never knew what it was. Stopped being able to lift his arms, couldn't eat, couldn't keep his head up. Dreadful.'

'I'm sorry he suffered.'

'I'm sorry remembering it. My mother's not well now. They say it's a cancer.' As though precluding further discussion, Frank placed both hands palms-down on the table. John noticed how the hair grew diagonally across their backs, burying in arrow-points under the little fingers. The tavern buzzed and clinked around them, and the floorboards creaked. The smell of beer and boots was very strong, sitting on top of the slow, warm air.

Frank looked up. 'Are you married?'

'I am. Are you?'

'No.' He appraised him. 'You must have children?'

'I have three daughters.'

'How old?'

'Twenty-three, twenty-two, eighteen. The eldest are both married – one is in Birmingham, the other in Dublin.'

'I'm gone twenty-eight,' Frank said.

'I shall be fifty in December.'

Frank shifted in his seat, stretching out his legs so that his heels ground along either side of the table. 'What sort of man are you, John?'

He laughed nervously. 'What sort of man are you?'

Frank spread his bluish fingers. 'I'm just a man who toils for his bread.' He lowered them again, examined them cursorily on the table. Then he held up his empty glass, the suds sliding greasily inside it. 'I'd like another drink. Are you having one?'

John looked at his glass, more than half full. 'Please,' he said. Frank got up again, shuffling sideways between the tables, placing his hand on John's shoulder and applying mild pressure, levering himself off towards the bar. After a moment John glanced over, seeing him standing leanly among the other men, collected by them. He saw him stroke down the corners of his moustache, put his hands in his pockets, rock on his heels. Then, bending his head back to his beer, John tried to recall the stab of danger he'd felt earlier when Frank met him close on the stairs, or the strangeness he'd been so conscious of outside on the step, but found in himself only a kind of luxuriant passivity. A desire to succumb, to drop under experience.

Frank came back. The sliver of foam reappeared in his moustache.

'You didn't answer me,' he said. 'About what sort of man you are. I think I can tell, as it happens.'

'Go on.'

'Clever, like I said. Brave, for coming here. But lonely, else you wouldn't have.'

'Could you tell, in the park?'

'I thought I could. I had to be a little brave myself.'

'You frightened me.'

'That's what I had to be brave for.'

They looked at each other. John thought again what he had missed by not seeing Frank naked at the river – the little triangle of skin at his collar invited, like an open window.

'Tell me something, Frank,' John said, liking to say the name, liking the way Frank's eyes widened in response. 'When you pretended to swim off, in the park. How was it you didn't look to see whether I was laughing?'

He seemed surprised. 'I was embarrassed. Did you?'

'Laugh? Yes.'

'That's good then. I like people to laugh, only it's easy to go wrong.' He paused for his drink. 'I'm glad I made you laugh. I supposed I had, when you wrote.'

Another look between them.

'Do you smoke?' Frank said. He brought out a pouch of tobacco and papers from his inside pocket – John saw for a moment his shirt curving away round his body – and began to make two cigarettes. John watched him sprinkle the tobacco, roll and nip the paper, bring each to his tongue to fasten it down. With one he made a mistake and began again. 'It's the beer,' he said, with a quick smile. When he was finished he tucked them behind his ear, curled over by the blond hair.

'I have something for you,' John said at last. He had been struggling for the right words; calculating the likely interest from the men at the other tables. But then he was mastered by his desire, to please. He handed over the cigarette case, wrapped in his handkerchief.

Frank received it with a soft exclamation. A man at the neighbouring table looked over briefly, returned to his talk. Unwrapped, the case glowed in Frank's hand, the gaslight flickering across it. He lowered it into his lap, beneath the rim of the table, looking down at it, so that the reflections on the brass wandered over his forehead. John heard the click of its opening and shutting. 'It's very nice, very nice indeed. Very smart,' Frank said. 'This is kind of you, John,' he added, looking up. Then: 'Aha!' He took the cigarettes down from his ear and the two clicks came again. There was something thrilling about the way his hands kept disappearing beneath the table.

'I'm glad you like it.'

'It's kind of you,' Frank repeated, slipping the case into his pocket. A look of determination came into his face. 'Tell you what, I'll just go and relieve myself, and then we'll have a walk with our smokes, how's that?'

While he was gone John paid the account at the bar, returning Frank's glass, and came back to his own two drinks still on the table, sitting and finishing one. The pleasant numbness created by the beer had only strengthened his feeling of passivity, of being washed willingly along into a new situation.

'I'll help with that.' Frank was standing behind him. He leaned over to pick up the full drink, the smell of him very close, his jacket brushing John's face, the buttons almost cold. John didn't turn around, only sat in this new proximity, staring at the tabletop while Frank took great consecutive gulps. 'There we go,' Frank said finally, speaking from the back of his throat. The empty glass was put down and John got up to meet his smile.

They were at the door when Frank swung back: 'The bill—'

'I settled it,' John said.

'You're being very kind,' he said, shaking his head.

They were on the pavement. Frank took out the case and offered John one of the two cigarettes embraced by green velvet, strangely dignified in their new setting. They stood smoking. It was still warm; almost dark. The group of men who'd been there when they arrived shambled off and a barman came out and collected the glasses. There was a crash and a swell of laughter from inside. Frank looked over the frosting on the window, his cigarette jammed at the corner of his mouth. 'He's blaming the landlady, look. As if it was the stool's fault.' He turned back to face John, breathing out a ragged sheet of smoke. 'Come on. Let's have a stroll.'

They began walking back the way they had come, side by side, following the ends of their cigarettes. There was anticipation in their apparent aimlessness; the emptiness of the streets, in the yawning lamplight, seemed an implication. John, walking at a slower pace than was natural, slipped with one foot off the kerb.

'Careful, John.' Frank flicked his cigarette stub away as he said it.

John stepped fully off the pavement, dropping his stub down a drain. Something occurred to him: 'When we met, you called me sir.'

'I was being polite, wasn't I, knowing what's good for me,' Frank said, looking over with a grin. In the lamplight his moustache had become very dark, but his hair shimmered where it was blondest. 'This is Emerald Street. Nice name isn't it? Here, here, and this is Emerald Court—' He reached sharply from his position on the pavement and took hold of John's arm, pulling him back onto the kerb and down a narrow passageway, scuffing his shoulder painfully on the brick. They stopped halfway and stood facing each other in the loose dark. The passage led out onto the Theobalds Road, from where came a low thunder of traffic and a haze of amber light. The rapid movement had made John breathless with surprise.

'This is what you want, isn't it,' Frank said quietly.

John had begun to nod, even though it wasn't spoken like a question, when Frank roughly took hold of his lapels with both hands. John couldn't help it – he started back, even raised his hands feebly in defence, his hat slipping, but Frank kept his grip, tightened, pulled, pulled him close, against his chest. His mouth fell on John's like a trap. John buckled under it, the hard mouth on his soft, wet on wet. Their mouths tasted of smoke and beer, the beer running liquidly under the smoke, one tongue to another. He placed his hands on Frank's cheeks, the new stubble like grit, then cupped them under his ears, then spread them on his neck, his fingers running under the collar. Their bodies were pressed close together. Frank's was lean, taut. John tried to make himself flat against it. They were hard against each other, John could feel Frank's cock hard against his. Everything was heavy, dense. The kiss became frictive, uneven – their lips were sticking and unsticking.

Frank broke off, looked quickly either side of the passage. 'We mustn't be greedy,' he said, his voice still quiet. He kissed John another time, pushing up against him, crushing them together. Air whistled through his nose. It was almost violent; John found himself shaking slightly. 'Not just yet, anyhow,' Frank grinned, coming away. 'Mrs Higgs won't take kindly to me bringing a gentleman back at this hour, especially not one as distinguished-looking as you. So, you'd better go that way and catch a cab. Will you write me a letter, John?'

'I will.' His voice came out weakened, unfamiliar.

'That's good. I'll see you again, John. I'll be swimming off now.'

John laughed. He placed one hand behind Frank's head and boldly leaned to kiss him. His mouth felt new again, warm and secret.

They backed away from each other, turning down their respective ends of the passage. John looked and saw Frank emerge onto Emerald Street and disappear. A sort of stunned relief that things could go no further was curdling already to disappointment; other schemes and scenarios accumulated untidily in his head. He came out onto the road, pushing up his hat, and looked behind him into the passage, to see what was visible. Only a vague darkness. The people walking past paid no attention to it.

He was about to hail a cab when he felt an overwhelming desire to urinate. Stepping back into the dark of the passage, which still seemed thick with their presence, so much so that at first he thought some others had entered it, he took out his still-stiff cock and waited for the piss to come. Finally it did, rushing and foaming on the flagstones, wet on dry. And he thought to himself, I am in love. I am in love. I am in love.

11 Gloucester Terrace

Paddington

13th July 94

Dear Mr Ellis,

I am writing to you, care of Mr Hazaldene of the <u>Contemporary</u>, to congratulate you on your recent article on Whitman in that magazine, which I read with great interest and admiration. How close we are in our response will be seen if you consult my own writing on the same subject. I have tried for many years to write about Whitman, saying all that he means and has meant to me, and yet it seems that you have succeeded on the first try — if it is your first try? I wish though that you had said more about the 'Calamus' poems: or, if you have formed an opinion, that you would tell me what you think.

Male comradeship clearly goes deep with Whitman, but I have never felt wholly confident in his meaning, even in 'For You O Democracy' or 'Earth, My Likeness'. He nowhere makes it clear whether he means to advocate anything approaching comradeship in its Greek form, or whether he regards that as simply monstrous. And yet this issue seems of overwhelming importance. Without clarification, I have felt unable to judge him in relation to the gravest ethical and social problems. Does Whitman imagine that there is lurking in manly love the stuff of a new spiritual energy, the liberation of which would prove of benefit to society? And if so, is he prepared to accept, condone or ignore the physical aspects of this passion?

I have ventured to write to you on this point, because I think I am correct to discern your sense also that Whitman <u>is</u> hinting at Greek feeling. For myself, I am more than ever inclined to believe that Whitman sanctions any form of passionate emotion in comradeship; and that he leaves it to the individual to form their own view of how that emotion should be expressed.

Yours very sincerely,

J. Addington

VIII

'Isn't she wonderful, Mr Ellis!' Angelica Britell turned to him, her eyes tight with pleasure, a few strands of dark hair streaming out from under her straw hat. 'You're wonderful, Edith!'

Edith batted the compliment away with her free hand and went on, her voice jumping in the wind: '"That is to say, the acceptability of women's suffrage depends on the wider acceptability of popular democracy. To admit women in their millions to the franchise is, in the eyes of some, to *compound* the *existing* dangers of democracy. So, if these two great causes are intertwined, the one depending on the success of the other, then we might fairly ask—"'

'Too many "depending"s,' Henry interjected.

Edith stopped dead, looking at her page, only slightly short for breath. '"Depends", "depending". Well, one can get too wrapped up in that sort of thing. Clarity over elegance, I've always thought.'

'"Guaranteeing"?' said Angelica. '"If these two great causes are intertwined, the one guaranteeing the success of the other . . ."'

'That's not quite the same thing,' said Henry. They were gathered round the pages fluttering in Edith's hand, newly conscious, now that they were no longer walking into the wind, of the heat of the sun on their backs. He reread the lines, in Edith's small, firm handwriting. There were several crossings-out already, some of them done in the last half-hour, on the move, the lines shaky, running away to the margins.

'I'll lose that bit altogether,' Edith announced, starting off again along the path, with Henry and Angelica following. ' "So, if these two great causes are intertwined, then we might fairly ask: what is the key that will open the door to both? Here I wish to quote from Henrik Ibsen, whose great works for the theatre, though they are not just that, many of you will know: 'An element of *aristocracy* must be introduced into our life. Of course, I do not mean the aristocracy of birth, or of the purse, or even the aristocracy of intellect. I mean the aristocracy of character, of will, of mind. That only can free us. From two groups will this aristocracy I hope for come to our people: from our *women* and from our *workmen*.' That is Ibsen. His—" '

'That's a wonderful quote, Edith. Perhaps you could do it a little slower.'

'Thank you, Angelica. I am more interested in your criticism of my argument at this stage. I do not plan to give the lecture as part of a walking tour, in a gale.'

'Of course, Edith.'

' "That is Ibsen. His argument is most novel perhaps, as it applies to women. For is there such a thing as an aristocracy of character, of will, of mind, among women—?" '

Henry tramped along, listening carefully. They were in north Norfolk again. The sky was still vast, bleeding bluely to the edges of his vision. The weather remained fine, if billowy – the long grass and the reeds sighed and whistled more plaintively. They had taken the same cottage, with the tree over the low wall. And they were walking with their new friend, Angelica, just as they had most of the days of their honeymoon. Angelica was at his side now, wearing a dress with thick blue and yellow stripes that put him in mind of a sailing boat. The image appeared: of himself on her back and them pushing off together into clear water, the dress spreading out behind like a wave running in to shore.

Angelica troubled him. She took no notice of his shyness, which is to say that she made no effort to overcome it. Henry was shy but knew himself to be interesting; Angelica treated him almost as an idiot, taking his silences at face value, talking to him as though he were merely a docile attendant on Edith's greatness – it was all, don't you think Edith is working too hard, Mr Ellis? and, you will make sure she gets to bed early this evening, won't you, Mr Ellis? He found himself in an invidious position, for to assert his significance would cost him much embarrassment, in pursuit of an uncertain goal. After all, what did he want from her? He could not tell whether she really believed him so negligible – he could not, for instance, bring himself to enquire whether she had read anything of his work – or had simply pressed home an advantage. The advantage being her expanding intimacy with Edith, which, in expanding, pushed him further out, made him a silent watchman on its perimeter.

He tried not to think like this. Edith admired Angelica. 'That woman is a tonic,' she had said quite emphatically when they shut the door behind them after their very first walk with her. She said Angelica had a good mind. She liked how interested Angelica was in her lectures, in her thought. She liked Angelica's clothes. She thought Angelica was good-looking – which she was, in a hard, jutting sort of way. She found Angelica amusing. They had long, coiling conversations. Angelica smoked cigarettes. She had a loud laugh that finished shortly on a snap.

Angelica was the only daughter of an upright Burnham family. She was in rebellion. 'I am an unmarried woman, Mr Ellis,' she had said to him, sending a shaft of pearlescent smoke up to the ceiling, 'And I am at my liberty.' Something about the way she said it had prevented him asking questions. Her home life was mysterious – he knew nothing about her parents, save that they were dreadfully upright. She had simply appeared that hot morning, the first full day of his honeymoon, knocked and begun talking to Edith on the step, in a green dress bursting with sunflowers. And she returned the next day, quite as if she was an old friend – of Edith's. And the next, and the next, and the next. And now he and Edith had reappeared, to see Angelica, to resubmit to her attention. Edith had insisted. Letters came from Burnham Market in coloured envelopes.

They stopped on a high ridge to take in the view across the flats. The tide was coming in, advancing rapidly across the mud; an old fishing boat seemed to sizzle in it. Angelica clamped her arms to her sides to keep her dress from flapping. A couple walked past and the man raised his hat. Angelica ignored him.

Edith took a breath of salt air, looked down at her conclusion. 'Shall I do that last bit one more time?'

'Yes, do,' Angelica said.

'"Where we see female ability, we must coax it into the light; we must all of us, where we find it, in whomever we find it, shelter and protect it from the slings and arrows of the world. But we must also look inward. We must look to ourselves. Self-development must be our creed. The development of personality. Freedom in individuality. Freedom to *be*. It is not by what they can seize, but by what they *are*, that women finally count."'

'Marvellous,' Angelica said, now raising a protective hand to her hat. 'Wasn't that marvellous, Mr Ellis?'

*

Two days later, they were back in London. Edith had decided she would come to Brixton for supper straight from the station. She was in an armchair, eyes closed, her neat little legs hanging over one of the arms, ankles crossed. Henry had already written to decline an invitation to lecture, on the usual grounds of incapacity, and was reading through the rest of his post. The gas made its noise, like air escaping through teeth.

'Are you comfortable, dear boy?' She kept her eyes shut.

'Quite comfortable, thank you.' He was examining a letter he'd been sent. '*You* look comfortable,' he added.

'Yes, I am. I'm thinking.'

'About what?'

'Vegetarianism. It seems a chore. But the arguments are good.'

'The suppositions.'

She smiled sleepily under her lids. 'Yes, the suppositions.'

There was a silence. He began reading the first lines of the letter.

'Henry, I've started thinking about something else.'

'What?'

'I'm thinking about Angelica.'

'What about her?' He looked over.

Her eyes were open. She pushed herself up in the chair, drew in her knees. 'She's so lonely there; she told me. It's difficult for her in that house. Her father calls her a new woman.'

'She is.'

'Yes, but he's forever getting at her. Pecking, she calls it. Always pecking at her, like a tattered old cockerel. I think it's terribly wearing. Henry—'

'Yes?'

'What do you think?'

'We must be kind to her.'

'We are being, I think. She's very grateful.' There was a pause. 'She's impressed by us. Our mode of living.'

'Yes.'

'I thought I might ask her to come and stay with me.'

'For how long?'

'Just a few weeks. To show her a different way. You'd help, wouldn't you?'

'Would I still see you on your own?'

'Of course. I would still come here.'

'What about your work?'

'I'll go on with it. You know she isn't an obstacle. She's interested.'

'Not as interested as me.'

'Of course not. It doesn't touch you, Henry. Henry?'

'No, it doesn't touch me. Of course I'll help. I am only a little spoiled with your company, that's all.'

'Thank you. I would like to do this for her. She might say no, of course.'

'Yes.'

'But I doubt it.' She smiled at him. 'We are not unattractive, you know. It is what we wanted.'

'I have never thought myself attractive.'

'I meant that we are an example. The New Life.'

'I had hoped it was enough to *be*.'

'That was naive of you. I shall have to read you my lecture again.'

He scratched an eyebrow. 'Not just yet.'

She laughed. 'Dear boy. But now I need to catch a train. And to use your closet first.'

He became hard as he listened to the plangent plummeting sound, thinning to a trickle, a drip. He still had his erection when she came back.

'I will write to Angelica in the morning,' she said, standing in the doorway. She took two quick steps over to him and kissed him on the top of his head. She rested her chin there a moment. He shifted, pulling his legs together, trying to conceal the ridge in his trousers – it was squeezing him tighter for the nearness and pressure of her, the

82

proximity of the imagined dampness under her skirt. He could not tell where she was looking.

'What a lot of freedom you have given me,' she murmured into his hair. 'It is a great gift.'

As usual, once she was gone it took some considerable time for the atmosphere in the room to settle around her absence. He stared blindly into it, or at it, frustrated-feeling. They still had not consummated their marriage and he understood now that they never would. On the second night of their honeymoon – the day they first met Angelica – he had climbed the stairs to the bedroom almost certain that something would happen, that they would make good on the night before. Instead, they had lain there in the swallowing darkness, silent. The long silence had rebuked and urged and then finally absolved them. All the nights following they had gone easily and familiarly to sleep – it was this that had come to seem the worst thing.

Henry told himself, as perhaps Edith told herself, that this failure only made their marriage more distinctive, founded it more securely on the bedrock of principle. But it still felt like a failure, and failure had brought with it a new and burdensome sexual fullness. He felt constantly in danger of spilling over. There were his strange feelings about Angelica, who sometimes induced an irritation so intense he longed to lunge out of his quiet and lay hands on her. And then there was this deviation of his, this peculiarity, tickling, warm: his desire to hear and see a woman urinate. A tender little curiosity, nurtured since childhood – nurtured, at first, without guilt – that had mingled somehow with his sexual perceptions, gradually rendering them strange and unaccountable. He could not trace it directly. In adulthood he had simply come to recognise it in himself, with the surprised, belated acceptance one gives to one's appearance as the mirror insistently shows it: as what is there, as what has settled, the shape that has mysteriously filled. He had accepted it, but he could not speak of it, to anyone.

He could see no plausible way of satisfying it. And yet after the honeymoon it had regained pre-eminence in his mind, like a stinging salve for his disappointment. He thought cringingly of his erection earlier, whether Edith had noticed and, if she had, whether it would have occurred to her to make the connection. He found himself, with the usual nervous twitch of excitement, imagining that he might, debating whether she—

In the enforced gap in his thoughts, he eventually became aware of another excitement, generated by the letter he'd been sent. He picked it up and read it properly. John Addington was something approaching a great, a famous, man. Certainly an interesting man. But what a strange letter it was. Perhaps not entirely surprising. But brave, extraordinarily straightforward. How odd, to depend so much on an answer, and from an entire stranger. And with Whitman the soul of candour.

He took down his copy of *Leaves of Grass* and thumbed through to the 'Calamus' poems, locating the ones Addington had mentioned. He smiled at 'For You O Democracy':

> *I will plant companionship thick as trees along all the rivers of America,*
> *   and along the shores of the great lakes, and all over the prairies,*
> *I will make inseparable cities with their arms about each other's necks,*
> *By the love of comrades,*
> *By the manly love of comrades.*

But he hesitated over 'Earth, My Likeness':

> *Earth, my likeness,*
> *Though you look so impassive, ample and spheric there,*
> *I now suspect that is not all;*
> *I now suspect there is something fierce in you eligible to burst forth,*
> *For an athlete is enamour'd of me, and I of him,*

But toward him there is something fierce and terrible in me eligible to burst
  forth,
I dare not tell it in words, not even in these songs.

And it occurred to Henry to wonder: of what was Walt afraid to speak?

*

Three days later, taking great pains, Henry wrote and posted his reply. He decided to enclose a photograph of himself. It seemed the sort of thing one author might send another. The picture he chose had been taken the week after he and Edith returned from their honeymoon. They had gone to the studio together. He was shown side on, sitting in a chair, one leg dangled over the other, a book open in his lap. He didn't exactly like it, but he felt some grudging respect for the pose: the angle and the arrangement of limbs and the dignity it conveyed. In reality he had been looking at a dirty corner of the studio where the toys for distracting children were kept. The book wasn't his either: he had made sure to obscure the spine. There were several more pictures taken that day, sliding out of the packet into his hand:

Edith's face in close perspective, hair brushed back, eyes bright and conquering.

His own face, dark, bearded, sombre, eyes focused elsewhere.

Edith in the chair, elbow planted, clever head cupped in hand.

The two of them: Henry sitting, looking up at Edith; Edith sitting, looking up at Henry.

The two of them, standing nervously side by side.

14 Dover Mansions

Brixton

21st July 94

Dear Mr Addington,

Apologies for my delay in responding. I have been away from London, holidaying in Norfolk with my wife and a new friend of ours. It is the place where we recently spent our honeymoon, so it is rapidly becoming a favourite with us.

Your questions about Whitman I am not sure I know how to answer, though you are quite right that I detect in him an openness to Greek feeling, and to its useful expression in the present. All questions of future society — its morality, the principles on which it should be based — are of deep interest to my wife and me. You must believe me on this point, and write again. I know and admire your work on the Greek poets, and on Michelangelo.

I have taken the liberty of enclosing my photograph, and I hope you will send me yours, which I would greatly value.

Very sincerely,

Henry Ellis

IX

The door opened a little way and a long inquisitive sliver of cap, eye, nose, mouth and dress appeared alongside it. When Susan saw who it was she stepped backwards with the door and became entire, the sun falling on her face.

'Good afternoon, sir.'

John came in with Frank following.

'Madam and Miss Addington went out separately, sir.'

'Yes, I thought they might have,' he said, handing over his hat. The floorboards in the hallway shone like cherries in the clipped light from the window above the door. The house smelled of polish and was very quiet; so quiet that John felt almost guilty for interrupting its Sunday peace. Susan seemed to him to have a proprietary claim on it.

She was looking at Frank with controlled expectation. He took off his cap and hung it on the crown of John's hat while she held it. 'Good afternoon,' he added.

'This is Mr Feaver,' John said.

She looked quickly at Frank again.

'We'll take some tea in my study.'

'Yes, sir.'

Upstairs, Frank stood magnificently in the middle of the room. 'She's a pretty girl,' he said, nodding his head towards the door.

John could barely look at him, he was so beautiful and so close. 'She is.'

'She knows I'm no gentleman, mind. Not that she'd have to be a genius to notice it.'

It was true that his accent was very strong in this room. 'It's no matter,' John said.

'So you say. I've never been in a house like yours.'

'This room is the only one that is really mine.'

'You've almost as many books as Mr Higgs in his shop.'

'Ah, well, these are only some.' He could not help saying this.

Frank arced his eyebrows. 'This is where you write?'

'Yes. Though I am only reading currently.'

'And who's this?' Frank walked over and plucked Henry Ellis's photo from where it lay on the desk.

'A writer; he sent it with a letter.'

'He's handsome.'

'A little too dark.' He smiled at Frank, and then added, 'My impression is that he is in love with his wife. I do not think he means to be admired.'

'By sods, you mean?'

John felt his face tighten. 'Is that what you call yourself?'

Frank put the picture back. 'I don't call myself anything. It's what people might call me, if they knew something.'

'Would they ever – know something?'

'Not because of anything I ever said. But here I am in your big house. It's not usual. People usually want to be a bit quieter.'

'I'm not ashamed.'

'Well, we've done nothing to be ashamed of yet, have we John?' Frank grinned. 'Nothing proper. You can't get nicked for a kiss, can you?'

John was about to reply that he didn't know, when Frank's breath was suddenly on his face. Their mouths at first were as dry as the day outside; then it became like drinking from a cup, the kiss like water, wetting their lips.

John escaped it. 'There's tea coming.' He pulled the bell, heard it ringing in the far-off of the house. They looked at each other. Frank patted down his moustache, grinning still. He put his hands in his pockets, his lean wrists showing; he was framed like a saint against the bright window. John seated himself in a chair and crossed his legs.

Susan backed into the room with her tray, apologising as she set it down and poured the cups. Frank said thank you in his accent. After she left they both listened to the diminuendo of her footsteps. When there was no longer any sound, John released a cramped breath. His heart was beating crampedly in his chest. The steam from the cups was waving in the light. The question was there. 'Will you take off your clothes?' He couldn't help from sounding pleading.

Frank laughed. 'Will you take off yours?'

'Not yet.'

He seemed to accept this. 'All right,' he said. 'What about the window?'

'No one can see in. And I want to have you in this light.'

'The girl?'

'She'll only come if she's called for.'

Frank nodded, like he was accepting an order. He took off his jacket and lay it over the desk chair, looking round the room. 'Like this? Stood here?'

'Yes, just there.'

Frank kept his eye, beginning to unbutton his shirt. He pulled it over his head, teasing the sleeves over each wrist in turn. His pale chest and stomach and forearms were cross-hatched with golden hairs that caught the light.

John's erection was visible in his lap. He pushed under his trousers and took its heat into his hand.

Frank, watching this, his mouth moving at the corners, took off his boots and socks and unbelted his trousers, pushing them down from the hips, stepping out of them on the floor. His shins looked almost hairless, clean and white, but the hairs regrouped above his knees, climbing up his thighs. He looked like an athlete, a runner before a race, his arms flexed at his sides, his toes subtly arched. Then he unknotted his drawers and dragged them down over his cock, which John saw now for the first time as it lengthened under the shifting fabric, actually stretching out beneath as if trying to avoid being uncovered, which it was at that moment, rebounding on the air, long and smooth and strong-veined and peeping pink.

Frank stood in the middle of the room, as he had only a minute ago in jacket and shirt and belt and trousers and boots, with his cock pointing at John.

'Turn around.'

Frank grinned, pivoted on his bare feet on the red-patterned rug, presenting his broad white shoulders, his lean tapering back, his pale buttocks, the glinting slopes of his thighs, the dents behind his knees. The light brushed along his outline. He was padded all round with the wide silence of an empty house, abandoned to the maid on a Sunday afternoon. 'You're not exactly what I thought you were,' he said, not turning or moving his head, his hands stretched at his sides, bluish fingertips probing the air. The rug was rucked a little around his feet.

John wanted not to speak. 'How do you mean?'

'You're bolder.'

I am only desperate, John thought. He stood and walked up behind Frank, placing both hands on his hips, somehow vulnerable, pimpled slightly in the cool of the room. He lowered his face onto his neck, pulling him close – the strangeness of all this naked flesh against his clothes reminded him for an instant of his children as babies – kissing in the crook of his jaw, the stubble cutting his lips, smelling of smoke. He let his hands run down the sides of Frank's thighs, the hair licking beneath them, bringing them up the backs, up over the incline of his buttocks. Frank turned and they were kissing again; there was his whole golden body beneath his hands, the hard cock; and Frank's hands were now at John's buttons, working quickly and blindly like a thief. John had the sense, the vague sense, that this was more than he had prepared himself for, but it was falling back, receding under the pressure of hands. There came another thought, fierce in its clarity: I would fuck this man in the street. And then they heard the clear, chill, imperious ring of the doorbell.

Catherine was examining the letters on the table in the hallway. John saw her look past him at Frank as they came down the stairs.

'Susan said you were with company. I got all the way to Anna's and found only the servants. She'd forgotten about me, clearly. I don't believe we've met?'

'Catherine, this is Mr Feaver, who knows my books. Mr Feaver, this is my wife.'

'Good afternoon, Mr Feaver.'

'Good afternoon, Mrs Addington.' Frank took the proffered hand. 'I'm a great reader of your husband.'

'We met in the park,' John put in.

Catherine looked closer at Frank. 'I see.'

Frank touched his moustache and looked at John. 'I must be away, sir.'

'Yes, thank you. It was very good to make your acquaintance.'

Susan came forward to open the door, holding Frank's cap. Placing it on his head, he turned to Catherine: 'A pleasure to meet you, madam.' He put out his hand to John. 'Thank you for giving me your time, sir.'

'Not at all.'

He walked to the door with him. Down the steps, Frank turned and tapped the peak of his cap with his forefinger, before sticking his hands in his pockets and striding off. Coming back inside, John quietly asked Susan to fetch his hat.

Catherine had moved into the drawing room. She was standing with one arm sharply outstretched, her fingers stood slantingly on the arm of the sofa. Her wrist was strained white. She was wearing a grey dress, almost silver, the collar wrapped strictly around her neck.

'Is this happening again?' she said. 'Just say.'

There was a great tiredness in her voice, like boredom: an awful, sickening boredom bringing her to the verge of tears.

'It is,' he replied, and waited.

Still the overwhelming impression was of boredom. It flooded to the corners of the room. He felt like a child caught in some wrong-doing, who must confess and be punished before life can unstop and continue on its way. Guilt burned under his skin. The image of Frank burned. He wanted to follow him, to leave the house before he was beyond finding. He called for Susan. She came in quickly and gave over his hat, quickly leaving.

Catherine said, 'Where did you find him?'

'I told you, in the park.'

'Today?'

'Another day. You will have to know him, Catherine.'

'Why?'

'Because I do not intend to give him up.'

She took her arm away from the sofa, rubbing her whitened fingers absently with her other hand: 'Why have you always brought them here?'

'So I can believe I am not ashamed.'

'But you are, Johnny. It is natural.'

'No,' he said. 'It is unnatural. It is unnatural to attempt to destroy the physical instinct, until every other instinct is withered and dead, and this one still persists.'

The boredom was now so intense that tears stood in her eyes. Her face injured him with its familiarity. 'I did not marry for this,' she said.

'Neither did I.'

'Oh, but you did.'

She came past without looking at his face and went out, her perfume staying behind like a guard. He listened to her climb the stairs. Then he put on his hat and left the house, turning rapidly in the direction Frank had taken and seeing with a jolt that he was only a few yards away, poised at the end of the street, opening a brass cigarette case that winked in the sunshine.

11 Gloucester Terrace

Paddington

25th July 94

Dear Mr Ellis,

Thank you for your interesting response. I think that if I were to call your attention (and that of your wife) to any subject with pressing implications for future society, it would be this one we have so far called Greek feeling; or, as it is becoming known, sexual inversion. It is a terra incognita; and yet this eccentricity of nature throws such an extraordinary light upon previous conceptions of sex.

I am at this moment reading among those Continental medical and forensic authorities who have taken up this subject in recent years — Casper—Liman, Tardieu, Carlier, Taxil, Moreau, Tarnowsky, Krafft-Ebing. If you are interested in inversion as it manifested in Ancient Greece, I have written a book on the subject, privately printed, a copy of which I could send you.

Congratulations on your marriage. I hope it may prove as true a source of happiness as mine on the whole has been to me.

Very sincerely,

John Addington

PS I enclose a photograph of myself. It is not as nice as yours.

X

'Is it socialism or India tonight?' Henry asked, as they came into the room. They were at Ted Carpenter's lodgings near Charing Cross, held in a clench of afternoon heat.

'India tonight, socialism again tomorrow, feminism Friday,' Carpenter replied, taking a seat. His shirt was open at the neck, showing dark hair that sprang about the buttons. His trousers bagged. He wore sandals on bare feet. The window behind him was pushed out to its furthest extent. A tree spread shining leaves like polished wares beneath the hot white sill.

Henry sat across from him and thought how nicely Carpenter was in conflict with the scene. It wasn't just his garb. The room was too small for him, too carpeted, too busy with pointless ornament. The sun was a London sun. It steamed and baked, became distracted in plate glass, veiled itself in dust. The noise outside was wheels, beaten pavements, croaking water pumps; it was shouts and door slams and the constant chitter of harnesses. There was a smell of grease slowly browning the air. Carpenter's face was stained by northern weather, his hands were rough from work. He had the quality of a countryman dragged from the plough. But this quality was lent keenness and distinction by his surroundings. He had lectured last night to four hundred. Excitement sat in his face, at the corners of his eyes. Applause had rubbed him to glowing. The city was a whetstone, against which he must strike off sparks.

'How is Edith?'

'Well,' Henry replied.

'She plans to lecture on women?'

'Yes.'

'She is my rival, then. Though there is still a little novelty in a man urging the independence of women.'

'There is.'

Carpenter chuckled. 'I had forgotten how unforthcoming you are, Henry. You are a danger to a man like me, who likes to talk.'

It was something beyond Henry's usual shyness, with Carpenter. It was Carpenter's voice, so exquisitely modulated. His age: he must be fifty; there was grey singed in his dark beard, in his hair. His manners: money and Cambridge, worn with his workman's clothes like family inheritances, gold rings. He was handsome, all in all, and knew it. Henry felt the easy pressure of his charm, applied now and then by a look or a touch. It was not unpleasant to feel it. With Henry at least, the charm seemed aimless, perhaps even a form of reserve, though he sensed that with someone else it might tug and pull. When they first met at the Society of the New Life, years ago, Henry had been shy like this, but Carpenter had brought him out. He always did bring him out: theirs was the kind of friendship that was simple, because they agreed on so much. But it was always like this at the beginning.

'Is George well?' Henry asked. George Merrill was the young man Carpenter lived with. There was no secret about it, if you knew Carpenter. Merrill was a workman of some kind; he spoke with a thick, halting Sheffield accent and smoked a pipe.

Carpenter looked pleased. 'Yes. He is kept busy; we farm a little, and there are always people. He cooks – he is becoming quite famous for it. Meanwhile I have been trying to put down what I believe about love and marriage. How they might come of age.'

'I read the pamphlet,' Henry said.

'Well, I had you and Edith in mind. New relations between the sexes. You are living separately, aren't you?'

'We are.'

Carpenter tilted his head. 'Do you find it easy, to give Edith her freedom? To stand a little aloof?'

'I do.' Henry patted the sweat on his back, feeling vaguely irritated by the question. 'I don't think Edith could live another way.'

'It is very good of you.'

'You suggest in your pamphlet,' Henry said, 'that there is also a role for those like yourself.'

Carpenter smiled. 'It is not all about men and women. There is a place for me in the future, I think.'

'And that is how you think of yourself? As belonging to an intermediate sex?'

'There are lots of words now, ones we needn't be ashamed of. Invert, Uranian, Urning, homosexual. The intermediate sex is my phrase. Our role in the New Life will depend on the blend within us – the body of a man and the soul of a woman, or the body of a woman and the soul of a man. We are a kinder race, unconcerned with propagating ourselves. We see differently.'

Henry pictured George Merrill in his braces and cap, his pipe fixed under his heavy moustache, and could not associate him with the soul of a woman.

'You think me mystical, Dr Ellis. I can see it in your face.'

'Souls are undiscovered by science.'

'So are many things.'

'It is more – lately I have been corresponding with John Addington. Do you know him?'

'Not personally. You have been writing to him about these matters?'

'He has been writing to me. He wrote at first about Whitman – about the "Calamus" poems. Wanting to know if I agreed they were about men loving men. Passionately.'

'What did you say?'

'I prevaricated. I suppose you think they are?'

'You forget I met Whitman,' said Carpenter.

'I had forgotten. When was it?'

'In '76.'

'And?'

'We spent the night together.'

Carpenter had kindness and mischief in his eyes. Henry stared past him at the window, the summer's day. 'You're blushing, Henry,' Carpenter said, the look in his eyes carried over into his voice. 'I don't wish to shock you. Only it seems pertinent. And you cannot be surprised.' He spoke sonorously to the ceiling:

'Here to put your lips upon mine I permit you,
With the comrade's long-dwelling kiss or the new husband's kiss,
For I am the new husband and I am the comrade.

'What did you think that meant? I read your article of the other week: "Morality is the normal activity of a healthy nature." It is an admirable thing to have written.'

Henry pulled at his beard. 'I do not know how I could have overlooked it in Whitman.'

'What else has Addington said?'

'He has gone on to address the whole subject – the state of understanding.'

'Are you surprised by him?'

'By his boldness. I am not entirely surprised by his interest.'

'It is more obvious, when a man's subjects are the Greeks and Michelangelo's sonnets to Tommaso.'

'Yes.'

'I do not know him,' Carpenter said. 'But I've heard stories, that he and his wife are unhappy. That she doesn't approve of his writing in the way he does.'

'He was kind about her, in his last letter.'

'I'm sure he was.'

A fly found the open window and came hesitantly into the room. They followed it with their eyes as it was repelled by the closest wall, then by the desk and a china ornament.

'Men write to me, you know,' Carpenter said. 'There are lots of men, picking up the clues we leave. I am not sure if Addington means to leave his, or if he cannot help it. I do not think Whitman could help it. Men wrote to him and it made him unhappy. He frightened himself.'

'You wrote to him. He was not unhappy to meet you.'

Carpenter laughed. 'No, he was not always unhappy to meet men like me. But he did not like to attract attention.'

'Do you reply to your letters?'

'Of course. My clues are deliberate.'

'What do they write to you about?'

'Their lives. Imagine, Henry, if you had no one to describe your life to. That all its meaning was a dark secret.'

'What do you tell them?'

'Different things – that the world must change, and not they.'

'I see.'

Carpenter leaned forward and put a warm hand on Henry's knee.

A few grey hairs stood out crookedly on it among the dark. The fly made a sharp blurred sound against a hard surface somewhere. Outside, the shining leaves swayed under the sill. 'Your marriage is important, Henry,' he said. 'People like you and Edith, and people like me, expressing our needs and feelings, finding the right arrangements: this way we might aid the expression of thousands of others.'

'I know,' Henry said, looking at Carpenter's feet in the black sandals, flat against the heavy carpet. He had developed an odd uncertainty about whether the hand was still on his knee: the feeling was all one, as if his knee were a rock and Carpenter was flowing everywhere warmly around it.

'Of course you know,' Carpenter said, taking his hand away and leaving an absence. 'But believe me when I tell you that I understand, that sometimes it is hard enough simply to live for oneself.'

*

Powder hung in the air like a blessing, sparkling in the lights. The man climbed, the different muscles in his body standing out under his skin. On the platform he dusted his hands another time and see-sawed on his feet where the sparkle settled. In the audience they were absolutely quiet, tamped down: they could hear the creak of the boards under the man's weight. The three rings hovered in line. He looked ahead, stepped back, punched forward and sprang, the boards making a loud ripping sound; his hands were on the first ring before they had registered that he was falling, falling; he swung forward, back, forward and was falling again, higher then lower, landing on his hands again, then drawing his whole body up behind, feet pointed at the rafters, his knuckles white with powder or pain, then curving back, releasing, making a circle over the far-below ground, a sped-up clock, catching himself an instant on the final ring, then once more a circle, heels landing smack on the platform on the other side. They roared, the lid lifted on them, bubbling up.

Henry clapped with the rest. The heat, held back by suspense, returned, along with the pain in his knees where they were forced against the chair in front. He noticed a woman two rows down, her face half-lit, all smile. He allowed himself to watch her, seeing how closely she watched the acrobat as he stood bowing in the lights, a sheen of sweat on his chest.

'It makes me ill, watching this,' Jack Relph said into Henry's ear, his voice becoming loud as the applause fell away.

Henry saw the woman was laughing at something her friend had said, and yet her eyes were still on the man. Her friend was looking at him also. He realised they were laughing at the bulge in his trunks.

'It wakes me up,' he replied.

'It'll do that all right.'

It was the interval. The auditorium was mostly empty, gone slack, the lights up. Henry and Jack were in their places, allies of the left-behind cloaks; both of them had swung their legs over the seats in front.

'How's married life?' Jack said. 'Not that you're doing it very conventionally. I have had a time explaining why two people would marry and then carry on living in separate houses, leagues apart. And I am in the theatre, Henry.'

'We're happy.'

'Of course you are.' Jack's smile gathered above his green velvet collar. 'And *married life*?'

'Happy.' He did not carry on lying, though he had been prepared to; instead he merely changed tack: 'Edith has our friend, Angelica, staying with her.'

'The famous Angelica. I would like to meet her.'

'She cannot easily be avoided.'

'You said "our" friend.'

'Yes.'

'Is she yours?'

'Perhaps not yet.' He thought of the day when Angelica arrived at Edith's flat; of her trunk lying tensely in the hallway, like something waiting to pounce.

'You don't like her?' Jack said.

'I like her. She and Edith have grown very close. They are both very active.'

'And you are steady, is that it?'

Henry looked down over the seats. On a few rows men were sitting and puffing out smoke. The smoke squatted before stretching out in fingertips towards the stage, above which the acrobats' rings slowly pivoted.

'Henry?'

'I must keep a little aloof,' he said. 'Edith must be able to have friendships without me.'

'How is Mary?' Jack said. 'She made good company at your wedding.'

'I'm sure she is well.' Henry had not thought about Edith's friend Mary recently – he experienced a small flicker of worry now as he tried to recall when he had last seen her. At the same time, he noticed the two laughing women returning to their seats. Nodding in their direction, he said, 'They were looking at the man's parts in his costume.'

'His parts?' Jack smiled. By now the women were presenting only their backs. 'Are they rough?'

'No, I don't think.' He studied them. 'Do you imagine it is usual, for women to notice?'

Jack smiled again, his teeth drawing out like a string of pearls. 'It was rather obvious.'

Henry looked at him. 'Have you read Edward Carpenter?'

The smile drew in. 'Yes. He's your friend, isn't he?'

'I saw him the other day. Have you ever written him a letter?'

'Why would I?'

'He talked about leaving clues. For certain kinds of men to read.'

More people were returning to the auditorium. It felt hotter already. Jack glanced behind him. 'He's not the only one to do it.'

'He said that too. It's interesting. I have never thought so much about it before.' Henry had the same feeling with Jack as he had with Carpenter, that he had not asked enough questions. That bare facts had stood in for understanding.

'It is not usually thought about,' Jack said.

'Carpenter is clearly thinking a great deal. So is another man of whom I am aware.'

'Who?'

'John Addington.'

'Oh, yes.'

'You know him too, for that?'

'Yes.'

'It seems admirable.'

'So it is, though it frightens me a little.'

'It is useful to be frightened,' Henry said. 'It shows us what we daren't approach.' He reflected. 'I am more and more convinced that sex holds the secret.'

'To the future? You *are* brave.'

'Merely frightened.'

The audience was pressing back in, waves of chatter driving along the rows. Henry and Jack pulled in their legs and stood to let people past.

Jack turned to him: 'So what are you going to do?'

But the lights went down and the applause began, sweeping all possibilities away.

*

He wrote to Addington the next morning. Overnight, an idea had planted and grown in his mind. The more he considered it, the more obvious it became: that it was not sufficient simply to distinguish sex from marriage, as he and Edith had tried to do. Only a larger conception of sex, one that comprehended and encompassed deviations – men loving men, for instance – could constitute a new system of morality. Didn't true freedom, he thought now, depend on this? A study of inversion could establish scientifically that sex was not defined by procreation – it would be a step towards proving that it was an instinct that took countless forms, all within the range of human possibility, all conducive to happiness. And this – to show this! – would be to expose the sterility of current social arrangements: their killing of individuality, liberty, naturalness; their burden of guilt and shame. It would be to satisfy Whitman: to uphold morality as the normal activity of a healthy nature. It would allow for the positing of wholly new forms of relationship, of relation between the sexes, of roles and functions. It would be a basis for the New Life. It would make Henry Ellis a figure of the future.

He itched to share these thoughts with Edith, but felt also the new embarrassment they had about discussing sex questions. He was sure that he wanted to write on inversion – already he hugged it like a secret, the closer for his desire to be the one to tell it. But he couldn't tell it alone: it would be only too easy for the world to shout him down, crush him out. To effect some sort of partnership would be to share the risk. Carpenter was too eccentric and blatant a figure, too well-known for taking extreme positions, to make a satisfactory partner; besides, he hadn't the temperament for scientific investigation. Addington's reputation, however, was still strong and broad enough to offer protection, even if further injury would undoubtedly be done to it. It seemed that he was preparing to publish on the subject anyhow – by doing so he would make the subject purely his own, destroying himself and retarding the advance of knowledge in the process. For Henry to come in, another married man, would be to both their advantage.

Still, could it ever be safe? Addington was almost certainly an invert. If he were to be discovered in a public lavatory, or in some kind of brothel, all would be lost.

Henry wrote out his proposal. Looked at it, pristine in its envelope. If Addington agreed, he would keep their contact to a minimum. If there was a scandal and no book yet existed, he should be able to say that they had never met – it had been a correspondence only, an exchange on a subject which engaged him as a man of intellect, medically trained, committed to reform. In that event Addington would have to fend for himself. But in the meantime, Henry would work to make him free.

14 Dover Mansions
Brixton

28ᵗʰ July 94

Dear Mr Addington,

Last night, at the Empire, investigating a new company of acrobats, it occurred to me to wonder whether we might perhaps collaborate on a work about sexual inversion. It is a subject that has become of increasing interest to me, partly through finding how it exists to a greater or lesser extent in persons whom I know, or know of, and whom I love and respect. Your letters have been a further spur. The attitude of the law, which I still do not understand in its full complexion, certainly seems an injurious one.

Have you already heard of Edward Carpenter's pamphlet, <u>Sex-Love and its Place in a Free Society</u>, which has recently been published? He is a friend of mine, from our working together at the Society of the New Life, and, like ourselves, a great admirer of Whitman. I can send you my copy — it shines a sidelight on these topics.

Please do send me your work on inversion in the Greeks, which I would be very glad to read.

Ever yours sincerely,
Henry Ellis

XI

How his eyes had ached. He could not read after dark. His hands jittered. His parts itched. His head hung from his shoulders like a corpse from a pole.

John was sent to Dr Wells. Dr Wells took the measure of him. 'You have made a mania of your ideals,' he said. 'Be practical. It does no good to stifle instinct. You must take a mistress, or you must find yourself a wife.'

(Even now, in memory, he could count the folds in Dr Wells's waistcoat.)

His father, Dr Addington, who had been told everything, agreed with Dr Wells.

They were leaning over a bridge, looking into the green water.

In Venice, they'd eaten peaches, juice dripping.

Jolting along, atop a carriage in the dark; the warm air, warm-smelling.

He'd said, 'Catherine, there are things you must know about yourself. Your temper, for instance.'

Had he been cruel? It was so long ago. He had decided on marriage. He had decided on Catherine. She seemed sensible.

'You are like a broom,' she laughed. 'Always coming across my way.'

He could not stop thinking about her. He plotted how it might be done. But hadn't she calculated his next move, as much as he had? She did not pretend to be surprised, when he asked her, as they looked into the green water. If he hurried to be in love, she hurried to meet him. Or so he told himself, in these days when memory had become merciful.

They married in September of that year, 1870. A clear morning, long ago. He was a doll propped in this position and that, ringed by a controlling attention. There was a photograph: of him and Catherine seated next to each other, surrounded by bridesmaids clutching flowers. The bridesmaids were looking down at them. Here you are, they seemed to say. We have managed it again.

To Brighton for the honeymoon. The fog like steam coming off the sea. Obscure behind glass windows they foundered on the wide white bed. Ignorance brought shrinking into the light. An argument of limbs. And then it was finally done, three days late.

Then children. A family. The end.

He had asked, above the swirling green water: 'Could you manage to be content with me, all through life?'

This time when John knocked, Frank opened the door, wearing a blue shirt and braces. Again, there was the transition from light to dark, the hallway, the closed door, the stair. The same feeling seeding in his stomach as he climbed.

It was a plain room at the front of the house, clean, the single bed against one wall. There was a washstand, a chest of drawers, a table with Frank's cigarette case on it. A morning paper: John could see that the print had smudged down a whole column on the right-hand side.

Frank pulled the curtains to, clinking on their rails. The room became dim and brown. They undressed where they were standing, vaguely concentrated. John had not thought for a long time about how he appeared without clothes – he had seen, dreamed, only the other – but he allowed his fidgeting anxiety to be submerged beneath the supreme fact of Frank's returned nakedness, brown-coloured in the dimness, as though painted all over with Mediterranean tan: a curtain flapped in the breeze and white light discovered the top of his thigh, the side of his cock. He came over to John and kissed him, the kiss like a snare, curving up and under his top lip. In that first instant there was something vigorous and clean in the contact of their skin, the warm sliding of their limbs, the pressure of their lips. They went over to the bed and Frank lay on his back, his feet planted and his knees up. John spat three times into his palm and wetted his cock. Frank closed his thighs round it and John began to push and retreat. The pressure, the warmth and tightness of it, he felt almost in his head. His cock slipped and stretched. Frank's body opened under him, the pit of his stomach and the slow rise of his chest; his arms were flung back, his head tipped slightly forward, watching the movement. John spat again. He sucked in air. The insides of Frank's thighs were inside his head. Their warm blind pressure. The high, vanishing feeling. And then he began to spill, like a glass left under a tap, running over in small steady waves. It layered in the hair on Frank's stomach.

He stayed on his knees a moment and then sank onto the bed, into his old self. They lay there, wedged tightly, shoulders overlapped. Then Frank spat, rolled onto his side, nudging at John's hip so that he rolled too. He put his arms round his chest and pushed his cock between his legs – John felt it like the snout of an animal, a dog's insistence. His lips were on John's neck, the moustache burning on it. And the cock moved between his legs like something trapped. John watched it over the curve of his stomach, the skin rolling backward and forward, the head a strangled pink. Frank's arms were tight around him, shifting as he found his place, the hands clambering and sticking – he could feel the sweat on the palms. Frank's breath collected in his ear. It began to shudder, condensing in his ear, like the wet between his thighs. The hands shifted again on his chest, the fingers curling in the hair. He looked down, saw the cock push, retreat, push retreat push. Frank's voice came in his ear, one low flat note. The arms tightened. Semen lanced out, over the edge of the bed, landing in streaks on the floor.

John was hard again, sore so soon after. He could feel semen running in a thin tepid stream down his thigh.

'That was good,' Frank said at last, in a half-whisper. 'I didn't know if you'd let me.' His cock remained pinned between John's legs, swollen, like a fattened finger. His arms were still tightly wrapped round John's chest, his voice in his ear.

'Why?'

'Because before, it was me who had to take my things off. I thought perhaps it would be all your way.'

It was true he had taken what he had seen was in his power, to satisfy himself. 'No,' he said.

'Good. That's good.'

They lay quietly. John looked at the semen on the floor, then closed his eyes. The curtains lifted, warm air flowing in, bearing the smell of the street. They could hear the chant of traffic on the main road. It was hot, somehow hotter for being naked on the bed. The heat outside seemed aimless, it leaned up against the windows and walls.

He realised he'd slipped into sleep when Frank got up, easing himself from between his legs and stepping over him onto the floor, his testes dangling lopsidedly.

'Do you want something to clean yourself?'

'Not yet.'

Frank walked over to the table and came back with his cigarettes. He smoked sitting up on the bed, while John smoked on his back. Frank talked about his work – the book they were setting and the trouble they'd had. The smoke drifted in silken blue clouds across the room. He wanted to know about John's elder daughters, what their husbands did. John told him about Janet going to Cambridge.

Frank lit another cigarette – he had a way of squinting as he drew on them – and asked, 'Your wife. How was she, after I'd gone?'

'She saw right through us.'

'Did she?' He looked down at John with a furrowed eye, through the smoke.

'It was inevitable. Though I'd hoped it wouldn't be so immediate.'

'She knows about you?'

'We're old. It would be a long time to keep a secret.'

'You've got children.'

'Yes, I managed that.'

'When did she know?'

It was a great relief to talk so casually of what he had never told anyone. He found the words came easily. 'After three years. I still wanted very badly to be as I should, nor did I stop trying. She understood, eventually – that I was trying. And then I wasn't even doing that, really; only watching, apart from the world. Writing with more daring than I lived. Rotting against my tree in the park. It's only this past year I decided I had wasted my life.' John looked at Frank. In the brown light the hair on his lip and chest and legs was darker. His ribs lay like shadows under the skin. 'Have you always known what you wanted?'

Frank's face became quite still. 'It's easy enough to find, once you know to look. There's plenty who've accepted their natures, if you call it that. I'm sorry for you that you hadn't.'

'There are people now, medical men, who would try to explain it.'

'And what do they say?'

'That it is not wilfulness. That we are not to be blamed for wanting. But that it is not a sign of health. We are degenerate.'

Frank made a faint smile. 'Nice of them.'

'Have you never been frightened?'

'Never of myself.'

'Of the law?'

'The law, sometimes. Other men. Gentlemen.'

'Have you read Whitman?' John asked.

'I know he's a poet.'

'He is a prophet. Men loving men – it is a bridge between the classes, he says.'

'Does he really.'

'What is this, if not that?'

'It's not always like this.'

'It might be.'

'It might.' Frank sounded unconvinced. 'Is he a socialist?'

'Of a sort. There is Edward Carpenter also. You know of him?'

'I saw him speak once, in Bishopsgate. Are you a socialist?'

'Of a sort.'

'Are you?'

John laughed. 'Is it so impossible?'

'I believe you,' Frank said. 'Just I expect it isn't socialism as I understand it.'

'I believe in humanity. In the beauty of it. That is my route to socialism.'

'I don't see much beauty. That's mine.'

'These are two sides of the same coin.'

'If you say so, Mr Addington. Where do you get all your money from?'

'My father made investments. I live on the interest – that and what I earn from my books.'

'So you're the problem. People like you.'

'Yes. But we are also the solution, if enough of us alter how we think.'

Frank laughed. 'God forbid it should have nothing to do with you.'

There was a short, willed silence. Frank appeared to bring something to the fore of his mind and push it away again. He lay down on the bed, shuffling his shoulders for comfort. 'Mr and Mrs Higgs will be back any minute,' he said, looking at the ceiling.

John was aware of his cock filling – their hips and thighs and legs were pressed together. 'Should I go?'

'You needn't. Like you said, it's hard keeping secrets if you're with people long enough. Anyhow they're free-thinkers. So long as I don't make a parade of myself they won't complain. Like I won't go on about them and their books and the funny sorts of people they have coming round.'

A few minutes later they could indeed be heard on the doorstep. Mrs Higgs's voice, northern-sounding, perfectly clear. The door shut.

In the renewed quiet, in the excitement of their presence, wishing to assert something in the clean, spare room, John brought Frank off slowly with his hand. At the end Frank arched his neck, the Adam's apple very large and tender in his throat, making the same noise as before, a long low note, like a hurt. And John knew that he loved intensely this moment of surrender; that he wanted to witness it again and again.

11 Gloucester Terrace
Paddington

6th August 94

Dear Mr Ellis,

If it were possible for us to collaborate on the production of an impartial and really scientific study of inversion, I should be very glad. I believe, as presumably do you, that it might come from two men better than one, in the present state of public opinion. And I truly think it is a field in which pioneers may not only do excellent service to humanity, but also win the laurels of investigators and truth-seekers.

It seems to me first that we must find a way of connecting the historical and medical aspects of the phenomenon. Do tell me what you make of my work on the Greeks, a copy of which I enclose here (please take great care of it). I anticipate it forming the basis of any historical discussion. I will say, after some preliminary reading, that the modern Continental authorities seem quite ignorant both of history and fact. The general notion that sexual inversion is the product of some sort of mental degeneration allows them to see the problem as not of an individual's own making, which is some advance — but really this is just as false as the idea that it is purely sin and vice. They not only do not know Ancient Greece, they do not know their own cousins and club-mates. It is in this last regard that I might be of further help, gathering material on the lives of inverts in this country. Should we meet to talk this over? We would have to agree on the legal dimension: I couldn't take part in any book which did not show the absurdity and injustice of the English law. You say you do not know it in its full complexion. It is very simple. Any act of 'gross indecency' between males, in public or <u>in private</u>, is a Misdemeanour punishable with two years' incarceration and hard labour.

Connection <u>per anum</u>, with or without consent, is penal servitude for life.

Very truly yours,

J. Addington

PS Thank you for sending Edward Carpenter's pamphlet. It is a most useful work.

14 Dover Mansions

Brixton

10th August 94

Dear Mr Addington,

It is a great relief to me that you are willing to co-operate on this proposed work. I have for some time been interested in questions of sexual psychology and sexual ethics; those relating to inversion are some of the most pressing, it now seems to me, and shed light on all the rest. I have begun and am absorbed in your <u>Problem in Greek Ethics</u>.

I share your doubts about the modern theories, especially the idea that inverts must necessarily be morbid. And I agree that you should begin gathering testimony from British inverts, if it is in your power to do so. I am glad Carpenter pleases. If you were to write to him, I'm sure you would find that he would readily be of assistance.

You suggest a meeting. I am ashamed to say I suffer a great deal from a shy nature, and am convinced I am most coherent and useful on the page. It is unorthodox, but could you conceive of carrying out our project — at least in its initial stages — by correspondence? I could begin by sketching out a plan for how I think the book should be organised. Have you given any consideration to the matter of inversion in women?

Very sincerely yours,

Henry Ellis

XII

The two women entered on the last ripple of a conversation. It had carried them out of the hot dusty white evening into the small, flickering restaurant; it played over their faces; it animated their fingers in their gloves. They are happy, Henry thought, watching Edith and Angelica being directed to the round table at which he and Jack were sitting. The walls were lined with mirrors and they moved through them in consecutive pairings, like dancers, unequal in height, Edith's small hat a recurring prediction of Angelica's larger one. Henry expected Edith to be happy – he thought of her as one of those rare people on whom happiness has been bestowed as a lifetime gift. Angelica he didn't – she was too dissatisfied, blocked. Often in her smoking, for instance, there was the sense of her emitting steam, generated by some obscure internal activity. But now, carried in on this ripple of disappeared conversation, she did not look happy merely in the temporary sense. It was there in the tolerant way she looked at him as she seated herself opposite, the candle flames bowing to her and standing again: that she was happy. It was in her smile. She was wearing primrose yellow.

'What were you talking about, when you came in?' He smiled at them both. Edith was on his right. There was a band playing in the corner, and he had to speak louder than he liked.

'Just now?' Edith said.

'Yes, as you came in.'

'I don't – oh, it was someone in the street. It was silly.'

'You looked happy.'

She smiled at him distractedly, as she picked up and put down the cutlery. There was a run of sweat by her ear, catching the light. 'It was just a silly thing.'

'I don't believe Mr Relph and I have been introduced,' Angelica put in.

She and Jack were introduced.

'What an unusual jacket. You look as though you read Oscar Wilde, Mr Relph.'

'As do you, Miss Britell.'

'We are both of us too obvious in our attachments. It is embarrassing. I suppose you admire Burne-Jones?'

'With some hesitations.'

'Ah, we cling to our hesitations. Where would we be without them?'

'Far gone.'

Angelica laughed – a single loud noise, like the snapping shut of a case. 'Far gone! God forbid we should ever be that.'

Edith tapped Henry's leg under the table. This was Angelica in her favourite mode.

'What do you permit yourself to be far gone in?' Angelica asked.

Jack paused, smiling. 'I suppose the theatre. I write about plays for my living. Even if it is a bad one, I never feel I have wasted time.'

'Yes, I see that.'

'And yourself?'

'You would have to ask my father. It is his pet subject.'

'Angelica is still having a bad time,' Edith said to Henry.

Angelica remained looking at Jack, waiting to give her explanation. 'He's threatening to end my allowance if I don't leave London and go back to Norfolk. I am far gone in city life, you see, without a guide. The usual thing, straight out of a novel; that's what's so irritating about it.'

'How old are you?' Jack asked.

She curled her lip. 'Thirty; and I have grown rather unfortunately into my brain.'

'Always dangerous.'

'Very.'

'How long have you been away now?'

'Only three weeks.'

'A month,' Edith said.

'A month, then.' Angelica noticed the tentative approach of the waiter, casting her eyes down to the menu. 'Far too long for a woman of thirty, I'm sure you'll agree.'

They ordered.

'What will you do?' Henry asked her.

'I won't go back. I'll find work.'

'What sort?' Jack said.

'There will be things at the Society,' Edith replied.

'What things?' Henry said.

'Typing, I expect.' Edith looked at Angelica for support.

Angelica took it up: 'Typing. Perhaps the accounts. We've discussed it. And if not, there are other possibilities. I might make use of my German.'

'And where will you stay?' Henry directed this question at Angelica.

'With Edith.' Her face was clear of doubt.

He turned to Edith: 'For how long?'

'For as long as is necessary, Henry.' She had a stubborn look.

'And is your father a strong-willed man, Angelica?'

'He is. But I am stronger.'

Jack raised his glass: 'Chin-chin.'

'And your mother?' Henry persisted.

'Oh, she is entirely under the cosh,' Angelica replied. 'She's confused, really. By women.'

'You should give her complimentary tickets to your lectures, Edith,' said Jack.

Edith took it seriously. 'Do you think she would come?'

Angelica laughed. 'No. Besides, if she did I'd have to sit next to her and explain every other word.'

'Are they written yet?' Jack asked Edith.

'Not all of them. Angelica is being a great help.'

The food arrived and the conversation was temporarily lost behind steam and the performance of appetite. It came in and out as they ate. Edith had a habit of raising her hand to her mouth while she chewed, as if something were always at risk of falling out. When she was also listening, with her eyes fixed on a person speaking, it suggested that what she was keeping back might be words, that she was protecting some impression or response. Henry knew – he was fairly sure he did – when she was only chewing. Watching Edith now, deciding which it might be, he thought again how odd it was that he had seen her naked, mostly, and that it did not seem to make the difference it ought. But then perhaps this was life? That, on its own, this was just a commonplace sort of knowledge, like knowing the way to somewhere. It must be so, and yet it did not make it any less interesting, the invisible fact that almost all the couples dining together in this room had seen each other naked, that they went to bed together night after night.

His eye followed the green cuff of Jack's jacket next to him as it moved across the white plate. With Jack the invisible fact was folded over on itself; a secret beneath the secret. He looked around the room, at the men talking and eating and drinking and smoking. Were any among them like Jack, or Carpenter, or John Addington? Who were they, these men? He thought about his last letter from Addington, agreeing to his proposal that they write a book together, a proposal Henry hadn't yet told anyone about. It ended with a reference to the law. 'Connection *per anum*' was the phrase used. There was something about the baldness of this, the baldness of the link between the act – fascinating in its crudity, as an expression of human need – and the calculated viciousness of the penalty, that horrified him. Accompanying the letter was a printed manuscript in a packet: Addington's work on inversion in the Greeks. He'd only had time to read the first chapter, time enough to wonder at the existence of this thing so loudly unasked-for by the world, the disciplined, eager solitude that must have produced it. In the photograph Addington sent of himself he was in profile, his eyes lowered, lips hidden between heavy moustache and beard.

Henry looked at Edith, her hand in front of her mouth, watching Angelica. 'I had told him,' Angelica was saying, 'that I didn't want to go. I hadn't been unreasonable about it – I had simply said I didn't want to go; they could do very well without me. And I went into the garden for a cigarette. It was a lovely day, and I was standing there smoking, and then he marched out and snatched the cigarette from my lips – he burned me, not that he noticed – and said, "I don't recognise you as my daughter."' She stopped and took a gulp of wine, candlelight rolling like a lozenge in the glass. 'And my lip was swelling from the burn, and I looked at him, and I said, "You have no hold over me whatsoever," which isn't true, for all the obvious reasons, but it put a stopper in him. And then I reached over and took back my cigarette and went into the house with it. I went to my room and wrote to Edith. My lip was hurting terribly by then.' She looked at Edith across the table. 'You'd already written, hadn't you, saying to visit. So I took up the offer, and came down the day after next.'

'It was the same with my father,' Edith said. 'The expectation. Only it was made worse by my stepmother, who wanted so badly for us to be friends, except it was friendship on her terms – calls and teas and charity bazaars, and shopping and – it sounds so unlike me, doesn't it? But it was like that. And I was reading, reading, which they weren't interested in, and then I saw Mrs Percy's advert, wanting help with her pamphlet, and I jumped. I've not seen either of them since, or hardly. My stepmother sends little cards – she sent one after my novel came out, saying she'd seen the reviews and that she was pleased for me. That was kind of her; and yet it didn't make me want to be kind in return. I'm not sure I know why that is.'

'She hadn't earned it,' offered Jack.

'It's like something Henry and I talked about the first time we met,' Edith went on. 'Do you remember? We talked about surety. That we would accept heresies, if they were backed up by proofs. But of course the proofs have to be found, and sometimes we have to be brave enough to be them ourselves. When people don't understand that – or won't understand it – you can't wait for them, can't walk back and stand at their side and try and nudge them along. You've got to push ahead, you've got to be ruthless. We British are used to being ruthless, of course, but only the men. The women aren't. We don't grab. We *shouldn't*. But we have to, to make some room for ourselves.'

'We must conquer a new world,' Angelica said.

'Yes, yes, that's it. But for all of us. Not just for women, though we'll have a new place in it.'

'We must have plenty of room.'

'Yes, plenty of room.'

They smiled at each other and laughed.

'I hope you're getting this down,' Jack said. 'For the lectures. It would make a fine peroration.' Henry could hear the wine spreading in his voice.

'I'll do it,' Angelica said. She asked the waiter for a pencil and began writing on her napkin. They watched her. She was entirely unselfconscious, one hand pinning the napkin, the other pushing the pencil; she paused after writing a few words, looked up, her eyes shifting between them, and then started writing again, till the cloth was grey with argument. 'I think that's it,' she said, handing it over to Edith.

Edith took a moment. 'As usual, it looks a lot less clever written down.'

Their plates were taken away and their glasses refilled.

'I'm curious,' Henry said – he had not spoken for a long time, and he had the usual sense of his voice struggling into action, not entirely welcome – 'as a point of interest, about where the limits on a woman's ideal liberty lie? There must be some, as surely as on men.'

'Ideal, meaning we are conceiving of a world where women's lives are no longer limited to drudge work, motherhood, marriage?' asked Edith.

'Yes.'

'The New Life, in other words.'

'Yes. But there must still be restrictions of some kind, limitations.'

'No murder, even for women?' Edith said. 'No matter how deserving the victim? Is that it?'

Angelica laughed.

'No.' He felt irritated, knowing himself to blame, for beginning to speak before he knew what he wished to say, speaking only because he was sick of his own silence. 'The law – we would expect it to have been reformed in its worst aspects – would apply indifferently to men and women. What I meant is –' he paused, seeking the right formulation – 'do women still have special obligations, over and above those they share as equal members of the community? To children, for example? As men might be responsible for physical defence.'

Edith replied instantly: 'Yes, I think so – and as far as they should be considered as limitations on liberty, I don't disagree. Though of course motherhood might expand one's sense of self, of individual capacity. And we must remember, also, that not all women are, or will be, mothers. We are not.'

'We are at perfect liberty.' Angelica smiled, showing her teeth.

Jack took a quick drink from his glass, and, stamping his napkin to his mouth twice, said after the second time, 'Henry, was what you really meant, about sex? Whether there should be any restriction on it?'

'No.' He looked quickly at Jack on his left, feeling the eyes of the two women on him. He spoke again: 'Though that is an aspect. Whether a woman – whether she should have total sexual liberty.'

'She should be free to give her love as a gift, to whomever she chooses,' Angelica said, in a rush.

'And the man?' Jack asked.

'It is mutual.'

Henry had been looking past Jack's head, away from Angelica, as though something of great significance were happening at the front of the restaurant. With difficulty he brought his gaze back round. Angelica was staring at him. She was ugly tonight, he decided. She did not suit yellow. 'And what if the woman gave her love wantonly?' he said. 'Without care, as she was drawn.'

'Of course liberty can be abused.' Angelica was staring fiercely; the candlelight reinforced the black of her eyebrows, shadows collecting in the hollows beneath the bone.

'We agree there. Children born from thoughtless matches, from instinct, might suffer for it.'

Edith leaned forward: 'And what about contraceptives, Henry?'

'Any woman who is of good character will seek contraceptives for sound purposes. It must be a considered act. If she were truly wanton she—'

'I think that is foolish,' interrupted Angelica. 'I don't believe a woman should give herself carelessly, without thought, but women do, such women exist. If sex is considered as a pleasure why would you not make it safe from consequences in every kind of case? It follows logically.'

The music from the band became very noticeable, naggingly familiar, and Henry heard a burst of conversation from the next table – enough to make him worry that they themselves could be overheard. Edith was looking at him fixedly; Jack was examining his cuffs. Henry's eyes now found a spot above Angelica's head – a mirror showed his dark face and the dark heads of the two women. 'Perhaps I attach insufficient importance to spontaneity,' he began. 'I think so highly of marriage.'

'And yet you are not married!' Angelica said loudly.

His voice momentarily snagged in his throat. 'We are,' he said finally, trembling on the brink of a laugh. He looked blankly at Edith.

Edith spoke to Angelica. 'What do you mean? Jack was there.' She paused, eyes narrowing. 'I don't know what you mean.'

Angelica seemed stricken; she had thrown her head back and was staring at the ceiling, her chest visibly rising and falling in her dress. Then she looked back at them. 'I would like to pay for the meal,' she said.

'You can't,' Edith said.

'I would like to. I will do it now.'

And she got up, leaving behind an empty chair, her gloves folded on the tablecloth next to Jack's wine-smudged napkin. The music continued, and Henry recognised the tune.

At the door, as they were given back their hats, Jack said to him, 'I'm sorry, Henry. I shouldn't have said that – only you did mention it, last week. I saw immediately I couldn't add anything.'

Outside, the warm, shiftless air swaddled them. Jack went over to Angelica and Henry heard him begin another apology. She looked almost ill. The two of them began to move off down the street. At its end Henry could see the scurrying shapes of people and traffic, the hard glare of electric lights.

'It's so hot,' Edith murmured, taking Henry's arm. Her hat skimmed his shoulder. He said nothing; it occurred to him how uncomfortable he would be, trying to sleep in this heat. Their shadows leaned across the cobbles as they walked. After a moment Edith said, 'I don't know what she meant.'

They reached Cambridge Circus. There was a great mass of people outside the tiered and turreted theatre, illuminated under the lights, the smoke a fraying canopy above their heads. Dozens of windows scrutinised them, as if the pavement were the stage. Henry and Edith pushed through, still hooked at the elbows, through the din of voices and swirl of beer and smoke, the heat almost unbearable, coming out at the edge to be confronted by the clap and jangle of traffic, the raw smell of the road. Henry noticed Jack and Angelica waiting on the other side, standing awkwardly, their outfits oddly bleached by the blur of electric light, with people streaming past. He glanced at Edith. 'Will you come home with me tonight?' he asked. There was a howl behind them, cutting into the noise. He looked at the two solitary people waiting together on the other side of the road. Another cab whirred past. 'Will you read to me?'

Edith turned her face, with something like pity lit up on it. 'Not tonight,' she said.

Part Two

October–November 1894

XIII

'Who is he, Johnny? Really?'

They were standing in his study. The lights had been turned up, and John could see them both in the window, his face, ripped in the middle by the red tip of his cigar, and the back of Mark's head and shoulders, spectral against the outside darkness. There was no fire lit and it was cold. From downstairs there came a murmur of laughter; he could hear Frank's voice, which meant that Mark could hear it too.

John pulled on his cigar, tasting of confidence. 'He is my secretary. He's helping organise my papers.'

The smoke floated out and sagged on the air. Mark stared at him over it. 'You can't expect anyone to believe that, Johnny. He speaks like a cabman.'

John laughed.

Mark bunched his beard in his hand. 'You know, Catherine wrote to me about this.'

'I'm not surprised.'

'I'm afraid I wasn't surprised either. I'd been expecting something.'

'Well, you knew about him already. He is the man I met in the park; I told you about him the day we spoke in the garden.'

Mark took this in. 'The man from the park –' he made a grimacing smile – 'and here he is, installed in your home. Your secretary – the man from the park. You have brought him into your family. Who is he? What does he want?'

'He is a compositor. He lived in Holborn, above a bookseller. Is that sufficient biography?'

'He has not asked you for anything?'

'No.'

'But you have dressed him; given him the run of your house. You are paying him some sort of wage?'

'Yes.'

Mark looked at him intently, his tongue travelling nervily across the underside of his top lip. 'You are intimate with him, aren't you? It is not even sentimental. He is well-made, I'll—'

'Well-made! I am pleased you noticed. I am pleased to hear you say it.' John ground out his cigar. He tasted confidence, knowledge. He felt easily capable of this conversation.

'In your own home. How can you, Johnny?'

'I love him. I desire him. Can you bear to hear that?'

Mark leaned against the lip of John's desk. His suit seemed to hang off him, not to touch flesh; John saw there were mud spatters up his trouser legs, dozens of small round spots dried the colour of ash.

'I can bear it,' Mark said. 'Of course I can. I can even understand it. But what does it mean? You have him here, your compositor. What now? He is a prisoner. You have no work for which he is capable. He is embarrassed every time he opens his mouth. Louisa and I can be polite, for your sake, all your sakes – other people will not understand, or will understand too well. You cannot flaunt him. You cannot have him where you wish. Are you to spend the years of your maturity scuttling down corridors after midnight, terrified of the servants? I assume this is what you are doing. Unless –' he gestured with his hand – 'you satisfy yourself here, under the pretence of sorting materials for your autobiography?'

John suppressed his desire to snap back and shock. It wasn't even that. His desire, almost physical, to speak of what he and Frank had done, were doing. He worried that his experiences would not be fully legible until then, even to himself. He wished to make them permanent, whole, to give them a place in the world. Every day, memories tugged fiercely for release. Words, details, salivated on his tongue. He imagined sitting Catherine down and forcing her to listen to it all come drooling out. There was a part of him that resented her, for tolerating Frank's presence in the house, even as he delighted in it. He sometimes feared she did not truly understand what it was she tolerated. He wanted her to know. He wanted to be sure that she knew.

Instead he said, 'It is a pretence, yes. I am writing something else. He really is assisting me with it. I am writing – co-writing – a book about our impossible subject, Mark. It will prepare opinion for a change in the law.'

Mark stood up, away from the desk. 'And who is your co-author? Surely not Mr Feaver?'

'He is called Henry Ellis. He is medically trained, interested in sex questions. Of progressive opinions. You may have read him – in the *Contemporary*. He is a newly married man, happily so.'

'What is he like?'

'We have yet to meet. He tells me he is very shy. Perhaps it is a precaution. I would not hold it against him.'

'You will put your names to this book?'

'Yes, we are agreed on that.'

'Catherine does not know?'

'She does not.'

'You have not considered her,' Mark said. 'Not in any of this.'

'I have spent so long considering her.'

'Only to make a mockery of your life together? Of your sacrifice, and hers?'

'An empty sacrifice. We gained a little respectability, and lost humanity.'

'You are not showing much humanity now.'

Cigar smoke, sour, coated John's mouth. He saw that there was nothing to drink in the room. 'It is unavoidable,' he said. 'I must be honest finally. What did she say, in her letter to you?'

'She does not wish you to be unhappy,' Mark said.

'I know.'

'Why did she agree to him coming here?'

'I did not give her a choice.'

Mark noticed the mud on his trousers and brushed at them half-heartedly, sighing. 'It is so difficult,' he said. 'Men and women. Marriage. All these long years of it, twining over and over. There is so much one no longer notices, one simply turns towards the light that is given. If one were to cut it away, even a section, what would one see?'

John smiled. 'I saw the swimmers in Hyde Park.'

'Are they very beautiful?'

'Yes.'

They stood looking at one another, the moment flaring up between them. In the gap they could hear the voices from downstairs. Eventually Mark said, 'Louisa has made me a far better man than I would otherwise have been. We have achieved great things together. The university, Newnham, women's education, have been well-served by us in partnership. I have not given her all of myself. But I have given all that I could. I can say that before the universe.'

'You are stronger than me. I am weaker.'

Mark wrinkled his brow. 'What do you speak about? You and Mr Feaver?'

John considered. 'Nothing of great significance. It does not seem necessary.'

'It is a passion, then?'

'Yes, but it is more than that. He is so simple, so unencumbered. He is not self-conscious like we are. It is like drinking water from a stream.'

'Water from a stream,' Mark repeated, in a distrait tone of voice.

John saw an opportunity: 'Would you write about yourself? For mine and Ellis's book? It is one of the things Frank is helping me with, finding men who will give an account of themselves. There are men he knows.'

'I am sure.'

John ignored him. 'We have a few cases already. It would be anonymous, of course.'

Mark looked troubled. His forehead creased again. 'What would I write? I have no experience.'

'That is no matter. You would write about your feelings, your wants. When you became aware of them. How you have lived with it.'

Mark clicked his tongue. 'I will consider it.'

John felt his confidence returning. He went to his desk and crouched to unlock one of the drawers. 'Will you take these?'

Mark squinted at the photographs John fanned out in his hand. Of dark-haired youths, all of them naked, their bodies supple, tanned, languidly posed, some showing enormous, lolling penises, others full, welcoming backsides; they leaned against rough whitewashed walls, stretched beneath trees, stood on the seashore, waves washing frozen at their feet. He looked up at John with amazement. 'If they were found?'

'You would make sure they were not.'

'I cannot take them.'

'Are you sure?'

'Yes, I'm sure. Put them away.'

The drawer was locked. When John turned around, Mark was waiting to speak: 'You are taking great risks, Johnny.'

'No substantial change has ever been managed without risk.'

'You are not Gladstone saving Ireland. What you are suggesting is even more impossible.'

'It is still the law. It is still men in Parliament, whose minds must be changed. And there are others who think as I do. There will be more before long.'

'That is as may be. But the law has not yet been changed. What you are doing now – what you are doing with this man, here in your house – is foolishness. It is not part of your campaign.'

'No, it is not,' John said. 'It is only my poor life. Let us go downstairs now. Our wives will be wondering where we are.'

When they came into the drawing room, Catherine was sitting in her armchair; she had taken off her bracelets and piled them on the small table next to her. Louisa and Janet were sitting on the sofa. Frank was sitting on the floor, his back to the empty chair next to the fire, hugging his knees. He was wearing one of the suits John had paid for. The fire danced in the grate, its reflection burning in bright points on the crystal decanter and the glasses crowded round it, playing over the polished fronts of Frank's shoes. It trembled in the glowing surfaces of Catherine's bracelets. The room was warm – too warm after the chill of the study. Everyone's faces were slightly pink.

'The great men return,' Louisa said, on her usual note.

'I hope you've managed without us,' John said.

'We've managed. But this is Janet's night. One of her last with the family. You might have put off your disquisitions.'

'It was not so long, Louisa,' Mark said quietly, sitting down next to her. He poured himself a drink and sipped from it.

'Don't pretend we've missed them,' Janet said. 'I must get accustomed to spending all my time in the company of women – though there was Mr Feaver here too, of course. Only he is not so talkative as Mark and Papa.'

John went over to the armchair Frank was leaning against. Frank shuffled a little way from it.

'We have tried to get Mr Feaver to take a seat, but he prefers the floor,' Catherine said.

In response Frank gave a low laugh and hugged his knees tighter. Janet laughed in sympathy. She was looking so much like Catherine these days, John thought: she had the same severity of line, a high clean forehead and strong nose, the same appraising eyes; her black hair was shorter, gathered up at the back in the fashionable way. Her sisters had more of himself in them, physically: the wide Addington mouth he had grown his moustache and beard to cover, the same wide-spaced eyes. And yet there was an echo of his personality in Janet that he had only just begun to catch.

'We've discovered that Mr Feaver has never visited Cambridge,' Janet said. 'That he is not at all a university man.'

'You knew that, dear,' he replied, glancing at Frank, who was rubbing at a mark on his shoe. 'Mr Feaver came up another way.'

'Yes. I had forgotten.' She seemed to weigh her words. 'I said he ought to join us when you deposit me at Newnham. You know Cambridge well enough to show him the colleges and the Fitzwilliam. While Mother helps me sort my room. You'll only get bored otherwise.'

'And what does Mr Feaver think?'

Frank turned his head. 'It would be a pleasure, sir. If it wasn't too great a trouble, and you didn't mind me missing work.'

'Of course not.'

'We will likely be about our business,' Louisa said quickly. 'Janet should expect to encounter us first in our official capacities. Though I will look for you at your matriculation, as I looked for your sisters.'

John was acutely conscious of his foot that was closest to Frank. He was already too warm next to the fire; his calves seemed to swell under the hot cloth of his trousers. He wanted to touch the ruby lobes of Frank's ears. Across from him Catherine was observing Janet, her chin propped in her hand. The first night Frank had been in the house, a month ago, John had lain in bed, his body tense with want, waiting for her to fall asleep. He always knew when Catherine was awake. That night especially the silence had felt shared, mutually comprehended; it became like something unbearably precious balanced between them. Her stillness and his was only a form of heightened attention. He began to dread Frank having gone to sleep, his door being locked – he imagined having to carry the strain across another long day. And then she had spoken, spoken without moving, in the surety that he was awake to hear her, her voice like a dart across the pillow: 'Just go.' He had gone every night since, though only after first making a show of retiring to his and Catherine's room. Frank was down the corridor, in one of the rooms reserved for guests. John slept there, waking and dressing before the servants got up; Mark had been right to suspect that he spent his time trying to avoid their notice.

'You're interested in spirits, Professor Ludding,' Frank said unexpectedly from his place on the floor.

Mark's expression changed. 'In psychical research, yes.'

'My father is dead two years now. I wonder about him.'

'About his existence after death?'

'I suppose that's it.'

From his position John could only see the side of Frank's face, the corner of his mouth; his expression was hard to read.

Mark looked merely patient. 'It might be possible to establish contact,' he said, 'with the correct medium. But, as I frequently remind your employer, I am by no means settled in my mind as to the reality of the life beyond.'

There was a pause. The coals tinkled.

'What was your father's name?' Janet asked.

'Also Francis,' replied Frank.

'What did he do?'

Frank hesitated – it was over before John had time to panic: 'He was a clerk.'

'You liked him, of course?'

'I did.'

Janet shaped her lips, but nothing came out. Instead she looked at Frank earnestly. They were all looking at him earnestly, as at a new baby in its basket. John felt extraordinary pride in the fact of his possession.

'And your mother?' Louisa said.

'She's alive, but she's not so well as she was.'

'I am sorry to hear it.'

There was a well-intentioned silence. 'I didn't mean to have everyone talking about me,' Frank said.

'Of course you didn't,' Janet said. 'It hasn't been like that. How about we play a game? What could we play? Oh, look at you all – where is your sense of duty to the departing girl? I must be obeyed. This is the very last time in my life I shall be able to tell Mark and Louisa what to do. And Mr Feaver must be amused somehow, else he will flee the house.'

She opened the partition doors and led them back to the dining table, which had been cleared of its things, sombre in its abandonment. The light was starker, the air freer away from the fire. Lewis appeared at the door to see if he was wanted, before retreating. Janet picked out a small ball of red wool and placed it at the centre of the table. As she explained the rules, John wondered if she would ever be so unthinkingly imperious again; whether her childish powers of command would survive the dislocation from home, the knowledge of her smallness in the greater world.

The game was simple: to win, a team had to succeed, by lung power, in blowing the wool over the opposite end of the table. The individual closest to the wool when it rolled over must perform a forfeit. Seated at one end were Catherine, Mark and John; at the other, Janet, Frank and Louisa. They began all of them by blowing rather feebly, surprised at how quickly the little ball whisked in various directions. They laughed at its strange stallings and hesitations when it was buffeted by too many contrary winds, and at its sudden rushes for the edge, which had to be furiously resisted. And of course they were soon laughing at themselves: the unexpected difficulty in sending breath in the same direction at the same time; the way one side pushed in together, all blowing manically, when the ball approached them, the other team also bunching and leaning, lips working, opening and pursing in grotesque kissing shapes. It was difficult, also, to maintain momentum when people kept breaking off to laugh, their breath stuttering and collapsing, or to take in air. Once it had been noticed how oddly Mark contorted his cheeks, and the way his beard fluttered in the face of an enemy advance, it was even more difficult. Finally, John's side achieved an absolute advantage, the ball constantly being urged forward and the opposing team unable to push it back more than an inch or two before it leapt close to the edge again. They were blowing, laughing and cheering on the outbreath, the others blowing and wailing, as the ball came closer and closer. Frank dropped onto his knees, bringing his mouth almost to the table, blowing madly at the ball as it quivered there, his cheeks like bellows. They were in such high spirits that this flagrant breach of the rules added to their enjoyment. It was not enough: finally, with a great relieved whoop from John's side, the wool went over into Frank's lap – he had to fall back onto his palms at the very last moment to avoid it going into his mouth – and he stood up with it scrunched in his hand, grinning, tossing it onto the table in mock disgust.

'What children we are!' Louisa said, her hand on her chest. They were all smiling, catching their breath, in some way disarranged. Frank briefly put his hands on his knees and bent over them, before coming back up, still grinning. His hair had flopped out of its parting and he pushed it back.

'You must pick a forfeit for Mr Feaver,' Janet said, very pleased with her success.

They hesitated, before Mark cried out, 'Stand on your head!'

Frank's grin disappeared, and he put his hands on his hips. His face was still flushed. It looked for a moment as if he were offended, but then he said, 'I'll need to go into the drawing room.'

The fire had sunk. They stood in a half-circle and watched while Frank pulled at the corners of the rug to straighten it before positioning himself in the middle. Their shadows were squeezed up against the walls. Somehow – perhaps it was the way Frank had taken it – all the humour had dropped from the situation. It had the air of a challenge. John wanted to say something, to dispel the atmosphere, but could think of nothing that wouldn't expose him. Frank crouched and put out his hands, the arrow-head hairs visible on their backs, but then had second thoughts and stood again. 'I can't do it with this on,' he said, handing his jacket to Janet. He returned to his crouch, putting out his hands again, and slowly bowed his head to the ground, like a Muslim at prayer. He ground his head into the rug, working onto the crown, setting his hands widely parallel with his pink ears. Then, after a moment, with a short expulsion of breath, he tipped forward out of his crouch onto his head and hands, his knees drawing in and briefly touching his elbows before his legs went waveringly up, the glossy tips of his shoes winching in a salute to the ceiling, his trouser legs slipping to show his socks, his laces drooping like tiny nooses.

It was only a moment, before his legs began to quake and he

folded to the ground; only a moment that his body stood like an exclamation mark in the room, the firelight lapping eagerly up it, dark shadows shrinking into the folds of his white shirt. Only a moment, when it seemed to John the most miraculous thing he had ever seen.

Dear Mr Ellis,

I am grateful to you for your provisional sketch of our book's contents. I quite agree that I should handle the earlier sections, viz. the Greeks and the transition in history from the Greek, through the Roman and medieval periods, to present times. It will necessarily be superficial, given the absence of much of the material one would want. The great thing, I think, will be to signal the importance of the Justinian Edict and the theological basis thereafter for prejudice and persecution. After that, the task will mainly be to emphasise the persistence of the phenomenon, in spite of it. It occurs to me that it might be sensible to name some eminent historical inverts, those whom we can identify with some certainty.

I agree also that you should handle the chapters on the <u>nature</u> of sexual inversion. That would be expected from the medical authority in our partnership. I have almost completed my reading in this area, and will be happy to share with you my verdicts.

And I agree with your argument for not, after all, dealing with female inversion. You are right that the absence of a legal penalty for it will blunt the force of the critique we make in this book, and right that it would create a great deal of additional research, which neither of us can easily take on. The study of the male case will anyhow shed considerable light on the issue as a whole.

Finally, I have done as promised, and begun seeking, with assistance, autobiographies from living inverts in this country. I enclose a copy of the questionnaire I have drawn up in order to elicit these confessions. If you approve, please rely on it when you come to approach inverts of your own acquaintance. I have already written to Edward Carpenter with a copy, and he has agreed to collect some cases for us. He has also invited me to visit him at his house at Millthorpe, which I hope to do in the coming months.

Believe me very truly yours,

J. Addington

14 Dover Mansions

Brixton

20th October 94

Dear Mr Addington,

Your letter gave me great pleasure. I am glad you are making such progress, and that you approve of my plan, hesitant as it was.

Your questionnaire seems to me excellent, covering every point of real interest and containing nothing superfluous. I shall certainly rely on it, as you suggest; and I am pleased Carpenter is to be involved. Now I am more advanced in my own research, I see how important it is that we should publish the responses of British inverts. As far as I can tell, in the whole of English medico-scientific periodical literature, not a single case of sexual inversion has ever been studied, however briefly. (Of course, sexual perversions are mentioned in discussions of episodes of insanity.)

Sincerely yours,

Henry Ellis

XIV

The grey afternoon light was slung like a net through the window, capturing damply within it the table, which held glumly to its little set of blurred reflections; the dusty-looking floor and the scattered sections of rug; the sideboard with its brandishment of books and photographs; the sofa and the two chairs huddled together in the front part of the room next to the hallway. Henry and Edith were also captured, grey, the light cold and not quite clean on their faces. The window had been closed ten minutes before and the room still had an outside smell: cold rain, wet leaves, dirty trailings of smoke. Henry refrained from his letter, which he was writing at the table, and gazed at the raindrops stalled on the windowpane. A small warped circle of water was lying on the sill. Opposite him Edith was taking notes, *The Story of an African Farm* open under one hand.

They were at Edith's flat. It was familiar to Henry – he moved about it quite freely – but he felt no sense of possession. It was hers. This was how it should be, he reminded himself. And yet it had been *theirs*, an insistent voice shot back at him – hers and Angelica's. He had visited several times in the weeks since Angelica returned to Norfolk, on each occasion looking for changes she'd wrought. There was the obvious thing – a new vase the two women had bought one afternoon, placed in the middle of the table – and one other: a pair of red leather gloves abandoned on the sideboard. The vase vaguely unsettled him. Was it something Edith would have bought for herself? – he had never thought of her as acquisitive – or something Angelica wanted, or something that only made sense in the light of them both, the result of some inscrutable interplay of personality, mood, environment? He knew nothing about vases, which made it harder to tell. The gloves he had pinched between his fingers, briefly sniffed.

Nothing else? Nothing in the flat. What had been Angelica's room, with its settle bed, had boiled down to the bare sum of its original contents. He could find no trace of her there. But Henry discerned some change in Edith, in the way she related to her surroundings, to the flat itself. He had a sense, hard to shake, that she was inhabiting a space grown larger around her, that somehow she had become smaller within it. He could only liken this to his memories of his father being away at sea: his perception, even as a small boy, that his mother felt the distances more keenly, from wall to wall, door to door, without her husband's intervening presence. This was not a reassuring parallel, and he attributed to his recognition of it his feeling that the flat was indeed changed somehow, notwithstanding its appearance. He felt this even without considering the question of Angelica's letters, no longer visible in the coloured envelopes he remembered from before. Edith referred to them still, but she did not write to Angelica in his presence. She did not move the red gloves from their place on the sideboard. He registered these things like a tremor, a skipping heartbeat.

Angelica had fought hard against her father all summer. The three of them – Angelica, Henry and Edith – had spent long afternoons together, in various parks, in the brimming heat. Angelica would allow a certain number of letters to arrive, usually several from her father and one from her mother, and would carry them everywhere, unopened, until she found that she could face reading them. Henry and Edith would be getting on with their work, stretched on the ground or propped on their elbows, when there would come the sound of a paper knife and they would glance up to see Angelica opening her envelopes, pressing down the springing squares of paper onto the grass. Reading them, she would frequently be stirred to speak some sentence or paragraph, with that snapping laugh of hers, and shortly they would be drawn back into the saga, strategising together. His and Edith's relationship felt focused, consolidated, by having Angelica as its object of interest, as perhaps it would have been by the birth of a child. On one occasion, when Angelica was reading a letter from her father and Henry and Edith were lying parallel to each other on their elbows, Edith had begun to run a finger down the prominent vein on the back of his hand, following it over the wrist bone, stroking the underside. They had exchanged a smile, while Angelica's voice went on, receding into the summer noise of the park – the soft roar of a fountain, the smack of deckchairs – and the shared smile had broadened into total understanding.

There had been something delicious about that London summer freedom, as it quite unexpectedly appeared to him; in the feeling that the days were widely open, the city limitless, life noisy and beckoning, all in contrast with the closed, still, sulking provincialism represented by Angelica's family. Angelica would sometimes reply to her letters there and then, in whichever park they were sitting, but more often she would refuse to. It was her way of dropping them back into her bag, unanswered, that seemed so delicious, as if it really was that simple – a moment's decision whether their day should be interfered with or not. Henry felt, with Angelica, what he hardly ever felt, which was young.

He had, in those particular sets of hours, a strong awareness of their being a trio, of their being friends, that had previously eluded him, and which seemed so impossible a prospect after that disastrous dinner in Soho. And on one occasion at least, the evening he had told Edith and Angelica about his and Addington's project, it seemed as though he and Angelica were the two who understood each other best. They had been here, in this room, arranged over the sofa and chairs. Angelica was first to speak. She was in one of the chairs, her dress – lapis lazuli, brocaded – falling over its front like a curtain. 'I am surprised, Henry,' she said. 'Forgive me, but I would not have expected it. It is a very considerable undertaking.'

Edith was thoughtful. 'Are you committed to it, Henry?'

'Yes.'

'John Addington is an invert, you think?' Angelica said next.

'I am fairly sure.'

'It does not trouble you?'

'No.'

'You go further in my estimation. Your friend Jack – is he an invert?'

'He has told me so.'

'I thought perhaps he was. How interesting. There was a man I knew—'

'You did not tell me,' Edith interrupted, 'about Jack.'

'It is private,' he said. 'I know nothing about it.'

Edith picked at her nail and then looked up as if jolted by a thought: 'And why did Addington ask you?'

'He didn't,' Henry said. 'The book was my suggestion.'

'Why? You have never told me you were interested in the subject. You told me nothing of this.'

'It is obvious why,' Angelica said.

'Why?' Edith repeated.

'It is unjust,' Henry said. 'The legal penalty—'

'But it's more than that, isn't it?' Angelica said.

Henry bloomed under her approval. He explained. Edith appeared more satisfied. Still: 'Are you sure it is wise?' she asked.

'I imagine Henry has considered the risks,' Angelica said.

Henry nodded, not looking at either of them.

'There,' Angelica said, sucking quickly on her cigarette. 'You see. He has considered.'

But then, when this evening was finished, as with all the others, it was Edith and Angelica who remained, who got to describe it to each other after Henry had gone. His returns to Brixton often felt like withdrawals, sometimes like expulsions. He would picture Angelica at this table – the table he was sitting at now – cigarette smoke like a gauze over her face, her letters scattered before her. He feared then that he had served only as a sort of distraction and that those moments when Angelica put her stack of envelopes away in her bag were only pauses, breaks from the business of life, resumed when he was apart from them. That the freedom he had been drinking up so parchedly was limited after all.

Angelica's collapse, when it came, surprised him totally. He had grown so used to her father, holding him in his mind so familiarly, condescending to his foolishness and bad logic and childish grievance, that he never imagined him actually gaining any sort of advantage, achieving any assertion of will. He was confident Angelica would hold out for ever – he remembered the naked confidence on her face when she had said at the restaurant, 'I am stronger.' It was hard to imagine that face crumpling into remorse. Hard to imagine her walking defeatedly up to the Norfolk house, crowned by one of her hats, in one of her wonderful dresses.

They still didn't know what had broken her resolve. Edith said only that she thought Angelica was worn down – that she'd fretted for her mother, who was really blameless in everything. Edith said she'd been as surprised as Henry; more so, considering all the time she and Angelica spent together. Angelica simply announced her decision one morning over breakfast, and was gone by the afternoon. They had neither of them, Henry or Edith, seen her since: it had been over a month.

Today, at the table in the grey light, they were anticipating unsought guests. Edith's father and stepmother had written to say they were coming into town and wished to make a call. They hoped they would have the opportunity of meeting Henry at last. Edith called it a bore and a waste of time, Henry's especially, but she didn't suggest he not be present. Instead they agreed to give them tea. The window had been open to air the flat. Earlier they had tidied, bearing down with excessive energy on small tasks – Henry found himself picking things up and putting them down again in the same place. If he wasn't looking forward to the meeting, he rather enjoyed the preparations for it; they had given his and Edith's togetherness a coherent shape it hadn't possessed since Angelica's departure. It helped, he knew now, to have someone or something bring them into definition, like throwing a stage light, giving them a role.

'Let's put away our things,' Edith said abruptly. 'They'll be here any minute.' She stood and looked down at her notes from a height; seeing something, she scratched out a word and substituted another, before picking up her book and papers and placing them in a drawer in the sideboard. When she turned back she saw Henry still sitting there. 'Don't – don't be too quiet,' she said, 'and don't worry about us living apart. Let them think what they will.' She looked at him quickly. 'You might like them, you know. I might like them. Isn't that a frightening thought?'

They moved to sit on the sofa, Edith slightly curled in the right-hand corner. It was some minutes since the guests were due. Henry had an unsatisfied feeling, thinking of the letter he'd put away and the work he could be doing. The time ached. It was darker and Edith put on some lamps; the room looked crooked, the light falling unevenly.

There came a knock. Edith got up and Henry, turning his head, stared down the dark hallway to where she was opening the door. There was a novel arrangement of shapes, a musical fretting of voices, higher and lower – he could hear the nerves in Edith's – and the guests were led into the room. Mr Vills was short like Edith, in fact barely taller, military-looking, with grey hair shorn closely to the sides of his head and whiskers cut into thick wedges that came down to his chin. He moved with a curious sideways rocking motion, like a toy with a round bottom. His wife was the tallest of the family, and she stooped as if in compensation; her hair beneath her hat was threaded with white and there were faint lines at the corners of her mouth. Henry bent to shake their hands, submitting to their assessments. They sat down, Mr and Mrs Vills on the sofa, and Henry this time in the chair to the left. Edith laid out a plate of shortbread, which her father reached for, and went to make the tea. Henry and her parents looked at each other with frank embarrassment. He drummed his nervousness on the sides of his legs.

'Well, Mr Ellis, you and Edith have been married now how long?' Mrs Vills said. She had a soft south London accent, the sort familiar to him since childhood.

'Since June,' said Henry, smiling feebly. He smoothed his knees.

'We were so pleased when we heard. You are also a writer,' Mrs Vills said encouragingly, as if reminding him.

'Yes.' He looked over at the window and cleared his throat.

Mr Vills leaned forward, plucking at his trousers. 'We have read some of your articles, Mr Ellis. You are a vigorous arguer. I found myself quite taken along with you before I rightly knew where I was.'

'Thank you.' He nearly asked, 'Which have you read?' but prevented himself. 'Thank you,' he repeated, more meaningfully than before, taking in Mrs Vills as well.

'And what are you working on currently?'

He scanned the cornicing for inspiration. 'Something on the criminal. The criminal type.'

'Oh, well. That *is* interesting,' Mr Vills breathed. 'And what do we know?'

Edith came back into the room with a tray. 'What are we talking about?' she said briskly.

'The criminal type,' said Mr Vills, taking his cup and saucer. 'Mr Ellis's project.'

'Let's not,' said Edith, pouring three more with a look.

Henry had an access of confidence: 'I am interested in the work of Cesare Lombroso. An Italian, obviously. He sees the criminal type as identifiable, but there is a corollary – that what is not willed, cannot be punished, at least not in the same way.'

'Oh, I see, yes,' Mr Vills said.

'Henry is interested in responsibility,' Edith said in her explanatory voice, seating herself in the other chair. 'We both are. We believe in the maximum of responsibility, where it can be freely exercised without injury: responsibility for oneself, one's own development and pursuits, and responsibility for the health and progress of the community. One leads into the other, or should.'

Mrs Vills's eyes followed this somewhat uncertainly. 'I see.'

Mr Vills had taken another biscuit. 'You're lecturing, Edith,' he said, through crumbs.

'I am only saying—' she began hotly.

'It is a question, dear,' Mrs Vills interrupted. 'We heard you were beginning to lecture.'

Edith's eyes smiled, but her mouth only trembled slightly. 'That's right. Next month, commencing November fourth at Hanway Hall.'

'Will you be attending, Mr Ellis?'

He nodded. 'Call him Henry,' Edith said.

Mrs Vills sipped at her tea. 'The lectures, Edith, they are for women?'

'Yes; but I want to address men also. They are about relations between the sexes; love and marriage; work and family-raising.'

'And marriage,' Mrs Vills said. 'Edith told us you do not live here, Henry?'

'He does not,' Edith replied.

'Where do you live, Henry?' her father asked.

'Brixton,' Henry said.

'Brixton! Do you see each other often?'

'Yes, Father,' said Edith. 'Often. We can work together quite easily, you see.'

Mrs Vills looked between them, her eyes seeming to touch softly on each of their faces. Henry under her scrutiny felt that same unusual awareness of his maleness – almost of his sexual nature – that he had experienced on his wedding day. He glanced at his hands cupping his knees, the hairs on the lower parts of the fingers, the hard knuckles sticking out; he was conscious of his pale ankles under his socks, of himself as a series of hidden gaps and hollows, stretches of skin over bone. He reflected on the gaps in knowledge between the people in this room – what Edith knew of him and he of her, placing them together on one side, looking out from their shelf of hidden experience. Mr and Mrs Vills looked out from their own, the secret place they had taken themselves. Once we are entered into marriage, Henry thought, none of us ever truly meets again.

'Do you still see your friend Mary?' Mrs Vills said.

Edith smiled. 'She was at our wedding, but no, not so much. We have another friend, Angelica, who was staying here until recently.'

'I'm sorry about Mary. She was nice, I thought.'

'Yes, she is. Angelica too.'

Mrs Vills drank from her cup. Mr Vills, swivelling in his seat, said, 'It's a pleasant room.'

'You don't employ a maid?' Mrs Vills asked.

'No. There is hardly a need,' said Edith.

'It is a little dark, Edith,' Mrs Vills responded, looking round her with more attention, 'and small, if you were to have a family.'

There was a short pause. 'Yes,' Edith calmly said, 'we have often thought it would be a little small.'

'Have you?'

'Yes,' Edith replied.

Mrs Vills turned her placid, touching gaze on Henry.

'Yes,' he said.

They were clearing away the things. Edith was standing with plates stacked in her hands.

'Have you really thought that? About children?' Henry demanded. His fingers were pushed uncomfortably into the looped handles of the teacups. They dangled from his hands.

'Don't look at me like that. You were being terrible, going on saying "Yes" in that deadening way of yours. I could see both of them drifting away – I didn't want them to feel vindicated in their way of doing things. I could see that's what she was feeling so I said it to surprise her, to give her something to think about. You saw how she changed after that.'

'Yes.'

'Henry—'

'Yes! Yes! Yes! I'm sorry, Edith. I am a poor excuse for a husband.'

'You are not.'

He found himself foolishly tearful. 'We do not understand our marriage. It is unconsummated. You talk of children only to score a point over your stepmother.'

Edith adjusted her fingers around the stacked plates. 'That side of it – after this time, I did not know you wanted it. I don't –' she sighed, glancing away – 'I don't think that I do. I thought we were agreed. We are so much to each other, Henry, it is hardly necessary, surely. We always thought so, when we began.'

'We did not think it through. What are we to each other, Edith? There is something that comes between us.'

'Henry,' she began.

'Why do we not see Mary? Has she also been pushed out?'

'How do you mean?'

'By Angelica.'

She chilled. 'I told you that my women friendships were of the greatest importance to me. I said you were the only man I had ever truly bonded with. I told you. There has been no change in me. I thought, and Angelica thought, that with you and me as we are, and now with your book – we thought you might know something of what it is to prefer the company of your own sex. Something more than you could tell me before we married. Is that right, Henry?'

The cup handles pinched his fingers and he had an impulse to fling them off to the corners of the room. 'You have discussed this with Angelica? That is why she said we were not married.'

'So she explained to me. It was wrong of her.'

He took this in. 'I have no personal interest in the book,' he said, trying to keep his voice from cracking. 'It wasn't from some personal interest that I committed to it. You have misunderstood. I should have anticipated that you might. I should have foreseen what it would be like to share you.'

'But Henry,' she almost shouted, 'you never did have me to yourself. It was on that basis that we married, that we thought up our marriage. No two people need be everything to each other.'

'You have become everything.'

She stared at him defiantly. 'I do not want to be, to anyone.'

Anguish locked in his throat. 'You are. I am only loneliness without you.'

She stared at him still. 'Then we should never have married,' she said, quite plainly, putting down the plates.

XV

The train thud-thud-thudded on the track. John felt it in the soles of his feet, in his knees, his forehead as he touched it briefly against the glass. Catherine's perfume dragged at his nose as he watched the rapid rolling-out of the landscape under the wide unblinking sky, all of it clarified and hardened by bright autumn light. A troop of men carrying baskets on their shoulders were trailing up a field, lost to his vision before he could guess at their purpose or destination.

Frank shifted in the seat opposite. It was the smallest movement; he merely moved one leg slightly to the right. But John understood immediately that he had done it to free his scrotum, to let it drop away from where it had stuck. He pictured the two globes in their loose snug skin, brushed with dark hairs; he felt in his mind their soft weight, their liquid fullness in his hand. He closed his eyes, opened them again and stared hard at the unravelling world outside. He had not anticipated this, obvious as it now seemed: that the arrangement he'd devised would expose him quite so ruthlessly to the play of his desire. Frank's continual presence had not inured him to its effects, as he thought it would; rather it had dramatised the distinction between their two relationships, the public and the private, investing the switches between them with overmuch significance, conferring on each a peculiar new eroticism. In company, John was constantly beset by impressions, seeing Frank doubly, as now, his outward appearance limned by secret knowledge. And when they were alone, some unspecified charge carried over from their official interactions, some stored-up social friction that made their lovemaking fierce and oddly abject on John's part. Four nights ago he had let Frank penetrate him, his whole body expanding around it, centring upon it, so that while it lasted it was the great returning undiminishing fact in his life, that he was being penetrated by this man.

Catherine closed her book and lay her hands on it. The dark blue stuff of her dress neatly seamed John's trouser leg. She spoke to Janet, who was sitting opposite her, next to Frank. 'What are you worrying about, dear?'

Janet laughed. She looked very smart in her hat and jacket, bought specially. 'I was looking at you and Papa, and thinking – oh, I don't know what. Being sentimental. I was imagining you both at my age.'

'Not so hard to imagine,' said Catherine.

'Not hard at all, actually. Harder to imagine Papa without his beard, but I've seen photographs.'

'If it weren't for the photographs I would struggle to imagine it myself,' John said. 'I remember the *feeling*, however, of going up to Oxford the first time. I hope you will be a little braver than I was.' He saw that Frank was quietly smiling, very golden in the light falling on the window; his new suit looked well on him.

'Braver than me also,' Catherine added. 'Not that I had yours or your sisters' chance, and though you are brave already. Girls are brave now as a matter of course.'

'Do you feel brave, Miss Addington?' Frank asked, his voice surprising them as usual.

Janet hesitated, facing her parents. The sunlight meant that she had to squint. 'Yes, I do, I think. I don't know if it has anything to do with how other girls feel. I just feel prepared, somehow, for anything.'

'For anything!' laughed Catherine.

'Well, anything in Cambridge, at any rate,' replied Janet.

The platform was a maze of bags and luggage trolleys, densely thicketed with smoke and servants, mothers, fathers, slim young men with thin moustaches, and several women of Janet's age and demeanour. Above the smoke the air and the sky were sharp, the sunlight cool and transparent. Susan the maid, who had travelled with the luggage, met them in the throng; they eventually oozed outside, joining the line for a cab. When theirs came, the three women got in, and, once everything was safely stowed, John and Frank waved them off. It had been decided in line with Janet's original suggestion that the men would walk into town and appear at the college in a few hours' time, when she was set up.

He and Frank were some way down Hills Road before John began to feel his strange tension dropping away. It had gathered while they were standing outside the station, amid the kicking of horses' hooves, and the clattering away of carriages, and the restless noticing, questioning, asserting chatter. He'd felt uneasy, watching the moustached young men and the quiet absorptive look that came over Janet's face, especially when the cab set off, carrying her towards the future: it might in that moment have been the gallows. Frank seemed also to have visibly relaxed, his hands jauntily in his pockets, eyes darting at the shopfronts. The sky ran ahead of them and was squeezed into a bright gap between buildings far removed.

'Janet's a good girl,' Frank said, looking at him sidelong as they walked.

'I hope so.'

'You're alike.'

'Is she like Catherine, do you think?'

'I expect, but that's not my business.'

They halted at a crossing. People collected around them: a woman was standing with martyred patience, a small child gripping either hand. The new Catholic church bulked on the left, the stone very young and crude under the sun. The children were looking at it. So were John and Frank. 'I think I understand Catherine less and less,' John said. With his eye he followed the steeple up. 'A little less each week.'

'Does it bother you?' Frank asked.

John turned to see him: the lean, known, knowledgeable face, under the smart unfamiliar hat. In the background the intersecting road stretched away, profusely hung with the spreading branches of trees. The leaves, backed by sunlight, glowed like opals. 'I can't tell,' he said.

The road cleared and Frank started across. John caught up with him and they kept their pace down the street. The town proper was beginning – ahead of them was indeterminate bustle. 'I was friendly with a man who moved to Cambridge,' Frank said. 'I never knew his name though, else I'd look him up and ask him to fill in your question-naire. He was an interesting case.'

'What did you call him?'

'Oh, he had a name, just it wasn't his real one.'

'Would I like these men, whom you were friendly with before?'

Frank shrugged. 'Perhaps you'd know them.'

They went first to the Fitzwilliam Museum, admiring it initially from the outside, the stone beautifully sun-struck, each hard line showing as freshly carved. Inside, in the large, quiet, damasked picture rooms, they stayed mostly together, pausing in front of paintings John remembered or that Frank took a fancy to. Then they walked through the Greek and Roman gallery, echoingly empty, drifting like devotees between the busts and statues, the miraculous fragments, making circuits round a chosen few. In all of it, John was careful. Careful not to perform his erudition, careful not to propound – careful not to draw attention to distinctions, careful not to assume. He watched Frank, carefully, to measure his effect; to measure the effect of the building, of its contents. He liked seeing him looking, liked the way his eyes flared and narrowed as he concentrated, liked how he could not help coming closer and closer to what interested him. He was pleased that the questions he asked were intelligent, and that he himself was able to answer them, while Frank glanced between his face and the object under discussion.

There were several small moments of breathing proximity, when, standing side by side, John was aware of the heat gently beating from Frank's cheek and could almost feel, as though by his senses he had taken a mould, the quantity of Frank's body under his clothes. In the classical gallery they separated, so that at one point John found himself in the aisle ranged through the statuary, at the far end of which Frank unexpectedly appeared between two male nudes, as if – the thought irresistibly occurred – to complete the line. Frank must have seen this thought in John's face, because the next thing he did was imitate the pose of one of the figures, setting back his shoulders, extending a leg and gesturing with his right arm, his palm elegantly open. In response John burst out with a laugh, a high full laugh that fell into the room like glass, shattering on its quiet still surface, pieces flying to every corner.

'Which of us do you prefer?' called Frank, grinning, wildly careless.

'You in the middle!'

Frank laughed. His hands were on his hips. 'That's because I still have all my parts!'

'It will do, won't it,' Janet said, surveying her rooms: the one they were standing in, with its two rather worn armchairs and writing desk, a rug in front of the fire, and a second, visible through an open door, containing a single bed and Susan, who was placing clothes in a wardrobe. Several of the pictures from Janet's room at home had been hung about on the walls.

John could tell from her face that she was pleased. He and Frank had just arrived – they were like additional pieces of furniture, unfamiliar in the new surroundings. 'It's very nice,' he said, exchanging a glance with Catherine, who was standing with them, a thick, wiry-looking blanket folded over her arms. She had been holding it when they came in: he was beginning to wonder if it was for warmth.

'She has a good view,' Catherine said, lifting her arms in the direction of the window. It gave out onto the college gardens, silvery-jade in the dying light. John and Frank looked together. Two young women were seated on a bench, their skirts seeming to plant them in the ground. As they watched, one leaned her head on the other's shoulder.

'No sign of Mark or Louisa?' asked John.

'None,' Catherine replied.

'They did say we wouldn't see them,' Janet said.

'I thought perhaps they might have relented from duty, for the sake of old friends,' John said. As usual he felt Frank's quiet presence like a pressure. To lessen it, he added, 'Mr Feaver is much taken with Cambridge.'

'Is he?' said Janet.

'Yes,' said Frank, picking up the cue. 'Yes, miss. It's very beautiful.'

'And did you see the Fitzwilliam?' Janet asked.

'Yes, we did.'

'Did you admire it?'

'Yes, miss.'

'I hope Papa didn't fuss you with facts. Names and dates and patrons and so on. Never giving you a moment to make up your own mind.'

Frank's lips crinkled. 'No, miss.'

'I'm not sure that he didn't. It would be very out of character.' She paused. 'You are smiling, Mr Feaver. That means Papa is guilty.' She looked at her father, her eyes flashing with enjoyment. 'Papa, how could you?'

John laughed. 'I restrained my lecturing instincts, as it happens. I could hear your criticisms in my head. If Mr Feaver is better educated now than he was before, it has nothing to do with me.'

'I don't believe you. Look at Mr Feaver. He looks like a man who's been bombarded. When he walked in here I thought I could see relief on his face.'

John laughed again; Frank was laughing too. 'A moment ago you thought he might only have been fussed. Now it is a matter of bombardment.'

'That's because your dissembling suggests that the crime was much greater than I supposed.' As she came out with this, Janet's mouth split into a wide grin. Her face was childlike. She was delighted.

Catherine's voice sheared through their laughter. 'Janet, you are showing off. Today is not a day for teasing.'

They went quiet and looked at her. The wiry blanket was still over her arms, but now she was hugging it to herself. Seeing Janet's face, which had been shocked back into its similarity with her own – the smile vanished, the high blank forehead reasserted, the long nose drawn back down – she seemed to soften. 'We are leaving you here. For the first time.'

'I know that,' Janet replied, sounding mournful herself.

'We should say our goodbyes,' Catherine said. 'You have your appointments, and we should not be home late. Susan is finished putting away your things.'

John noticed that Susan had joined them, standing by the door into the other room, her hands clasped. He thought he detected a trace of laughter on her face too, though it had been replaced by readiness. 'Yes, we should take ourselves away,' he said to Janet, 'even though you are very amusing this evening. No doubt to remind us of what we shall miss.'

They collected their things and made a note of what to send down in the week – another blanket (the one in Catherine's arms, it turned out, had been rejected for being too rough), some more spoons, a book that had been left behind. Eventually the chatter cancelled itself and they faced each other again in the sitting room. He and Frank were nothing like new furniture, John realised; they were merely impermanent incursions from the past. The room needed them gone, all of them bar Janet, in order for it to become hard and strange, before it became something else.

Perhaps Janet saw this. 'Goodbye, Susan,' she said. And then, 'Good-bye, Mr Feaver,' putting out her hand to Frank, who took it solemnly.

'Goodbye, miss,' he said, his hand still over hers. 'Don't let them bombard you.'

She had faltered slightly when he held on to her hand, but now she smiled, seeing Frank's grin. 'Goodbye, Papa,' she said, turning to him next, the smile still on her face, so that there was something incongruous in the way she hugged him – not letting go, her hand pinching his shoulder and her face and nose pushed into the crook of his arm. When she came away there were tears in her eyes. She was childlike again; emotions were shifting like playing cards on her face.

John held on to her shoulders, the plush of her new jacket. He tried to think of the house without her in it, of her empty chair at the table, of a third bedroom pretty and stale with disuse, but all he could picture was Frank, Frank; he imagined going back to the house with him, to that widening, encompassing space, the greater freedom they might experience. He was shocked at himself. 'Goodbye, darling,' he said, touching along her jawline with the fronts of his fingers. 'You must enjoy it.'

She smiled under his touch. Her tears were a tremble beneath her irises. 'Yes, Papa,' she said, her voice quiet. Then her eyes shifted: 'Oh, Mother, don't!'

Catherine was sobbing, the blanket bundled up under her chin, her face buried in it. 'Mother, don't, don't,' Janet continued, beginning confusedly to pull at the blanket. Catherine seemed to hold on more tightly, burying her face deeper. Her sobs were loud and rasping; John had only heard her cry like this two or three times before. He recognised the set of her shoulders and – now that Janet had succeeded in dragging the blanket out of her arms – the way her mouth fell open to emit that rasping noise. He was embarrassed for Frank and for Susan, both of whom looked astonished.

'Mother, please,' Janet said, her voice almost breaking.

Catherine stood with her chin on her breastbone, tears tracking down her face. She had stopped sobbing. Her breath was coming quickly in little gasps and then shuddering out in whistling sighs. Her hair had fallen from behind her ear on one side. Eventually she looked at them. The expression on her face was one of silent accusation, as though she had been discovered in a hiding place against her wishes.

'Catherine—' John began.

'Please, John,' she interrupted. 'Susan, Mr Feaver – I'm sorry.' She briefly closed her eyes, and tears signalled in the lashes. 'I'm sorry.' Her long pale hands were pressed to her sides, the ringed fingers extending. 'Please, John,' she said again, this time without cause, and held out her arms to Janet.

It darkened all the way to the station. They sat in silence, in the shadowy, darkening interior of the carriage, John and Catherine across from Susan and Frank. Frank was by the window and the light from the lamps periodically flooded across his eyes. His hat covered his head in darkness. Cambridge was spun out in silver and grey, the colleges ghostly like the hulks of ships seen from the water. Thinking of

Janet, John put his hand down where he thought Catherine's was resting, but found only the seat, cool and coarse.

When they got back to the house, Catherine sent Susan and the other servants to bed. She kept John and Frank in the hall. The lights were dim; her face was etched white above her blue dress, above the gleaming floorboards. She appeared exhausted, but no longer bored, as on the day Frank was first discovered in the house. It was as though she had spent some hours in hard physical activity. She took them in like some mountain peak she had ascended, looking back from the slopes.

'We are three, then,' she said. She spoke just above a whisper. Her face was composed. 'We are the three of us alone. So I release you. You may do as you like. I only ask that you do not give the servants reason to suspect, any more than they might already. We must pretend, but let us not pretend any longer between ourselves. I am giving you this freedom; in return I expect that you will bring no public scandal on this house. This house shall remain without blemish. The reputation of your daughters, John, shall remain without blemish. So will the reputation of your wife. I have been your wife too long to suffer any worse than I have suffered already. You will grant me this, if you are any man at all.'

And then she turned, giving no possibility of reply, and the skirt of her dress dragged slowly up the stairs like the carcass of an animal.

26th October 94

Dear Mr Ellis,

First, I am grateful for what you say about the questionnaire. I took some pains to draw it up.

You will find enclosed my close notes on the products of our fellow investigators' labours. I shall precede these with some general observations here.

Tardieu I think we need barely concern ourselves with: he is occupied almost wholly with collecting what he thinks are physical manifestations of inversion (dimensions of the pelvis, shape of genitalia, inability to whistle etc.). This is foolishness, though there is a link with Paolo Mantegazza's notion that in inverts the nerves of pleasurable sensation, which ought to be carried to the genital organs, are in some cases carried to the rectum. This falls down on the point that not all inverts practise Venus _aversa_.

In Moreau and Krafft-Ebing, simply put, the phenomenon of sexual inversion is usually regarded as a psychopathic or neuropathic derangement, inherited from morbid ancestors, and developed in the patients by early habits of self-abuse. These authorities do not any longer hold inverts responsible for their condition. In their view, these are matters for the physician rather than the judge, for therapeutics rather than punishment. There are many points to make here. The most obvious is that many inverts are healthy in body, and, apart from their abnormality, are in full possession of their mental faculties. We might ask: how does the theory explain the known fact that most boys practise masturbation in their youth without ever becoming inverted, even when, in our public schools for example, this self-abuse is often in fact connected with some form of sexual inversion, either passionately Platonic or grossly sensual? Krafft-Ebing would no doubt reply that these boys must not have a hereditary taint. But it would be absurd to maintain that all the boy-lovers of ancient Greece owed their instincts to hereditary neuropathy complicated by onanism. The invocation of heredity in problems of this kind is always hazardous. We only throw the difficulty of explanation further back. At what point of the world's history was the morbid taste acquired? If none but tainted individuals are capable of homosexual feelings, how did these feelings first come into existence?

The arguments of Ulrichs seem to me, on the other hand, to be excellent. Ulrichs, who is himself an invert, seeks to establish a theory of sexual inversion upon the basis of natural science, proving that abnormal instincts are inborn and healthy in a considerable percentage of human beings; that they do not owe their origin to bad habits of any kind, to hereditary disease or to wilful depravity; that they are incapable in the majority of cases of being extirpated or converted into normal channels; and that the men subject to them are neither physically, intellectually, nor morally inferior to normally constituted individuals. To deal with them as British law does, therefore, is no less monstrous than if you were to imprison the colour-blind.

In those countries — e.g. France and Italy — where inversion is permitted, and the law intervenes only to protect the young (with a protected age for boys, as for girls), to preserve public decency (barring resort to the street or open spaces) and to punish rape, there has been no surge in inverted practices, no spreading moral infection. Give abnormal love the same chance as normal love, subject it to the wholesome control of public opinion, allow it to be self-respecting, draw it from dark slums into the light of day, strike off its chains and set it free — and I am confident that it will exhibit analogous virtues, chequered of course by analogous vices, to those with which you are familiar in the mutual love of male and female.

Yours very truly,

J. Addington

XVI

Henry wrote to Angelica. He didn't tell Edith, which meant that when Angelica failed to reply there was no one to whom he could express his sense of outrage and panic. It was as if something had been stolen from him that he could not prove he ever possessed. The letter had been short:

Dear Angelica,

I fear there has been some misunderstanding between us — between you, Edith and myself. Edith and I are truly married, if not in the sense the world expects. But we miss you. It is hard to explain why you are necessary to us.

I hope you will forgive this letter, from a well-meaning friend.

Yours,

Henry Ellis

He was embarrassed to have written it. It had been done after a visit to a tavern with the men from the Society. Edith had gone home after the meeting, and he had stayed out, to stand in the murk and reel of the bar, to stand with his beer until he felt bold enough to essay his opinions, to answer questions, to think. By the time he got back to

Brixton he had written and rewritten the letter in his head; he put it down on paper as soon as he was inside, folded it and stuck down the envelope. The next morning, he felt he owed it to himself to send it, to honour the impulse. Perhaps he was still under the influence of drink. It certainly seemed now to be a very incautious letter – he and Angelica had never written to each other before, had never even been alone together for more than a few minutes. He hadn't known how to explain the letter to Edith, so had said nothing. If Angelica had replied he would surely have told her about it. But she had not replied.

Why hadn't she? His first reaction was to be hurt. He was unimportant, as he always suspected. Or he was unpalatable. Her indulgence of him over the summer had been only that. He was still the man in the restaurant: bullying, hidebound. She could not bear him. He could not bear himself. When these thoughts possessed him he stared at the mirror, spitting insults at the long, dark, insolently disregarding face.

And yet perhaps this was not it. Perhaps she did not know what to write, could not find the words. Perhaps she was sunk in depression. Perhaps – and here came the panic – she was not allowed to write. Perhaps she had never received the letter. Perhaps her father was keeping her prisoner. And yet this idea, though it was forever circling back, could not sustain itself. He could not picture Angelica a prisoner. Miserable, or contemptuous, or both, brooding in a high-ceilinged room, her complexion slowly spoiling in smoke, her letters arrayed like evidence – this he could see. He could see her lip as she read his letter, and her brown-black eyes criss-crossing it. This he could see. But not Angelica as a prisoner.

Perhaps Edith had told her not to reply. In which case Edith knew about the letter, but had said nothing, as Angelica had said nothing. Or perhaps it was only Edith to whom Angelica wished to write, and as usual he was trying to penetrate their intimacy, presuming on it.

Perhaps he needed to let them alone. Perhaps this was what Angelica wanted him to understand.

It was odd, his reluctance, or inability, to speak to Edith. They were still in their routine, still together-working; they discussed subjects with the same amicable intensity, enquired after each other's work. They still went for walks, in coats and carrying umbrellas now, under lowering skies, the streets turned greasy and black. But they were not as they had been. Their relationship had become like the river – smooth and constant, but sluggish, opaque. They were standing on opposite banks, watching it go by. He dared not interrupt it – smash its calm, swim across – for fear of forcing some irrevocable change, for fear of losing even his current unloved place, or worse of struggling, flailing, of Edith not coming out to meet him, not even outstretching an arm.

So he went on working. This way he could feel himself secure, feel his grip close on something firm and real. His intelligence, when he focused it, felt hard, sharp – like a cutting tool. The subject – inversion – was beginning to shape itself under the scalpel of his attention. He could almost see it whole, finished, shaped: a compact argument, faultless in every line. He anticipated its entrance into the world, saw himself a public man, carried over the chasm of his shyness by a new, fulfilling strength, complete conviction, the great moral advance for which he and Addington formed the vanguard.

It was only when he lost his focus – when he grew tired or fretful, as in the first days when Angelica's reply did not come, or the times when Edith seemed most inscrutable to him, that work, the subject of the book, became another source of fear. His thoughts travelled to locked rooms, to underground lavatories, to passageways, to fumblings and flickerings in the dark. There was so much loneliness and anger and lust, seething and boiling under this inadequate covering of words. He felt its furious pressure, under the surface of life.

He was walking towards Edith's flat. Towards Jack, who would have arrived there by now. Jack had agreed to answer Addington's questionnaire, but asked to do it in person. He hadn't explained why. Henry told him to come to Edith's. It seemed somehow safer to have him there.

The two of them had met first at medical school. Jack was taller, thinner, more angular even than Henry: his face seemed to be trying to break out of its skin. Henry was not long back from Australia, and Jack had the same air of having spent time somewhere difficult, only in his case it was the airless village nearby Reading where he had grown up. In the end Jack's career in medicine lasted only a few months: Henry could still picture him aghast, peeking at a section of torso set down between them, his nose shrinking, pushing his knife about. Jack said later, as he hadn't at the time, that he never intended to make a doctor, that it was simply a route into London his family approved of. He began writing for a living, scraps at first, anonymous pieces in the lesser journals that he would point out if he was pleased with them. Later he became addicted to the theatre, sometimes seeing two shows a night, running from one to another, arriving perspiring at his seat, and started to write reviews.

They continued going about together. Jack would often wait for Henry outside St Thomas's at the end of the day and they would stand smoking on Westminster Bridge, watching the ships track up and down the brown water. For a year they talked of going to Paris and then they did. They stayed at a shabby old boarding house run by an English woman so long abroad that she spoke her native language with a French intonation, with strange, jolting emphases. Henry accidentally caught sight of her early one morning, squatted over a chamber pot in a shallow room off the staircase. He remembered large white legs, limp black socks, heavy scuffed shoes under a stretched work dress, the sound dancing between whitewashed walls on which the morning light was hanging in squares. It was high summer. Paris in his mind was still bright, golden streets, gazed at from the swimming, greenish shade of a café awning. It was the smell of a city evening outdoors – the smells of the city warmed up, stirred and thickened into a perfume: dust, manure, smoke, fruit, candlewax, coffee, wine. And the constant noise, the French tongue lapping round, soothing him with its great indifference. He and Jack saw everything they wanted to: churches, galleries, buildings; streets whose names, dripping with blood, had been taught them by Carlyle. On their last day, they spotted Verlaine with his bald head bowed into a newspaper – it was Henry who spotted him – and walked up and down the street three times to see him properly. Neither of them dared go over.

Women were never mentioned. Not by Henry because he was too shy – it was one of the things he liked about Jack, that he did not talk about women. There was none of that barking, snuffling, wet-nosed camaraderie he had hated at school and that frightened him, in its adult form, on his father's ships. He was not made by Jack to feel like an oddity, as though what feelings he had were irredeemably childish and virginal for not being roughly expressed. He never wondered about Jack's quietness. He was not then in the habit of thinking about other people. It was not that he didn't care – with the exception of Edith, he had never cared for anyone so much as he did for Jack at that time – only that he saw other people purely as they presented themselves to him, as if he were a backcloth receiving a projection and this was his sole purpose, to show them to themselves.

This flat, comforting incuriosity was temporarily broken when, several years after that trip to Paris, Jack made his confession. There was, if Henry recalled correctly, no prompt. They had eaten at his flat; he knew this, because there were crumb-flecked plates on the table. He had no memory of Jack's face as he spoke, only of himself anxiously pressing crumbs to his fingertips. Nor could he remember exactly what Jack's words were. He hadn't asked questions; he had merely accepted the short statements he was given. The conversation changed Henry's whole sense of his friend, and changed nothing at all. It had explained some traits and habits – it did not at that time suggest to his mind the possibility of other, unknown ones. Jack's projection gained a little clarity of outline, a little depth. They went on with their lives.

It was now nearly eight o'clock. The air was damp and odorous; it seemed to smear itself on Henry's face. He rubbed at his cheeks with his coat sleeve. The sky was yellowish where it wasn't black; smoke uncoiled under the lamps, like bandages peeling away from wounds. The pavement was covered by a thin layer of dirt and his boots stamped a pattern on it. At the far end of Edith's street was a tavern – its friendly note sounded false and tired, like something out of an aged music box. He rubbed his cheeks again. He was nervous. He did not want to hear Jack speak about himself. Everything was easier in outline, projected, tacitly understood. Except one couldn't work with outlines, could do absolutely nothing useful with them.

When he arrived, Jack wasn't there. 'He has perhaps got lost,' Edith said. She led Henry into the sitting room, pre-eminently herself: scent-less, hair brushed back, blouse, cravat, jacket, skirt. He saw there were papers piled on the table under the survey of the new vase, and that the red gloves were still on the sideboard.

They sat on the sofa. Edith settled her skirt. 'Well, how are you, dear boy?' Her face fell into its familiar state of expectancy – her grey eyes under their heavy lids were intent on his face. She was eager, still, to hear what he had to say. That had not changed.

'It's filthy outside,' he said complainingly, feeling the air on his cheeks again. 'I've been thinking about our sunny little cottage in Nor-folk. I worked so peacefully there – by that tree, rustling over the wall.'

'It will be bare now, like a skeleton tapping. We should go in the spring. When I have finished my lectures.' She gasped. 'Imagine that, a world when I am no longer thinking about my damned lectures! When neither of us is.'

He smiled and asked the usual question: 'How do they do?'

Edith was editing. She had close-to-finished versions of each. He had read them and listened to her speak them all, making suggestions. He admired her immensely.

'They are as they are. The flaws seem permanent.'

'Don't pick at them. If they are indeed flaws, then they are mine too.'

'Yes,' she said, 'only I am stupidly proud. I find myself wanting to have the appearance of knowing everything. It is harder for a woman, to lecture on subjects she only half-understands. How is your book? I think Jack is brave.'

'He is. I don't know if I am brave enough to hear what he has to say – I do not want to have to pity him. The book is proceeding. Addington and I make our separate ways.'

'You do not need to pity Jack. You can sympathise. That is different.'

'I know. Possibly I am in a pitying mood.'

'Who else do you pity?'

'Angelica.'

Surprise flashed on Edith's face. 'It's nice of you to care for Angelica,' she said. 'You grew to like her better, didn't you?'

'I did.' He hesitated – there was something still that held him back from admitting about the letter. 'I learned to see what you saw in her.'

'I wonder for me if it didn't work the other way: that I learned to see her as you did at first.'

'Which is how?'

'You thought her, didn't you, a little too inclined to see only her own way. You thought she didn't notice you.'

'And now you think so?'

'Yes. It doesn't ruin her for me. But perhaps it makes her going away easier.'

'You do miss her?'

'Of course.' She examined him. 'Is there something you want to ask me, Henry?'

'What does she write in her letters? You say so little.'

'You have never asked. I didn't realise you wanted to know. Saying that, it's not—' There was a knock at the door. She did not cease from looking at him, only broke off her sentence and sighed. There came two louder knocks. 'It is very frustrating. But here is our friend Jack, getting frustrated on his own account.'

'I think we're due a fog,' Jack said as he came in, taking off his hat. He found space for it on the table and folded his coat over a chair; underneath he was wearing his green jacket with a deep blue necktie. He tidied his parting. His large, long body was knotted at various points like a magician's ever-lengthening handkerchief: by prominent elbows, wrist bones, knuckles, kneecaps, ankles. Behind him the window showed gloom and the smudged reflection of lamps.

'Filthy, isn't it?' Henry said from the sofa. He could tell immediately that Jack was nervous and thought Jack would notice that he was equally so. They knew each other too well to make this kind of exposure, at this point in their lives. Yet there was no way of avoiding it; it had the inevitability of a section of corpse on a bench.

'It's too early for fog,' Edith said.

'It's not, we had one this time last year,' replied Jack. 'I remember because I was reviewing *A Woman is a Stranger* at the Adelphi and could barely find my way there. It wasn't as if I was coming from miles off – I had dined on the opposite side of the street. I ended up sleeping backstage rather than risk going home.' He was still standing by his things, smiling at Henry in twitches.

'Sit down,' Henry said, patting the arm of the chair on his left, feeling the medical manner he had once cultivated settling on him and resenting it. He did not know how to manage this situation.

'Shall we have tea?' Edith asked. She was standing too.

'No –' he glanced at Jack, who had taken the chair – 'should we get on? The sooner we've had done—'

'Yes,' Jack said. He shuffled back against the cushions, casting one long leg over the other. He closed his eyes and for a moment Henry thought he was going to remain like that. But then he turned his head abruptly: 'You're sure you don't mind, Edith? Henry has given me some idea of the questions. I've decided there's no point being shy. You'll know me better than any woman should know a man who isn't her husband – better than any woman would want to know her husband, I expect.'

'I'm sure.'

'And you, Henry? I'm serious.'

'Of course. You cannot shock me,' Henry lied, not meeting Jack's eye. He felt in his jacket for the list of questions and unfolded it in his lap. 'Edith, you'll transcribe?'

'Yes.' She sat beside him with the materials.

He hemmed. 'Are *you* sure, Jack? I don't want to embarrass you.'

Jack was rubbing his forehead with the back of his hand. 'I'm sure.'

Henry waited until Jack's eyes rolled up under the ridge made by his fingers: 'We know your age and profession. How would you describe yourself in appearance? The state of your health.'

'Excessively tall. Slim. Not an unpleasing face, for those who can see up that far. Manly enough – if that's what you're driving at. In good health.'

'Your interests?'

'I like the theatre, music, paintings. I read.'

'What about your family?' Henry asked. 'Are you aware of any history of illness? Any other instances of inversion?'

'Not illness. There was an uncle, I think, who was inclined that way.'

'How do you know, about the uncle?'

'We once had a conversation. When I was a boy.'

'He told you about himself?'

'Yes, in so many words. He was a great-uncle. On my mother's side.'

'When did you become conscious of sexual feeling?'

'At school. I admired other boys. Two or three. "Admire" is the right word. I looked up to them. I wanted to be noticed by them, be useful, make them laugh. It didn't seem unusual.'

'When did it come to seem so?'

'Quite a long time later. There was only the one boy by then. I wanted to be close to him – to sit next to him and feel my knee knock against his, that sort of thing. I was doggish about him. Following him around, doing things for the sake of seeing him. Thinking through things I could say to him the night before.'

'Did you have any physical encounters in this time?'

'No.'

Henry felt his heart pick up pace. 'Did you masturbate?'

Jack's eyes flitted in Edith's direction – Henry could hear her pen scratching. 'From when I was about fourteen. I found otherwise I had trouble.'

'Emissions?'

Jack held his gaze for a moment, almost defiantly, as though expecting Henry was about to call the whole thing off for a joke. But then he answered, in the same level tone. 'Yes. And erections, during the day.'

'Do you still?'

'If I am on my own too long.'

'Are women attractive to you?'

'No. There were opportunities. There was a girl when I was young; before I met you, Henry. She was very eager. We would lie down together, with my arms around her waist, and I would feel nothing.' He laughed. 'I would smell her hair. I like women. I appreciate beautiful women. But in the same way that I appreciate beautiful scenery.'

'You have not considered marriage?'

'It wouldn't be fair to the woman. It would be a kind of trap. A horrible one. And –' he smiled slightly – 'as there seems no immediate danger of the race dying out, I leave marriage to the people who like it.'

Henry looked down at his questions, his heart blundering in his chest. He saw, over the top of the paper, Jack uncross his legs. The sound of Edith's pen went on for a few moments and then came to a stop. 'What sort of man attracts you?'

Jack made a small noise in his throat. One finger arched itself on his knee. 'It was older men, at first. Ten years, twenty years older. Boys my own age were too similar – to me, I mean. Anxious, havering, over-eager to talk. I could do all that just as well on my own: asking why, how, what to do about it. Older men were no longer interested in those questions. I have since changed my mind. I like men my own age, sometimes a little younger.'

'What sort of looks?'

'They can't be too short. Dark hair. Intelligent teeth. I can't bear bad teeth on a man.'

Henry's heart had steadied a little during these answers, but now it began to lurch about again. There was a thin sweat across his palms. Meanwhile, Jack seemed to be growing calmer – he sat there with his hands on his knees, his lips trembling with what might have been amusement. Edith's pen scratched. Henry formed the words. 'What physical acts,' he said, 'do you perform?'

Their eyes met. Henry's looked an apology, but Jack returned something like relief, or surrender. 'I don't think I know the Latin,' he said.

'No matter. I will supply the terminology.'

Jack nodded. 'Often it is only that we pleasure each other by hand. But I like –' he hesitated, and the finger arched again on his knee, and there was the same look of surrender – 'taking a man in my mouth, and him returning.'

Henry looked at the arched finger. He realised he had only the Latin. 'And is there, connection *per anum*?'

'Not frequently. Sometimes.'

'And—'

'I prefer the active role.'

'Ever the passive?'

'Yes, if the other wishes it.'

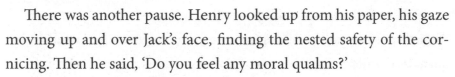

There was another pause. Henry looked up from his paper, his gaze moving up and over Jack's face, finding the nested safety of the cornicing. Then he said, 'Do you feel any moral qualms?'

'No.' The answer came out baldly. 'None at all. I did once. Now, I cannot see where affection between people of the same sex differs from love as it is ordinarily understood. Everything I have ever read in books or seen in plays; everything I have seen in my life of ordinary love, I have known in inverted form. It cannot ever seem unnatural or abnormal, because it has been natural and spontaneous in me.' Jack's eyes were soft with tears.

'Thank you,' Henry said. 'That is the end.'

The tears spilled down Jack's cheeks, but he made no effort to clear them. 'Of course,' he said, 'there is a barrier between the ordinary and myself. But I am sure there is less nastiness between men than there is between men and women. That is how it appears to me.' Edith's pen took this up, while they sat without speaking. Jack finally produced his handkerchief and patted his face with it. Afterwards he stood and put out his hand. Henry rose to grip it. 'Thank you, Henry. I won't stay. Thank you. This book of yours – it is a very noble idea. It will do a very great service. I wanted to say all this in person. I hope it wasn't embarrassing for you.'

'No, no.' Henry looked at his friend's hand clasped in his own. His friend who preferred the active role. Intelligent teeth.

'I wanted to say it out loud. I wanted – I don't know what I wanted.' Jack smiled and frowned; his handkerchief was balled in his left hand, bits of it sticking out in tufts between his fingers. 'I don't know what I wanted. I wanted this. Goodbye, Edith. I hope I will see you both soon.'

When she had let Jack out, Edith came back and stood at the opening into the hallway, leaning against the door frame. 'How interesting life is!' she said. There was a note of bravery in her voice.

Henry, still on the sofa, twisted to look at her. 'Yes,' he said.

'Do you pity him?'

'Perhaps more than I thought. Differently.'

She bent her head back, squeezing her eyes shut. 'You realise you didn't ask, whether he has someone.'

'That is not one of the questions.'

'I know.'

'Should I have done?'

'Oh, Henry,' she said. 'Yes, you should.'

XVII

John was waiting, and had been for some time, first sitting and now standing, first patiently and now impatiently, for his wife to come downstairs to speak to him in the drawing room. He was standing against the mantelpiece, which pushed firmly at his back. The room stared dully at him. The window was blinded – by the thick yellow fog that in the course of the morning had sidled up to the glass and spread itself on it. All the lamps were lit but the room remained dim. The gas in its different mouths whispered and hushed. The warmth from the crumpled fire in the grate was reaching only as far as his ankles.

He stared dully back at the room. At the green sofa, the little tables and the photographs and the pink flowers and the lamps, at the pictures on the walls, the books shuttered in their cases; at the patterned armchair to his left and the folding doors with the thin lines of light running down where the hinges were and again where presently they were joined; at the bruised gold scuttle and poker and tongs to his right, at the other armchair, at another small table with another vase of flowers on it, white flowers this time, and more books and pictures behind glass, and then at the window, crowded and pressed upon by the dirty leering fog. The clock ticked eagerly behind his shoulder. It was evening. He could hear the servants moving round the house.

Catherine had said she would be down in half an hour – this when he found her at her dressing table an hour ago. He had sat here, on the sofa, with the newspaper – it lay where he'd left it, open-armed, embracing a cushion. He did not know why she'd kept him waiting. Of course, he could have rung for Susan and sent her up with a message. He could have gone up himself. He could still do either. Perhaps what prevented him was also stopping Catherine from coming down: the knowledge that he was about to say something irrevocable. A couple married as long as they had been could know many things without ever talking about them. Sometimes it was the need to speak which signalled trouble.

This room he always thought of as Catherine's. He remembered saying to Frank that only his study belonged to him properly. Now he had gained his own bedroom: after Janet went to Cambridge, after Catherine's statement in the hallway, he had moved into the other guest room, continuing – with less trouble now – to sleep with Frank, rising early. But really it was silly to think of any rooms belonging only to him, or only to Catherine. All the rooms were Catherine's – her taste, her decision and supervision – and they were his also. She made them for his use, and he gave her the right. They had fitted themselves to him. They were – as she was – the inevitable backdrop to his life. As inevitable as his father had been. He had not chosen his father either, but he had lived in him comfortably for years.

It had mattered that his father was a doctor. As a child he liked the comings and goings at the house – the front door opening on a patient was like the beginning of a story – and he liked his father for being so wanted and necessary. It meant that when Dr Addington was with his children, they felt themselves superior, that their claim on him had been weighed and found significant. John, foolishly, could not even now imagine a higher authority than his father, who had been dead seventeen years. He had sat in this room; John remembered him here, somewhere between the sofa and the armchair – it had been arranged differently then. He saw him opposite: his matching eyes, the same wide mouth. Younger. Another time, in another room. His kind, stern face. 'It will pass,' he'd said, with all his authority. And John had gasped with relief, tears streaking down his cheeks.

This morning, when he was working at his desk, Frank had addressed him from the doorway, already wearing his hat. 'I'm off out,' he said, superfluously. 'I've some questionnaires to collect, and I want to visit my mother.' They smiled at each other. John held out his hand, and Frank, closing the door, came over and took it. Frank's thumb rubbed gently in his palm, scratching with the nail. 'Can I have some money, John?' he said. 'For Mother.'

He had given him the money. It thrilled him, to have his love extending quietly and secretly, like an underground stream, into the far corners of Frank's life, fructifying it. He thought happily of poor Mrs Feaver, of his being able in this way, without trouble or awkwardness, to ease her suffering, to show gratitude for the great gift she had given him. And he thought of Frank, the money sitting close in his pocket, proof of his love, warm against his thigh.

He moved away from the fire, stooping purposelessly over the newspaper. What was Catherine doing? He paused to listen; he eyed the bell. When he'd told her that he wished for Frank to live in the house, she had said close to nothing. It was almost as if – except he had gone into it, to be sure – she did not remember the man he was talking about. She made no allusion until that first night, when she spoke to him across the pillow, her voice like a dart.

'You're mad,' Frank had said, when he first outlined his plan, when they were sitting in bed together in the plain room in Holborn. 'You know, John, you're not as safe as you think.'

'I have never thought myself safe; but am I not entitled to live?'

Frank laughed. 'Course you are.' His cigarette bloomed orange under his moustache, withered white. 'It's just what you expect from living.'

John had never felt safe. As a boy he possessed a photograph of Lysippos's *Athlete*; he remembered sitting by the fire one evening, entranced by it, the soft white curves of shoulder and thigh, and then his father's voice behind him, kind but stern, calling him away. He remembered feeling that he had done something not only wrong, but odd. The advent of desire was like the quickening of a blade – he was the blade, and he was the prickling flesh against its edge. How hard to be both, to not see a way to being neither. Away at Harrow he watched as younger boys were made the tawdry playthings, the bitches, of their elders; he had seen small babyish faces forced open-mouthed into hairy, swollen crotches. He dreaded the turning out of the lights – the pregnant silence, and then the first fleeing shapes, the tusslings and creakings, the soughing of sheets. Desire was like a knife at his throat. He was the knife, waiting in the dark.

He was never touched. But he wanted to be. He read the *Symposium*; he fell in love with the possibility of love between men, chaste, clean and elevating. He went to university. A friend, leaning his head against his knee, his curls tense around his fingers. A friend, showing him a photograph. Mark, clean-shaven, serious-faced, following the drift of his eye – the half-concealing hesitancy of his noticing smile. John's ideals strained to accommodate it all, to render it pure.

He was the knife. His eyes began to give him trouble. He woke spoiled in the night. His hands shook. His parts itched. He could not read after dark.

He told his father. 'It will pass,' his father said.

It did not pass. He left Oxford and he went to Dr Wells.

How lonely he had been, in the first years of his marriage.

In the middle years.

In every year.

But it was worst at the beginning, before the children. It was not Catherine's fault. She had not known how lonely he was. How could she, when they were so much together?

He could see her, walking beside him, laughing. He had been so cruel.

Where was she? The fog was dreadful. He went over to the window to look at it, could see scarcely beyond the glass. It hung there like a curtain. Yellow, poisoned. There was brown in it. Everything seemed muffled by the curtain; the city was only a suggestion behind it, a hidden amplitude. He could hear next to nothing – the sound of steps, perhaps, that may have been coming from the street or from within the house.

Why had she still not come downstairs?

It had been impossible. His familiar torturer: lust. Beckoning to him constantly. Wafting under his nose. A year or two into his marriage he had turned down an alley near Trafalgar Square and seen daubed on a wall two dripping cocks, stuck together, with underneath the words: *Prick to prick, so sweet.*

It was impossible. Eventually he paid a soldier; they went to a room near his barracks and John had him undress. That was all. He sat in a chair and watched him undress; made him stand there, turn about. He lived on it for a year. And then he paid another. Again a shabby, shadow-stalked room, and this time he allowed himself to touch and be touched. Afterwards they smoked and the soldier told him about his life. It was the first time John had ever spoken on equal terms with a working man.

He found other men after this. Some were brought to the house. He wanted so badly to accommodate his passion, to domesticate it. Eventually Catherine noticed too much. He was assailed by remorse, was made sick by it. He explained to her as best he could – tried not to see her pained face, its shivers of distress. Told her he would exercise greater self-control. He did exercise greater self-control. But there was a third child: Janet. And he began to feed his frustration into his work, like so much wood into a fire. Poetry, of the kind Mark had once made him put into a chest and sink to the bottom of a river. His researches into the Greeks. Into the Renaissance, which blazed in his imagination as the rebirth of liberty, of sensuality, after the cold, sheer darkness of the Middle Ages. He discovered Whitman, another connecting fibre to the Ancients. He felt himself borne up by this large, simple man – as though Whitman had plucked him from the ground and placed him on his shoulder, the better to survey the world.

Hark close and still what I now whisper to you,
I love you, O you entirely possess me,
O that you and I escape from the rest, and go utterly off, free and lawless,
Two hawks in the air, two fishes swimming in the sea not more lawless than we.

This was the fire that leapt in his imagination. That pitched behind his eyes. He wrote with more daring than he lived. He began to attract controversy. Catherine suffered. She felt, she said, under suspicion: for what woman's husband wrote on subjects like these, and with such urgency of enthusiasm? But he found that he no longer cared a great deal about this. He was still almost entirely chaste; all was turned inward. Occasionally the flame would out. A hesitating flame, lighting on some figure. Yet he was essentially chaste. He had become an observer, an intelligence, a reader in obscure places – but also an agitator, stumping in his mind. And this was his undoing. For he was seized by the desire to write his book, *A Problem in Greek Ethics*. And he had done it, despite the madness of the enterprise: filled page after page with self-accusing sentences. This was it, the sign – the flag of surrender waved over his collapsing defences. He gave the book to Mark. He went down to the Serpentine, and was met by Frank.

O you entirely possess me,
O that you and I escape from the rest

Now; now was fog, yellow-brown, as dense and textured as cloth. A curtain hanging on the wrong side of the windowpane. It seemed as if it must be a very dim, dull world beyond; a great waiting emptiness. John was waiting to tell his wife that he must sacrifice her on the altar of his integrity; that in order to speak to the world – he knew it existed, still, beyond the windowpane – he must further shed the disguise it had bid him wear in the years of his quietude, must pose in its tatters, which hardly covered him. His and Ellis's book must be published. His name, his wife and daughters' name, must go forward with it. His reputation – as a writer, but most of all as a married man, a father – would be the book's first and last defence, its only recommendation. He believed that the book would do good, that it would impress on ignorance and intelligence alike the justice of its case. He trusted to the keenness of his pen, the force of his logic. But it would take time to work on the hard mass of public opinion. There could be no doubting that for some his name would become a byword for effeminacy, corruption, morbidity; it would be tainted, shadowed by suspicion, if not outright, outraged condemnation. For some, the appearance of the book would justify every sneer previously cast in his direction, confirm every implication.

It was the one thing Catherine had asked of him. That he should not bring scandal on her house. Their house.

He was the scandal, the knife.

Where was she?

There was a knock at the front door. Though it might as easily have come from inside. He could see no one, nothing at all. The yellow-brown curtain had not swayed. It had not parted even a chink. The knock came again, like the knocking of a ghost, and John heard footsteps in the hall, and the door being opened.

A moment later Susan came into the room. 'It's Mr Feaver, sir, he wants to speak with you.'

Frank was standing on the step. The fog rose behind him, gripping at his shoulders and stroking the brim of his hat. It crept in past his arms and reached round his legs. There was moisture in his moustache.

Watching Susan move away to the stairs, John closed the inner door behind him. 'What is it? However did you find your way back?'

'Never mind. Come out here – don't trouble about your coat.' He held out his hand.

'What are you doing?'

'Take it. No one can see.'

Which was surely true. He took it.

They walked down the steps, holding hands like boys. The fog did not move – it had to be entered into with every step, sealing round their heads. It had its familiar yellow taste.

They were at the gate, visible only as they reached it. 'What is this, Frank?'

'Shush.'

They passed through the gate and were on the street, still hand in hand. The fog encased them. John could see the stone underfoot and Frank, but no further. What must be the street lamp figured as a brighter, faintly glowing patch of yellow in an indeterminate space higher up. They listened: there was a distant fall of hooves, slow and muted as a funeral march. A pale faraway shout. The sky lurked, massive and obscure. Their two heads looked at each other beneath. It was like a dance, John thought; you saw only the one face, all else blurred to insignificance. Frank put his hand up, the cold fingers on John's cheek. He kissed him very softly, dropping his lips onto John's, letting them hang tentatively first on the top and then on the bottom. John accepted it, remaining very still, stupidly afraid of attracting attention. The world gaped around them. At last he began to kiss back. He put his arms around Frank's neck, his body loosening, drifting. Frank pressed, kissed. A deep, dark, drowning kiss.

The world gaped.

They came up in Gloucester Terrace, heads bobbing in the fog, the well-used pavement under their feet.

The day had been made perfect. It had been ruined. When they went inside, Catherine was waiting in the drawing room. John could tell her nothing now.

XVIII

Travelling to Holborn Viaduct was like journeying to the centre of the earth. The train from Brixton seemed to move under rather than over ground: the fog pressed round it with the solidity of packed dirt. And arriving at the other end, stepping onto the street – 'stepping' in fact being too active a verb, for what amounted to a kind of hesitant merging – was to be confronted with a landscape gaseous, vaporous, oddly lit, obliquely cavernous. The fog was chill, it touched your face and squeezed itself out on your tongue like a smelly, greasy piece of dishcloth. The patch of pavement underfoot was your only surety. Henry merged out of the station on his, looking with everyone else – the people he was definitely aware of, lit from behind by the station lights – along where the street should be, trying to impose remembered co-ordinates on the dimensionless yellow mass. A cab gradually came into view, the horse's hooves sounding individually, ominously, like a policeman's knock. Clop. Clop. Clop. Clop. A man with a lantern was walking in front – like Charon, gently steering his boat down the Styx.

At the spot where the man and the cab disappeared back into the fog, Henry was able to isolate dark shapes and small areas of brighter yellow. Eventually he was able to connect them and see that they were people. Another moment, and they were boys, bearing lamps. One presented himself. He was aged about fourteen, his face gnawed into an uneven maturity; his jawline and chin were fuzzed with soft hair that showed angelically in his light. 'Where're you after, sir?'

Henry said, and a few others nearby stated their own destinations. He was pleased and surprised to hear a woman repeat Hanway Hall after him – she and her friend could only be going to Edith's lecture. The boy considered and said in a dignified fashion who he could take without general inconvenience. They set off behind him, five of them, shuffling like a chain gang. All of them coughed, the boy most frequently. As they moved, their surroundings altered and veered, became close and then distant: people, post-boxes, carriages, buildings, walls, windows with lights in them. Henry wondered about the two women who were going to Edith's lecture. It occurred to him to make conversation but he didn't, even though he always found that fog gave him confidence, by putting other people at a disadvantage. After a while they were the only three still in transit. One man had been deposited at a corner, and another directed to the opposite side of the street, the boy throwing his light as far as he could onto the road, and spitting into it at the same time.

As they with difficulty navigated an unsuspected crater in the pavement, the woman who'd spoken earlier said to her friend, 'I hope she's worth it.'

'If she isn't,' the friend replied, 'let's make up for it by having something nice to eat after.'

When they got there, with a scattering of coins and commendations for their guide, the fog was snuffing about in the entrance, seeking out corners and the bottoms of skirts. The man at the door shooed it out, waving his arms. The hall was surprisingly full. Henry knew most of the tickets had sold, but he hadn't expected so many people to face out the weather. Or was that being entirely honest? He hadn't truly believed – even when he had been told to expect it – that so many people would be willing to hear Edith. Not because of any limits on her talent, but because of the nature of her message. He was glad, very glad, to be proved wrong. The audience was mainly women, most of them young. None of them paid him the slightest attention.

He seated himself a few rows from the front, conquering his desire to bury himself at the back – he thought Edith might be encouraged if she could see his face. The air was damp and the lights turned right up. Ferns had been placed artistically; one cast a slender, sloping shadow on the wall behind it. He could taste fog. After ten minutes, a spry young man came quickly and quietly onto the stage, followed by Edith. The audience was surprised into applause, each row surprised by the one before it, so that when the man signalled for quiet it had only just attained coherence. He was David Creake, from the Society. Edith sat down on a chair next to the lectern – Henry watched as she placed her notes in her lap, continuing to grip them with both hands, and then began to stare reverently at the back of the room, somewhere above the heads of her audience, her lips pinioned in the beginnings of a smile. She was wearing a long skirt and a wide-sleeved jacket, to which was affixed the gold brooch she'd worn on their wedding day.

Creake stepped close to the front of the stage, saying in his clever, carrying Scotch accent, 'Ladies and gentlemen – and, certainly, that order of precedence is justified this evening – thank you for being in attendance, thank you for resisting all inducements, powerful as they must have been, to stay indoors, in order that you should come here and listen to Mrs Ellis speak. She will address, in this, the first of her six lectures, what I'm sure you will agree is one of the most pressing of the great questions demanding our attention at this time of change and development: the relations between the sexes. Mrs Ellis, who I am proud to consider a friend, is the author, as Edith Vills, of a very notable novel, *A Woman's Journey*, and of many articles in those publications willing to shelter and nurture the intellectual seeds of the New Life. Mrs Ellis is one of the most fruitful sowers of those seeds, a most avid pursuer of truth, a reaper of the harvest, and it is with great pleasure that, without further delay, I commend her to your attention – Mrs Ellis.'

There was united applause while Edith stood and approached the lectern. It was surely too tall . . . Henry was relieved to notice there was a box for her to stand on. When she did, she looked out proudly over the top, catching Henry's eye, it seemed to him, for a second. The applause dropped away, and in the abrupt silence they could hear the rasp of her notes as she spread them out. She looked up again. 'Thank you,' she said quietly, too quietly, almost to herself. And then, loudly, clearly: 'The modern woman understands herself better than she knows: her soul recognises what it is that it strives for, the sympathies it seeks, the causes it leaps to defend. But her mind, her *intellect*, may block the way. Ideas, precepts, imbued in her as a child, like the training wire applied to some tender growth in a glasshouse, often prevent her following her natural leanings . . .'

As she went on, Edith gained strength. She looked less frequently at her notes, and made generous gestures, her arms extending out from the sides of the lectern in their wide sleeves, like wings. Her face, the large, canopied eyes under the sleek rise of hair, was wonderful to watch as it shaped itself to every word, every emotion. And her voice! Her voice struck him as it had on the morning of that first day, as they boarded their train to High Wycombe – hard, like a long, plain surface against which the chosen words were thrown, rebounding through the air.

'. . . and between the sexes there should be no barriers to understanding, none of the mutually upheld expectations, hesitations, politenesses that prevent two souls entering into honest relation. None of the brutalities either. Women really free would never countenance for their mates the many dishonourable and unclean types of men who today appear to have things all their own way, nor consent to have children by such men; nor is it difficult to imagine that the feminine influence might thus lead to the evolution of a more manly and dignified race . . .'

She was marvellous! He could see that she was. He felt himself affected by her, with the others; he watched her face, delighting in her hard, active voice the more for knowing it at its softest and lightest, spoken into his ear or up to his face, as she rested her head in his lap.

'. . . If it should turn out that a certain fraction of the feminine sex should for one reason or another not devote itself to the work of maternity, still the influence of this group should react on the others to render their notion of motherhood far more dignified than before. There is not much doubt that in the future this most important of human labours will be carried on with a degree of conscious intelligence hitherto unknown, and such as will raise it from the fulfilment of a mere instinct to the completion of a splendid social purpose . . .'

The women sitting in his row were transfixed. They looked up at Edith with devotion. He looked up at her. He felt furious, bitter, that he could not properly desire her. And then he remembered – it really was as though he had forgotten, such was the sharp flavour of his disappointment – that, even if he could, Edith would not properly desire him. His marriage was a kind of taunt.

'. . . We must conquer a new world. Together. For all of us. It will be like this world, only women shall have a different and larger place in it. A place we will have freely made for ourselves. And we will live alongside our menfolk on a new and different basis. This is the vision we must keep in our sights. It will not be easy in the reaching. But reach it we shall.'

It was over. The applause was enthusiastic, people turned to their

friends and said things under cover of it. Creake made a few conclud-
ing remarks. There was more applause for Edith; she was back in her
chair, smiling gratefully at them, her rigidity melted away. And there
was a final round as she and Creake left the stage. As soon as they disappeared from view, chairs were pushed back, pleading on the floor;
voices accelerated into volubility; hats were adjusted, coats and gloves
buttoned, mufflers knotted, veils lowered, bags and cases and an old
lady lifted. Henry waited patiently to escape his row and patiently to
get out of the aisle into the entrance, smelling London dampness on
the mingled coats and mufflers and hats. He had arranged to meet
Edith outside on the street.

In the entrance he saw Angelica, wearing a red-and-gold patterned
dress that shimmered at the openings and endings of her coat, like
Christmas decorations in the folds of a tree. She held in one hand a
silver cigarette case. Behind her, outdoors, the fog sat and slowly
drifted.

She had seen him now. The people around him continued through
the door. But he stopped.

'Wasn't she marvellous?' Angelica said, before he could open his
mouth.

'Yes.'

'I knew she would be. That peroration.' She laughed – snapped.
'Straight from the napkin, wasn't it?'

'Yes.'

She looked at him dissatisfiedly. 'I saw you, from my seat. It didn't
look as though she had your complete attention.'

He could not keep the irritation out of his voice: 'I have heard it
many times previously. Edith had only me to practise it with.'

'Yes, poor Edith. But it is what you are for, Henry. Let's go outside. I
like a fog.'

On the pavement, she lit a cigarette.

'Why didn't you answer my letter?' he said.

'I didn't want to.' She looked at him brazenly, as she pulled on her cigarette. The hot rapid glow of its tip, too, seemed a provocation.

He would not rise to it. 'Does Edith know you're here?'

'She does not.'

'I didn't mean to offend you. With the letter. I meant nothing—'

'You didn't offend me.'

'I meant nothing beyond what I said.'

'You did not say so much.'

'That is what I mean.'

'Well, I apologise, if that's what you want.' She dropped her cigarette onto the pavement where it burned out forlornly between them, quenched by the fog hanging soddenly about their heads. 'It was ill-mannered of me, I know.' Her eyes slipped away from him. 'Where's Edith?'

'She's coming out here.' He hesitated. 'She'll be pleased to see you.'

'I will be pleased.' Her voice softened. 'Have you plans, Henry? Could you let me have her for the evening? There is so much I want to say.'

Again he hesitated. 'Alone?'

She was almost imploring: 'I would be so grateful. There are things I couldn't tell anyone else. I'm sorry about the letter. We are friends still, Henry, I assure you.'

He looked at her. He felt liberated by this conversation, by the fog, into a lucid honesty. He wanted to say more, before Edith arrived, and put a little humour into his voice to carry them through it: 'Surely we have never been friends, Angelica.'

She considered him. 'Do you realise that you wield your shyness like a weapon? You wouldn't let me like you. Not at first.'

'I didn't notice that you wanted to like me.'

'You see only what you choose, Henry. Will you let me have Edith tonight?'

'She is not mine to dispose of. But yes, you must have your talk. Of course you must.'

'Thank you.' Her eyes slipped round him again and he began to perceive that she was anxious. She looked back: 'How is your book? I have been thinking about it, and have concluded that you are dreadfully brave, for a man who can't hold a person's eye for a minute.'

He laughed, raking a hand through his beard. Someone came out of the building and he reassured himself it wasn't Edith. 'Perhaps it's in compensation,' he said.

'Perhaps.'

'I do believe it is useful to be frightened.'

'Why?'

'Because it shows—'

Angelica's face became dramatically inattentive. 'Edith!'

She had appeared just behind him. He swung to see her.

'Why are you here?' she said to Angelica. Her voice was straitened. Her hand closed on his elbow.

'I came to see you. You were wonderful.'

'That isn't it.'

'I want to have a talk with you. Henry has offered—'

'No.'

'Dear—'

Edith's hold on his elbow tightened almost to hurt. He was stunned. She was pulling him away. 'No, Angelica,' she said.

Angelica's voice was desperate. 'Edith. Henry—'

They were turning blindly into the fog. It wrapped itself around them. Henry took in Angelica's face as they turned. Her mouth was astray, her eyes bright with tears.

Edith stumbled almost immediately, dragging on his elbow, her skirt sweeping the ground. She staggered upright. They kept walking. Her hand was still tight on his elbow. The pavement changed underfoot, darker to lighter stone, here dirtier, here cracked. Pale lights orbited in the fog. People thrust out of it and then disappeared. Objects leapt into obviousness. The sounds of the city came to them dead, like echoes.

Henry thought of Angelica, abandoned, swallowed up.

He looked for somewhere to put his hat, cleared a space on the table among Edith's papers. A dribble of wet ran down from the crown. The flat was perilously quiet. 'What is it?' he said. His voice quavered.

Edith was standing with her back to the door frame. Her hair was flattened and sticky-looking where it had been under her hat. The gold brooch protruded on her jacket. 'Surely you can see,' she said.

'What do you mean?'

'Don't shout. I am so surprised. She gave no clue.'

'Why wouldn't you speak to her?'

'We have not spoken for nearly three months.'

'Your letters—'

'We didn't write. I pretended. We argued. That's why she left.'

'Her father didn't summon her?'

'No. I'm sorry to have lied to you. Don't—'

He shook his head and she backed away. The tears he stemmed with his fingertips. 'Why did you argue?'

Edith was silent.

'Edith—'

'We argued,' she said with horrible energy, 'because Angelica wanted me to give you up. To give up our marriage. And I couldn't.'

'Give me up?'

'Henry, look at me.' Edith's hand was over her mouth. She removed it and he saw how it shook. 'I am an invert,' she said. 'Angelica is an invert. We love each other.' Her eyes enlarged on the last words.

He could not speak.

'Are you not relieved?' she said. 'That I did not give you up?'

Eventually he said, 'You may still.'

'No I won't. I hurt her terribly. I hurt myself. I did it because I love you too. You see that, don't you? You understand how it is possible.'

'It is not possible.'

'It is possible. You know it. You love me and you do not.'

'I love you.'

'And you do not.'

He groped for his hat. Gazed at it: the dark crown, speckled with moisture, the wear along its brim, the threads showing. Red gloves on the sideboard. 'I did not understand,' he murmured. 'You love her?'

'Yes, Henry.'

He read her expression, turned, and left.

Part Three
February–September 1895

XIX

In the afternoon, Edward Carpenter measured their feet. They stood outside, on the grass that began at the back of the house, and John and Frank took it in turns to take off their boots and put out their feet, while Carpenter crouched and laid a measure along them, lifting the heels gently in his hands, squaring off at the tops of the toes. While he did this they looked down the garden, at the green fields stretching away to recline under the soft, rain-filled Derbyshire hills; at Carpenter's nimble head in his felt hat, shiny in patches like fur; at the hair on his neck and on his careful, clean, practised hands. They looked at each other anew in these surroundings. They looked at George Merrill, who looked at them, pulling at his braces and smoking.

The day was wool-grey and wet. Their feet went cold and damp-feeling back into their boots. The air was clear, sharp as medicine, going all the way down. There was a stream at the bottom of the garden, the water noisy and purposeful, splashing past oily rocks. Occasionally parties of sunlight roved over the grass, over the determined little stream and the stretching fields, which sent up a glitter in response.

Carpenter was measuring their feet for sandals. He was quaintly proud of the pair he wore over his stockings even now, in February; the leather was very black with use, smooth, the soles comfortably dented, showing the shadows of his toes. He promised he would have theirs made by the end of their visit. 'You'll not want anything else,' he said. John could not help noticing that Merrill still wore boots.

The house was long and low-ceilinged: the downstairs rooms slid into each other, without a corridor. There were flowers placed about in vases. The kitchen and sitting room were warmed by wood fires that smelled of the outside. That evening they ate together at the plain deal table: porridge, ham, vegetables, buttered bread. Merrill cooked, wearing an old blue apron, his pipe in his mouth. He worked, not slowly, but with an air of slowness, deliberation. Carpenter talked and refilled their glasses. At one point he got up to take down a bottle and slipped his arm round Merrill's waist, keeping it there, his fingers delving behind the apron, while he finished his sentence.

They were a handsome couple, though it was odd to think that way. Carpenter, about John's age, was better-looking even than his photographs: slender, well-proportioned, his beard lighted with grey, complementing his tanned, angular face and mobile brown eyes. Merrill was younger and wiry; good-looking, albeit more crudely or nakedly so, with a large dusty moustache which fell over the corners of his mouth. He spoke, when he spoke, with a stutter, though he tried to mask it by not removing his pipe, the suggestion being that he was pausing merely to talk around it, shifting it on his tongue. There was some superficial resemblance between the four of them, John noticed: him and Carpenter with their beards, their years, their educated speech, and the two young men with their moustaches, their accents. This resemblance had not been mentioned. At first, Merrill and Frank had been halting with each other, tensely alert in their proximity. But as the day went on they began to talk, and after the meal Merrill announced that they were going to the pub in the village.

They were gone an hour already. The table had been cleared. There was only one lamp in the kitchen, and the light from the fire disported on the ceiling. The spaniel, Bruno, pushed his black muzzle into John's lap, tipping his head and looking up with a single avid eye. John brushed a scrap down onto the flagged floor. He rubbed the dog, feeling the warm skin travel loosely back and forth over the little ribs.

'How do you manage with your young man?' Carpenter said, across the table.

'Frank?'

'He's a lovely creature.'

'He is.' Belatedly, John realised that this last phrase referred to the dog, which he was still fussing.

'You get on well together?'

'We do.'

'Where did you meet?'

'The park. The Serpentine.'

Carpenter winked, almost imperceptibly. 'What is his trade?'

'He is a compositor. Where did you meet George?'

'He followed me off the Totley train. We'd noticed each other. He knew what he wanted –' he held John with his bright eyes – 'wanted it right there and then. That was three years ago. And he has been living here a year.'

'He is from nearby?'

'Sheffield. He had a hard time, poor boy. Raised in a slum – he took me to see it. His father drank.'

'And you get on?'

'We do. He is so unlike. You understand. He has not all these layers –' he pulled at his collar – 'separating him off. I could not have imagined it as a young man. I was near thirty before I first found a friend. Even then I thought I was a monstrosity. Was it the same with you?'

'It was the same,' John said.

'We owe so much to Whitman. Did I tell you I visited him?'

'You mentioned it in a letter. I am envious beyond belief. What was he like?'

'Common sense beautified. I will not have said in my letter, that we went to bed together.'

There was a look of amused pride on Carpenter's face. John was shocked – or was it envy still? Both. That Whitman should have revealed himself, in the most direct way, and to someone else, in the unreachable past. 'How did it happen?' he said.

'We were talking late. I was young, it was around the time I mentioned, when I found a friend –'76. We got up for bed and he kissed me, as if it was the most natural thing in the world, which is how it felt to me. We went upstairs. I drank him up, swallowed him down, and went to sleep in his arms.'

John laughed and looked at Carpenter wonderingly. 'What did he taste like?' he said, surprising himself.

Carpenter laughed back. 'Sweet, like age.'

'I wrote to him once,' John said, 'asking him to explain the poems, assure me that I was not seeing more than I should. I was very bold. He replied with a terrible letter: he said I was deceiving myself. I did not believe him.'

'No, you should not have believed him.'

'Do you think he did it often, with men?' He felt elated.

'He told me he did.' Carpenter took a drink from his glass. 'You said Frank lives with you. Your wife accepts it?'

'She has no choice.'

Carpenter turned down his mouth. 'The condition of woman.'

'I cannot help it,' John replied, the guilt darting out.

'I do not blame you. I have three unwed sisters, without

employment. I'm sure your wife has been happier than they. And yet it is not so much. She knows about yours and Ellis's book?'

'No.'

'She will understand it?'

'I do not think.'

'She did not ask for it,' Carpenter said. 'But perhaps she will see something. She might be released also.'

'Released?'

'It is what some of us call the New Life.'

'I fear the New Life has come too late for Catherine.'

'Have you met Mrs Ellis?' Carpenter asked.

'I have not even met Mr Ellis.'

'I was forgetting. How strange you should not have met.'

'I like him in his letters,' John said. 'We seem to understand one another. And Mrs Ellis? Why do you mention her?'

'She is a very interesting woman. They are an interesting couple.'

'You mentioned her in connection with Catherine.'

'It was only – I think she would be impatient with this idea of your wife as having been sealed off in aspic, like a tin of beef.'

'She is fifty—' John grimaced, waving away the words. He looked down at Bruno the dog, lying on the stone floor, his front paws joined and his eyes morosely open, seeming bored of his own thoughts. He started again: 'I have three daughters. They have all studied at Cambridge, my youngest is there now. The wife of my closest friend is the principal of Newnham. I am not insensible to the position of women.'

'I did not say you were.'

'No. It is just – with Catherine, we are in a different time. For us it is still 1870. We know but do not understand one another, if you can conceive of that. It is our marriage, in this sense, that resembles a can of beef. What we are separately, what we have been, I am only just discovering.'

Carpenter angled the chipped nail on his thumb to the side of his glass. The skin on his hands was rough, like paper that has been wet then dried. When he was thoughtful, his face became concentrated, almost Christian, in its beauty. No one, John thought, would guess it of him.

'It was brave of you to marry,' Carpenter said. 'I could never have done it; for me the one fear was stronger than the other. The free lovers, though – I am not quite convinced by them. Marriage, it still seems to me, helps secure a woman's independence. Independence only of a kind, no doubt, since it depends on the husband.'

John felt tired by the turn the conversation had taken. 'Mine and Ellis's book,' he said, 'you believe in it?'

'Never more. It is high time for a clear statement. What good it may do! And I have enjoyed collecting cases.'

'We have twenty-six now. All anonymous. They have astonished me. Some make me want to weep; I want to seek these men out and speak with them. Others,' he smiled, 'make me jealous, make me see how much I have missed.'

Carpenter laughed. 'I think it may be best,' he said, 'to see both sides in life. To come through suffering to pleasure.'

'Have I read your case, among those you sent?'

'Yes. And George's.'

'Thank you,' John said. 'Frank and I have contributed ours. Do you have trouble?' he added. 'The two of you together in this place.'

'The milk boy I dread a little.' Carpenter's eyes smiled again. 'We are sometimes careless in the morning. Otherwise – if there are whispers, there are whispers. We do not advertise ourselves. Here we are among the animals, in the wild. A great many things could be happening. People will not worry themselves examining every possibility. Life is weary enough.' In the window behind his head, leaves of ivy moved like silhouettes; one came near and tapped on the pane.

'You do not think anyone would—'

'Report us?' Carpenter cocked his head. 'I don't believe anyone would be so cruel. I have made great friends with the vicar. But it is your book that will make us truly safe. Sound arguments. It must be impersonal, to a great extent.'

'Though it is a strategy that depends on a publisher.'

'Who have you tried?'

'Smith, Elder; Fisher Unwin; Williams & Norgate, and some others I forget – I have only enquired as to views and possibilities, though in fact we have a finished manuscript, or close to. I am yet to have a response.'

'Someone will take it,' Carpenter said, again pushing his thumbnail against his glass. 'These are different times.'

'Not different enough.'

'Not yet. In the meantime, we must live in the future we hope to make.'

John gave a laugh of approval. 'That is well said. Have you written it somewhere? I may borrow it from you.'

'I believe it is Ellis's phrase.'

Voices pierced the outside. Carpenter ran a hand through his hair. Merrill came in, laughing, followed by Frank. Bruno barked twice and wriggled round and between their legs, his tail striking out at them, contorting himself to receive swatting pats. The young men scuffed their feet and clapped their hands for warmth, expelling the scent of tobacco. The house became charged with their return. Even the plates and cutlery by the sink took on an unclear significance.

'Hello, Ted,' Merrill half-whispered, resuming his seat. He smelled of beer and smoke, of night-time air. He put his hand on Carpenter's neck and made him shiver. They kissed. Their eyes closed on it.

Frank stayed standing, watching the kiss. He took a small step backwards. 'I fancy bed, John,' he said, desire rising between them on a spring.

John woke into darkness. It was raining, and he listened to its patient wash. Frank was asleep, his breathing an undertone. They were both naked in the bed, warm. The skin at the top of John's stomach stretched beneath the semen dried on it. He touched it, taking a flake under his fingernail. Then he moved on the pillow, extending his hand so that it brushed the silk of Frank's forearm, brought up by his chin. He let Frank's breath fall over and over on his face. He rested in it, in the darkness. They would begin in the morning in the same place, for the first time.

He thought of Carpenter and Merrill in the next room. He imagined them naked also, the shape they made under the bedclothes. He listened for the sum of their breaths.

The rain fell. It would be streaking cold down the grey walls of the house, bending and beading the grass where Carpenter had measured their feet. It would be entering the stream at the bottom of the garden, quickening currents of broken moonlight.

His eye went beyond. Over the fields, their dense blotted green. Moving under the black softly pouring sky. He lay down beneath the ministering hills. He lay there and listened, to the livening earth.

11 Gloucester Terrace
Paddington

24ᵗʰ February 95

Dear Mr Ellis,

I am just returned from a visit to our mutual friend (I can now say), Edward Carpenter, with a pair of sandals in my luggage that are rather stiff. He is in good health and full of enthusiasm for our book. Of which I have some encouraging news: this morning I received a letter from Williams & Norgate, expressing some interest, and asking to see a copy of the manuscript when it is done. I enclose a copy of the letter.

Yrs ever,
J. A.

XX

The maid brought her out of the dark, like something hooked to the surface of the sea. As a catch appears first only as a slight alteration in the colour of the water, a change in its composition, so it was that he saw her initially as a blur in the blackness of the long corridor, a slipping stream of mottled white, before she broke into clarity on the doorstep. The brightness was such that she blinked, or perhaps it was surprise.

'Henry, you didn't write.'

'You do not reply to my letters.'

Angelica gave a pursed smile. 'Is that a reason to come all this way?'

'I like Norfolk, you remember.'

'You may take my place.'

He looked up at the house. 'Would your father have me?'

She repeated the smile. 'No.'

'Is he here?'

'He is not, thank God.'

She seemed quite unprotected without a cigarette; seemed young in the sunshine, in a white dress, hatless, her hair loose. The corridor leached the light behind her. Henry felt almost guilty. It was not comfortable to possess the advantage so clearly. There was the noise of a wagon on the road beyond the drive, and he turned to look at it, pushing up his hat. When he turned back she was much the same. 'I would like to talk with you,' he said.

'I did not think you had come only to look.' When he made an attempt to laugh she scoffed, staring at the foot of her dress. 'Don't mind me. I – let us go for a walk. Will you wait inside?'

He said he would wait where he was. While she was gone he walked up and down the drive, gravel splitting under him. It was early afternoon, and cool, despite the sun. The house was large and square, the bricks tightly packed like infant teeth. He saw the maid pass in one of the upper windows. Then, when he was at the far end of the drive, an older woman appeared in the doorway, dissolving into the darkness as he approached.

Angelica came out eventually in hat and gloves and jacket. 'Does Edith know you're here?' she asked.

He shook his head.

'You know she has not written to me since that night.'

'I know.'

They walked out the drive and into the village, passing a series of shops before Angelica took them down a lane leading to fields. A well-trodden path, marshalled by hedges and crossed by stiles, stretched towards some mingled treetops in the remote distance. They reached the first stile and Angelica put out her hand matter-of-factly; he gave her his own and she stepped over, a press of soft leather in his palm. On the other side, she said, 'My mother didn't want me to go walking with a man on my own. She wanted to accompany us.'

'I think I saw her,' Henry said. 'She came to the door.'

'Did she? I told her not to. She might not have been reassured.'

'Why?'

'You being so tall, with your black beard. I'm not sure I'd entrust my daughter to you, if I didn't know better.'

They continued on the path, their shadows running swiftly alongside like little streams. The fields absorbed them. In one a group of cows stood and lay in attitudes. The hem of Angelica's dress was patched grey with damp.

'You do not mention your mother,' she said. 'Did she understand you?'

'Only Edith has ever understood me.'

Angelica picked up some of her dress. 'How old was your mother when she died?'

'Fifty-six.'

'Mine is fifty-three. I think she is happy. I do not know how she can be. It makes me want to scream to look at her sometimes. But then I realise there is no point in my thinking differently to her, in believing myself different, when I am leading the exact same life. I sit in that house, and I speak to the people who come, and I read and go for walks, and I worry about my dresses.'

'You are not like that,' he said.

'To be unmarried is to lack the basis for independence. And yet I cannot marry, being constituted as I am. Unless I were to find a man like you, Henry – and you are rare indeed.'

Henry looked at his boots, reddening in the dust from the path. He saw Angelica's boots under her dress where she had lifted it, and her stockinged ankles. 'Why did you wish for Edith to leave me?'

She did not slacken her pace. 'Because two women can live together quite easily and go about together. Because it is simple for a man to live on his own – as you do already.'

'That is not it.'

She stopped short and faced him. Behind her were fields. Their two shadows froze and pointed, like arrows on a map. 'I wanted her to myself,' Angelica said simply. 'I did not see why she needed you, once she had me. I knew about your marriage. I thought, when you told us about your book, that you were permitting us, and explaining yourself.'

He sighed frustratedly.

'Why does it satisfy you?' she said. 'An unconsummated marriage.'

The words had never been spoken by a third person. 'I require nothing more,' he said.

She stared at him. 'I suppose I must believe you.'

They began to walk again. After a few moments, he asked, 'When did you first feel yourself to be differently constituted?'

'When I was a girl. It is rather a sad story.'

'In what way?'

She waved at the fields. 'Loneliness. Here, believing that I was the only person in the world to feel as I felt. Feeling unknown even to God.'

'Did you know at once, about Edith?'

'Not at once. Or –' she looked at him as if to judge his strength – 'perhaps I knew after that first day.'

'That she was receptive.'

She looked again. 'It was an understanding. She had her friend: Mary. We talked about her before too long.'

'I did not understand about Mary.'

'Mary did not want to share Edith either.'

'That is why we stopped seeing her.'

'Yes. Did you understand about us? About Edith and me?'

'I was jealous,' he said. 'I knew she cared for women. But I thought I mattered most.' They were nearly at the copse. The heads of the trees were in conference with a slow slope of white cloud. His feelings swarmed below. 'Why did she marry me?' he said.

'Shall we stop?' Angelica pointed at a clearing before the trees.

They sat, Angelica's dress rippling out and ending in a froth of lace. Henry watched as she lit a cigarette and poured out smoke on the clear air. The sunlight stuck on her cheekbones. She said, 'Are you really not sure?'

'Two women can live together quite easily.'

Angelica looked at the trees. 'She loves you, Henry. You did not imagine it. It is simply as you always knew, that there was an element missing.'

'But why marry?'

'You both know better than me. Because you wanted to prove it could be done, is it not? And you have proved it.'

'No.'

She smiled slightly. 'No, perhaps not quite.'

'We failed,' he said, 'to speak about it. About consummation. We made no decision. I did not think it necessary for us, but, after we were married, I became sure it would happen. And then it did not.'

The memory of that night – a thin stretch of turbid darkness – seemed to intervene between them. The thought of Edith, naked, expectant, stretched.

'It is not everything,' Angelica said. She rubbed her cigarette into the grass. 'You were right to think that. It was me who was wrong, assuming it invalidated the promises you'd made. You have proved to me already that marriage can be organised differently, that it can mean new things. It is not failure to admit to jealousy or misunderstanding. You are only at the beginning. You are an experiment.'

He put his hands out on his knees.

'And you were not a fool, Henry, not to see about Edith. She was shy with details, and she didn't hold, then, with categories, of the kind you and Mr Addington must discuss in your book. It was to her no great oddity to marry a man, if it were done in a new way. I am responsible, I think, for her beginning to see herself a little differently.'

'As an invert?'

'I expect we have read some of the same books. You know my German is good. They are dreadfully wrong-headed in places, those men. I hope you will say so.'

'They will not escape criticism.'

'Good. It frightens Edith a little, to be outside the usual run of humanity. She is not entirely easy with it. Yet it satisfies me.'

'Why?'

She held his eyes. 'I have a place. I am not merely one more woman.'

He did not struggle in her gaze but relaxed into the odd trustfulness they had willed between them. 'I understand,' he said.

They went some minutes without speaking. Angelica fidgeted with the stuff of her dress. There was an occasional breeze and the trees drew in breath.

Angelica gave up fidgeting. 'Henry, what are you here to say?'

'I want you to come back to Edith,' he said. Angelica lowered her eyes. 'That is, if you accept me,' he continued, 'and do not ask her to choose between us.'

She shot a glance. 'Do you accept me?'

'You are the missing element.'

'Does Edith think so?'

'I am sure that she does.'

'I can live with her?'

'If you both wish it.'

She laughed. 'Oh, I admire you.'

'Will you come back?' he insisted.

'What will it be like?'

'You haven't said, whether you accept me.'

'It is you and Edith who have made the choices,' she said curtly. 'Her to refuse me, and you to recall me.'

He said nothing. They could hear the trees gathering the wind, and the indecision of the birds among the branches. There was no visible activity anywhere. The sunlight was like a spell: the human world was put to sleep. Angelica returned to fidgeting with her dress. Her fingers made runnels in the fabric, smoothed it, pinched it into ridges, then started over again: pushing, flattening, pinching. She had begun to speak, was saying something about the walk, her fingers still working as if according to instruction, when she noticed him watching. She stopped her sentence. In her expression guilt and relief were mixed. 'I'm sorry,' she said quickly. 'I don't think – this is dreadful, but I don't think I can manage the walk if I don't relieve myself first.'

'Oh – of course.'

'I apologise.' She got up, gathering the skirt of her dress around her and shaking it. 'I think I will go over into the trees, if you don't mind facing this way . . .'

She left, and he shuffled so that his back was to the copse. He listened to the print of her footsteps in the grass. The fields in front of him thinned to the horizon, planed by the sky. He could hear still, and then he couldn't, Angelica's footsteps. The sunlight pressed the world down to a whisper. The fields whispered green beneath the sky and the sunlight subtly pressed. His mind wrestled out from under it; he looked over his shoulder, saw Angelica like a stub of white paint, put here, there, between the dim brown tree trunks. She did not turn. He watched the shape of her under the trees, in the dimness, white among the brown and green – saw her stop, half-obscured, and dip, like a swan settling on water. He looked away. His body sang beneath the sky.

When Angelica came back, he raised himself. 'It's catching,' he said.

He set off towards the copse. When he looked back she was sitting, staring at the fields. The smell under the trees was of dry earth and rot. He made for where he thought he had seen her stop. He looked back again – she was barely visible now. Twigs cracked under his feet. It was not as dim as it appeared from further off; light broke in from every direction. He calculated, searched. Saw what he thought was an area of damp ground, at the foot of a tree. Went over, crouched and pressed a finger to the black assenting earth. Smelled it. His heart rabbited in his chest. He stood, opened his trousers and manoeuvred out his cock, struck for a moment by the sight of it, so white, swollen and pushed out like a bulb. He took hold of it, pulled the skin once, luxuriantly, over the head. Then he began to frisk it, fast as he could, looking at the patch of soft damp ground. The feeling came quickly, catching over his head and constricting his throat, spat out in three bright slicks. He put his hands on the tree and shuddered against it. When it was over, he buttoned his trousers and carefully trod the slicks into the earth, before walking back to Angelica. His mind was a hot blank – like a pan taken off the stove and scraped clean.

Angelica did not get up, and so he sat down beside her. He could feel his cock coldly clamming. She reached out and touched his hand. 'I will come back,' she said. 'Since you both wish it.'

*

Already when Henry caught the train back to London the weather had turned, the sunlight wasting and the clouds moving in to mourn. The rain started that night, while he was lying awake in bed, with a sound like sheets being shaken out. It grew in strength until it roared, till he could see in his mind the lances of rain, striking at the street so hard that they splintered and jagged back into the air. After it was finished he lay listening to the glug and gurgle of the drains and the gutters, the silence of the shocked pavements.

In the morning it was raining again. He spent the day penned in by it, working in his flat, wondering if Angelica had written to Edith yesterday, after he'd left, or whether she would write today. He knew he would hear as soon as Edith had received a letter. But evening came without word. He made some tea in his sitting room and heard the ladder being set against the lamps. Warm light jumped at the window. The rain landed in amber streaks.

There was a knock. Henry went to the door, expecting Edith.

'Hello,' Jack said. He had pushed back his hat coming upstairs: water swelled on its brim and splashed onto his cheek as he spoke. 'I have come all this way. And I am a little drunk. May I?'

He entered the sitting room. His boots were dirty. The fibres of his coat were spined with rain. He blew some off his lip. 'There is some news,' he said. 'It will not seem like it, but it concerns you very much. It is about Oscar Wilde. You know who he is?'

'Of course I do. What concerns me?'

'Perhaps you saw he has accused someone, Lord Queensberry, of libel. That's what has been in the papers. What isn't in the papers is the nature of the insult, which I happen to know. Wilde has accused Queensberry of libel because he called him a sod. Sodomite. That was the word used. But, you see, it isn't a libel. He is. Wilde is. Everyone knows it; who knows him, I mean. I can't think why he's gone to law. They say he's mad on the subject.'

Henry felt an emptiness open up. 'I didn't realise you knew Oscar Wilde.'

'I don't.' Jack waved a hand, slightly upsetting his balance. 'But the theatre. These things are known. It's true. He is. And they're going to find out. There's a man, an actor, collecting information. Letters. Boys who might confess. He plans to give it to the defence. Apparently there are swarms of detectives going about doing the same thing.'

'You think it will—'

'I think it will cause the most awful stink. Your book—' Jack took out his handkerchief and stopped a trickle of water at the side of his face. 'They won't ever have had their hands on someone like this before, Henry. The man is famous. And they'll get him. They've got him already, I'm sure of it. The bastards have got him on a damn hook.'

XXI

These were John's days of dread. His months: March to May. When everything secret, hidden, whispered, was shouted, pasted, printed. When what was unmentionable was warmed in every maudlin, moral mouth. When what was nameless was become nothing but names.

Douglas, Queensberry.
Collins, Clarke, Carson, Lockwood, Gill.
Kettner's, Albemarle, Florence, Savoy.
Parker, Grainger, Mavor; Wood, Atkins, Scarfe; Shelley, Tankard, Conway.
Ponce. Bugger. Sodomite.
Taylor, the procurer.
Wilde, the seducer.

When everything that had been dignified, rationalised, was made gross and tawdry, was torn down and trawled through the gutter.

When the days had the steepness, the terrifying altitude, of a nightmare. When every prejudice uncoiled and rose from its pit, showing the inside of its ugly throat.

Leaders, letters, speeches. Handbills, placards, pictures. Chalkings on walls. Crowds on corners. Jeerers. Jurors.

When John felt himself exposed, sprawled on the slimed wreck of his privacy, at the world's mercy.

Except it was not his privacy.

You dined with him?
Gave him an excellent dinner?
Did you give him plenty of wine at dinner?
Did you give him whiskey and sodas?
After dinner, did you give him a sovereign?

When he could not sleep. When he wanted to run and run. When he took every newspaper, down to the lowest. Scoured them. Studied variations. Speculated on gaps, absences. Filled them. Cursed the questioners. Cursed the answerer.

Was he a literary character?
Was he intellectual?
Was he an educated man?
How old was he?
Was his conversation literary?

He had never met, never seen Oscar Wilde. Never talked of him, almost, but for the fact that he had seen one of his plays. Not one of the plays running at the time of the first trial, that were considered so amusing, that were at first carried on with Wilde's name taken off the bills, until they too were removed from sight. An earlier play.

You were alone, you two?
The approach to your room was through his?

What was there in common between this young man and yourself?
What attraction had he for you?

He had read some of Wilde's tales. Some of the essays. He had wondered. Of course that was the intention, the old intention. To raise a doubt. To make a signal. To make you wonder.

Did you kiss him?
Did you put your hands inside his trousers?
And then bring him into your room?
Sleep in the same bed with him all night?

He looked at Wilde's photograph. Large, elegant. Fat and sleek and fine. Clean, crisp, a wave in his hair. He read the descriptions of his appearance. Silk hats, fur coats, coach and four. Waved cigarettes. His tie a bright spill of colour on his shirt. A flower burst in his buttonhole. Read how he was crushed at the entrance to the court. How, after his arrest, prison told on him. How he creased, went shabby. Became thinner, older. How his hair lost its curl. How his face went white in the dock, washed red. John wondered whether the thought had occurred to him, too. That it was merely his portrait that was degrading in public. That somewhere else Oscar Wilde was still free and fat and fine. Clean and crisp.

What did you go there for?
Not the sort of street you would usually visit in?
You had no other friends there?
Rather a rough neighbourhood, isn't it?

He stood outside himself, saw himself arraigned. Heard the evidence. He felt, sometimes, reading the reports, as though he was being watched for his reactions, even when he was alone. He sought to control his reactions even when he was alone.

Did you take the lad to Brighton?
And provided him with a suit of blue serge?
You dressed this newsboy up to take him to Brighton?
In order that he might look more like an equal?

He began to worry that he and Frank could have been seen without their realising it, identified for what they were. He could not sleep for thinking about the day they had gone out into the fog, down his own front steps, outside his own front door, beneath the street lamp. What if they had been seen among the statues in Cambridge, heard calling to each other? What if he had been recognised?

In the night he sometimes wept. Frank's body next to him made him weep. It made him miss lying behind the high blank wall of his wife.

He read the reports. He saw in his mind's eye the boys. The narrowness of their bodies. Their charm. He found himself envying Wilde, for having had them. He heard their voices; their accents. He heard voices like his own, accusing them. He heard another voice like his own, denying them.

'Gentlemen,' Frank said. 'I always said it was gentlemen you needed to be afraid of.'

He added solid links to his chain of witnesses. He counted Mark Ludding, Edward Carpenter, George Merrill. Mr Higgs, Frank's landlord on John Street. Catherine Addington. Frank Feaver. Henry Ellis. Surely they could not find any of the others, from so long ago? He worried about his letters, the photographs in his desk drawer. He worried about the servants.

Are you prepared to contradict the evidence of the hotel servants?
You answer that the chambermaid's statement is untrue?
You deny that the bed linen was marked in the way described?
Were the stains there, sir?

He never doubted that Wilde was guilty. His denials fell dead on the page. The wit withered. The truth showed clear, like bone, picked clean.

I wish to call your attention to the style of your correspondence with
    Lord Alfred Douglas.
Did he read that poem to you?
What is the love that dare not speak its name?
Do you think an ordinarily constituted being would address such
    expressions to a younger man?

The letters arrived from publishers, all of them rejections. Some, like the one from Williams & Norgate, decorously avoided alluding to the present circumstances: beyond scope – ill-suited – list full – question of sale – commercial considerations – sincere regrets. Others were monstrous in their certainty. '*Even allowing that this should be a medical book, addressed to a qualified audience, which we do not allow,*' one read, '*it could not be made publicly available in any form without risking severe injury to public morals. It is a vicious subject. Even were its readership restricted to the most proper authorities, a danger would exist, for compositors would have to set it.*' This last did not even raise a smile. It made him so angry that he kicked the waste-basket across the room.

Why did you choose the words 'My own boy' as a mode of address?
Is it the kind of letter one man writes to another?
Do you think that was a decent way for a man of your age to address a
    man of his?

Was it decent?

Do you understand the meaning of the word, sir?

Catherine watched him. She watched, and she wanted him to know that she watched. She did not speak on the subject. The papers circulated on the breakfast table without a word attached. It was like embarrassment. There was only one occasion, when he was reading the reports in his study. She came in, closed the door behind, came no further. 'You promised,' she said, 'to preserve this house.' She looked tired. Thinner, older. It was on his lips to say that he had made no such promise. That, besides, promises meant nothing, nothing at all. Instead, he did not reply.

A letter came from Mark Ludding. He trusted John had abandoned the book – he could not regret that he had never returned the questionnaire; there could be nothing more dangerous. He trusted John had done nothing indiscreet. Had Mr Feaver removed himself? Was John being attentive to Catherine? He recommended burning all incriminating papers, including this one, please. What was happening to Wilde was unfortunate. But Wilde had been a fool. He had strayed from all moral sense. He had been sensual, self-indulgent. '*So much tasting leads to poison,*' Mark wrote.

A letter came from Carpenter. '*Isn't it a country?*' he wrote. '*There is a long campaign to fight.*'

These were the days, the months, of John's dread. But what he felt finally, when at last the wreck went down, was rage.

Do you find the prisoner at the bar guilty or not guilty of an act of
gross indecency with Charles Parker at the Savoy Hotel on the night
of his first introduction to him?

Do you find him guilty or not guilty of a similar offence a week later?

Do you find him guilty or not guilty of a similar offence at St James's Place?

Do you find him guilty or not guilty of a similar offence about the same period?

Do you find him guilty or not guilty of an act of gross indecency with Alfred Wood at Tite Street?

Do you find him guilty or not guilty of an act of gross indecency with a male person unknown in Room 362 of the Savoy Hotel?

And is that the verdict of you all?

And I? May I say nothing, my lord?

11 Gloucester Terrace
Paddington

25th May 95 aft.

Dear Mr Ellis,

Wilde is sentenced. Now it is over, do you agree that we should meet? I cannot think our interactions should any longer be limited to letters.

Yrs ever,
John Addington

14 Dover Mansions
Brixton

25th May 95 aft.

Dear Mr Addington,

I agree. Please appoint a place and time.

Yrs sincerely,
Henry Ellis

XXII

Henry knocked at the door of the house on Gloucester Terrace, which was opened to him by a pretty maid in a cap. While she hung up his things, he waited in a hallway on dark lacquered floorboards. He had put on his wedding suit and polished his boots to the point of extinction; tapping one shiny boot on one shiny board, he looked at the stairs, making their stately progress into mystery. He did not know what to expect. He was anxious to please; anxious to resist entreaty. He did not want to be charmed. He didn't know, in fact, whether John Addington was charming. He had never wished to know. He had recoiled from this meeting. It reminded him of being a child and being introduced to another child against his inclination; they were expected to get on and play – because they were children. He and Addington must get on, because they had written to each other, written a book together. He felt the tug of his old conviction: that everything was easier in outline, projected.

The maid came back and led him upstairs. They went down a corridor before she stopped at a door and knocked. A voice called to enter.

It was a study, book-lined. Addington was standing next to another, younger man. 'Mr Ellis,' he said, coming forward with his hand out. 'It is an honour, at last. You are taller than I realised. This is my secretary, Mr Feaver.'

The other man took Henry's hand. He was blond, with a moustache. 'Good day, sir,' he said, in a strong London accent.

They sat, Addington and his secretary on chairs in front of the desk, Henry opposite. The maid quietly closed the door on them.

'How is your wife?' Addington said. He looked older than his photograph, with purses of grey skin under his eyes, and two hard lines propping up his nose. The moustache in his beard was heavy and hid his upper lip; the bottom one was very pink beneath it. He was wearing a light checked suit. Behind him and Feaver and the desk, a window showed lucid blue sky. It was a pleasant day, though here, at the back of the house, they seemed recessed, distant from it.

'My wife is well, thank you,' Henry said. 'And how is Mrs Addington?'

'Very well. She is out. Let us call us by our names, Henry, if I may, since we are collaborators.'

There was a pause while Feaver brought out some cigarettes and, Henry declining, took one for himself and another for Addington. He struck a match and lit both. The smoke that poured from his mouth, under his squint, was intricate. He was extremely good-looking. It occurred to Henry that this man was not a secretary. Addington let his cigarette sit in his mouth a while before he breathed out. His smoke went faint as it passed into the light from the window. 'It is the worst thing I could have imagined, Henry,' he said. 'It is worse, in fact. The country has choked itself on ill-feeling. Gorged on misery and heavy morals. Laughed themselves sick. I have never known anything so ugly. It seems hard labour is not enough, for the crime, though it will likely kill him. I doubt even that would satisfy them.'

'It is something I hadn't foreseen,' Henry said, though in truth it was the realisation of his worst imaginings, too. There was in Addington's voice and movements a fast, palpitating quality that made him especially hard to look at – it was not nervousness, Henry didn't think, but rather some overactivity of mind, not wholly disciplined. It was as though he was kept always chasing after his thoughts.

'He will die there,' Addington went on, as if Henry had not spoken, 'solitary, nothing to read, no one to visit, an hour of exercise a day. Oakum to pick. And this is the law! The law, that births the blackmailer, nurses him, makes him fat. The law, that turns him witness – grants him pardon, when it suits, in order to secure the guilt of the sodomite. This is the majesty of it! And the Justice, for him to say that Wilde must be dead to shame. That he had never tried a worse trial. Does he know that little children are strangled and burned by their parents? That most nights old men die bundled in doorways? Does he know that women are raped in cellars and have their throats slit while they scream?' He stopped and sucked on his cigarette. It bobbed in his mouth.

Feaver, who had done with smoking, pulled out his cuffs.

'It is not humane,' Henry said. He could find nowhere safe to look.

Addington stabbed out his cigarette. He smacked his hands on his knees, coming forward in his seat, his voice still rapid and unravelling. 'To treat it as a sin beyond parallel. As if it would stain your tongue to speak of it. And then to speak and write of nothing else for months – only sideways, out the corner of your mouth, or with one word swapped for another, for a host of words which would be meaningless if you did not already know their meaning. To speak of him as if he is something alien, a vast impurity to be purged. They cannot believe themselves, if they are not imbeciles. They cannot believe half the things they say. And yet they willingly empty more filth into the pot.'

'Opinion has been very harsh,' Henry said. Again he did not say exactly what he felt, which was that the country had shown itself thoroughly reactionary. That it had thoroughly scared him. That the New Life seemed immensely distant.

Addington continued, once more as if he had not heard. 'They have destroyed a man, who three months ago they doted on, because they are afraid of what they might learn about human nature. They have learned enough and they have turned the key on it. We are near the end of the century and are as primitive as we were at its beginning. I'm sure we are expected to be grateful that Wilde will not be hanged – only left to be trodden slowly into his grave. At least before, we had the honesty to hang a man.'

He turned to Feaver, who passed another cigarette and lit it for him. 'I apologise, Henry,' he continued, blowing out. 'I have had no one but Frank – Mr Feaver – with whom to speak about it.' He blew out more smoke. 'What I cannot bear, is that all this should be as it is, and for nothing gained. I cannot bear what a coward Wilde was. It is what makes me angriest of all, him lying twice over. That he should lie about what he had done with those boys, I understand, though it was a trial of his own stupid making. But to invoke the Greeks in his defence. To drag idealism into it. Shakespeare and Michelangelo. A pure and perfect affection, indeed. The love that dare not speak its name, indeed. He has brought each and every one of us down with him. All my work. All your work, Henry. Every man who trusted us with his history. Our assertions of the blamelessness of our lives. All of it. It is all mingled in the dirty pot. The Greeks are made to justify the man who pays a boy drunk on champagne to share his bed, who deals with blackmailers as others do with their grocer.'

Addington's cigarette had burned down and as he took the last of it he winced, staring at the floor. 'I have heard myself again just now,' he said, glancing up, and then at Feaver, who was sitting very still. He took a breath. 'You had anyhow perhaps suspected—' He stopped again and looked at Henry. His eyes were imploring.

Henry realised what he was being asked for. 'I had thought, perhaps,' he said. 'But I did not want to presume—'

'No, of course. Of course. Well, you see how I am concerned.' Addington passed a hand over his face. 'I have never admitted it to anyone I am not intimately connected with. I am most grateful to you, Henry, for your largeness of mind. Now and before.'

Henry cleared his throat, his eye going to the window. 'It is,' he said, 'as I hope you knew long since, a subject about which I entertain no prejudices. Indeed, it is one in which I have an uncommon interest, beyond our book.' He looked from the window back to Addington and asked himself what he was prepared to say. 'I have a friend,' he settled for. 'He would not like me to name him, for he is a writer like yourself, albeit not occupying so high a place, but he gave us his history. He is down as Case Seven.'

'Ah.' Addington smiled in recognition. 'The admirer of intelligent teeth.'

Feaver laughed.

'Yes,' Henry said, joining slightly. 'That is him. I could not value his friendship as I do, were I prejudiced against him. And there is Carpenter, besides.'

'Carpenter is a good man,' Addington said. 'I hope he and Merrill will be safe.'

'And I am,' Feaver said suddenly. 'I expect you can see it already and are being polite, Mr Ellis. But John won't say it on my behalf, so I will. I am. Me and John and Oscar Wilde and Ted and George and Case Seven.' He sat back heavily against his chair so that it creaked. 'It's no use for you to know it, but there it is. John and me are Cases Eighteen and Twenty-One. Ted and George are Cases Five and Fourteen.'

Henry did not know how to respond. Feaver brought out his cigarettes and put one shakily in his mouth, passing another to Addington, who said, after a moment, keeping Henry's eye, 'We are grateful to you. It is no small kindness. It leaves only the question of how we are to publish our book.'

Heat crawled up Henry's back. 'We have been rejected by every publisher,' he said.

Addington crossed his legs. 'We have. Every publisher to whom we applied.'

The heat reached Henry's neck. 'No publisher will accept it. Wilde has made the whole subject anathema. We must wait and watch the public mood. It will be a matter of years, perhaps.'

'We cannot wait years. The book is written. It makes its case completely. It is needed exactly now.'

'They will arrest us,' Henry said desperately.

Addington laughed, looking pained, as though something were caught in his chest. 'We never feared arrest before, Henry. We knew the worth of our work. There is no crime being committed. Ours is a book designed to change the law. The law has claimed a famous man, but he is not the first man, nor will he be the last. Our waiting will only allow others to suffer as he is now suffering. Ignorance cannot be allowed to persist. It is a danger.'

'No one will touch it. It would be of more benefit to—'

'We cannot,' Addington interrupted, 'allow the public to judge only from this case. They will set their faces against us for ever. They must be shown that it is more complicated. More simple – that there are blameless lives.'

'It is when they have forgotten this case,' Henry said, 'that we have the most chance of appealing to them.'

'They will not forget this case.'

'The fury will be forgotten. When it has died away, people will ask themselves what it was all for. That is when we should publish. Science requires a rational audience.'

Addington raised his voice. 'The fury will not die away! If you believe that, you have not learned anything. It is ancient, and cruel, crueller even than I thought. This is where progress stops, Henry.

Progress will not encompass this. Not unless we try to force it on. It may make no difference, but we must try. It will never be easier in the future and it may be worse. It will be worse, for the men in the cells. We –' he gestured to himself and Feaver – 'may be those men.'

Henry was silent. 'But there is no publisher,' he said eventually.

'There may be,' Feaver said.

Addington took it up. 'Frank used to work for a publisher, a Mr Owen of the Watford Press. They are situated near Holborn and are in the business of publishing on brave subjects.'

'I have never heard of them,' Henry said. 'We have always known that the book requires a respectable publisher, if it is ever to gain a hearing. That is more true now, not less.'

'We know, now, that a respectable publisher is impossible, and we will not gain a hearing if we do not publish at all,' Addington replied. 'I have written to Mr Owen, and he is prepared to meet with us next week. I made so bold as to reply on your behalf.'

Henry felt as though he had been knocked back into his seat. There was no air in the room – only cigarette smoke, coiling. The blue sky in the window mocked. 'I see,' he said.

'Thank you, Henry. I will write with the arrangements.'

He had been overpowered; he needed to get out of this choking room. He nodded feebly.

'It is right, Henry. We cannot think of ourselves.' Addington extended his hand, smiling. 'Thank you. You are a courageous man. Do believe me when I say that I have always known it.'

Henry shook his hand. Shook Feaver's, when it was offered.

Downstairs, at the front door, Addington said to him, 'This is a dark time. But we must live in the future we hope to make, must we not?' Seeing Henry's look of surprise, he added, 'I believe that is your phrase.'

Henry was standing on the step, facing Addington, framed in the doorway. 'Yes,' he said. 'It is my phrase. I am grateful to you for reminding me of it.'

He was only a little way down the street when a woman, who seemed to have been waiting, crossed and halted him. She was middle-aged, dark-haired, with strong features, dressed in mauve and black lace. 'You were at my house just now,' she said, 'seeing my husband. I am Mrs Addington. What is your name?'

He told her. He saw her turn it over. She was impatient. 'What was your business?'

He looked involuntarily back at the house. 'I don't think I could say.'

'It is no matter,' she said.

Henry watched her walk to her door, knock, and be admitted.

XXIII

John came down the corridor in his nightshirt, one hand following the wainscoting. He could see himself, just, in the dark: mottled white, pale feet like fish moving in a pond. He no longer feared the creaking of the floorboards. His hand came to the break in the wall and went certainly to the handle of the door. Inside, Frank was still dressed, smoking by the window, his braces dangling from his hips. He turned and said, 'Hello, sweetheart.' The endearment was new.

John said it back: 'Hello, sweetheart.'

Frank threw out his cigarette and let down the blind. There was one lamp lit, by the bed, and he was in its light. 'I was thinking about Mr Ellis,' he said. 'He isn't what I expected.'

There had been no chance to discuss Ellis's visit in the morning; Catherine had returned almost as soon as he departed. 'In what way?' John said.

'He's no money, has he? Those boots. And so shy.'

'I expected him to be shy. I told you.'

'I know, but not like that. I've never seen a man shy like that.'

John went over to the bed and sat on it. 'I'm afraid it had a bad effect on me. I didn't mean to give us away. I'm sure we can trust him.'

This last phrase seemed to hang in the air. 'Why wouldn't we trust him?' Frank said, wrinkling his nose at it. 'You've written a book together.'

John was plucking at a seam on the bed linen. 'I know so little about him. He was hardly enthusiastic about taking the book to Owen.'

'I wonder whether I was sensible to remind you of Mr Owen. Ellis isn't wrong, is he? Wilde's fouled it up.'

'He has.'

'Don't do it then. Leave it. Don't see Owen.'

John said nothing. It seemed very lonely, the two of them in the small room, at the end of the dark corridor, in the big house, with night outside.

'Let him rot, John.'

'Wilde?'

'He knew what he was about. And he knew what'd happen if they caught him.'

'We know what we're about. We also know the punishment, if they were to catch us.'

'It's different with us. I know Wilde's kind. I know the sorts of lads he's been with. They don't all of them like it. They're doing it for money or food or drink. Wilde knew that. You said: blackmailers were like grocers to him.'

'I have paid men before.'

'You've not been that way.'

'I paid soldiers – two, a year apart. One I asked to undress.' He looked to see how Frank took it. 'The other I asked for more. Another time, I was walking at night and a man followed me. He caught up with me and said I'd looked at him; it was dark, and I couldn't be sure whether I had, whether he was telling the truth or not. He said he would bring me off for a pound. It wasn't – he wasn't offering, he was telling me. I was frightened, I said yes and we went into an alley. I thought he would take everything or kill me, but he didn't. He pressed right up against me, he smelled awful, and he took out my cock and he did it horribly fast. I must have messed all over his front. I was frightened, but I was thrilled by it all the same. I thought about it for months. I walked the same street over and over, hoping to find him again.'

Frank passed a cigarette, holding out the match, the flame veering and steadying. 'You think that makes you Oscar Wilde?'

John drew on the cigarette. 'I pay you.'

Frank breathed on the match and then broke it. 'I wouldn't be here if I didn't want to be. You're the first man I've ever taken money off and that's because I liked you already.'

'It was not all bad with Wilde, remember. He had Alfred Douglas. There was the letter read out in court. I think they cared for one another.'

'Perhaps, but a lord – it's different.'

'I said to Ellis today that there are blameless lives, that Wilde had dragged us all down with him. It isn't true. I don't think any of us are blameless – we haven't been allowed to be. It is all furtiveness, lies, greed, vice, hurting other people out of fear. Just look at how I am prepared to use Catherine, to hold her up as a shield. It is all an effect of the law. I bullied Ellis this morning. I will again. I will make him do what I need him to – his feelings don't come into it.' John disposed of his cigarette and blew some flecks of ash off the bed, leaving grey marks behind. 'Wilde was a great fool, yet I pity him with all my heart. To think – he has been in darkness for hours already. I cannot put him out of my mind.'

'You're thinking of yourself,' Frank said. He was leaning against the wall, hands in his pockets. His shadow bulked on the ceiling. 'You're scared, John. I'm scared sometimes. But it's only a book – you're forgetting. It won't save anyone. One book never did.'

John looked at the marks on the bed. 'Today I said nothing about Wilde's wife and children. But I am thinking about them also. His wife will take those boys abroad, doubtless she will change their names. I cannot help thinking that, if mine and Ellis's book exists, there might be men, even if it is only a handful, who read it, and see that they must never marry. Or there might be grown-up children who read it, and forgive their fathers. I don't think it is silly of me, to wish to spare people pain. The book may not change the law, not on its own, but it may spare people pain.'

'What will you tell your girls, when it is published?'

'I will remain married to their mother. We will tell them what I will tell the public: that I am a disinterested sympathiser, determined on reforming the law.'

'Do you think they'll believe you?'

'I hope so. It will be hard, when they see how I am attacked. It will be awful enough, for it to be suspected of me. If they believe it is true—' His throat throbbed.

'They mayn't be like that. You could tell them in secret.'

He swallowed. 'How can I be sure they are not? They will have read all about Wilde; perhaps they hate him as much as other nice persons do. I think, sometimes, of telling them. I have debated whether I might leave some statement after my death. That is where the idea of an autobiography came from. But I couldn't, without being sure that my memory would not become hateful to them as a result. The book, if it did some good, might allow it.'

'And Catherine? You have to tell her about the book, John.'

'I have tried.'

'You haven't. You've considered.'

'I'm afraid to do it. I'm afraid to do any of it.' An idiot tear fell onto his cheek and ran into his beard.

'Don't do it then.' Frank came and stood by him where he was seated on the bed.

He shook his head, then rested it against Frank's hip, crushing his tears against his trousers. They ceased speaking, listening to the quiet. Two men in a small room, down a dark corridor, in a big house, in a heartless city, on an island lashed round by cold sea. John rubbed his eyes softly from side to side.

After a while, he became aware of Frank's erection and looked up. 'I can't help it,' Frank said, with an embarrassed smile. 'Don't mind it.'

John unbuttoned him and Frank pushed it slowly, swollenly into his mouth, tasting of tears.

*

Ellis's gaze landed tremulously, like a butterfly, and took off again, before fluttering down somewhere else. John watched him while Mr Owen was speaking, followed his eyes as they went this way and that, looking first at the edge of Owen's desk, then at the bookshelves behind his head, then at Owen's hands, then at the waste-basket, then up at the cornicing, then over at the window. All in the space of a minute.

It was already difficult to recall the imagined Ellis, the person he had constructed from his letters. Last week, the real Ellis had stepped in front and blotted the light. He was not even alike to his photograph – this was what John had thought on meeting him again today. He was identifiable, of course – there was the dark beard, the long face and bulge of forehead – but there was no way of being prepared for the effect of his frantic eyes, his stoop and, at the same time, his height, his loping walk. Any handsomeness was obliterated by it.

And yet he, Ellis, was undoubtedly better today. He could not hold Owen's eye, but he was obviously listening, since he was asking useful questions in his rather high voice. Presumably he had nerved himself to it. As for Owen, John liked him. He was a big, square man in his sixties – grey-haired, with leaping eyebrows and thick fingers that he kept spread neatly in front of him like stationery. He was from York-shire, and John seemed to hear clear green spaces in his voice, the running of cold clear water. It was reassuring. It made up for the offices, which were small and mean, with brown, tobacco-smelling walls. The voice soothed his anxiety about Ellis.

'I agree,' Owen was saying, 'with that approach, sir. The book should be sent only to the medical journals, at least to begin with. Advertised only in them, too. The hope must be that they show themselves unprejudiced, and so doing set an example. Radical ideas, I've found, often gain their first acceptance in the medicals.'

'And the book would look sober?' Ellis said.

'Yes, sir. I would view that as essential. It will be a very respectable-looking book. We should set the price high. My buyers will stock it. They are careful people. It is also, as you no doubt realised, a definite advantage to have two authors for a book of this kind. A distinguished man of culture, like yourself, sir –' here he nodded at John – 'and a younger man well-known in progressive circles, like yourself, Mr Ellis. It is a perfect match, if you'll forgive the vulgarity.'

'You would not expect a large sale?' John asked.

'No, not to begin with. And we do not want it to be a sensation, Mr Addington, I'm sure you agree. But if it's accepted by the medicals, that is our way in, sir – and there the Wilde case might help us, by inclining the public to take an interest in such matters, rightly or wrongly.'

'Does it seem to you,' John said, 'that the public view might change?'

'It doesn't seem likely, sir, not immediately, though books I published thirty years ago, that were firebrand stuff, a child today might take out from a library. Change can be quick, much quicker than that. It may be there is a reversion of sympathy for Mr Wilde. There is talk of a petition, is there not?'

'Some talk,' John said. 'I would sign it.'

'Very good. As would I, were I not obscure.' He took his fingers off the desk and shook them at the brown walls.

'As would I,' Ellis said.

'You are not so obscure, Mr Ellis,' Owen said reprovingly. Ellis dropped his head, looking back at the waste-basket. 'Well, gentle-men,' Owen went on. 'I say it is time for facts to do battle with prejudice. Let us press our sympathies into action and publish your excellent book.'

Standing on the pavement with Ellis after signing the contracts, John was reminded of the morning his father died. He and the doctor had walked outside the house afterwards, just like this. There was the same bleak sense of anticlimax, something cool and disregarding in the day called upon as witness. Ellis was a doctor too, of course. The other had been better company.

They might have parted then, with scarcely another word spoken, had they not realised that they were both intending to visit the Read-ing Room at the British Museum. So instead they began walking together down High Holborn in the fine May sunlight, alongside the great clinking, rattling, shuddering current of traffic.

After some minutes, Ellis pointed and said, 'My wife lives on that street.'

'You do not live together?'

'No.'

'You have separated?'

'We have never lived together. We did not believe it necessary.'

'How do you manage?'

'We see each other often.'

'And why did you choose Brixton, for yourself?'

Ellis gave a small smile. 'Because people think it too far to visit.'

They came eventually into Bloomsbury Square. One house was badly afflicted with scaffolding, on which labourers shouted and ham-mered, while the other buildings, impervious, subjected to calm scrutiny the garden and the statue of Mr Fox. A white slice of the Museum was visible in the distance, like a promised treat. John found himself – perhaps it was Ellis's silence that demanded it – wanting a further talk. 'Will you tarry with me while I smoke?' he said.

They leaned against the garden railings, looking at the house under scaffolding. The hammering noise and the shouting were made hazy somehow by the sunlight, becoming a premonition of summer.

'I saw Wilde once,' Ellis said. 'In the Reading Room. I recognised him but did not think anything of it.'

'Why should you have done?'

'I'm not sure. I feel now I ought to.'

People came past – couples, and groups of young men, and women with children, and plodding scholars. 'Why should they care?' John started, in a quiet, wondering voice. 'What does it matter to them? It is all so – continuous. They howled and locked him away, and now they have gone back to whatever it was they were doing before. Never stopped doing, in fact. They don't care about me now. I walk among them, though I am as guilty as he was.' He paused. 'I am guilty in my happiness. I did not feel guilty when Frank and I visited Ted Carpenter. That is perhaps the only time.'

Ellis was watching the labourers with fixed attention. A man was climbing a ladder, a pail of something hanging from one hand. Some of it, whatever it was, greyish-blue, slopped over the edge and marked the pavement.

'Why did you want this, Henry?' John asked. 'The book was your idea. Though I do not think anyone would believe it.'

Ellis turned. 'It was mainly, that I am interested in sex.'

'There are easier subjects.'

'But we do not understand it. And suppositions,' Ellis said, looking away again, 'are not enough.'

John weighed this. Then he said, 'We are doing so much good, Henry. We have only to be brave.'

XXIV

Jack was eating with nervous enthusiasm, going rapidly back with his fork, his long arms folding like pinions, dipping his chin. Soon, Henry said to himself, he will be scraping his plate. They were in the refreshment rooms at London Bridge station. Henry had chosen not to eat. It was easy to talk – in a general way – because of the noise: every table was taken, and the mingled conversation, and the chiming of crockery, filled the space almost physically, densely; the white-aproned waiters moving swiftly between the tables seemed to cut through it, arriving to take orders in little rents of quiet that sealed up once they went away. It was early evening. The lights slipped round the brass fittings. Through the arched windows could be seen the platforms – the mill of anonymous activity, and the long shapes of the trains, the smoke parting to reveal them standing in their polish like exhibits.

Jack had written not long before, to say that he was going to France. It was a surprise. He had said a few times, on those evenings when he came to lie outstretched on Henry's sofa and despair – when Wilde was on trial and then after the verdict – that he might leave the country, but Henry hadn't taken it quite seriously. It seemed obvious now that he should have done. Jack had been so scared, and so contemptuous of the future. He spoke as if he were doomed. When Henry said this to him, Jack sat up on the sofa.

'I was born doomed,' he said. 'That's what I realise. I am walking blindfolded towards the edge of a cliff. I don't know how far off it is, or when I will go over, but I certainly will.' It was then that he had said for the first time, 'Unless I leave.'

Henry had never known him so abject. He could understand, of course, that Wilde's imprisonment would cause alarm. But somehow he had not expected it to go so deep, to threaten so much so entirely. Perhaps it was that, in spite of hearing his answers to the questionnaire, he could not imagine all the things Jack might be guilty of.

'Your French is dreadful,' he said now, as Jack took another fervent mouthful.

Jack swallowed. 'It will improve.'

'What will you do?'

'I can live for six months, perhaps a little more if I'm careful. Then I will see what I can make of myself. I may be able to review.'

'You have never made great claims for the Parisian theatre.'

'It may take on a new aspect, once I start drawing attention to its faults. Or once I understand French better.'

'You don't think you will come back?'

Jack was scraping his plate. 'I think not.' He looked up. 'You will visit, of course.'

'Of course.'

'I'm sorry it's sudden. It crept up rather, a dread that if I didn't—' He drew his knife across his plate again, edged some trace onto his fork. 'They will not notice I'm gone,' he said blandly. 'And yet I no longer feel safe. It is a nice problem.' At last he put down his cutlery. 'I am sorry for your book, Henry. It is not only me who is injured.'

Henry had not told him. 'It is going to be published,' he admitted.

Jack stared. 'When?'

'September.'

'September! Who would publish it?'

'The Watford Press.'

Jack screwed up his face. 'In Watford?'

'In Holborn.'

'I can tell that you don't think much of it.'

'They are prepared to publish.'

'It is craziness.'

'We have signed the contracts.'

Jack stared a while longer. 'I am in the book,' he said.

'You are anonymous.'

'Everywhere? In your notes? If someone were to search?'

'Everywhere. Anything that could identify was burned.'

Jack arched a finger on the table. 'Even so,' he began. Then he leaned across. 'It is Addington who has insisted on this, isn't it?'

Henry tried not to show an answer on his face.

'I understand,' Jack said, seeing one. 'I know how he has felt, these past months. How humiliated. How angry, with them all, with –' he caught himself – '*him*. That is natural. And it is always tempting to believe that some sense may be shaken into people, that they may be open to reason.'

'You believed in the book,' Henry interjected. 'When you came to Edith's flat, you wept. You thanked me.'

Jack sighed. 'It was so unexpected, to find myself – when you are used to silence, or to speaking in code, a little like we are now, with all the words dropped out, it was so unexpected: to speak freely. And it was possible to think that it might, that something might happen. I was grateful to you. I still am. But that was before the great dramatist took his bow. This book will not succeed, Henry. You have had your warning, your prevision – you should be grateful for it. You must exit that contract, as quickly as you may, before Addington destroys you both.' He sat back and picked up his napkin, seemingly only to have something to hold.

In Jack's hand the white cloth looked like a limp bird, with the life squeezed out. Henry said, 'Why did I sign the contract, do you think?'

'I think you are scared of him.'

'I am, I suspect. More scared, perhaps, that he may be right.'

'It is possible for things to be morally right, and practically wrong. Recognition of which fact keeps most people sane.'

'There is a name for it: hypocrisy. It is a justification for selfishness.'

'It is how we survive,' Jack said.

'That habit of mind calcifies. It is a bar to the New Life.'

A smile hooked across Jack's face, ear to ear. 'Does it ever occur to you that the New Life might be easier for some people to live than for others?'

'I do not think it easy for anyone. It requires a leap.'

'But the gap is wider if you are in defiance of the law, than if you simply choose to live apart from your wife.'

'We are not breaking the law by publishing this book.'

'No, but—' Jack's teeth shone in apology. 'I had forgotten we were talking of publication. What I wish to say is that you should not have involved yourself in this. God bless you for it, if I will not be struck down for saying so, but you should not. It is altogether different to your man-and-woman questions, your gas-and-water ones. You should have stayed in with your socialists. That is difficult enough work, but it is friendly in its way, and there is hope in it.'

'Something may still happen. We cannot know if we do not try.'

'You do not like attention, Henry. Martyrs attract it. And Addington has a martyr's potential. I tell you I understand him. Every day, we think: if only they knew. If only we could just point here, and say, "What of this man? You have valued him for his work, his wit, his friendship, his patriotism – are not all these things still true, even as he has held his secret?" And then the thought goes, "What of me? What if all the world is waiting for a man courageous enough to own to it? Could they call me a criminal, when my life has been blameless but for this spot?" I have had this thought many times. So will Addington have had it. The difference between us is that he has lost his check, which has kept him safe all these years. He is subject to a delusion: with this book, now, he is risking everything. And though I am sure he does not wish it, somewhere a quiet voice speaks: "If I am exposed, perhaps it will be for the good." That voice is your enemy.'

'It is too late to turn back,' Henry said with bitterness.

'It isn't too late.' Jack leaned forward again. 'There must be some means of extricating yourself.'

'It isn't so easy as leaving the country.'

Jack pulled himself sharply up. 'It is not easy to leave your country.'

Henry resisted the impulse to withdraw it. 'You are admitting defeat,' he said.

'Defeat in what?'

'It is a battle,' he answered, more uncertainly.

'Oh, Henry,' Jack groaned, picking back up the napkin and putting his face into it. He lifted his head: 'I am anonymous; I am going abroad. Your persisting with this book will make no difference to what happens to me, only to what happens to you.'

'Wait a while, and see.'

'I cannot. I must take my life as it is, and try to live it.'

Henry returned his look. 'I shall miss you.'

Jack dropped his eyes to his watch. 'And I shall miss my train.' He signed to a waiter. 'Keep with me, Henry, until I go?'

After paying, they came out into the station and walked arm in arm to the platform, where Jack went to consult with a porter about his luggage. Pale evening light dimmed as it filtered through the sooted windows in the roof. It seemed a later hour, even a different season, autumn or winter: in all this quick activity, these floating voices, there was the memory of nightfall, lock-up and bed. The Dover train arrived, snorting smoke, its long dragon tail of carriages stretched down the track. People started boarding; doors hung open all along the tail, like prised-off scales. Henry felt the tug of travel, smelled pleasure on the dirty air, heard it in the chatter of the trolleys, the irregular bumping heartbeat of trunks and cases. He thought of a boat, the great expanse of the sea, and then France, the inscrutability of a new beginning. He thought of the time he and Jack had gone over to Paris, how quickly it had all become known.

Jack returned, folding his arms and peering at something.

A family passed close by, and Henry noticed the little girl turn to look at them, these two tall, lean men, with their sad faces. 'I shall miss you,' he said again.

'And I you,' Jack said. 'What does Edith think, about the book?'

'She worries. She has always thought it a great risk. Angelica is wholehearted in its favour.'

'Why did she come back? Angelica.'

He hadn't expected the question. 'It was not for me to prevent it.'

Jack's body was half-turned towards the train. 'Listen to Edith,' he said. He took Henry's hand and held it firmly. 'Listen to the people who love you.'

Henry gripped back.

'Goodbye, Henry. Adieu.'

'Adieu.'

Jack turned and walked away down the platform. Henry kept watching him, his diminishing figure and hat, partially obscured by groups of passengers and shouldered luggage and drifting clots of smoke. There was a clanging somewhere, harsh and rapid. A whistle, vibrating on the air. Light falling softly from the sooted roof. Henry watched Jack arrive at a carriage door, where there was a man paused. It seemed to him, even from that distance, that the two men exchanged a glance.

XXV

In July, John's eldest daughter Maud and her husband Stanley arrived from Birmingham for a visit of two weeks. The family was gathered in the drawing room. 'How different you look,' Stanley said in his friendly, discerning way to Janet, who had already been home nearly a month. His hair was sticking up at the back, from taking off his hat. Luggage was being carried upstairs by the servants; there was the bump of a trunk. The garden, through the glass doors, swelled with summer light.

'Let me see.' Maud, larger and smoother, put her hand to Janet's chin, smiling. 'No, only fatter perhaps.'

Janet exploded laughing, slapping at her hand. 'You're dreadful!'

It was true that Janet looked different. After a year at Cambridge, her features had come into definition, like a mould that had set. And she was cleverer, more considering. John seemed to hold more interest for her – several times she had come into his study and pulled books from the shelves, asked questions about them. It was a pleasure for him to see her and Maud together. They had not always been friends – there was five years' difference, and Harriet, the middle child, had sometimes needed to parley between them – but now they got on well.

Catherine also took pleasure in it. She was lighter around them. On that first day, when Janet slapped Maud's hand, Catherine stepped forward and said, 'Now, now, girls. You are both too fat.'

John didn't know whether he would ever get used to it, in any of his children – used to them, to the people they had become. In Maud's and Harriet's cases, there were the usual alterations, recognisable to any father of married daughters: they were no longer his responsibility, they had had their experience. For him, though, there was another feeling, more uncommon: that these two young women were more experienced than he was. He watched them with the men they had chosen, in the seeming easiness of their relations, and found himself wondering, where did they learn it? To express love with a look, a dozen minute movements, as simple and delicate as a hand resting on a wrist. They had not learned it from Catherine and him. His elder daughters had found access to a realm that remained barred to their parents. And this made him anxious, that perhaps they could see this as clearly as he could. He supposed it was natural that parents should become different for their children, as natural as the other way round, but he did not believe it inevitable that the children should end by sitting in judgement on them. He did not want Maud and Harriet to perceive, in a way he hoped Janet could not yet, his inadequacy as a husband, to see through the paste of his marriage, discern how it was only modelled on truth. It was too late for him to change; an entire adjustment of his manner towards Catherine, an excess of affection and solicitousness, would have been wrong more flagrantly. He knew that familiarity was his best defence. Yet his behaviour was no longer familiar – not to him, who lurked behind it. In the company of his married daughters, John performed himself. One of his old selves.

The husbands they had chosen were acceptable to him. Harriet had married a mild, fastidious Irishman, ten years older, who had taken her to Dublin. Maud married Stanley, whom she'd met at Cambridge, and was about her age. Stanley's father was a manufacturer in Birmingham, and Stanley was due to take over the firm. There was something very attractive about him – his freshness, the permanent untidiness of his hair and feathery moustache, combined with the beautiful suits Maud encouraged him to buy, which he wore with a combination of pride and indifference, forgetting to button his jackets but looking satisfiedly at the brightness of the silk linings, stroking them with the back of his hand. He was slim and long-legged and spoke with a pleasant hint of Brummagem. John was embarrassed to recall how fascinated by him he had been. He knew he had been a poor father, not standing apart from his daughter's romance but rather entering into it. Envying her even. Yes, envying her. He had put himself in her place, imagined Stanley's body on top of him, the sleek press of it, those long legs parting his. He had watched Maud closely, as if by so doing he could extract knowledge to which he was not entitled. When they came to stay, he dallied outside their door, hoping to catch sound of something. He had disgusted himself.

That was before. During these two weeks he felt none of this, or little of it – just that ruffling breeze of pleasure deriving from the sight of any good-looking man. He was reserved, as was politic (after Wilde, you did not know what people might choose to notice). And the presence of Frank anyhow rendered the memory of this hopeless indulgence, and all those other hopeless indulgences, each of them entailing injury to his self-respect, unpleasant to him. When Maud and Stanley arrived, when they were assembled as a family in the drawing room, Frank entered to pay his respects and John had the opportunity to see the two men together. Frank was handsomer – he saw how Maud took him in – and was *his*. Of course, there was the usual provocation made by Frank's accent; John saw how Maud took that, too. There was only a few minutes' conversation before Frank retreated; later, Stanley said to John, in the respectful, confiding tone he adopted for their conversations, which used to thrill him, 'He's wonderfully well-dressed, your man.'

With Maud and Stanley in the house, in addition to Janet, John could not risk visiting Frank's room. He hated the nights lying awake, resentful as the house and the streets quietened, till he felt himself abandoned. In the mornings he was tipped into a different element. He seemed to swim through a bright succession of days, without Frank – visits, and parties, and trips. He stood in green gardens in a summer suit, sipping cold drinks or spooning ices, his straw hat pricking at his head. He watched fireworks explode in velvet skies. He watched young children chase and squeal. He watched young men flirt. He watched his daughters, the smooth shelter Maud seemed to provide for Janet. He watched Catherine be sought out, talk eagerly, link arms, laugh. He wished he was not married to her, so that he could be one of these acquaintances, could spend a happy hour in her company and then take his leave, think nothing of her until another year had passed, until another party brought them together again, for a charming afternoon. Mrs – what would be her name? This was where he stalled in his invention, for he could not imagine Catherine as another man's wife.

On one of these days they took the train to Cambridge and visited Mark and Louisa Ludding (again, Frank was not invited). It was extravagantly hot – Mark looked thoroughly uncomfortable in it, his beard like an absurdly inappropriate winter garment. They went out on the river: John, Catherine, Mark and Louisa in one boat, and Maud, Stanley and Janet in another. The water was crowded, cleaved into thin strips; oars thudded together and cast spray, boats nudged and mingled, there were cheerful apologies and abrupt intimacies, laughter spilling across. A hat fell into the water, floating like an ugly yellow flower, and was fished out on the end of an oar, borne aloft to cheers, the water dropping in silver beads. The colleges sat like so many enthroned princes on their banks, accessed by long spotless carpets of green – the river, with its noisy, cavorting cargo, was like some vulgar travelling show, passing under their notice.

Afterwards, as they walked to Newnham, John and Mark fell behind the others. There had been no intimate correspondence between them since Mark's letter after Wilde's sentence. John could not forget his bitter phrase: '*So much tasting leads to poison.*' Ahead of them, Maud and Louisa had opened their parasols, making bulbous shadows. Mark's eyes were narrowed by the heat; he lifted his hat and touched the inside all round with a handkerchief, then mopped his forehead. He put the hat back on. His beard pulled toward the ground.

'Won't you ask me,' John said quietly, 'what I have done, about the book?'

Mark looked down his beard. 'I have thought about it,' he said. 'And I have decided that I will not.'

'We have always discussed such things together.'

'I am sorry to disappoint you, Johnny.' He nodded at the others, who were turning into Newnham. 'I wish to think the best of you.'

'I will protect them.'

'And so that is what I will think.'

Another day, at home, the proofs of the book were delivered. John unwrapped the parcel on his desk. The pages, stacked white, looked like destiny. He stepped away and smoked a cigarette, assailed by doubt. Gradually the room, the volumes on his shelves, pushed back calmly and intelligently against any possibility of disaster. He went over to his desk again and turned the pages, his eye settling on sentences and paragraphs at random, all of them estranged by the passage to print.

Frank found him at it. 'Let me see,' he said. He had been out somewhere and smelled of the sunny street. John stood by him as he examined the proofs with a new intent, seeing not words but rather distances, angles, sizes – the printing of the letters. His hands moved across the pages with a brisk searching authority, as if they were cloth, or the flanks of a horse. He didn't speak; his breath made a fragile, rattling sound in his nostrils. He made several small notes on the brown paper used for the parcel. John had never seen Frank engaged in his trade: he delighted in what he did not understand, in being dependent on him differently.

Frank got to the end. 'They've done a nice bit of work,' he said, straightening his back and fingering his moustache. 'Funny to think I'd have been doing this myself, if I'd still been at Owen's. Hard to reckon what I'd have thought, setting up these pages.' He lit a cigarette, squinting at them. 'I wonder what the lads made of it. I'd have had to listen to them talk about it, making jokes. Listening and saying nothing.'

'You're assuming the book would exist,' John said, 'if we hadn't met.'

'Wouldn't it?'

'It would not.'

'So I am to blame then,' Frank replied, through smoke, and coughed. 'When will you tell Catherine?'

The morning before hers and Stanley's departure, Maud opened the door to John's study. He was at his desk. She brought a chair towards him and sat down. He saw, for a startling second, in her face, himself.

'Do you know I have been married two years already,' she said. 'I feel aged by it, in the nicest way. It makes me feel like home, life with you and Mother, was a long time ago. Does it feel that way to you?'

'Not always.'

'I am only twenty-four.' She gave him her hand and he weighed it like evidence, feeling the ring on her finger. 'You do like Stanley, don't you?' she said. 'You did not seem so interested in him this time. Never say, but he was a little hurt.'

'I like him more than ever.'

'Good.'

'You are happy?'

'Oh, yes.' Her eyes ranged distractedly across his desk. 'When shall we get to read your autobiography?'

They were still holding hands. 'Perhaps never.'

'I think Mother is anxious about it.'

'She should not be.'

'I am sure you will be kind.'

He pressed her hand by way of answer and let it go.

'You and Mother no longer share a room,' Maud went on, as if this was the conversation they were already having.

'We no longer sleep so well, at our age,' he said. 'Your mother must have told you.'

'She did.' A pause. 'I sometimes worry that we three girls are now a little over-educated for Mother, for her to be comfortable. I don't mean we are cleverer. Harriet and I are certainly no different, being married. It is only that we have all been to Cambridge. It should be a source of pride for Mother, shouldn't it? But I'm not sure it is.'

'I am sure it is pride she feels,' he said.

'You know her best,' Maud said, almost experimentally.

'I do,' he said conclusively.

'I wonder,' she continued, according to that logic of her own, 'what Janet will do. She has so grown into her looks. Cambridge has been good for her, of course. Should you let her do some form of work, if she wanted?'

'If she wanted.'

'I wonder what she will do.' Maud picked something off her dress and then looked at him directly. 'She is fond of Mr Feaver.'

'She has always been kind to him. I have thought well of her because of it.'

'Yes, she is very kind. Stanley has noticed it too. And I daresay Mother.'

Her gaze was unnaturally direct. The effort to see exactly what was being offered to him brought an ache. It was obvious she would come no nearer.

'You must be conscious of it,' she said.

'I shall be,' he said, unnerved.

'Thank you, Papa.' And she put her hand into his again, with its ridge of alien ring.

After Maud and Stanley had gone, he asked Frank, 'Do you think perhaps – have you noticed, that Janet is fond of you?'

'She can't help it,' Frank said.

XXVI

Henry could not cease from thinking about that time, years ago, when he had seen Oscar Wilde in the Reading Room at the British Museum. He remembered a large man, with a great mop of hair he kept having to push behind his ears, absorbed in his book, making notes. That was all. Before, Henry had only ever thought of it when he saw a play notice somewhere, or a new photograph of the playwright in a window, the hair shorter. Now, he could not stop returning to it in his mind, this little picture of absorption in the Reading Room. He had a stupid, infantile regret: that he had not gone over and warned him, that no one had warned Wilde of what was coming.

It was mid-August. Long, light-filled days. He and Addington were done with the proofs, with sending them back and forth between Brixton and Paddington and Holborn, following twisting lines to the high ground of inserted phrases, crossing chasmic deletions along straighter ones. The book would be published in a little over a month. Henry still believed in the objections he had made in Addington's study, that Edith had echoed afterwards: it was foolish to publish now; they should wait for a braver time. Nor had he forgotten the things Jack had said. He was conscious of all the danger the book posed to his prospects. But he remembered, too, how he'd felt during those three months when Wilde was on trial, as the mood grew murderous, seeping darkly over a thousand news-stands. When the sentence was delivered he had succumbed to a blissful feeling of *escape*, from a commitment – the book – that had come to feel more and more a weight, pulling him under, down beneath the surface. This despite knowing that Wilde did not deserve his punishment, that the injustice was precisely what the book was intended to help prevent. And so, ever since Addington unexpectedly blocked the way, insisting they could not abandon the cause, Henry had been aware that behind the logic of his arguments against publication, behind his ready sympathy with Edith and Jack's warnings, bubbled that initial, shaming feeling of deliverance, trapped like air. To this self-knowledge was added the expanding element of possibility. The book might, *might*, be a success of some kind, a spur in the nation's conscience. Which would put him on the side of right and clear his path for the work to come. He did believe – as did Angelica – in the value of what he and Addington had written. In the New Life. Wilde had not ruined that for him. And how could they know what would happen, if they did not try?

*

'Is it to make me happy, Henry?' Edith had said in March, when Angelica wrote to say that he'd visited and requested she come back. Edith was holding the letter in her hand.

'Of course,' he replied.

She looked down at the letter for so long that she seemed to be reading it again. Then she looked up. 'You dear boy,' she said.

Viewed from one angle, their life together – hers and Henry's – continued now much as before Angelica's return. They had never recovered the state of being that existed before they were married, what had seemed their entire intimacy of thought and action. Their lives no longer twined – they overlapped, and what Henry was over-lapping with was not Edith's life alone, but her resumed life with Angelica. Their life – Edith and Angelica's – appeared to him settled, interior. It was based on a mutual dependence the two women seemed half-baffled by: Henry saw in each a fierce desire to take decisions and pass verdicts, and then an exasperated, helpless recourse to the other for their verdict and assent. He was excluded by this, but not from everything. His knowledge of Edith was a key. It meant that he and Angelica could sometimes tease her together, complain at her little faults and raise their eyebrows in code, and this way they themselves were easier, took some open pleasure in each other. At these moments, it came back to him, as it did with particular smells and sounds (the stale sunshine stored in the fabric of a deckchair, the shushing of a fountain in a park, the nibble of a paper knife): the warm, fleeting feel-ing of last summer's friendship. Yet, whereas he felt then that Angelica provided him and Edith with an object of interest, a point around which they could collect themselves, it now appeared that he fulfilled that role for Edith and Angelica.

He was fixed at the centre of their life, but found himself wanting to squirm, to slip into some further, protected realm. He was painfully conscious of how much remained hidden from him. He was certain of Edith's happiness – but what did it consist of? He knew she loved him and valued his company, placing as few demands on her as it did; he knew she felt similarly about Angelica. Edith possessed them both. He understood the quality of her affection for him – where it was fullest, and where it tapered to nothing. He did not know precisely the quality of her affection for Angelica. He could not be certain where it ended. The two women were not shy of revealing their intimacy to him, in their manner of speaking to and about one another, in the conjunction of all their plans, but there was no physical contact between them. They did not hint at what lay beyond, but he could recognise some anxiety on their part, that it was perhaps too close in view. There were separate beds made up in Edith's flat, and Angelica's room was full of her own things. Was it for show? He supposed they kissed. He supposed, supposed, supposed.

Ever since the day he had gone into the copse after Angelica, he'd felt threatened by sexual need, keener than any he'd ever known. Perhaps it was how Wilde had felt, before he gave way utterly. (Was he, perhaps, feeling like this when Henry had seen him, absorbed in his book?) It was how Carpenter and Addington had felt; how many of the inverts who'd submitted their histories had felt: desire burning you up, too hot to touch. He understood this: what it is to burn, and to dare not touch. Except, by following Angelica, by touching the ground, by doing what he had done, he had, like all these men, given way. Or nearly. And ever since, his imagination, for so long so closely kept, was loose, dancing out ahead of him. Some nights, he simply sat, held in the grip of his desire, unable to move for fear or ignorance of what he might do. He did not know where to take his desire. He often wondered about the man he'd seen – or thought he'd seen – exchange a glance with Jack on the platform at London Bridge, boarding the Dover train. Were they together in Paris? Had they jointly planned their escape? Or had Henry simply been privy to one of life's vivid offerings, that Jack might or might not have had the courage to accept? Jack mentioned no one in his letters, and so Henry did not ask.

*

One hot thickened evening he was sitting up at home, in his now familiar state of repressed eagerness, of willed and unwilling inactivity, when he noticed, through the window, the woman he had seen on the morning of his wedding day. He could not be positive it was her – it was dark, and she was lit only by the lamps, the small filtered glow of the houses, but it was her shape, and she moved the same way, drunk, with heavy, weighted steps. He saw her stop, put her hand out against a wall, her head nodding and her hair falling forward before she threw it back again. It was her, he was almost sure. She remained there, as if stopping for a purpose, and he was seized by a chill compulsion, ghostly, impersonal. He withdrew quickly from the window and almost ran out the flat, down the stairs, two at a time. Only when he came onto the street did he feel some of his madness. The lamps pooled light across the pavements. On the side opposite the woman was still leaning against the wall. He stood, the warm air clinging to him, hearing faint movements in the houses. He did not know what he was doing. He took a step forward, tried to make the woman perceive his waiting, define his purpose. She seemed to notice him.

'What is it?'

There was irritation in her voice, that was slowed by drink. He could see that she had turned fully to face him and was staring across with a heavy tiredness. He said nothing. He was frightened; all his breath seemed caught in his chest, to have expanded and turned solid. He could see her face, the features hung on a look of dull disdainful curiosity. Her hair came over her shoulders, holding some of the light from the lamps. His heart thumped like something trapped under ice. If he could just walk over to this woman, it would be easy to impose himself and his wishes on her. He could ask of her what he could never ask of his wife, what he had taken from Angelica only in secret, treacherously. Possibility pierced him all over.

The woman pulled her shawl round her shoulders. 'I've given you nothing to look at,' she said, almost to herself, and began to walk away with heavy steps, down the street, glancing across to see he wasn't following. He watched her go. Then he came in off the street, climbed the stairs, went back into his flat and located the small, shattered piece of her jewellery he'd picked up from the ground on his wedding day. He sat down and masturbated with it tight in his spare hand, pricking the skin.

In the days afterward, he dwelled on how near he had come. How easy it was, and how fiercely difficult. And he began to feel, curiously, a sort of interested admiration. He found that when he remembered himself – breathless from the stairs, unbuttoning, teasing an after-image of the woman into eager liquid life, the piece of jewellery cutting in his hand – he was amazed. It intrigued him, this private, ungovernable sexual nature of his, the strange satisfactions it had invented for itself. He thought about a book he could write, while knowing that all his possible futures floated still in the unknowable aftermath of one definite event. There was the book he had written, *Sexual Inversion*. He carried it with him through the declining summer, heavy and shifting, like a bomb in his pocket.

XXVII

The book was published. It was between green boards, and had on the title page:

SEXUAL INVERSION
BY JOHN ADDINGTON AND HENRY ELLIS

The morning after he received his copies John woke as usual before the servants, leaving Frank in the tenderness of the bed. He went down the corridor, dressed, and then quietly opened the door into Catherine's – their – bedroom. At first he stayed on the threshold, allowing the darkness to separate. The room had acquired a different smell, or its smell had grown unfamiliar. He entered, stopping again when he discerned Catherine's head on the pillow, her hair splintered across it. Narrow shelves of light obtruded on the floor from beneath the curtains. After another moment, he moved with resolution towards his wife. She opened her eyes, and he saw them startle. 'Johnny?'

It was the sound of his youth. It was a trespass, to rediscover her now in her warm innocence. He stood by the bed. 'I have something for you to look at,' he said in a whisper. He nestled the book into the bedcover, green boards and gilt, saw her look down at it and secure it with her hand. He wanted to touch her hand. 'I will come back in the afternoon,' he said.

He went to the park, down to the river. It was a beautiful September day, tinctured with autumn. He sat against his tree and watched the men undress. The shrunken shapes of their clothes haunted the grass. The sunlight did not strike and glance at the water, but simply lounged on its surface, kicking in occasional bright bursts. The men swam alongside it rather than under it. John had for the first time brought a bag and towel, thinking he might strip and swim, but knew now that he would never. He watched as they came out. He followed the water as it channelled over eyes, down necks, stomachs, cocks, legs. Threading hair; tracing muscle, vein. He watched them dress, the clothes coming back to life, gripping with their claims.

He ate breakfast at his club. Read the papers. Smoked. Drank coffee, then wine. Smoked. Lunched. Smoked. Closed his eyes and fell asleep. He woke with the impression, sharp and distinct, that the men spotted round him, seated in their own chairs, at their own tables, clothed in comfortable suits, in comfortable good manners, had each received a copy of the book and were steeping in their animosity, waiting only for a signal to turn him out. The feeling lingered and in response he asserted himself, ordering more coffee and talking to a waiter he liked. He tried not to think about Catherine, waiting for his return. He had asked Frank to take Janet out for the afternoon. This brought more guilt.

Catherine was in her – in their – room. She was seated by one of the windows; her hair was behind her ears, her rings were knotted on her fingers. The light showed him the lines woven under her eyes, stitched across her high white forehead. The book was elsewhere, on a table. His and Ellis's names glittered on it.

'You have done it then,' she said, standing.

'Done what?'

'Crowned your selfishness. Not content with ruining your own family, you have ruined another man's. Does Henry Ellis have a wife?'

'Yes.'

'Two families, Johnny.'

'He is not, if you think – he is not like me. That is not why.'

'I do not care. You will have cajoled him into it. You know this will be the undoing of him.'

'I do not know that.'

She glared at him. 'You must know. To publish this now, after Wilde. You looked ill all those months. And still you went ahead with this. You have rushed to do it. You have done it regardless. When did you begin?'

'We first corresponded last summer.'

'There has never been an autobiography?'

'No.'

'And I have so feared it! I was right, though, to detect in you some mania for exposure. Except you were not brave enough to do it on your own.'

'Ellis is necessary. Without him, I would have the effect of an eccentric.'

'Why must you do any of this?' she cried. 'God knows I have not prevented you from gaining your pleasure.'

'The law is unjust.' He raised his voice in turn. 'The morality is unjust. It cannot continue. It is too late for myself and Wilde – though my life was spoiled long before his. Other lives can still be saved.'

'You seem to me quite happy in your spoiled life.'

'I am as happy as I am able. But you are not. It is your life too I am thinking of.'

She raised her eyebrows. 'Is it? I have not noticed.'

'I know how badly I have wronged you.' He stepped towards her. 'Through no will of my own, Catherine. No animosity. It has been the fault of my nature. You know how I fought it. You will see, in the book, for how many others it has been the same.'

'I have been reading through your book. It has been like breathing a bag of soot. I am –' her voice broke – 'filthy from it. I found your history. Case Eighteen. You are recognisable to me. I have read all about your misery, your loneliness. Thank you, for waking me this morning and pressing this record of your adulteries into our bed. As if, when I wake, I am not sufficiently reminded.'

'I could not find a way—'

'Yes, this is much easier, much. You cannot tell me you intend to proclaim yourself a sodomite –' she spoke the word as if it were glass and she was cracking it between her teeth – 'by publishing this book, so you publish it without telling me. You cannot tell me, truly, about yourself – so you write it all down in your book, for me to read. And both ways, what you cannot tell me, you show me as you show the world. The only thing that separates me from anyone else, any person in the street – my only compensation for being your wife these twenty-five years – is that I have not had to hand over money for my humiliation, but have obtained it *gratuit*.'

'It is not humiliation,' he said. He studied her expression fearfully. 'No one who reads this book in good faith could imagine that the wife of a man constituted as I am—'

'They would not think of her at all,' she snapped. 'She does not come into it. I know how you felt as a child. Your longings. Your photograph that you fidgeted over, until your father bid you stop. I am sorry for you. Do you know what I wanted as a girl? A husband who loved me. A man in a blue necktie, with polished shoes. You say you were lonely –' her voice broke again; the tears in her eyes brokenly reflected the window – 'I was lonely,' she went on, 'and I was not free to go into the streets, to go with soldiers to their dirty lodgings. I was not free to bring strange men to this house. I was not free to install in it a man of another class, twenty years younger. Not free to share a bed with him – not free to send him out with my silly daughter for the afternoon. But it is you who have been lonely. It says so in your book.'

He came closer, close enough to touch. He looked at her, the dark hair behind her ears framing a white forehead, tortured with lines. 'You are right,' he said. 'It is unjust. I should not have married you – I know it. We should both have been free to pursue our happiness. We were not. We are both victims. It is what the book is for. It is for you as much as for me.'

She moved as if to shove him. 'Tell me: is the injustice that I have suffered the stuff of a book? To whom can I tell my history? Except to you, who will not record it. Who is to blame for it.'

'Please, Catherine. I have always respected you as my wife.'

She gasped – a dry, parched sound. Put her hands up and pressed her eyes. He could hear her breathing. He stepped back; the floor-boards creaked.

'Do you remember our honeymoon?' she asked, revealing her face. 'Do you remember those first nights? How you had me undress, be still, move, touch you here, there, open wide, wider. Dress, undress. Lie differently on the bed. Look. Don't look. With you on top of me, staring at me. Kissing me with frightened eyes.'

He prickled with shame. 'I was without experience. I did not know how to go about it, I could not make myself.'

'You did not know; I did not know. I forgave it. We had our two girls. Then you tell me how my parts – it is not my fault – disgust you. How you delight in a man's. I must realise that you will never want me. We agree that everything of that sort is over between us. Three years pass. I have, in my loneliness, taken to my heart that my husband does not love me as he ought. I have taken to my heart what is strange and horrible – that his feelings are for his own sex. And then, one night, without warning, you are on top of me, you are pulling up my nightdress—' She stopped, searched him with her eyes. Her voice was low but distinct. 'You are on top of me. Your breath is in my face. You have your beard by then. It scratches. You do not speak. You do not look at me. You are just a weight. I am merely a pit dug for you to empty yourself in. I am merely flesh, fitted to receive your waste.'

He stood on the wreck of his privacy, feeling it slide beneath his feet. 'You don't understand.'

'I understand,' she said. 'You have always told me what I do not understand. I understand that I am not what you wish me to be. I am not a man. But I have been woman enough, when it has suited you.'

'Forgive me,' he said.

'You do not want my forgiveness. That is where we misstep, every time. It is the world's forgiveness you want.'

'Yours first.'

She pointed at the book. 'This first.'

'What do you want, Catherine?'

She straightened, became remote. 'I wish for us to separate. I will not divorce you – I will not describe your adulteries and allow the police to take you. I will not pretend to any adulteries of my own. We will separate.'

'It is too late,' John said. 'It is too late for this.'

'It is not. It has not been too late for you. But we must think first of our children. They know nothing about this book?'

'No.'

'You must write to them and tell them of its existence. Make whatever excuse you like for it, or none. Do not mention my decision. It may be more understandable, if they are given time to consider my position on their own. We will tell them at Christmas, when we have made our arrangements.' She watched his tears. 'Johnny, did you think

I would never do this, because I cared too much about the world's opinion? Or is it simply that you trusted to my love? Don't answer,' she interrupted, when he moved to speak. 'Please don't answer, Johnny. I am too tired. I have spent so long in fear for you. Fearing with you, or so it once seemed. I have dreaded your disgrace, your being made to suffer – I have ached with the dread of it. It has made me old. But you are not frightened now. You wish to take greater and greater risks. That is your business. You may do it on your own. You and Mr Feaver. I will not exist for your sakes.'

He put his head in his hands. Darkness swam up at him. He reared out of it. 'If you do not stay with me—'

'People will know, but you have decided that they should know. So there is no reason left to pretend.'

'The book will be seen only as an attempt at self-exculpation.'

'You made your decision,' Catherine said.

'It is too late for this.'

'It is not.'

And he had to admit, that it was not.

Part Four
December 1895–March 1896

XXVIII

It was a cold December, hard and scraped. The days were numbed and distanced from themselves, and the bare trees made black, petrified protests against soot-stippled skies. Oscar Wilde had been in prison seven months, and *Sexual Inversion* by John Addington and Henry Ellis out on sale for nearly three. Nothing had happened. The book had been published between green boards with gilt lettering; it could be purchased, and yet nothing had happened.

This was not the complete truth. The book had been shyly advertised in several of the medical periodicals and received quiet notices in two. Both reviewers had taken the book seriously and discussed it soberly. Both recognised the force and intelligence of its case, commending the approach taken by the authors. Neither mentioned Wilde, though both expressed the view that the subject as a whole deserved further consideration. This was undoubtedly something; but the notices, even small as they were, had prompted no correspondence, no publicity, no mention, no fuss or comment of any kind. It was silence enough to make Henry wonder whether they actually existed, whether some earnest prankster – or Mr Owen perhaps, wishing to reflect well on himself – might not have written them up and pasted them into the copies of the journals he and Addington had been sent. It was indisputably the case, however, that some people had purchased the book, unless this too was a ploy of Mr Owen's and there was no basis for the monthly tallies of sales he had sent since October. But if these tallies were imaginings, they would surely have been calculated to be more flattering.

Henry felt himself stranded, as though he had been tumbled and torn at before being hurled onto a calm and unfamiliar shore. He looked out from his new place with the weak sense of salvation appropriate to the shipwrecked. He had expected . . . not this, not nothing. Not for the book to form, to swell briefly in suspense, and then fall noiselessly into vanishment, like a raindrop slipping from a leaf into a pond. This was not disaster, but nor was it success. The book had sold only a handful of copies. Henry had taken on new commissions: an essay on Nietzsche and another on Zola. He'd surrounded himself with fresh material. He was wheeling dutifully between his tasks, but could not conceive of starting out boldly on the further exploration of sex he envisaged – a study of its personal, self-generated aspects – while still stranded, as he felt himself to be, between catastrophe and deliverance. He stood on the calm, lonely shore and looked out, at a grey seethe of sea and an unbroken horizon.

How to explain it? Since Wilde's sentencing, there had perhaps settled some general complacency. The monster was dead, his head had been paraded through the streets. Or there had been a deliberate forgetting, a resolute shutting of eyes, a pretence that no such monster ever existed. Either way, Owen was clearly right in his judgement that the book would be safe in the medical journals, buried under the massive discretion of the doctors. It made Henry regret Jack, living in Paris with his bad French, chased out of his own country by fear. He wrote to him, remarking on the quietness at home and enclosing cuttings of the two reviews. He was careful not to make it seem as though he felt in any way vindicated; he did not want to suggest that he had been correct to ignore Jack's warnings. In his reply, Jack wrote, '*I'll grant that the quiet is surprising. But do not trust it.*'

Henry hadn't seen Addington since the book was published; indeed, they had barely communicated, only exchanging letters when the reviews appeared. Their relationship – it could not be called a friendship – had no reason to persist, but its falling away had contributed to Henry's sense of dislocation. He supposed it was natural to feel something. When he'd imagined the terra incognita of the future, Henry had relied on Addington being there as his fellow explorer, or at least as a landmark, a co-ordinate by which he could navigate. Instead he was alone.

Edith and Angelica invited him to spend Christmas with them. For several days he wondered what to purchase as gifts, and then one afternoon bought two things on impulse, quite cheaply, from a jeweller in Bloomsbury. When the day came, he arrived at Edith's flat around twelve. It was like all the other days, cold and hard. The pavements were speckled with frost and the trees had pulled on long gloves of silver. When passers-by greeted him, their breaths unfurled like scrolls. Above the tavern at the end of Edith's street the lamp was lit, and Henry watched a young lad emerge, four pots of beer carefully juggled against his chest, looking very sombre and pleased as he handled his commission.

Edith opened the door. She hugged him. Henry put his cold face down into her hair which smelled of nothing but her. 'Merry Christmas, dear boy,' she said into his coat.

Angelica was in the sitting room, wearing a green dress with a red bow at the neck. She smiled. The fire was lit. There was a small Christmas tree on a table – tapers burned among the hangings. Angelica kissed his cheek, bringing a waft of perfume and heat from the fire. 'Merry Christmas, Henry.'

Edith poured them all a glass of wine. They sat by the fire, which fogged the windows. 'When we woke this morning, the frost was so thick we couldn't see out,' Edith said, and Henry had a sharp image of the room they were in, shadowy and blue-white, the two women in their nightgowns, sealed away in a wild privacy. The wine was good and he held it in his mouth, savouring the moment. His face grew warm. They had ordered dinner from the tavern. It came at half one and they laid it out on the decorated table. Angelica had made ivy knots to put among the candles, dusting the blossoms with flour so that they resembled flowers. They ate cheerfully and Henry felt his spirits lifting to meet the women's. More wine was poured.

Edith raised her glass. Their plates were still in front of them, streaked with gravy and scattered with bits of meat. Her face was flushed, and there was happiness on it. 'I would like to say to Henry – congratulations. This year you published your book, fearlessly, on a subject no one has dared come near before. And it has succeeded, has been praised and has sold – in spite of the naysayers, of whom I'm sorry to admit I was one.' She searched out his eye, the glass still held up. 'I should not have doubted you. Merry Christmas. To Henry.'

'Henry,' Angelica echoed.

Tears crept at the corners of his eyes, drawing the candlelight. He looked between the two of them. 'Thank you,' he said, and then remembered to pick up his glass. 'To my wife and her dear friend. Thank you for your hospitality.'

They toasted.

'To Oscar Wilde,' Angelica said a moment later.

'To Oscar Wilde.'

Afterwards, they had pudding. Contentment reached deeply into him like a thief, stealing away every anxiety. They returned to sit by the fire. The light outside was beginning to fail already, almost to freeze. There was laughter in the street.

They exchanged gifts. In the jeweller's he had bought Edith a new brooch – it was golden like her other, but in the shape of a lion in profile, raising one paw – and Angelica a bracelet of old silver. Edith pinned on the lion. 'I shall call him Henry,' she said. She helped Angelica fasten the clasp of the bracelet, rolling back her sleeve. Once it was done, Angelica turned her wrist this way and that, looking intently. In the light from the fire he could see the delicate hairs on her arm. 'It's lovely, Henry,' she said, still looking.

They gave him a large box, wrapped in pink paper. Inside was a pair of new boots. The reflection of the fire ran over the polished black leather, and the inside of the box gave off a rich smell of it. He took them out and turned them over in his hands. They were like big polished stones, sea-smooth. 'Try them,' Edith urged.

He put them on. They fitted, the leather tight and comforting. He rotated each foot from the heel. The firelight licked up the leather and the smell rose like cooking. 'Thank you,' he said, for the fourth or fifth time.

'I have wanted you out of those old boots as long as I've known you,' Edith said.

For the rest of the evening, the boots sat in front of the fire, like the haunches of a glossy black cat. The smell of new leather filled the room, while they played games, and drank wine, and ate cakes from a bag. Angelica loosened the red bow at her neck. The lion called Henry raised his paw in friendly salute. Beyond the window it turned to dark, and the lamp man came. They put their heads out and wished him a merry Christmas as he stood on his ladder, watched him reach in and light the lamp, his hands in thick gloves. Candles burned in some of the windows on the street. Above, the stars stared brilliantly. The cold was intense and lingered in the room after they shut the window.

He had agreed to stay the night. A pillow and blankets were laid on the sofa. The fire was banked up and the lights turned out. Edith and

Angelica went into their separate rooms. He felt strange, undressing, putting on his nightshirt, with the lights still showing under their doors. He lay down, his thoughts slurred by wine, listening to the separate sounds they made, and went into the black, held tenderly between happiness and grief.

When he woke in the morning, he was shaking with cold and his head ached. The windows were shrouded with frost, and the light was blue-white and shadowy, like in a prison of ice.

XXIX

Christmas lay dead in the house. Its silence communicated to every room, embalming each in turn. Reminders of past existence were everywhere: the tree, its tapers burning like tributes; the gifts unwrapped and then forgotten, keeping their unintended positions; the ivy run through the house – along the mantelpieces, between the banisters, down the centre of the dining table – that resembled the tactless growth on a grave. The cold outdoors – its blank hostility, the frail, colourless, cloudless skies – sealed them in, in the remote, insisted privacy of the graveyard.

Three months before, John had written to his daughters as Catherine demanded, notifying them of the book. He explained that Ellis was also a married man, that they were both motivated by a desire to render justice where it was due. He stated that the book was not savoury reading, and that he did not expect or desire them to approach it. Each of the girls had replied in similar terms, surprised at his secrecy but blandly congratulatory. None said they would read it. He was sure they must have discussed it between them, though Catherine claimed they had not involved her, and that she'd told nothing of her intentions.

The knowledge that he'd given yet another clue to his nature made him see clearly that he'd long been comfortable, by necessity, with his daughters – as with his wife – appreciating that he was not a usual man. What he could not accept was the idea that Catherine's disavowal of him, prompted by his crossing into explicitness, would be repeated by his children once it was declared to them. So, for three months, John had opposed Catherine's plans. The near silence the book was received with, which in different circumstances might have infuriated him, gave him encouragement, and a justification. The quiet, and the two polite, dignified reviews, suggested that the subject might yet, in spite of all, become respectable, and that an educated section of the public might still be receptive to reasonable argument. This delicate possibility needed to be sheltered from scandal, allowed to slowly bloom and seed itself. It made it even more essential that he remain decently married. The delicacy of the moment inhibited his writing to Ellis: he did not want by some careless suggestion to initiate a development that might endanger it.

But Catherine would not change her mind. She was insensible to John's every urging. It was as though she were a vessel that had spilled its precious, irretrievable contents, and now stood beyond reproach or blame, beautiful and empty. She could do no more. She had been one thing and was now another. This did not stop him assailing her, pleading. Even the appeals to her motherhood achieved nothing. Frank told him to leave her alone. He was relieved, John could see, that Catherine had taken this step. It removed guilt, or removed it to a farther place. Frank felt happier now Catherine had struck back; it had been a reproach to his manliness, of the kind John had long inured himself against, to persist in humiliating a woman, the mother of grown daughters. He tried to make John see that they had been freed, all of them, but John could not understand Catherine's decision as anything but a disaster, for his book and his children – for himself. The weeks frittered into Christmas, and hope finally crumbled, leaving him high and exposed. He felt like a building marked for destruction, the last to be cleared from a street already ploughed away, in which he was the one petering piece of life. Frank's encouragements, his blandishments, were so many intrusions, echoing trespasses. Then Frank was gone, to his mother's house for a week, and John was left to face the end.

Janet was first to arrive, from Cambridge; then Maud and Stanley from Birmingham; and finally, Harriet and her husband Terence from Ireland. There was a trace of Dublin in Harriet's voice now. The house creaked and stretched accommodatingly; the servants flowed from room to room; the four women from subject to subject on the current of their returned intimacy – all subjects save one. The house was warm and snaked with ivy, the tree large and brilliant. Christmas Day was strung out on laughter. Outside was cold and clear, the element in which they were suspended.

And then on the 27th, the daughters were told, in the drawing room. The partition doors were closed against the dining table and the view onto the garden. Stanley and Terence were dispatched on a walk. The girls sat on the sofa, which was too small for them, so that they were forced to occupy different depths. John and Catherine sat either side of the too cheerful fireplace. He watched the reflections from the fire lap in darkening waves over the stones in her rings, and waited.

Catherine held herself strangely, her back at a distance from the chair. 'It will not surprise you to learn,' she began, 'that your father's book, which he kept secret from us, has caused me great pain. I believe he has told you its subject, but I must ask –' her fingers contorted in her lap, as if the fervid rings were strangling them – 'whether any of you has chosen to read it?'

There was only the ribboning of the fire.

'We have all three of us read it,' Janet said. She did not look at either of her parents, but at the fire between them.

Catherine's silence was like the short sharp shock after a cut, before the first brimming of blood. 'Then you understand,' she said. Her eyes travelled ravenously across the three faces, dwelling on each and extracting an answer. 'You understand.' Her mouth convulsed, twitching up to show desolate teeth.

The three girls sat wedged, vivid. John saw that they were holding hands tightly. 'We are to separate,' he said in desperation. 'Your mother and I.'

Catherine was staring at the children aghast, as at some monstrosity she had made. 'If any of you had a life such as mine, in this house with your father and Mr Feaver,' she said, 'I would take you away.'

'Papa?' It was Harriet.

'I cannot argue,' he said. They all turned to him. Tears formed like cataracts and he hid from them in his blindness. 'Please forgive me.'

The tears fell and he saw them again.

The girls were looking in panic at Catherine. And now in a rush they were rising, tearing their fingers apart, the sound of their dresses like a sudden intake of breath. They were fleeing. They were fleeing after their mother, while behind them their father came crashing down.

As the days passed, the house became less a graveyard than a single tomb, containing something mouldering. The subject of the separation was not returned to. No one confided in him. All of them inhabited the shape, the impress of their old togetherness, fitting their own death mask. The New Year was toasted in solemn simulacrum of good cheer. The weather grew colder and harder and brighter; there were small, choked flurries of snow that froze on the pavements. Finally, his elder daughters and their husbands departed. Each time, as the cab pulled away, the wheels left fine prints on the frost.

When both her sisters were gone, Janet knocked at his study door, walked across to the bookshelves and leaned against them, her black dress rucking at the shoulder.

'No one has spoken to me,' John said. He was at his desk.

'I am here now.'

He watched her nervously. He did not recognise the expression on her face.

'It could not entirely be a surprise to us,' she said. 'We knew something of it.'

He nodded and years of silence rolled away. An opening faced them, deep and obscure. He found himself asking: 'What did you think of the book?'

'It is shocking to read about. But once you are used to it, it is a little like reading about Ireland, or socialism.' She paused. 'It is a very rational argument, Papa.'

Already he needed a different answer. 'And what of Mr Feaver?'

For the first time, she looked embarrassed. 'He did not tell me, but I knew. Naturally Harriet didn't, having never seen him. Maud, I am not sure. She said she did not.'

'You are fond of him?'

'Of Mr Feaver?' She straightened against the bookcase. 'Yes, I am fond of him.'

'He is mine, you see.'

Her eyes widened and her voice became hard. 'Yes, Papa. He is yours. It is understood. He is what you have now.'

'Can you forgive me?'

'I think we might hate you, if Mother told us all.'

'You might.'

'I do not know if we can forgive you,' she said. 'And my sisters have their husbands. One can't be sure how they will respond. They might refuse to visit.'

John began to weep.

She looked at him from where she stood. She was trembling. 'I am very sorry, Papa,' she said, 'if you have suffered.'

He was speechless.

'I am very sorry, Papa.'

She trembled, and her eyes blazed, but she did not advance a step.

XXX

January. Cold and fog and rain. Henry put on his new boots like armour and walked through the bleary streets to assist his thinking, or to wear off the stiffness that came with too much thought. He had one of his long essays – the one on Nietzsche – to deliver, and spent the rest of his time cramped at his desk, trying to inch out from beneath his burden, word by word and line by line. He had hardly seen Edith and Angelica since Christmas.

Towards the end of the month, he came home from his exercise to find a letter. It was a blessedly clear, dry day, and he had even succeeded in working up some warmth. He knew the handwriting on the envelope as Owen's, and assumed it was the monthly sales tally arrived early.

Dear Mr Ellis,

I write to inform you that Mr Robert Higgs, a bookseller on John Street, was arrested this morning after selling a copy of Sexual Inversion to a gentleman who later revealed himself as a policeman in plain clothes. He has been charged at Bow Street with publishing an obscene libel.

I cannot see a mite of justice in it. I know Mr Higgs and expect he will make a good fight. You may wish to instruct a solicitor.

I have also written to Mr Addington.

Yours sincerely,

Philip Owen

Finishing it, Henry pushed his tongue roughly around his teeth and suddenly coughed. The absurd thought came that he might have consumption and he touched his tongue, almost hopefully, to see for blood. It was still early in the afternoon, and so he wrote a letter to Addington and hurried out to send it. The reply came by the last post.

My dear Ellis,

I have received a letter. I too note its air of washing hands. The issue is clearly serious. I will go now to see what I can find out, and will write.

Yrs

J. A.

He would not hear again until morning. He considered going to Addington's house, or to Edith and Angelica's, but dismissed both possibilities on the grounds that they might make him feel worse. He preferred to have a few more hours with his own fears, without other dangers being brought into prospect, quite possibly more serious than any he could imagine for himself. So he went out again and walked. He became angry, that he had been singled out for this, through his own fault. And then he remembered that it was truly the fault of all these other people behind and before him, going through life picking up prejudices like flowers from a verge, never giving them a thought though they stank of death. He mused on the necessity of dealing with a solicitor, and then on Owen's letter. He wished he belonged to the common herd, nuzzling in easy ignorance. Then he hated himself for this wish. Returning to his flat, he took out a copy of *Sexual Inversion* and read in it for an hour. He could not believe he had put his name to it. To think that recently he had begun to fear only obscurity! He had been paid in full now. But the thing was – it kept pulling him up short – that the book was right. It was right. Disgusted, he went to bed and barely slept.

In the morning, a letter came from Addington.

My dear Ellis,

After writing yesterday I went immediately to see Owen and discovered that he had left some hours before — for France, it appears. I would not have predicted it of him. Mr Feaver is most surprised. I do not know whether we should make attempts at pursuit.

The situation as I have gleaned it is thus. Mr Higgs was indeed arrested and charged with the offence mentioned. He will shortly be released on bail, at which point we will know the date for his first hearing. Curiously, I am acquainted with him very slightly — he was once Mr Feaver's landlord. He is, as we know, a bookseller, but merely from his sitting room, and is well-known locally as a radical. He stocks many of the books Owen publishes, hence him receiving copies of ours. In addition, he and his wife are members of the Legitimation League, a body which exists to encourage the legitimisation of bastard children and reform of the divorce laws. Further, Mr Higgs is editor of a magazine, The Adult, which advances these positions and others. None of this would appear to account for his coming to the attention of the police.

The situation is undoubtedly horrible. It seems, however, as far as I can tell, that the police intend only to charge Higgs, and not ourselves as authors, or even Owen as publisher (though this must have been his fear). Apparently the book was not on show in Higgs's window, and, considering that it is a private house, I struggle to see on what grounds the police can charge him with endangering the morality of the public — by doing so, what they are really saying is that there are no circumstances at all under which our book could be regarded as proper. And so we are as damned as Higgs, even though they have not proceeded against us.

I confess, I see some opportunity in this. I shall write again as soon as I hear that Higgs has been released.

Yrs

J. A.

Henry turned the letter face down on the table. He had never heard of Higgs, but he knew of the Legitimation League. Higgs would have friends who would relish a confrontation with the law. These friends might well be the reason for the police paying him attention. And why was Feaver friendly with Higgs as well as Owen? It was like a conspiracy, except what conspiracy would be as self-harming as this one? There was also Addington's suggestion that this might all be an 'opportunity' of some kind. He thought of his essay on Nietzsche, which had been his terror for weeks, with longing and even sat down with his papers, seeking the oblivion of work. It was useless. He wrote to Edith, giving her the bare details and asking if he could visit in the evening. Her reply came along with another letter from Addington, informing him that Higgs had been released and that his preliminary hearing would be in four days' time. Addington asked that Henry attend it with him.

Henry wrote back, the words appearing on the page as though from another's pen. He had never been inside a court. It was a side of life he could not bear to be associated with. For so long he had thought of the law purely as a candidate for reform – leading a paper existence – that it was somehow claustrophobic to think of it as erected into a building, a series of rooms manned by officials versed in its language and habits, something that would close its doors behind him. Those doors had closed behind Oscar Wilde, and he had never come out again.

*

He was surprised to find Edith alone.

'I thought it should just be the two of us,' she said, taking his hat carefully off his head. 'So I sent Angelica out.'

He looked gratitude at her.

'Is it very bad?' she said, once they were facing each other on the sofa.

He told her what he knew.

'Oh, Henry,' she said, when he had finished. 'It was too great a risk.'

'On Christmas Day, you said I had been right.'

She rested her forehead on her fist. 'I know. It seemed – well, you know how it seemed. It was pleasing to be wrong. I don't like to be cautious. But in this instance we have been proved correct. I wish we hadn't been. And yet, how proper: that you should be fighting on this side.' She half-smiled. 'How noble it is.'

It was appalling, to see his muddle reflected back at him. 'What shall I do?' he asked furiously.

'Is there anything that can be done? How will they defend Mr Higgs?'

'They must say that the book is not a deliberate affront to morality – that it is a work of science.'

'So they will ask you and Addington to speak in its defence.'

'That is what I expect.'

'And if you do not?'

'It would be an admission of the case against us.'

'Well then Henry, you must.'

He watched the fire. 'Even if Higgs is found innocent, I have been accused of obscenity. I am grouped with every purveyor of literary garbage – every crank and faddist and pornographer.'

'Not everyone will think that way. You will have supporters. You say Mr Higgs has friends. Well, so do you. And Mr Addington is well-known.'

He continued to watch the fire.

Edith continued: 'Angelica, for instance, will think this heroic. She will say it is an opportunity.'

He turned. 'That is the word Addington used.'

Edith considered this. 'Angelica has a campaigning temperament,' she said. 'It has often occurred to me. She is a great personality, but she has no proper object. She has always envied us our writing.'

'She should write.'

'She cannot. She is all at odds with words on a page. She needs something to fix on.'

'You think my book would be that?'

Edith reached for him. 'Henry, I know you best. You will trust in me, won't you? Trust in my love for you?'

He slid wearily down the sofa towards her and let his head be held against her breast. She stroked his hair. Her heartbeat welled under his ear like a pledge.

'Dear boy,' she murmured, her hand combing and recombing his hair. He kept his eyes shut, his thoughts mingling with and being dispersed by the blackness, the caress, the feel of Edith's blouse against his cheek and the feel of her heartbeat, his consciousness of the uncomfortable way his nose was flattened. 'Why did you do it?' Edith's voice said from far away. 'Why did you want to write the book?' He sat up and looked at her, his face tingling. 'I know,' she continued, 'about the truths of human nature and liberty and a new morality. I agree, of course I agree. But why this book?'

'Addington wrote to me.'

'But it was your idea.'

'I thought you had abandoned your notion that I am an invert.'

'I have. Yet I still suspect that it has something to do with the two of us, with—' When he looked away, she quietly said, 'Can you forgive me, Henry?'

He had never known her so vulnerable. A powerful desire to close the distance between them swept over him. 'You are assuming,' he said, 'that, simply because I am not an invert, I have no sexual peculiarity of my own.'

'I have had no way of knowing,' she said, surprise quick in her voice. The room was changed, as by the appearance of a guest.

'Perhaps not.'

'I do not like to—' She was unsure of him. 'It can be nothing that is against the law?'

'It is not.'

'Then you should not worry.'

'Your own peculiarity is permitted by the law. Has it made a great difference?'

She settled her eyes on him. 'No,' she said.

'Do you feel ashamed with Angelica?'

'No, not now.'

'That is freedom.'

She nodded. 'You know you are free, Henry, to do what you will.'

'It is not so straightforward.'

'I will find you someone,' she said impetuously, putting her hand out into his lap, the palm facing up. 'Someone who understands, whatever it is—'

He laughed in dazzlement, looking down at her palm. 'Doesn't it seem strange to you,' he said, the laughter suddenly spent, 'that we thought we were happy before?'

XXXI

On the third of February, at Bow Street, John and Ellis watched from the benches as Mr Higgs was committed to trial. The court was cold; the benches and the fittings and the order sheets were cold. Breath showed thinly in the air. Ellis seemed calm – calmer than his letters had suggested might be the case. He was quiet, holding his knees together, in his shabby coat, smelling slightly of frying. For the first time, John noticed the spindly lines of grey in his beard.

John absorbed his surroundings: the surprisingly low ceiling; the magistrate sitting leisurely beneath the royal arms; the system of inter-locking gates that separated the lawyers and the clerks, making prisoners of them. There was a murmur of conversation. The sound of pages being turned, which reminded him of examinations. Almost directly in front of him and Ellis was the dock, a bench on a raised platform contained by a lattice of green iron about the height of a gar-den gate.

It was with him still: the feeling of waiting for the curtain to go up. John had felt it ever since receiving the news of Higgs's arrest. Even when he told Catherine, even when she replied bitterly that this was where it had always been leading; even then, the feeling had persisted:

of anticipation. The house on Gloucester Terrace was being sold; they had found a purchaser and Catherine was departing soon, to stay initially with Maud and Stanley in Birmingham. It was as though the stage had been set, every last preparation made, and all that remained was for him to step forward into the lights and meet his audience, those spectators whose presence he had sensed and dreaded for so long.

When the case was called he noticed Higgs, standing up from a place where he hadn't seen him; a bony woman – Higgs's wife – was sitting anxiously in his shadow. Ellis's attention shifted to Higgs a fraction later. Their concentration on him as he stepped into the dock was a pressure jointly exerted. John could not have seen Higgs more than three or four times in his life; the most conversation they'd ever had was on that first occasion in the doorway. Naturally, he hadn't seen him at all since Frank left his lodgings. In fact, John realised he had never even seen Higgs without a hat; he was surprised to discover that he had hair the colour of dampish straw. He stood now with his back to them: in his early thirties probably, heavy-framed, his body thick and bolted in his suit, his neck wide and innocent-looking. Behind the fencing of the dock, it seemed as if he was there for inspection, a human type. They – John and Ellis – inspected him.

The charge against Higgs was read. That he had sold and uttered a certain lewd, wicked, bawdy, scandalous and obscene libel in the form of a book entitled *Sexual Inversion*. The prosecution was invited to make out their case. The barrister stood up. He was handsome, confidently sculpted out of middle age. 'The Crown's case,' he said, 'that this book represents a danger to public morals is nowhere more clearly stated than in the book itself.' He held up a copy, which had pages marked with stubs of yellow paper. 'I should like, with apologies to all present, to read some examples of its contents, by no means the nastiest, but entirely representative of its tenor. I have selected from what the authors term its "case studies": the testimony of men professing, indeed boasting of, criminal vices. You will note that this material, made worse by the appending of self-serving apologisms, is presented without the slightest attempt at condemnation.'

He opened the book. '"Case Three".' He had a good, clear voice, which he altered now as he read, contriving to pinch it so as to communicate his distaste, putting one hand to his brow and narrowing his eyes, as if the words were printed very faint. When he came to a Latinism, he pronounced it punctiliously. '"A medical man, Irish, aged thirty. Although up to the present he has no wish or intention to marry, he believes that he will eventually do so, because it is thought desirable in his profession; but he is quite sure that his love and affection for boys will never lessen. In earlier life he preferred men from twenty to thirty-five; now he likes boys from sixteen upwards; grooms, for instance, who must be good-looking, well-developed, cleanly, and of a lovable, unchanging nature; but he would prefer gentlemen. He does not care for mere mutual embracing and reciprocal masturbation; when he really loves a man he desires *paedicatio* in which he is himself the passive subject. He has thus described his attitude toward the moral question involved: 'As a medical man I fail to see morally any unhealthiness, or anything that my nature should be ashamed of. If not carried to excess, it is a far more healthy practice than self-abuse. And I trust that some day it may be taken up and discussed as a medical question in connection with its benefit to health, both physically and morally, and become a recognised thing.'"'

It could not help but sound shocking in the cold stillness of the court. The barrister looked out towards Higgs, his lips a firm line. Then he opened at another page. '"Case Eleven – Englishman, aged thirty-four, of no profession. He has had intercourse with three women in the course of his life, but simply as a matter of duty, to see if he could be like other men. He did not like it, and it did not seem natural to him. With men, the age preferred is from eighteen to forty-five, or even up to sixty. While preferring the educated, he makes the following interesting remarks concerning his instinctive impulses: 'I like soldiers and policemen for the actual sensuality of the moment, but they have so little to talk about that it makes the performance unsatisfactory. I like tall, handsome men (the larger they are in stature the better), very strong, and as sensual as I can get them to be, and I like them to practise *paedicatio* on me, and I prefer it done roughly, and I rather prefer men who are carried away by their lust and bite my flesh at the supreme moment, and I rather like the pain inflicted by their teeth, or elsewhere.'"'

There was a stifled laugh behind. John resisted turning. Hearing them being read aloud in this way, these poor men's honest, trusting answers, seemed a violent destruction of privacy. His feeling of anticipation had been shredded: it was like a rag at a window, through which a cold wind blew unavailingly. He felt he was being watched for his reaction. Ellis had bowed his head and was looking at his boots.

'Case Eighteen.'

John jolted in his seat. His case. Ellis raised his head, and John saw that he recognised it, too.

'"Englishman, independent means, aged fifty. He was strongly advised to marry by physicians. At last he did so. He found he was potent, and he begat several children, but he also found, to his disappointment, that the tyranny of the male genital organs on his fancy increased. Only more recently has he begun freely to follow his homosexual inclinations. He has always loved men younger than himself, invariably persons of a lower social rank than his own –"'

He no longer felt cold, but hot, too hot. He felt himself watched. The room narrowed and squeezed him. Ellis was sat like a rock. Higgs presented his back, the span of his collar.

'"– The methods of satisfaction have varied with the phases of his passion. At first they were romantic and Platonic, when a hand-touch, a rare kiss, mere presence, sufficed. In the second period: inspection of the naked body of the loved man, sleeping side by side, embracements, occasional emissions after prolonged contact. In the third period the gratification became more frankly sensual. It took every shape: mutual masturbation, intercrural coitus, *fellatio, irrumatio*, occasionally *paedicatio*, always according to the inclination or concession of the beloved male. Coitus with males, as above described, always seems to him healthy and natural. As a man of letters he regrets that he has been shut out from that form of artistic expression which would express his own emotions. He has no sense whatever of moral wrong in his actions, and he regards the attitude of society towards those in his position as utterly unjust and founded on false principles."'

How wishful these words seemed, read in this room, by that remorseless voice – how like a child's boasting bravery. At the touch of power they became toys, which John had pushed across the page. Had he tossed his life away, for the sake of these words? For the sake of sex? The sheer madness of it rushed at him: to have hazarded his freedom for the sake of those short periods of abandon; for the slick repetitive motions of his cock. *Irrumatio, fellatio, paedicatio.* For these he had eschewed study, art, friendship; he had sacrificed all the comforts of a home, the dignity of a marriage. He thought bitterly of Frank – of his commonness, his foolish infatuation with clothes; of the redness around his urethra and how ugly it sometimes looked with dregs of semen rising up in it. There was no comfort in Ellis's presence next to him, this uncongenial stranger he was chained to. Or in the presence of this other stranger, standing like a scarecrow: Higgs, on whom his life depended. The barrister had continued speaking, but now closed the book and held it up. 'I repeat,' he said, 'that all the justification for Mr Higgs's prosecution is here, as clear as day.'

The magistrate asked Higgs some questions of fact – could he confirm his address, could he confirm that he had sold a copy of *Sexual Inversion* on this date, etc. John could not see Higgs's face. He watched the burly body in the blue suit, the large hands that rested on the dock, and heard Higgs's voice make short, impatient-sounding replies. When asked how he pleaded, Higgs answered, 'Not guilty,' in a loud voice. Next, the defence counsel stood. He was a tall, sandy man – to look at him, he might have been Higgs's uncle, also on account of the familiar, apologetic way he undertook to prove at trial that *Sexual Inversion*, the book for which his client was arraigned, was a legitimate work of science, whose honest and honourable purposes could not be guessed at from the bowdlerised reading given today. The magistrate accepted this, and assigned a date for the trial: the 19th of March, in about six weeks' time.

The business was now done, and the chief actors rose and left the room. The court would resume after lunch. They saw Higgs's face as he came out of the dock, eyes cast down, wearing an odd swallowing look. Mrs Higgs pressed after him, thin elbows and wrists. Ellis stood. John remained in his seat – he did not want to get up until he had regained some self-control. He reminded himself that the street waited outside, and Frank at home; he was pleased, now, to have Ellis here, looking down from a height.

Ellis seated himself again. 'They will be cruel,' he said tiredly. 'They make no pretence at understanding.'

John nodded. He willed his heart to slow.

'You know Mr Higgs,' Ellis said.

'Barely.'

'What is he like?'

'I really do not know. I will write to him. We must offer our assistance.'

'Please, gentlemen.' A man at the door beckoned.

They stood. 'It is a different case to Wilde's,' John said. He was speaking his thought aloud, to give it reality. 'We can tell the truth.' He caught Ellis's eye. 'I do not know about you, Henry, but that is a great relief to my conscience.'

*

That night, he told Frank about the hearing, and about how he had felt when his case was read out, not giving every specific. 'It's the most terror I have ever experienced,' he finished. They were sitting fully clothed on Frank's – their – bed, backs to the headboard.

Frank's knees were drawn up, and he bowed his head against them, looking into the vee of his thighs. 'I'm sorry, John,' he said. 'About Owen and Higgs. It's my fault.'

'You could not have predicted the mania of the police. I did not.'

'I should have guessed there'd be trouble.' Frank looked up. 'I should have known Higgs would get copies. He's always had funny friends.'

'I was overhasty, perhaps, in dealing with Owen. I did not give you, or myself, time to consider. Or Ellis.'

'Poor bloke. I'm sorry for him too.'

'He's all right. He knows he must stick to it.'

'Poor bloke.'

'It really is an opportunity,' John said. 'We must remember. If the court is forced to accept that the book is legitimate, then de facto they admit the needfulness of the debate. It will be allowed as a question for science. The publicity will be great – we will have the police to thank for that. People will read the book. They will think about Wilde in his cell. We will gain friends. Reason will be seen to be on our side. The wheels of progress will turn.'

Frank puffed at his moustache. 'That's very well, but what if they find out about you and Catherine?'

'Perhaps they won't.'

'They will.'

'So be it. It is done. It was my mistake, to imagine that in some way things could remain the same. It is right that I give it all up. I wish to stand in that courtroom uncompromised.'

'You could ask her to stay in the house, while this is going on.'

'I will not.'

'They might start looking for something, John. If they can prove you're a sod, that means the book's as bad as you are. Doesn't it? What if they get something on you, like they did with Wilde?'

'I don't believe they will go so far. It is a different sort of case. And if they did, I cannot think who they could find. I have lived a cleaner life than Wilde, wisely or no.'

Frank stared at him. 'There's me.'

'Yes,' he said, discomfited. 'There is you.'

'So what if they find out about the two of us?'

'If it is hopeless, I will not lie like Wilde did. I will own to it.'

'And what if it isn't hopeless?'

'If they have any evidence at all, it is hopeless. I will own to it.'

'They'll arrest you,' Frank said on a note of panic, 'like they arrested him. And then they'll arrest me.'

'Only if they have evidence.'

'You were just saying how scared you were today.'

'That is the reason for being honest, if it becomes necessary. The law frightens us into lies: it is how the country is allowed to pretend, most of the time, that we do not exist. The whole idea of the book was to confront them with plain truth.'

'What about Mr Higgs? If you're found out, he'll be the first of us jailed, all for selling a book. Two years, you said it might be. There's his poor wife.'

'I have asked him here for a talk. I'm sure he understands the risk, why it is worth taking.'

'Does he?' Frank stared again. 'I've driven you mad.'

John glanced away. Their feet were very close together, but not touching. 'Why did you approach me,' he said, 'that day in the park?'

Frank rubbed distractedly at his eyebrow. 'I said, didn't I? You looked lonely.'

'So you offered to be my friend.'

'You know I did.'

'You could tell.'

'Of course. From the way you were looking.'

He eyed Frank. 'What did you want?'

Frank answered immediately. 'I wanted a rest, John.'

'A rest?'

'From work, day after day. Sixteen years I'd been at the printers, since I was a lad. A rest from worrying about Mother and having to take care of her. From men – from needing it all the time, and having to go out and find it, and having to take it from whoever I found.'

'And I looked lonely.'

'You looked kind.'

'Have I been kind?'

Frank laughed and took out a cigarette.

'Have you rested?' John said next.

Frank lit the cigarette and emitted some smoke. 'Yes, I've rested.'

'Does that mean I have served my purpose?'

'You haven't said why you wanted me. Am I still rough enough for you, sir?'

'Please—'

'Perhaps you will soon want to replace me with someone still in his workman's clothes, who hasn't picked up good manners.'

'It is nothing to do with your clothes or your manners,' John said exasperatedly. 'It is your character.'

Frank raised his eyebrows but smiled complicatedly at the same time. After a moment John touched his face. 'Where'll we live,' Frank said, accepting the hand on his cheek, 'when Catherine is gone, and we leave this house?'

'Where should you like?'

'The country. Like Ted and George. Somewhere far out, where we won't get trouble.'

'Would you farm?'

'I reckon I could. And we could get some lads to work for us.' He gave a quick grin.

'I'm not sure I am fit for the country,' John said.

'Paris then. Or Italy somewhere.'

'Why not London?'

'We wouldn't be breaking the law in those other countries. I'd like to see what it's like.'

John reached over for Frank's cigarette case. 'As would I.'

'So?'

'I would rather see what it was like in England.'

'John—'

He looked at Frank's pained expression. 'What is it?'

'This trial. You're risking it all. Everything.'

'I cannot help it.'

'Yes you can,' Frank said. 'Just you won't.'

XXXII

Two days after the hearing at Bow Street – it was a bitterly cold morning, and windy – the pretty maid led Henry off the step and, this time, into Addington's drawing room. A loud voice on the other side of the door was revealed as Higgs, already arrived and sitting in an armchair to the right of the fire; Addington was on the sofa opposite. The room was grand, impressively feminine, but had taken on a provisional, masculine air, as though it had been annexed out of necessity, with Higgs an unlikely conqueror. Addington rose when Henry entered.

'Henry, this is Mr Higgs. This is Mr Ellis, my co-author.'

'Pleased to meet you, sir,' Higgs said, standing and gripping painfully on Henry's numbed fingers (he was evidently one of those who found Henry's handshake unsatisfactory). 'I'm very sorry for this trouble.' Under his hair, his eyes were very sharply blue, like something precious turned out of some thatch. There was reddish stubble above his lip and on his chin.

Henry took the other chair. The warmth from the fire stung his cheeks.

'I know your writing, Mr Ellis,' Higgs said.

'Thank you.'

'The New Life,' Higgs said, nodding intimately.

'Yes.'

'I was just saying to Mr Addington,' he continued, giving one more nod, 'that this Inspector Sweeney, as he's properly called, who's the one that arrested me, was a regular at our meetings. I expect you know the Legitimation League, Mr Ellis, seeing as we're very much of your opinions. And perhaps our little magazine, the *Adult*, of which I am the editor? Anyhow, I was just saying to Mr Addington: I considered this Sweeney a friend of mine. I still can't give up thinking that at least some of his opinions were his honest own.' Higgs had turned his big hands out on his thighs, the palms red and crossed with lines.

'I'm sure some of them were,' Addington said. 'There is a great deal of hypocrisy in this case.'

'When Sweeney came in to buy your book, gentlemen – Harris, he'd said to us his name was – we had a nice chat, like we were used to having. He asked for your book and said was it good, and I said yes it was, it made a very good case, and he said what a tragedy what had happened to Oscar Wilde and I said yes it was, that a man should be able to do what he likes in private, so long as he isn't hurting anyone, and we wouldn't ask for anything less for ourselves – and he agreed with that. And then the very next day, there he is putting cuffs on me. Talk about hypocrisy—' Higgs stretched out his angry palms. 'Who's abusing British liberty, a couple of fellows and some women having dinner once a week at the Holborn – private room, mind you – and producing a magazine, or the police putting spies in plain clothes and arresting a man for selling a scientific book?'

'They spied on your dinners?' Henry said.

'Once a week at the Holborn. Sweeney always had a place. Some of our members have anarchist opinions – it's common enough as you know, Mr Ellis. Apparently too common for the police not to be interested. So they spied on us. Expecting us to be plotting explosions no doubt, rather than worrying about bastard children. We reckon your book was just the excuse they were looking for, since they couldn't find out any wrongdoing but wanted to smash us up anyways.'

'But the book was not exposed for sale,' Addington said, 'in the window or anywhere else? How did they know that you had it?'

'I asked that. We'd sold a few copies you see. One had gone to Liverpool, to a young man living with his parents. Apparently they found it on him, his parents that is, and complained to the police, who messaged to the police here, and there was their excuse, served up nice and hot.'

'A young man?' Addington said.

'It's an attack on freedom of speech, sir,' said Higgs. 'We saw that's what it was straight away.'

The door opened and Feaver came in, rubbing his hands vigorously together, a cigarette beneath his moustache (again, Henry had the feeling of having joined some male encampment). He was beautifully dressed. 'Hello, Mr Higgs,' he said, quickly plucking the cigarette from his mouth.

Higgs stood up promptly, shaking his hand. 'Mr Feaver, you're well?'

'Oh yes, very well, once I'm warmed up. I've been out seeing my mother.'

'How is she?'

'Still ailing.'

'I'm sorry to hear it,' Higgs said. 'I did not realise – it was a great surprise, when Mr Addington reminded me we'd met before, of the connection. My wife had your forwarding address, of course, but I didn't think to – it's no small trade, exchanging your lodgings with us for ones here.'

'No,' Feaver said, looking at his hands and rubbing them again.

The smile wobbled on Higgs's face. He looked back at Addington. 'Will your wife be joining us?'

'I'm afraid she is out,' Addington said.

'Terrible mess this, Mr Higgs,' Feaver said. 'Not how I'd have predicted us coming back together. I never would've thought Mr Owen had it in him, to do a flit like that. He was always so principled. How're you bearing it?'

They sat, Feaver on the wing of the sofa. Higgs hooked a finger under his collar. The loud tone of aggrieved innocence regained in his voice. 'I'm all right, thank you, Mr Feaver. I don't blame Owen for it, he's too old for this trouble. I'm angry, which is a good thing. It's anger that's got me where I am, you know, about the wrongs I'm keen on righting. So I suppose I expected something of this sort eventually. The cause of your book, gentlemen, isn't one of mine – though I'm all sympathy, as I've said – but there's a principle at stake here that affects us all, isn't there? Free speech. Which means I'm prepared to fight for it. And I have friends, a good number of friends, who are backing me to the hilt. They've formed a committee for my defence, paying my costs, and that's a relief. I don't mind telling you gentlemen that I don't fancy a sentence, nor does my wife quite rightly, but I know my duty, and I'm told I have a very good chance.'

'You know you have mine and Mr Ellis's full support,' Addington said.

Henry nodded. He pushed his hands under his thighs. He looked at the polished fronts of Feaver's shoes, one of them twitching above the floor.

'I do think,' Addington continued, 'if you will forgive me for saying it, Mr Higgs, that this trial is a very great thing for us, a definite opportunity. For our particular cause, as well as the larger. I said to Mr Ellis the other day that we can tell the truth and win. This is a scientific book; it has been reviewed as such in two medical journals. They cannot outlaw a subject from investigation because they wish it did not exist. You may rest assured that myself and Mr Ellis will rigorously defend our intentions in court. You may call upon us both.'

Henry's hands sweated under his thighs. 'Yes,' he said, looking nowhere in particular.

When at last he was able to make his excuses and leave, Henry stepped out into the hallway, finding the maid waiting there. In the minute it took her to fetch his hat and coat, he stood on the black floorboards, with Higgs's indignant voice rising and falling behind him. He coughed, and again did the foolish thing of touching his tongue for blood. The rest of the house was quiet. There was a drifting smell of perfume. He could hear Addington now through the door. The maid returned.

He was on the street, already shrinking from the savageness of the weather, when he heard the maid calling his name. Feeling in his pockets to see what he'd forgotten, he turned to see not the maid but Mrs Addington coming out the gate, dressed for a walk. She came up to him slowly, glancing at the ground, as though careful of treading in something.

'Mr Ellis,' she said again, when she was near. 'I hope you don't mind if I talk to you a while.'

He belatedly lifted his hat. The cold pincered his forehead. 'I don't mind.'

'I'm sorry we haven't talked properly before now. It seemed again that my only opportunity was to hail you in the street.' She was standing a little way from him. Her face was strong-featured, as he remembered, the forehead and nose very distinct even in the shadow of her veil. 'Shall we go through the park?'

'Whatever you wish. You won't be too cold?'

'I will not,' she replied, making a narrow smile of politeness.

They walked to Hyde Park in silence, as though they had agreed not to speak until they were at a safe distance from the house. Henry's face was roughed and then slowly numbed by the wind. Her perfume, the one he had smelled in the hall, came to him in cold traces. There was something untoward about their being together, he thought. Near-strangers, a man of his age and a woman of hers. As they entered the park, the city dropping back, their walk acquired the air of an assignation.

It was at this moment that Mrs Addington said, 'You came today, no doubt, to confer. The other man was Mr Higgs, the bookseller? You see I am forced to guess.'

'I am sorry your husband did not inform you.'

'My husband and I are shortly to separate,' she said. He darted a look at her. The wind dimpled her veil against the upper part of her cheeks. 'You will understand why that is, though perhaps you will wonder why it did not happen long ago. He has not told you?'

'No.'

'No. He has not told you because he does not want you to be alarmed. I will leave at the end of this month, and am not prepared to lie about my absence. It will be a sign to the prosecution, that they should dig deeper, as well as a form of evidence in itself. You know the life my husband has led, Mr Ellis – the sort he leads.'

'I do.'

'I am telling you this, because I know that my decision – for of course he did not want it – has removed a check. Our marriage, our family existence, imposed certain bounds on him. That is all gone. My husband is a zealot, Mr Ellis. Now he is free. And he is no longer ashamed. That, too, imposed certain bounds. He thinks this trial offers him vindication: it is his whole life he sees himself defending. When he told me about Higgs's arrest, he was excited; I could see that in

some way it was what he wanted. I cannot believe, on the other hand—'
She stopped herself. 'My husband said that you do not share his
weakness?'

'No.'

'You may tell me the truth.'

'I do not share it.'

'Your wife is a true wife, then. I was going to say, I cannot believe
you are willing to endure the same risk for – intellectual reasons. They
will find out what my husband is. He will be a second Oscar Wilde.
And they will see you as an apologist for the both of them. They will
suspect you of the same crimes. You will cease to be published. Your
wife will suffer terribly. Do you have children?'

'No.'

'That is a blessing. But when you do, they will grow up in the shadow
of it. They will hunger if you cannot earn. You may need to go abroad.
And your wife – she will feel it the most. All for the sake of my husband's vanity.'

The trees around them were thinning and the Serpentine was
revealed on their left, lying like a dagger, its silver surface stropped by
the wind.

'I assume you sympathise with his condition,' Mrs Addington continued, as they began to follow the empty path by the water. 'In spite of
myself, so do I. At times it has been like watching torture: to see a man
so wretched. But he is self-deceiving. I do not say he has bad intentions. He had no bad intentions towards me.' They approached a bench
facing the river. She gestured at it and Henry nodded, slightly
unwillingly.

The bench was damp. He looked across to the far bank, where the
reflections of the trees bled into the water like dye. 'I can do nothing,'
he said. Mrs Addington did not reply. Her body was tense next to him,
her neck rigid – it might have been the cold. There was still this

troubling intimacy between them. 'Perhaps you think I don't believe in the book,' he started. 'I do. You say that I sympathise with your husband. I do. And with the thousands who are like him. I could not disown the arguments we've made. It would be intellectual suicide.'

She looked at him impatiently. 'You are young. You can commit a dozen such suicides.'

He shook his head. 'I cannot.'

'Why this, Mr Ellis? Of all subjects, why choose this? It is such a sordid, squalid subject.' She stared at the blade of water. 'I am ashamed to speak to you of it, for you to know that it has touched my life, the lives of my children.'

'There is nothing shameful in it,' he said.

'There is.'

'My wife is in love with a woman,' he said.

'Mr Ellis—'

'It is the truth. They live together. I live alone.'

She studied his face. He met her gaze as long as he was able – she was so close, and there was so much grief in it. 'I did not know of the existence of such people until I was nearly married,' she said eventually. 'You do not believe you will ever meet such a person. Does my husband know about your wife?'

'He does not.'

'You have not told him?'

'It was not my secret. Perhaps I have been ashamed,' he added.

'Why have you allowed it?'

'We are living in a new way. Edith has her full freedom.'

'I cannot understand a husband tolerating it.' She was a thing of hard lines, angled against the freezing wind. 'For months, I have been thinking of her. Your wife. Thinking how she might be protected. But it is you who needs protecting.'

'Please do not consider me.'

'You are sacrificing your happiness for someone who cannot love in return. They are not grateful. They only come to hate you.'

When the wind broke off periodically, the cold set to work from the inside, seeming to have fixed on the bones in his fingers, where it swelled and throbbed. 'My wife does not hate me,' he said.

'You have been more understanding, perhaps. But are you content?'

He balled his fists in his coat pockets. Grey clouds were being harried across the grey sky. 'No,' he said.

'Then you will come to hate her.'

He brought his hands in his pockets between his thighs and crushed them. His eyes watered in the wind. 'Surely you see,' he said, 'that your unhappiness, and your husband's, would not have come about if society took a different view?'

'Society will not take a different view, Mr Ellis. This new trial is proof enough of that. Mr Higgs will lose his case. My husband will be exposed, and, if he does not flee, will be imprisoned, along with his friend Mr Feaver. And you will be ruined. Unless you choose otherwise.'

'You cannot be sure of any of this,' he said.

She bit her lip for warmth. 'I spent far too many years of my life imagining how it might be different, and none of it came true. Life is what it looks like, Mr Ellis. Regret eats into everything, eats and eats until there is nothing left. Do not make my mistake, I beg of you.'

'But you are about to change your life. You have made a great decision.' He felt admiration for her as he said it.

She swung her head and glared at him. This, her anger, the new tone in her voice, was the most dreadful intimacy of all. 'Too late,' she said. 'I have given up my position. I have brought disgrace on my daughters. I have suffered the presence of Mr Feaver in my house. I have abandoned my husband at the moment of his greatest danger. It is the end of my life.'

He recoiled from her.

'Do not mislead yourself,' she pressed, 'about what can be changed.'

Some black leaves slithered past.

'You must—' she said, her voice near frantic. 'You must save yourself, and Mr Higgs.' She rose from the bench. Her whole body seemed to shudder. 'And you must save my husband. Because I cannot.'

XXXIII

Men appeared outside the house. Different times, not every day, never more than one. They would sidle past, sidle back, looking in at the windows, or up at them, smoking stubby cigarettes, writing in stubby little books. They were journalists; at least, some of them were. One stopped John by the gate. He had a sore at the corner of his mouth. 'Mr Addington, sir, would you answer a question for the *Daily Chronicle*?' He tracked him down the street a few steps and then stopped, decorously tipping his hat. Another man followed Frank to his mother's and home again, not asking any questions and trying not to be seen. Frank came in wild. 'It's not the papers,' he said, tearing off his gloves. 'It's fucking spies.' But to John it did not seem to matter whether the men were there today or yesterday, whether they were journalists or spies. The fact of their existence fell like a shadow, and he could not slip its reach. The world was standing over him, craning its neck. At last it had found him out.

It was the beginning of March. Their names – Higgs and Addington and Ellis – danced in newsprint, column to column, paper to paper, evening to morning.

The headlines were like so many signposts, pointing the way, the content of the articles a prefigurement of the destination. Most of them cheered Higgs on to his destruction. He was an immoralist, the enemy of marriage and religion. Why exactly was he a sponsor of bastard children? He and his wife, it was implied, lived in the loosest possible arrangement. They mingled with plotters and bomb-throwers. Ellis, meanwhile, was a pornographer, a kind of mad physician, possibly a perpetrator of the crimes he analysed. John, owed some lingering respect, was, as usual, written about with winks: a '*distinguished writer, with a brilliant style, though not renowned for his judgement*'; '*an author whose attainment of the very highest rank has been hindered by an eccentricity of subject and theme*'. (There was at least no mention of Catherine.) Whatever their individual characters and intentions, it was obvious Addington and Ellis had managed to write a disgusting book; the *Chronicle* said it ought never to have been conceived, never mind printed, calling it '*worthless as science even if the science it professes to advance were worth studying*'. It did not appear that anybody had actually opened it, but that was no matter.

John read with a burst and then a steady seep of relief the few items that were published in their defence. There was W. T. Stead in the *Review of Reviews*:

> *It may be alleged that such questions should not be discussed and that this one should therefore be buried in impenetrable silence. The answer to this is that, seeing as the current legislation makes one theory of the Psychology of Sex the basis for passing a law which sends citizens to penal service, it is impossible to*

shut out another such theory from public discussion. Mr Addington and Dr Ellis's inquiry goes to the very root of the theory upon which one section of the Criminal Law Amendment is based, and if the conclusions they have arrived at are sound then the principle of the current legislation is unsound, and will have to be modified, for the same reason that capital punishment is never enforced upon persons of disordered minds.

And George Bernard Shaw in the *Contemporary*:

Fear of being suspected of personal reasons for desiring a change in the law in this matter, makes every Englishman an abject coward, truckling to the vilest vulgar superstitions, and professing in public and in print views which have not the slightest resemblance to those which he expresses in private conversation with educated and thoughtful men. The hypocrisy is much more degrading to the public than the subject of Mr John Addington and Dr Henry Ellis's book can possibly be. In Germany and France the circulation of such works has done a good deal to make the public in those countries understand that decency and sympathy are as necessary in dealing with sexual as with any other subjects. The prosecution of Mr Higgs for selling this book is a masterpiece of police stupidity and magisterial ignorance. But it is fortunate that the police have been silly enough to select for their attack writers whose characters stand so high; and I have no doubt that if we do our duty in this matter, the prosecution, by ignominiously failing, will end by doing more good than harm.

Carpenter wrote a letter to the editor of the *Saturday Review*:

Sexual Inversion decently, straightforwardly and scientifically investigates a social issue of the greatest importance. That Messrs. Ellis and Addington should possibly, by the outcome of the Higgs case, be left with a slur upon their names and their book is a gross scandal. The line of battle is deploying itself towards a great general engagement — which must be on us before *long — and in which the proponents of freedom against tyranny will have to stand by and aid each other.*

The Free Press Defence Committee, formed to argue Higgs's case and support his costs, included Stead, Shaw and Carpenter as well as two dozen other men and women, some of whom John had heard of. A dinner in Higgs's honour was planned to take place at the Holborn Restaurant. Several members of the committee paid calls on John at home. He welcomed them into the drawing room or his study, where they were voluble in their outrage, acute in their criticisms of the case, and – most thrilling – clear-eyed about the problem of inversion and the attitude of the law. Some of them confessed to having invert friends. They shook John's hand heartily and told him that together they would strike a blow for freedom. After so many lonely years, he gulped at these kindnesses. Courage burned in his stomach; hope made him adamantine. Phrases he could use in court appeared magically in his mind; he heard his voice speaking them and scrambled to write them down. At the same time he was dubious, as one is dubious of all good fortune. He was conscious that these men and women were defending a principle: free speech. Even at this moment of greatest transparency, he did not admit to anyone the truth about himself. No matter what they said or believed, no matter even what they might suspect, he knew that most of these people would not have publicly pledged their support, and certainly would not have visited, if it was him, John Addington, who was the accused, and the charge was of committing a sexual crime. Worse: he did not think that many of them would have pledged support now, were it not that he and Ellis were both married men. He did not think they would have visited him, were it not for Catherine, whom none of them saw, but who, for just a little longer, made him safe for sympathy.

When these visits happened, Catherine remained in her room. If she read the newspapers, if she noticed the men outside, she did not mention it. She had abdicated. It would be some time yet before the household was dissolved and the house given over to its new owners, but Catherine was leaving for Birmingham. She intended to come back to London in the autumn, take a separate house, and live as a private, retired lady. It had not been said, to John at any rate, but the likelihood of this surely depended on the result of the trial, beginning in two weeks' time, and on events that might follow it.

The day of her departure was sharply beautiful – one of those feints with which spring teases its arrival. The stripped trees stood gratefully in it, like whittled survivors of disease brought out to air themselves. Frank went early to his mother's. Maud and Stanley, who were to take Catherine, arrived in the mid-morning; Janet had received permission to come up from Cambridge. They were quiet, all of them, speaking in short, hushed sentences: an observer would have guessed that death was in the house. John had not seen Maud since Christmas, nor had they written to each other. She was clumsily uncertain with him, as though he were the one who was dying.

Sunlight sharded into the rooms. Catherine was upstairs. The girls went to her, leaving John and Stanley in the drawing room. There could be no doubt that Stanley knew everything; his embarrassment was an itch neither of them could scratch. They sat in the room, swaddled in male silence. John looked at Stanley on the sofa, where he was mortified into dignity, his jacket open, flaunting its vermilion lining. He imagined going over to him, pulling off his boots, unknotting his tie, easing him out of the jacket, out of his shirt, his trousers and drawers, down over the long legs. He imagined him naked in this room, helpless on the sofa, in the stark daylight. He imagined flattening his forearms on the tops of Stanley's thighs and taking his cock into his mouth, its stiff weight cradled on his tongue. I pity him, he thought. His is a life without experience.

A cab stopped outside the house; footsteps rumoured overhead. Stanley excused himself. The servants bore down some trunks – the door into the hall was open and John saw them carried out. There were sounds on the stairs. The cascade of a woman's dress. Catherine came swiftly past. She did not look. She was a flash of profile, framed for a moment, like the Queen on a postage stamp. His wife. John went to the window to see her go down the steps. While he was watching, Maud and Janet entered the room.

They stood there, silent and pale-faced, like avenging ghosts. He almost sank to his knees before them. But Janet stepped forward and held him up. She held him up, her head against his shoulder. And then Maud, too, was holding him up, and he was holding them, and they were hair and smell and grip and tears.

'We are abandoning you,' Janet said.

'It is best,' he said to them, into their hair, over and over. 'It is best.'

They left him and he returned to the window, watched them get into the cab. The blinds were down but when the door opened he saw Catherine on the seat. She was looking the other way; he couldn't see her face.

The door shut. The cab turned, curved, the light slipping off it, dropping behind on the road, and he was in warm breathing dark; he and Catherine were just engaged, they had left Venice and were travelling the Mont Cenis Pass overnight, seated up on the box, jolting along in the warm-smelling air. He turned to her, night sky flying out behind her head, and said gravely, 'Catherine, there are things you must know about yourself.' He explained her faults, each in turn, and how they might be rectified. She nodded and promised, and nervously pressed his hand.

*

After an hour, Susan the maid found him in his study.

She bobbed. 'Sir.'

He knew, seeing her face. 'Yes, Susan?'

Her face deepened. 'I was very sorry to see Mrs Addington go, sir.'

'Thank you, Susan.'

She twisted her hands in front of her apron. 'Of course we know about your trial, sir.'

'Not mine, Susan.'

'The trial involving a book of yours, sir.'

He noticed a flush high on her neck. 'What is it, Susan?'

She gripped her wrist. 'I know why it is you've separated, sir.'

'Why?'

'I've seen it.'

A needle dug in his chest. 'Seen what?'

'You and Mr Feaver, sir. I knew from the first time I saw him with that cigarette case.' Her eyes were wide. The flush on her neck had spread. He could see that she was in awe of herself. 'I've seen it, sir, and I'm not about to give you an opinion on it. I don't wish to part with my position, least not until we all have to. I only wish, sir –' she closed her eyes for a second – 'to be given more in my wages each week till leaving, and then three months' wages after that.'

He was silent.

'It's not much,' she said quickly.

'And if you do not have it?'

She shut her eyes again. 'I'm not threatening nothing, sir. It's only fair, sir, for living here, knowing what's going on and not having an opinion, with a trial and everything on top. There's a man outside the house, and he's asking—'

The needle dragged. 'A journalist?'

'I don't know, sir. He offered to pay is all I know.'

'What did you say to him?'

'Nothing. I wanted to speak to you first.'

'That is good of you. Is it only you, or do the others—'

'It's only me, sir. They might've been asked, but none of them knows like I do. I've never told a soul.'

He assessed the probability of this. 'I will make sure you are paid,' he said.

She bobbed. Her eyes were very white. 'Thank you, sir.'

She left, closing the door gently behind her.

XXXIV

When he received his invitation from the Free Press Defence Committee to attend the dinner in honour of Mr Higgs, Henry's keenest desire was to refuse it. He always refused such invitations, whatever the merits of the person or cause: the prospect of an evening in unfamiliar company, where he would be expected to make conversation, filled him with a horror only doubled by the further prospect of speeches and toasting, the bad theatre of cheering and hear-hearing. To endure such an evening now, in these circumstances, being personally connected with the speeches and toasts, would be impossible. Since Higgs's arrest Henry had been tiptoeing through life, trying to go unnoticed even by himself. He did not want to have to translate his thoughts into words and actions, or confront the infeasibility of doing so. He did not want to wake his fear, which he had forced into an outer darkness where it uneasily slept. He saw the papers – all those headlines, his name budding beneath – but did not read them. He did not write to Addington and did not think about Addington's wife. He did not think about Higgs. He turned down every invitation, declined every call. He pretended not to see the journalists who came to Brixton, or to hear them as they called after him on the street. It was futile, he knew, this tiptoeing through uproar: soon all eyes would turn on him; there would be dead silence, a court would wait on his voice, and on Addington's voice. But he could not bring himself to prepare for it.

Edith and Angelica both, however, declared it impossible for him to avoid the Higgs dinner. He resisted this logic as far as he was able, until at last he accepted the invitation on behalf of the three of them. In his reply to the chairman of the committee he stated that he did not wish to be made anything of and would under no circumstances give a speech.

It was Thursday, a week before the trial. When they entered the private dining room of the Holborn Restaurant, chatter broke on them. There were around thirty people congregated in a foreground made by three tables. The room was shadowy, windowless and panelled, the white tablecloths grainy in the gaslight. Smoke cobwebbed the air. Henry was in front and trying to see a place where they could stand unobtrusively when – 'Dr Ellis!' shouted a delighted voice, which Henry knew he would hate for ever, and the general conversation began to sputter out, as heads, cigarette ends, the bowls of pipes and the moons and half-moons of spectacles were turned on them, and there began a round of deafening applause. Henry weltered in it, looking at the ceiling towards the back of the room. He felt Edith's arm push under his. The noise stopped and she led him in, heavy hands landing on his shoulders and back. The next twenty minutes were awful, faces coming up and introducing themselves, grabbing his hand and pumping answers out of him. There were people he recognised and admired, each of whom he would have worried for weeks about meeting, following on each other like separate trials. Edith and Angelica tried to help, but the well-wishers batted away their women's niceties and aimed straight at Henry.

It was Addington who interrupted. He must already have been in the room, and have suffered his own applause. He came over and linked Henry's arm, saying something, and the siege was withdrawn.

The two of them faced Edith and Angelica, encircled by sound and curiosity. Henry felt oppressed by Addington's nearness. 'John,' he said, the first name unfamiliar – he was sure he had never called him it before – 'this is my wife, Edith, and our friend, Miss Britell. This is Mr Addington.'

Addington shook hands. He looked tired. The purses of skin under his eyes showed darker in this light, and the lines stood out on his face. But still he radiated his strange, teetering energy. There was, Henry could see, something attractive in his expressive eyes, in the rapid movements of his head as he addressed first Edith, then Angelica. And yet he was careless of his effect, the charm was not calculated. He was speaking to Edith now of an essay she had written; Henry saw how pleased she was. Then Henry became aware of Angelica, standing next to Edith but oblivious of her. She was watching Addington's face intently, words shaping between her lips. When an opportunity arrived, she fell on him hungrily.

'Mr Addington, I must say how important yours and Henry's book is. It is so very important.'

Addington smiled at her, the skin under his eyes bunching up, giving an odd impression of pain. 'Thank you,' he said. 'I am so glad you think so.'

'This –' Angelica swept an arm across the crowded, resounding room – 'all of this. Intellect is on your side, Mr Addington. We are all on your side. The trial will be a vindication.'

She was wearing a gold dress, striped with a darker gold, that glimmered in the smoky light like brass by a dying fire. Her manner was intent. Addington seemed intrigued by it. He thanked her again and in a preoccupied way brought out cigarettes and offered them.

'I must tell you,' Angelica said as she took one, 'that I am an invert.' She made no effort to lower her voice; perhaps she even spoke louder to be sure of being heard. Henry saw Edith look round quickly at the people nearby, her face tightening and her lips. He did not see Addington's reaction – he was too rigid with surprise. He felt, however, Addington's head move slightly in his direction.

'Tell me,' Addington's voice said, also a little louder than before.

'I have known since I was a girl,' Angelica said. 'Once Mr Higgs has won his case, I wonder whether you might consider taking account of the female invert in a new edition. I would offer my own history, and could provide others—'

'Angelica,' Edith intruded.

'Yes, Edith?' She was impatient of the interruption. Her dress glimmered. Her cigarette smoked.

Edith did not say anything, only looked tensely. Angelica regarded her with spreading disdain. In that taut second, the scene grew like a blot, to cover everything. Henry felt that he and Addington were covered by the consciousness of it.

Angelica returned her gaze to Addington. 'Will you consider additional material?'

The smile like pain was back on his face; some of his teeth were showing from under the heavy lapping moustache, showing the dim, grainy colour of the tablecloths. 'We –' he inclined to Henry – 'will of course consider it.' He paused. 'I am grateful to you, Miss Britell. I would very much like to speak more of this, in private.'

'I have much to say,' Angelica replied, catching Henry's eye.

Edith, next to her, looked at Henry at the same time. 'Perhaps we should find our places,' she said.

'Yes,' Henry said. And to Addington, out of embarrassment, without thinking: 'Is Mr Feaver here?'

Addington blinked. 'He is not.'

'I should so much like to meet him,' Angelica said.

Addington gave her a startled look, on which followed another smile.

Edith was about to add something when a great cheer went up, filling the room like a flame. Higgs and his wife had appeared inside the doorway. The room tipped towards them. Angelica, next to Henry now, was clapping loudly by his ear, smack smack smack. Glasses were raised high, their contents tipping. The room roared. Higgs was standing, straw-headed, his face childish, like a boy on his birthday, simultaneously proud and shy of his prominence. He was holding out his hands against the applause to deprecate it, looking oddly as though he were warming them. Mrs Higgs was hollow-cheeked, her neck and body pulled out like wire. They both looked young. She tangled her hands, her eyes ranging across the faces, and smiled only once, when the applause stopped. When they were ushered into the room, Henry watched her flinch as the claps landed on her husband's shoulders and back, as the heads craned in; he saw the patience she put on as the well-wishers laid their siege.

Addington linked his arm again. 'We should go over,' he said.

Henry looked at Edith and Angelica, who had begun to whisper.

They went haltingly across the room, with Edith and Angelica behind. When they reached Mr and Mrs Higgs, the crowd parted, seeing the significance. More applause broke out, not general, but enough to ring them in, making them fumblingly formal with each other. Henry saw Mrs Higgs bear up her patience again. But when he shook her hand, and their eyes met, he was shocked to see that she hated him.

'I'm sorry,' he said, involuntarily. There was talk all around them.

The hate dropped from her eyes. 'Nobody has said that yet,' she said. Her accent was northern.

'I don't know what else to say.'

She nodded. 'Thank you.'

Higgs, speaking to Addington, seemed nervily inattentive, both to Addington and to his own words – as though he were expecting to be called away at any moment. 'I'm all right,' he was saying, 'I just need it over with, so's I can catch my breath. I never imagined it. I've had let-ters, kind ones mostly, and it's not so bad, when you see all these people, but you do—'

They were asked to take their places. The tables were in a horse-shoe. Clumped at the corner of one, waiting for people to spot their names on the cards, Henry heard Higgs say to Mrs Higgs – they were slightly ahead of him – 'His wife's not here.'

'Course she isn't,' Mrs Higgs said back.

They had been placed at the top table. 'I said in my letter,' Henry muttered to Edith, 'that I wasn't to be made anything of.' But she didn't hear him, or she chose not to reply.

Higgs had been put at the centre of the table, facing out, with the chairman, Mr Holyoake, on his right, and Addington on his left. Henry, diagonally opposite, was between Holyoake's wife and Walter Crane. Mrs Higgs was in view, a few places down from her husband. Edith and Angelica had been placed at opposite ends of the table, both on Henry's side, so that they couldn't easily be seen. The food was served: chops, the grease queasily reflective on the plate. Henry chewed slowly, strangely concerned he might choke. Crane was at first eager with questions, but Henry could only manage semblances of replies and after a while Crane gave up. To avoid attracting any further inter-est, Henry concentrated on his plate, yellowish with grease, chewing carefully. Occasionally he raised his head and looked about him, like an animal compelled to search for predators. In any other circum-stances, the people assembled in this room would have impressed him as the best in London, but now he could see them only for what they were: socialists, secularists, republicans, anti-vivisectionists, free-lovers, suffragists – earnest agitators of every stripe, who had set up shop on the unpopular side of every argument. There was not a single doctor or official man of science among them. No one who might give confidence.

He looked across the table at Addington, who was deep in conversation. His wife must have left their house by now. His family must be broken up. How could he sit there, knowing the danger he was in? Henry felt a sharp thrill of anxiety, worse for being long suppressed.

The meal was finished. Now there would be speeches. Henry coughed to clear his throat. Two men spoke first – Mr Bax and Mr Foote. Both played variations on a theme. The arrest of Higgs was a grave affront to liberty and an insult to common sense. A scientific work had been traduced; knowledge was being denied. Higgs's virtues – foremost his courage in facing the charge – were enumerated. Mr Foote referred to Henry and Addington, and their sterling qualities. There was more applause, and Henry looked down at the table.

Finally, Higgs stood to much cheering, his face childish again while it lasted. He spoke at first with a tremor in his voice, thanking everyone present, especially his wife, and concurring fully with the points made by Bax and Foote. 'I will conclude,' he said, 'by concurring also with the praise given to my friends Mr Addington and Mr Ellis, and adding my regrets that their beneficent book should have become the subject of this odious action. It's a disgrace, that a British government should be interfering with free speech, in people's private affairs. That policemen should spy on decent men and women, deceive them, earn their trust just to betray them.' His voice had got louder, worked up – he looked at a waiter crossing the room with fierce suspicion. 'All for having ideas in their heads that haven't been put there nice and tight by the proper authorities.' There was thumping on the tables, which Higgs accepted with a heightened mixture of shyness and pride. 'I very much hope,' he said, more loudly still, his voice almost squeaking, 'and trust, that this action will be repulsed. I trust it will, and for the rest of my days I'll be proud of my association with the defence of a great principle.' He sat down violently, as another cheer went up, and the tables rattled and the gas jets waved. Henry saw that Mrs Higgs's face had softened into relief. The acclamations slowly ended. Henry thought of home, of the darkness of his flat and of his essay on Nietzsche that still wasn't written. Sitting down to it, filling his mind with it, would be like taking draughts of a cold drink.

But Addington was standing. There was applause again, waves of it crashing. He was smiling that awful smile, the purses of skin drawn up tight under his eyes, a cigarette pinched between his fingers just above the table, the smoke climbing to be cleaved by his beard, touching each end of his moustache. Higgs, close by Addington's elbow, shifted in his seat and tilted his head to see up at him, his face pink from his speech, puckering slightly in the smoke. The applause died. Addington cleared his throat, wetted his lips. Henry stared at his hand on the tablecloth. He heard Addington's voice saying, 'Ladies and gentlemen. I had not declared to my friend Mr Holyoake any intention to speak. Indeed, I had no intention; but it seems impossible to listen to so much kindness and not make some response. So, if I may contribute something for myself, I would like to endorse the sentiments expressed this evening. I am grateful, of course, to Mr Higgs, for enduring these arduous circumstances with great fortitude, in defence of the book my friend Mr Ellis and I have written. The charge against Mr Higgs turns on the nature of this book. It is called lewd and obscene, liable to corrupt anyone unfortunate enough to turn its pages. But it is not that. It is an honest attempt to comprehend a human peculiarity. And it is, especially, an attempt to address a grave injustice, the severe legal penalty inflicted on men who have done no wrong other than to be born.'

There was a small hesitating pause. Henry continued to stare at his hand on the tablecloth. Until it ceased Addington's voice had been practised, urbane. When it recommenced, it was in a new tone, which only began to tell in the second or third sentence. This tone was softer, more like his ordinary speaking voice, and yet harder, quicker, edged with intent – it was as though the words were spurs, digging, and the voice was being hurt out of its decorum, forced into a new pace. The change made Henry raise his head, but by then the sentences were sufficient for that. 'An invert,' Addington said, 'when he first becomes aware of sexual stirrings in his nature, realises that he is unintelligible. Should he attempt to tell a teacher or his parents about these feelings, the inclination, which for him is as natural as swimming to a fish, is treated by them as corrupt and sinful; he is exhorted at any cost to overcome and trample on it. So there begins in him a hidden conflict, a forcible suppression of the sexual impulse. The more energetic is the youth who has to fight this inner battle, the more seriously must his whole nervous system suffer from it.'

Addington's eyes moved restlessly round the room, as though he were counting heads; he had finished his cigarette and was leaning on his outstretched fingers, which stood slender and white on the table. Higgs was looking at them, preternaturally still. Henry wanted to make Addington stop. The tone was wrong. The matter. It was too intimate, too near. The silence in the room was not pregnant with applause; it was like a bruise, darkening.

'Some persons prolong this inner conflict and ruin their constitutions in course of time,' Addington continued. 'Others arrive eventually at the conviction that an inborn impulse which exists in them so powerfully cannot possibly be sinful – so they abandon the impossible task of suppressing it. But just at this point begins in earnest their suffering. For whatever relationship the invert achieves, his fear that his secret might be betrayed or detected prevents him from ever attaining simple happiness. Trifling circumstances, which would have no importance for another sort of man, fill him with dread: that suspicion should awake, his secret be discovered, and he become a social outcast, excluded from his profession.' Addington leaned back from his fingertips. His voice was heavy. 'Perhaps the invert is married, for that is by no means avoidable. In which case, he must make further deceits. He must betray the trust and mock the love of the woman who has pledged herself to him, the mother of his children, who has spent long years with him. He must risk ruining and shaming his dependants. He must lie in order to live.'

He stopped. His eyes roved about. They glittered. The room palpably shrank from them. Higgs was unresponsive, propped in his chair like a figure of wax. Henry glanced down the table at Mrs Higgs, who was waxen too. He could not see Edith or Angelica without drawing attention to himself by the effort. Addington seemed for an instant to realise: to see something in his audience, see himself reflected. But it was too late. And this also could be seen in his face. He went on. His voice now was the voice with which a man berates a lover, the voice of a man who sees that love is lost, who is filled with longing rage. 'It is only one,' he said, the voice pushing resistlessly into the darkening silence, 'who knows the mental and moral sufferings to which an invert is exposed, who knows the never-ending hypocrisies and concealments he must practise, who comprehends the infinite difficulties which oppose the natural satisfaction of his sexual desire – it is only such a one who is able truly to understand the purpose of the book that Mr Ellis and I have written.'

The light sat in his eyes, rose lightly over their surfaces. There was a jump in his throat. 'You all know the name of Oscar Wilde,' he said. 'But I cannot forget, though it was not reported, that the initial cause of Mr Higgs's arrest was a young man in Liverpool. I do not know his name – if I did, I would not name him. A young man in Liverpool, who purchased a copy of *Sexual Inversion*, and whose parents, discovering it, reported the book to the police. This young man no doubt considers himself alone in the world. He sought knowledge, and he sought assurance that he was not damned. And he has been damned. He has been damned.' A single, large, shining tear rolled down Addington's face. Then another, and another. Quick, slipping tears. They watched the tears, seemed to hear them slip and fall into the silence. All except Higgs, who still did not raise his head, who seemed insensible. Addington failed to produce a handkerchief. He thrust his face at them. His voice shook hideously. 'It is, ladies and gentlemen, a great tribute to yourselves that you are here in tacit support and approval of such an effort as Mr Ellis and I have made. It is not likely that such men as I have been describing will ever receive the kindness and toleration I perceive to exist in this room. It is not likely. But it is greatly to be credited. Thank you.'

The applause came like rain, different strengths mingled – strongly and then abruptly not. Higgs's face melted into an expression of terror; his hands moved together mechanically. Henry's chop rose in his throat to choke him. He tried to swallow, to clear his throat. Addington was back in his seat, smiling gingerly at the corners of his mouth. Patting his face with his handkerchief. This reckless man. This heedless, reckless man, entirely without shame. Henry looked at Mrs Higgs and saw that she had forgotten to clap. The applause coming from somewhere on his right was loud, and he realised he could hear Angelica in it. She was looking at Addington with joy, with nothing less than joy on her face. Smack smack smack.

The applause finished. There was a tentative quiet, on the brink of sound, like at the end of rain. And Henry became aware of heads turning in his direction, chairs scraping, a low mutter. And then that voice, that hated voice, went up again. 'Dr Ellis!' And the mutter became a surge, spilling into his ears. Thump thump on the tables. There was a hand on his shoulder and another on his arm. The room began to simplify – the cobwebbing smoke; the panelled walls hugging shadow; the smears on the tablecloth. Higgs and Mrs Higgs. Addington with a fresh cigarette glowing in the darkness of his beard.

Words sweated in Henry's mouth, trickled sourly down the back of his throat. His eyes went up to the ceiling. His fingers curled on the table. Applause crashed around his head. He leaned forward, to get out of it, trying to see Edith. There she was. He showed her his face. She looked past him to the other end of the table, dismissing something with a sharp movement. Then there appeared a small smile of forgiveness, releasing him. She stood. The noise flung itself up in a wave and fell back. She was standing; the lion pinned to her dress raised a golden paw.

'Gentlemen,' she said. 'On behalf of my husband, I would like to—'

He closed his eyes.

*

Outside, the night air rushed to touch their faces consolingly. They walked in the direction of Edith's flat, Edith keeping hold of Henry's arm and Angelica a step behind. It was as though something terrible had happened.

As soon as they came in, Henry went to use the closet. He stood shaking out the drops, listening to the silence in the flat. He did not want to see it, the silence between the two women. The taste of tonight's meal was in his mouth. His cock, held between his fingers, was bunching back on itself. He jogged it, hearing nothing from outside the door. A single drop formed and fell short of the basin. Why was he here? He hadn't needed to come home with them. It always transpired, whenever he examined it, that he had only himself to blame.

Edith was standing in front of the sofa and Angelica behind. They were not quite looking at each other. Neither had taken off her outdoor things. Only one lamp had been lit. Henry waded into the silence and stopped. The women weren't quite looking at him either. He wanted to leave. He parted his lips. Edith was closest. 'Thank you,' he said to her. 'For your speech. I could not—' He had said this much already, immediately on their being allowed to stand up from the table, and had broken off at the same point. 'I could not have done it,' he finished.

'I wanted to speak,' Angelica said. 'But Edith insisted.'

'I am his wife,' Edith said.

'But you did not want to speak. Not on the subject. It was all generalities, Edith. The book might have been about anything; Henry might have been anyone. And coming after Mr Addington's speech—'

'That speech!' Edith raised her hands.

'It was a magnificent speech,' Angelica said.

Edith pushed her hands down the sides of her coat. 'Even you must see that he went beyond anything that might have been permissible. If he speaks like that in court, he might as well pass the sentence himself. The prosecution will sing hosannas to him. Probably they will arrest him straight after. And what will happen to Henry then?'

'He spoke beautifully,' Angelica said.

'He all but admitted that he is an invert. He almost said the words.'

'Is it so very stupid?' Angelica said. 'To admit it? How else will anything be achieved?'

Edith shook her head raggedly. 'Clearly you have lost all sense of what is judicious. To say to Addington that you are one, surrounded by all sorts of people. With me and Henry standing right there beside.'

'Why shouldn't I have done?' Angelica said. 'Why shouldn't you? What are you afraid of?'

'Of him! Addington. Of Oscar Wilde in his cell. I'm afraid of Henry being caught up in it.'

'It is not just Henry,' Angelica said.

Edith glanced at him, and then turned. 'I am afraid for myself, yes. I do not want to be singled out and punished, Angelica. I could not bear it. It would be a waste. I do not want to be an invert if that is what it means. I would rather be only a woman.'

'A woman who loves women.'

Edith glanced back at Henry again. 'Yes,' she said. 'Who has a husband also.'

Angelica curled her lip and locked her hands in their black gloves. 'You must not think we are immune, because the law does not apply to us. Each time inversion is pronounced unnatural, we are condemned too. That's what you understand, isn't it, Henry?' Her gaze swerved to him. 'That it all connects. We must all be free, or none of us is.'

'Angelica, please,' Edith said. 'Do not encourage him to suit yourself.'

'That is what I am not doing,' Angelica said, her voice flat as a knife. 'And Henry can speak for himself,' she added.

'He cannot,' Edith said.

The silence in which he stood was risen up to his neck. It pressed on his throat. Angelica came a little nearer, curving her hands over the brow of the sofa. 'That's right isn't it, Henry?' she said. 'That all of us must be free?'

His silence pressed on his lips. Angelica stared at him. Edith would not look.

'You told Edith that you had a sexual peculiarity of your own,' Angelica said.

Silence was forcing itself between his lips and down his throat, choking him. He breathed fiercely through his nose. He turned his eyes up to the ceiling.

'What is it, Henry?' Angelica said. 'Henry? Tell us.'

Whorls in white plaster, connecting to other whorls. He could not lower his eyes.

'It is not our business,' Edith shouted.

'He is your husband,' Angelica shouted back. 'And I am your wife.'

They drowned in silence together. He lowered his eyes. Angelica was waiting for him.

'Please go home, Henry,' Edith said.

'Yes,' Angelica said. 'We call each other wife. And she is more my wife than yours, Henry.'

'Stop—' Edith moved towards her.

Angelica held up a black hand. 'I'm not sure about either of you,' she said. 'I do not think you understand what you have begun. I'm not sure you understand yourselves – you were brave enough to marry, but only because you made each other feel strong. You presume to show us all the way, but look how reluctant you are, to follow where it leads! Did you understand, Henry, that your book was meant to challenge the law? That you were confronting the law? Mr Addington understands it. He understands that life cannot be lived without confrontation. It is the same for you –' she looked at Edith almost wildly – 'you are forever saying that women must develop their personalities. And yet you wish to wind yours back. True development does not respect comfort.'

Edith laughed. 'Comfort! It is easy for you. You have never done anything. Your father pays your allowance and dares not cut you off, and you live here, and you lecture me and Henry. We must earn for ourselves. Our work is important – it goes beyond our self-conceptions. That is why, since we cannot get out of this awful trial, Henry should talk to Mr Addington and make him swear not to speak again as he did tonight. We cannot afford to take unnecessary risks.'

'There are necessary risks,' Angelica said implacably. 'As Mr Addington understands.'

'Necessary to him, perhaps,' Edith said.

'Why do you dislike him?'

'I do not. I liked him when we spoke tonight.'

Angelica sniffed. 'Then why are you determined to see this trial as a disaster?'

Henry wanted to say, 'Because it is.' And the words came. 'Because it is a disaster,' he said.

'It is an opportunity,' Angelica said.

'That is what Addington thinks,' he said. 'You and he were both wrong before, about publishing the book; it should not have been published so soon, it should not have been published by Owen and it should never have been in Higgs's shop. All of this happened because Addington thought too much about himself, about his own case.'

'How could he not?' Angelica said.

'It has deprived him of his judgement. He seeks to make good his wrongs. You asked me about a peculiarity that I may have. I did not answer; but it is not important, not on its own. It is only relevant in the general, as it relates to the principle. Freedom is the principle, and it is threatened by this trial. I do not see any opportunity in it. The mass of opinion is against us. We are supported only by people of our own stamp. No authorities have come forward to—'

'None of that matters,' Angelica interjected. 'You and Mr Addington can speak the truth. There is so little truth spoken on this subject. You will be believed.'

He thought of Addington's wife, sitting by the Serpentine, a victim to the wind. How she had shuddered, her whole body shaking, when she stood up. 'Addington will tell the truth,' he said. 'That is the problem. His truth is very different from mine. He has lost his check. The prosecution will very likely have found things out about him. He will speak as he did tonight. It will be worse. If facts are presented to him, he will admit to them.'

'And so he will drag you down with him,' Edith said, appalled. 'You will be made to speak and answer questions, in the wake of him, or before him, when all the while he is planning his martyrdom.'

'He has never considered me. He does not consider himself.'

'You must plead with him,' Edith said.

'It would be no use. Even if he moderated – if they have discovered his secrets, they will bring them out. They will know about the separation from his wife. That will go to confirm everything else.'

'There is Mr Higgs,' Edith said. Her voice was quiet. 'He will end in prison.'

Henry pictured Mrs Higgs.

'What can be done?' Edith said.

'I can't bear this,' Angelica snapped. 'You are such dreadful cowards.'

Edith turned to her. 'It is a man's life, Angelica.'

'It is all supposition, everything you say,' she protested. 'I can't bear it. Henry – it is too late to do anything other than tell the truth. Please. You must try it.' She had come round the corner of the sofa and was now nearer him than Edith was. The light shifted on her face, sharpening its urgent expression. Response welled in him, a painful instinct to satisfy her.

Edith cut in. 'Angelica, we must save Mr Addington from himself.'

'You will not save him,' she said, whipping round. 'You will spoil his chance.'

'There is no chance,' Edith said. 'That is what Henry is saying.'

Angelica's eyes darted. 'You are joining forces against me.'

'We are not,' Edith said.

'Henry,' Angelica said, coming closer still, so he could smell her perfume, tired and dirtied by the restaurant. 'We must go on. It is too late for anything else.'

He would not look at her face. She stayed there, waiting, the hazed shape of her like a pressure behind his eyelids, until, furiously, she was gone. He saw her stalking away to her room, into the dark unlit parts of the flat. From the dark came the sound of a door closing.

Edith was watching him. 'What can be done?' she said, quietly but insistently.

'I do not want to think of it.'

'You must.'

He sat in one of the armchairs, exhausted. Edith lit more lamps, each one appearing suspended in the windowpanes, a planet. Silence emanated from Angelica's room. Henry put his hands lengthways over his ears and closed his eyes, tried to let his thoughts flow out to new solutions, but they were dammed, as he well knew, in one place. Occasionally in the past weeks there had been a trickling advance in a new direction, but he was always returned to this same spot.

He went for some paper from the sideboard, laid it on the dining table and began to write a letter to Addington. Edith came over. When he was done she picked it up to read; meanwhile he started a new page, and wrote an identical letter to Higgs, excepting for one further sentence. After signing he put the pen down and, looking at what he had written, said, 'Higgs will not continue once he receives this. He will look to make an agreement with the prosecution. We will be spared the trial.'

'If he does not?' They were speaking in low voices, almost at a whisper, conscious of Angelica in her room.

'I observed him tonight, and his wife. I am sure that he will. But if he chooses to persist, I will be free of all guilt.'

'No,' Edith said. 'The guilt will be worse.'

He placed two fingers on the pen and rolled it on the table.

'The book will be banned,' she said.

'You asked what could be done,' he said with impatience, leaving the pen rocking. 'It will be banned anyhow.' His voice broke on the last words.

Edith put both his letters into envelopes and set them in front of him. 'Write the addresses,' she said. Afterwards, she put them inside her clothes. 'I will post them. In case you should change your mind.'

He nodded.

'And I will tell Angelica once they are sent,' she said.

He nodded again.

She frowned at him. 'Go home, dear boy.'

Under her supervision, he put on his coat and hat – there was something doomed about the gestures. Then she came with him to the door. As he was about to open it, she lightly touched his sleeve. 'Henry,' she said, 'what is it? Your peculiarity?'

He told her. Outside, the night air consoled, but he did not regard it.

XXXV

John opened his eyes on shallow morning light and shut them, pressing the lids tenderly with his fingers. His head ached. He was in his own bedroom; now that Catherine had left, and Susan sprung her blackmail, he and Frank no longer shared a bed even for some hours of the night. Though of course they were still suspicious enough: two men alone in the big house, with the mistress gone; taking meals together, spending time behind closed doors. The servants fulfilled their duties but carried about with them – perhaps it was John's imagination – an atmosphere of sublimated defiance, traitorous supervision, as though they were waiting on usurpers, all the while hoping, perhaps working, for a restoration. It was to destroy this impression, of the house anticipating Catherine's return, that John had asked for it to be packed up, though the coming of the new owners was some weeks away. There had been several days of lifting, shifting, folding and stowing. Already the house felt hollowed out; already it was amplifying sounds and emotions, which seemed to stop and lodge in its corners.

When he returned from the Higgs dinner last night, John had described it to Frank without mentioning his speech. It had felt, the speech, like an injury he didn't want fussed over – an honourable hurt, to be privately, proudfully tended. Now he listened to his voice again, saw the faces, tilted the picture this way and that. He really hadn't intended to speak. It was perhaps the wine he had drunk during the other speeches, or the unanticipated effect of the speeches themselves, the sense they had given him of being included in a community of feeling; more delicately, the sense of being trusted, of being, in some odd fashion, respectable. When he'd got up from his seat, he hadn't known what he was about to say. But on beginning, seeing all those faces turn and open to him, he'd accepted their abandon of passivity. And with that acceptance came the words, the phrases and arguments, formed silently in his mind over decades, drip by drip, suddenly revealed like stalactites in the pitch dark of a cave. He watched the faces of his audience, felt them in his command, and then – then he had gone deep into that dark part of himself, seen only words and phrases, dazzled by their quantity, the shapes they took, their cutting clarity. When he came out again, he saw that something had changed: that his listeners were no longer so passive, that they were unsure. It was too late. He must continue speaking: he must make them understand. His voice had begun to shake, he had to force his mouth around the words. The silence became something terrible that he must fill, that he must prop up with words. He had glimpsed Ellis and his expression of pained concentration, had become aware of Higgs's stillness. He must write to them both today, begging pardon if he'd indulged himself. He hadn't managed to speak to either afterwards.

There were some people who had spoken to him, who had been kind, but not many. He had embarrassed them, inevitably. It was the principle they cared for. Free speech. Not many of them cared for the subject. He knew this; it was why, in the end, he spoke as he did. But they had been embarrassed. It was what it would be like, he perceived, to be known as an invert, if the law was ever changed – free from the threat of imprisonment, but, at best, a source of embarrassment, difficulty. Ellis's friend had been sympathetic. Miss Britell. He recalled the brandished pride with which she had said, 'I am an invert.' She was not really Ellis's friend, though; she was his wife's. Mrs Ellis: a small, boyish little woman, clever and direct, who looked furious when Miss Britell made her declaration, interrupting and trying to give a signal. There hadn't been time to consider it, but of course it explained something about Ellis, if his wife was an invert. The odd, lonely quality of his interest in the subject; the something dogged about it, as if he were fulfilling a duty. They made an interesting trio, Ellis and his wife and Miss Britell, walking round together. He was reminded of siblings: the awkward forced unity, the awkwardness never quite covering the mutual dependence. Though as they left they had seemed all at odds with one another.

The door handle turned and Frank slipped into the room in his shirt-sleeves and socks. 'I thought it couldn't hurt for a moment,' he said, getting under the cover, fitting John's thigh between his knees. Then there was a noise in the corridor and Frank lifted his head. They listened to the sound of footsteps. 'Did you shut your door?' John whispered.

Frank nodded. The footsteps receded, came back, and receded again. 'I can't wait to be gone from here,' Frank said at length.

'It's not long now.'

Frank released John's thigh, rolling onto his back. 'We may end somewhere worse.'

'We won't.'

'So you say.' He propped himself on his elbows and listened. 'That bitch,' he said. 'She was probably come to spy.'

'She has given up spying. Otherwise, I will ask myself what I am paying for.' John's chest tightened on the joke.

Frank didn't laugh. 'I'll go back to dressing,' he said, and left.

John's headache recollected itself. He washed at the basin and put on his dressing gown, parted the curtain and peered at Friday. Six days before the trial. He wondered if Catherine was counting. Poor Frank.

He thought again that he should ask him if he wanted to leave London, leave the country even, so that he was safe from harm. Except the possibility must have occurred to Frank already, and he was still here. Anyhow, John could not ask. He faced his eye to the placid street. The daylight was strained weakly through cloud. He imagined prison, thought what Oscar Wilde would give to stand at a window in his own home and look down idly at the street. Though this was no longer really John's home. Loss tunnelled under him, and he felt as though he were looking at a memory, stranded above it. A man smoking a cigarette walked by on the pavement and looked up.

Dressed and downstairs, he decided he did not want breakfast – he was too restless, and the memory of last night's meal sat too heavily. Frank had gone out. John ordered coffee to be brought to him in the drawing room, where he could read the newspapers and the post. The room was mainly packed away. The sofa and the armchairs, and the dining table beyond the folding doors, formed islands on a waste of carpet. The walls were bare; the bookcases were removed; there were no photographs or flowers. The chandelier hung in icy splendour, and the clock on the mantelpiece ticked indignantly. John was still sitting there when the late-morning post came. He saw Ellis's handwriting on one envelope and opened it first.

My dear Addington,

I find that I cannot face the prospect of defending our book in court. Please do not think that I repent of any of our arguments or wish it to be thought that I do. I continue to earnestly hope that we shall win the case. I am simply unfit for controversy, as I should perhaps have anticipated long ago. I feel my weakness severely.

I have written to Higgs to this effect. Please forgive my cowardice, and believe me Yours very sincerely,
Henry Ellis

He sat back on the sofa and stared. Then he reread the letter and then sat back. His mind chased between possibilities while in the background, like the noise of a machine, his anger and humiliation dinned. He stood, looking for himself in the mirror over the mantelpiece, but saw only a vague indication of its shape on the wall. He wheeled round. It was as though he'd dreamed the room into a useless unfamiliarity. But there was Frank through the window, coming up the path. He met him at the door and gave him the letter as he was stamping his feet on the mat.

'What's this?'

John went upstairs to his study, numb. Frank followed, still in his hat and coat, the letter in his hand. Inside the room, he put down his hat, pushed the door shut, and leaned against it as he read. Beyond him, beyond the letter and the door, could be heard the sounds of the house being dismantled.

Frank looked up. 'I'm glad,' he said. He even smiled.

'You're glad,' John said coldly.

'I am.' He seized his moustache between thumb and forefinger. 'He's taken it out of your hands, hasn't he?'

'No.'

'He has. You'd lose for certain if you went ahead without Ellis. Mr Higgs isn't a fool.'

'Higgs is a man of principle.'

Frank smirked. 'I like to think I'm a man of principle, but I'm not a fool, and neither's Mr Higgs.'

'I should never have trusted Ellis. I should have done this on my own.'

'Maybe he's not comfortable letting a man be put away for the sake of a book.'

'I will make him retract it,' John said. He saw how easy it would be.

Frank's face dropped. 'You mustn't, John.'

'I will go and see him now. This will be corrected by the afternoon.'

Frank came forward and took firm hold of his wrist. 'It's a blessing,' he said. 'It's been taken out of your hands, John. If Higgs makes a deal, we're safe. If they've got anything on us, they'll put it in a drawer, won't they? Won't they? They won't bother with the fuss. All this hanging round our necks, it'll be gone.'

'The book will be banned. They will destroy every copy.'

'It would likely have happened anyhow – least we'll stay out of it.'

John shook his wrist free. 'I did not do this so that we could go into obscurity, to some out-of-the-way corner. The author and his secretary. How can you wish it?'

Frank sighed. 'You said if the book helped a handful of people you'd be happy. A handful got sold. We wouldn't be any freer, would we, if Higgs got off. The law wouldn't change on his account.'

'It would be the beginning. Without this, there's nothing. Oscar Wilde will be all of us.'

'I'm scared of prison,' Frank said, grabbing hold of his wrist again. 'I grew up scared of it. I know blokes that went in. You've never worked like they'll make you work, John. They hate sods. Let Ellis and Higgs make the decisions. If they want out of it, let them.'

'I won't be their captive,' John said. Frank's fingernails were digging. 'If I believed this trial was hopeless, I would not risk it. But it is not. We may succeed.'

Frank stepped away. 'They *know*,' he hissed. 'The law. There's no way they've not found out somehow, from someone. You said you won't deny it.'

'I will not.'

Frank looked at him despairingly. 'You're dooming me.'

'They may not come for you.'

'And then where'll I be?' Frank spread his right hand, showing clean fingertips. 'I'm spoiled for work. You've made someone else of me.' He stared at John a moment, then walked stiffly over to his hat.

'Where are you going?'

He crammed the hat onto his head. 'To see Mother. I'd like to see her a last time. She'll be too sick for visiting prison, and she'll be dead before I'm out again.'

He slammed the door. John heard him clatter down the stairs and go out. Into the succeeding quiet came the sound of a crate being dragged over floorboards. He pinched the bridge of his nose, breathed deeply, then went to his desk and wrote a letter to Higgs.

Dear Mr Higgs,

Mr Ellis has given me reason to believe that you will have received a letter this morning, stating his new intentions with regard to the trial. I kindly ask you to pay it no notice. It is an attack of nerves. I plan to speak with him shortly, and will come to you directly after. Please be at home this afternoon.

Yours very sincerely,

J. Addington

He sent Lewis out to post it, and to fetch a cab. When it arrived, he asked to go to Victoria. The roads were bright with morning traffic, brisk and chattering; the greyness of the day was cut by reins and whips, hats and women's dresses. For a time, they followed behind an omnibus and John tried to concentrate on reading the advertisements while a small girl on the top deck slitted her eyes at him.

At Victoria, vehicles and people dispersed themselves like insects, as though the station were a great stone that had been lifted from them. Stalls made fixed points in the scurry, like insects long since squashed. The cab pulled up by a hot-potato man, who watched John as he got out, waving one of his wares encouragingly. John ignored him. Inside, he bought a ticket to Brixton and boarded the next train. Images – listening faces, Frank cramming on his hat, Ellis, Higgs – moved consecutively through his mind as the window showed the city staggering down to the penny-coloured river, coming back up on the other side sparser, first flecked and then strung with green. The houses gradually turned inward, presenting their backs in long lines of comfortable indifference. The sky acquired a purged look. He looked at it and at the backs of the houses, and failed to imagine him and Frank living here. I must drag Ellis out of this place, he thought. Here is where courage dies.

Ellis's address turned out to be only a few minutes' walk from Brixton station – a mansion block on a featureless street. His flat was on the second floor; John climbed the stairs and knocked. The door opened guardedly, with Ellis keeping as much of himself behind it as possible. When he saw John, he winced.

'What is this, Henry? Let me in.'

Ellis retreated into a small sitting room, cramped with books and stacks of paper. There was a desk, and a murky kitchen visible through a door; the room smelled of frying, like Ellis's clothes. John stopped behind a chair. Ellis stood by the window; his shirt was open and showed his clavicles resting under white hairless skin. He asked nervously if John would like tea.

'No, thank you.' He attempted to hold Ellis's eye, which was still trying to escape into the kitchen. 'Why would you write that letter, Henry?'

Ellis would not look at him. 'Have you seen Higgs?' he said.

'No, not yet. Why did you write the letter? You said you hoped we would still win the case.'

'I do.'

'But you must see that your decision makes it far less likely. The prosecution will make hay with it. Higgs may reconsider his position.'

Ellis touched his forehead. 'I'm sure he will not. As long as you and he make the defence, I am confident all will be well.'

'I have told him you will retract your letter.'

Ellis looked at him for half a moment. 'I cannot retract it.'

John wanted to hit him. He said, 'Your wife gave an excellent speech last night. She will surely be a support to you.'

'My wife lectures. It is her business to speak.' Ellis coughed, and John saw the swell of his tongue go round his teeth.

'Does Miss Britell know of your decision?'

Ellis raised his eyebrows. 'She may by now.'

'She will be very disappointed that you have chosen to do something so injurious to our cause.'

'It is a pity she did not write the book.'

'You did, Henry. You owe it a defence.'

'How is your wife?' Ellis said abruptly.

'She is well. I am grateful for her sympathy.' He waited to see if Ellis would ask anything else. Then he said, 'Henry, you are committing an error. You are failing your friends, failing to live up to your ideals. The trial will be uncomfortable, I know, but it will be justified by the result.' Ellis was staring at the floor. John studied him. 'You think that we will lose,' he essayed. 'You are convinced.'

'No.'

'Well, what is it? I do not accept shyness as a reason. You have always been shy.'

'But that is it.'

John put more force into his voice. 'Henry, you are deserting us. I am not certain that Higgs will continue in your absence. Our work will be for nothing.'

Ellis looked at a point over John's shoulder. He seemed as though he might be about to cry. 'Please,' he whined.

John was filled with disgust: for Ellis, and for this dirty room he had been forced to beg in. Anger leapt in his voice, carried it to a place of conviction. 'If we must do without you, so be it. Higgs is a man of principle – we shall face this together. And when we succeed, we will remember that you made ours a harder, lonelier path. The world will remember it.'

Ellis blinked at the spot over John's shoulder. John, after a slight hesitation, turned and walked out, charging the silence behind him with shame and disgrace.

On the street he looked to see if Ellis was at his window, but he was not. He strode to the station and boarded a train back to the city – the houses tumbling out of their privacy, cluttering and decaying; the green withering; the sky muddying – and disembarked at Holborn Viaduct. He walked downhill from the station, the grinding traffic long since past its morning freshness: it was as though the day itself had been driven over too many times and was reduced to enduring the hours as they came. His legs took him swiftly to John Street, to the shabby house on the corner where Higgs lived. He knocked sharply on the door and then knocked again – the sound was swallowed by the wood. He came off the step and looked up at what had been Frank's windows. Pieces of the day held on the glass, with darkness pooled behind. He wondered if Higgs had received his letter. It was now after three o'clock. He gazed down the street: children were playing at the bottom. Hunger flitted in his stomach. Had Higgs received his letter? If he hadn't, where could he be, to not receive it? Might he have got Ellis's letter and immediately fled, him and his wife? John envisaged standing here for hours, the gradual fastening of disillusion. He mastered himself. They must have gone out briefly. He would wait.

After nearly an hour, when he was faint from smoking cigarettes, he perceived Mr and Mrs Higgs approaching. They were walking a little apart; neither showed any sign of recognising him until they were practically at the house. Higgs looked shy. 'Mr Addington,' he said, holding out his hand. 'My apologies. I got your letter, but I'm afraid we already had an obligation.'

'Please don't worry,' John said, raising his hat: 'Mrs Higgs.'

She inclined her head: 'Good afternoon.'

'Please come in,' Higgs said, opening the door with rapidity.

They went into the dark hallway, the stairs opposite leading to Frank's old quarters. Higgs opened the door into the sitting room. Shelves had been built against every wall up to the ceiling, each filled with books, so that it looked as though someone had set up home in the corner of a library. The smell was of a library: paper and must and hard effort. 'You see it, Mr Addington,' Higgs said. 'Our little enterprise.' He gestured to a chair. 'Please sit. Rhoda will fetch us some tea.'

Mrs Higgs went out and they sat. Higgs squeezed his hands together and licked his lips. His blue eyes were very distinct. 'So,' he said, 'you've been to see Mr Ellis already. We were most surprised to get his letter.'

'I've seen him.' John had decided he would be entirely honest. 'I'm afraid he is insisting on his decision. But we should not give it much mind. If he treats us so lightly, we are better off without him. The case is so weak that—'

'We aren't fools,' Mrs Higgs said, entering with a tray supporting some pink china and putting it joltingly down. 'My husband faces prison. Your book's nothing to do with him, rightly considered, but it's him that's in the dock. And now you're telling us to keep on, when your friend won't, and he wrote it. When it's your speech last night which will have frighted him off. I'll tell you something, it frighted us too.'

She seemed to hate him. He regretted his awful confidence at the dinner. 'I did not mean to frighten anyone,' he said.

'You lost your head,' she said. 'We know what you are. Just like we knew what Mr Feaver was. We don't care neither. But you can't go waving it around.'

'I understand,' he said, feeling his face colour. 'I will be careful. You mustn't – I do not think my speech has anything to do with Mr Ellis's decision. He is afflicted by a terrible shyness. His decision is regrettable. However, it should not be allowed to dent our confidence.' He turned to Higgs. 'I am sure you agree – the principle of free speech. You said last night, how proud you are to be defending it.'

Higgs's mouth was trembling with eagerness to speak. 'It's a great principle,' he said. 'Course it is. But if Mr Ellis won't defend it, I'm not so certain, being quite honest, whether it'll prevail in the court. Which –' he turned his hands out in supplicancy – 'gives me to thinking I might best serve it a different way, naturally being more use as a free man.' As he finished, they became aware of the screeching of the kettle on the stove. 'For God's sake, Rhoda,' he snapped.

Mrs Higgs went out; the kettle attained a further agonising pitch and then subsided.

'I fail to see how anything but a robust defence will serve the cause,' John said.

Mrs Higgs came back into the room empty-handed. 'Well,' Higgs said, 'without Mr Ellis, him being the medical man, the jury might not see the free speech aspect so much – they might view it all as bearing on the question of – of sodomy. They might think I'm involved in some way, that I need punishing. People don't always make the proper distinctions.'

John drew himself up. Mrs Higgs's stare was disconcerting. He focused on her husband, tried to impose on him. 'I cannot see what it is you want to do,' he said, putting on an air of bafflement.

Higgs became alarmingly impatient. 'Oh come off it, will you? Mr Ellis said in his letter, about your wife. She's gone, hasn't she?'

John's voice struggled through a blackness of surprise. 'Ellis wrote about my wife?'

'He did. He said the prosecutors likely know everything – that likely they know other things as well. Things that'll make your evidence worse than worthless. So we've decided I'll plead guilty,' Higgs rattled on, not giving John chance to recover. 'We went to see my counsel – that's where we were just now. He thinks if I plead guilty and give assurances, I'll get off with a fine. A big one, but the committee will help me pay it – they'll understand what choice I was left with.' He stopped to judge John's face. 'I'm sorry for your book, Mr Addington. I am. Only I can't be expected to risk my life for it.'

John stared at the empty cups on the tray. 'I will go back to Ellis,' he said. 'Please do not take another step. I will make him see, I promise you.'

Higgs eyed him sympathetically. 'I think perhaps it's too late. It's beyond that now.'

'No. No it is not. Thank you –' he nodded at Mrs Higgs. 'Please wait to hear from me again.'

'We'll do no such thing,' Mrs Higgs said. 'We aren't fools.'

He met her look, hate for hate. 'I will write,' he said.

Higgs stood. 'Thank you for coming.' He extended his hand. 'I know I'm a coward in a way. I do know it, Mr Addington.'

Returning to the station, John stopped at a drinking fountain. The water was cold and went coldly into his body, hollow as a bucket. Traffic ran ceaselessly past. The sky was wadding to a heavier grey. It was coming up to five. The station lights were throwing on the pavement, on hats and shoulders greasy with the afternoon. His legs took him on board another train for Brixton. The compartment was full: three men and two women besides him. They all negotiated their knees. He was pressed close to the window, against his reflection. The train steamed out and his face floated over the darkening river, lights beginning to bubble on the water; over the green spaces, draining colour; along the backs of the houses, which looked now like refugees from the city, camped on the road as night approached. At each stop, his face juddered to a rest, confronted by many moving others on the platform, and then was sped away.

He got out at Brixton again, his legs light and impersonal, as though they were trying to step away from his body. The platform was busy: he brushed coats, dresses, satchels, canes, umbrellas. There was another hot-potato man. The road thundered outside. He walked to Ellis's street, smoking. The sky was three shades darker, a closed oyster. A light showed at the window.

When Ellis opened the door, his eyes widened in horror. 'Why are you here?'

'I went to see Higgs.'

Ellis's face twitched. John followed him into the sitting room. There were sheets of well-inked paper on the desk, weighted by a pen. In the window the evening light looked bluer, oceanic; the buildings opposite were washed in it. Cool air entered where the sash was lifted. They resumed their positions from the morning, John behind the chair and Ellis by the window. Ellis coughed, keeping his hand over his mouth.

'Higgs wishes to settle,' John said. 'He will plead guilty. Our book will be obliterated without a word said in its defence. And this is what you wanted, isn't it, Henry? You knew, writing your letter, that Higgs would do this. Everything you said a few hours ago was a lie. How did you know about my wife? For God's sake, look at me.'

Ellis jerked his head up. 'I spoke with her.'

'When?'

'It was after our meeting with Higgs. She stopped me in the street. She told me that you had separated. Which you have never told me. You lied to me about it just today.' Ellis still wouldn't look at him directly. 'She told me I must save you from yourself.'

Tears started in John's eyes. 'I do not need saving,' he said, a rawness at the back of his throat. 'They may have no proof against me.'

'But they might.'

'That is my risk.'

'It is not only yours,' Ellis said in a high exasperated voice. 'There is Higgs, and me. If you have an impulse to suicide, we need not be brought into it. I did not want to publish the book, remember. You did not care about what I wanted. It was the same for your wife.'

'This is Catherine's revenge on me,' John said from his throat. 'She wishes to deny me my opportunity.'

Ellis looked startled. 'It did not strike me that way. I am sure she was thinking only of your interests.'

'I no longer have interests,' John said. 'Their price is too high. My wife saw this before I did, but clearly she could not see everything. I am an invert who has accepted his nature after a long struggle – but has accepted it at last. It is a fresh torment now, to carry on lying, to wear my old mask, to tolerate another minute of unhappiness. It is not living. I do not regret what has happened to my marriage, any more than I could regret wringing the neck of an animal halfway dead. And I cannot regret forcing you on, Henry, otherwise you would have left me where I am. So do not think you are saving me. You are not. The trial may save me. But if you keep with your decision, you will force me into a prison far worse than any the law controls.'

'This is what frightens us,' Ellis said. 'You are too absolute.'

'I have heard that before. I have an old friend, to whom I told the truth about myself when we were students. For years he went on arguing against me in terms of utility: how would self-candour tend to better results for my happiness, my family's, the world's? I listened to him too long, balancing the one thing against all the others. Now I understand that life is absolute. It is the only interest. The friend I speak of is an invert, yet he has not acted on his feelings, not once. He is a spiritualist; it distresses him that I will not entertain the possibility of an afterlife. It is the anticipation of a moral accounting that justifies all his niceties, his renunciations. Do you believe in heaven, Henry, or in spirits?'

'I believe in the future. In the New Life: in working towards it, even if one never sees it.' Ellis shot a direct glance. 'You are too personal.'

'And yet I have done none of this to obtain a purely personal freedom. I have tried to better my country. I have thought of thousands of others.'

'You have been reckless, out of personal need.' Ellis's voice was shaky. 'You prefer destruction to temporary disappointment.'

'Temporary on what scale?'

'We cannot know – it cannot be seen.'

'That is no answer, Henry. You should speak to your friend Miss Britell. She has an understanding of personal need. As does your wife, if I am not mistaken.'

There was a long silence. John took out his cigarette case and his matches, feeling the coolness of the air on his fingertips.

'They have nothing to do with me,' Ellis said.

'How can that be so?'

Ellis sighed. 'They have each other. I am an adjunct. I do not pry.'

'When did you first know about your wife?'

'Before we were married. Only, I did not understand quite what it would mean.'

'You did not foresee Miss Britell.'

'No.'

'It must have to do with your choosing this subject?'

'My wife believes that it does.'

'Do you agree?'

'I have always been interested in the subject of sex.'

'You said that before. And yet you chose to write on this aspect.'

'Yes, but I mean to deal with the whole. This book was only intended for a start.' Ellis glanced at his desk. 'I will be unable to continue if you or Higgs are on my conscience. I require serenity.'

'You do not require anything else?'

'I have no great expectations of happiness for myself. Mostly, I should like just to be left alone. To be invisible.'

Finishing his cigarette, John felt thinned out, as though he were a thing of smoke, extending on the air. 'I wish I knew how it feels,' he said, 'to be left alone. All my life, even in my deepest privacy, I have felt watched. All my life, there has been the fear of being seen, noticed, caught. It has never gone away.' He was trying to extend to Ellis, to absorb him. 'If you insist on doing this, you are taking away my chance. To say that *I see them*. I will have to continue telling lies, keeping secrets. You will have your peace and I will have my unpeace.' He waited. 'You are already invisible, Henry. You pass through the world unheeded. It is I who have to hide.'

Ellis said nothing. Then: 'The book could still be published in translation. Or we might try America. In the future—'

'I do not give a damn for the future,' John spat. 'Not a damn. You must allow me to speak in court.'

Ellis said nothing.

'I must speak, Henry. Please. I have sacrificed everything. I must—'

'No!' Ellis burst out. 'I will not do it. I will not.'

John's legs were trembling. It was almost totally dark beyond the window. Ellis pushed down the sash. It was only then, when the mutter of the streets was guillotined, that John realised it had been going on. Ellis turned back. 'What of Mr Feaver?' he said.

'What of him?'

'What does he want?'

'He does not want the trial. He wants to be left alone.'

'You have done all this in spite of him?'

John's mouth was parched. The trembling in his legs was violent. Something black and sinuous slid across his vision, soft and deep. He attempted to step forward, throwing a hand out onto the back of the chair. 'I need to sit,' he said indistinctly. He came carefully round the arm of the chair and sank into it. He was aware of Ellis approaching.

His legs pricked and jumped as though the chair were scalding hot. He closed his eyes. Blood swam into his ears, in and out.

He opened his eyes. Ellis was looking at him. 'What is it?'

'I haven't eaten.'

Ellis drew back. 'What would you like?'

John closed his eyes again. 'A hot potato,' he said.

XXXVI

'I haven't got a potato.' Henry looked about him for assistance, or cor-
roboration, as though there might be someone in the room he'd
forgotten about. 'I could go out for one.'

'No,' Addington said wearily, his eyes still shut. 'Anything.'

Henry went into the kitchen and cut the last slices of a meat pie. He
brought them out on a plate and handed it to Addington, who inched
himself up in the chair, the plate tipping in his hands. While he ate –
quickly, bits of pastry scattering over his beard – Henry watched
nervously from a distance, worried that at any moment Addington
might start up again with his insistence, his confessions and demands.
Addington was similar to his wife, Catherine, in that way, in the suffocating burden of intimacy each had heaved on him. The first visit,
several hours ago, had been bad enough, but he'd survived it – opening
the door to Addington a second time had felt like letting a murderer
back into the house. Though really it was Henry who was the murderer. Addington finished his meal, set down the plate, and stared
blindly. He looked now like Henry's destined victim: weakened, incapable of struggle. With the window closed the room was thick with his

presence, with their spent conversation, as though the things they'd said were stagnating in it and this was what Addington could see: the decay of their hopes. His face expressed a pure, dazed sadness, repudiated innocence. And yet he looked old.

Eventually, Addington started to brush the crumbs from his beard, plucking them from his lap and dropping them onto his plate. When he was finished, he raised himself and moved laboriously across the room. Henry remained where he was. Addington picked up his hat and turned with it held in both hands. 'About Frank – you must understand, all this was not in spite of him. It is because of him.'

Henry said, 'Yes,' though he didn't understand, and Addington left.

Henry stood in the room a while. Then he picked up the plate and took it into the kitchen to wash. The crumbs and flakes of pie became slimy in the sink. He went back into the sitting room and opened the window again. Cool air breathed gently in, and he leaned against the frame. Edith had written, not long before Addington came the second time, to say that she hadn't told Angelica yet about the letters, but she would tonight, and could he call tomorrow? Leaving the window, he wrote a reply, describing what had happened, and went to post it so that it would arrive early in the morning.

Outside, the evening was vastly calm, the encompassing all of London more intimation than sound. A tentative shiver of happiness ran over him. The street, pattered with deep shadow, had the smooth, still look of a stretch of river flowing under darkness, its reason made mysterious. At its end Henry found only the familiar post-box, except – except there was Addington: a little distance away, caught in the ambit of a street lamp, ringed by shadow, walking in the direction of the station so slowly, with such grave and aching deliberation, that the whole world might have been dragging on his every step.

Henry saw and could not look, and fled back down the street, back to where his happiness had briefly been.

*

The next day, he found Edith pallid and sleepless-looking. 'Angelica's gone,' she said flatly, as he came in.

'Because of the letters? Where?'

'Norfolk, of course.'

'Because of the letters?'

Edith threw herself down on the sofa. The room had a tired, ill-used feel to it. 'Yes, the letters. You know how she's been about the trial. It was awful. She called me all sorts of names. And you, obviously.'

'Did she?'

Edith tousled her hair. 'I don't want to talk about it for a minute. How are you? We have both been through the mill.'

He sat, bringing his hands tightly together. 'I wrote to Higgs this morning, saying that he should pay no attention to whatever Addington had said, that I hadn't changed my mind.'

'Good for you, Henry. It will soon be over then.'

He looked at his hands. 'I feel I have done something terrible.'

'You have.' He raised his eyes to her. 'There's no escaping it,' she said. 'Tell it all to me properly.'

He told her, and about his final sight of Addington.

'Poor man,' Edith said. 'Angelica was like that. Utterly defeated-seeming, like it was the end of her life. But it isn't. Not even for him.'

'Was it truly awful for you, last night?'

Her mouth slid sideways. 'Yes.' She sucked in breath. 'Yes, it was awful.'

'She'll come back, won't she?' Henry said.

Edith bit her nail. 'Angelica is so difficult.'

'But she will?'

Edith sighed. 'I think so.' She looked quickly at him. 'When you asked her to come back before – it was for you, as well as for me, wasn't it? You wanted us both.'

'Yes.'

'Do you love her a little, Henry?'

There was something so frank in her look, in her tone as she said it, that this felt like one of those moments of old, when they would meet eagerly in some shared perception, like two trickles of water joining on a windowpane. 'A little,' he said.

'That's good I think. That you should be able to feel for her as I do.' She took his hand and held it for a long time. Quiet penetrated the room, like grace. Then it was broken. 'In spite of everything,' she said, withdrawing her hand, 'I have found myself dwelling on what you told me the other night. About your peculiarity.'

Ambushed, he shrank back, flattening himself against the last defending wall of his personality. 'Do you think less of me?' he forced himself to say.

'I am shocked, certainly. I never would have thought—'

'No.'

There was an embarrassed pause. Edith made another effort. 'What is it, Henry? I mean, why is it?'

'I don't know.' He felt the wall breaking up. 'I cannot explain it yet.'

'Yet?'

'It is the sort of thing I should like to be able to explain.'

Edith shifted on the sofa. 'You have not asked anyone ever?'

'Asked anyone?'

She became embarrassed. 'It doesn't matter.'

'No, I see. I have never even – you are the first person I have told.'

'It is a relief,' she said musingly. 'To know that it was perhaps not all my fault. Our honeymoon night.'

'I did not mean for you to think it was.'

'No.'

'I would like to go back there,' he said, seeing in his mind the tree and the wall. 'To the cottage in Norfolk, as we planned. Do you remember we planned to, after you'd finished your lectures?'

Her face showed that she did not, but nevertheless she smiled. 'Yes, we should.' Then the idea seemed to strike another part of her brain. 'We should go,' she said, 'before the trial, don't you think? If it's available? Would you like it?'

'I would.'

'I'll find the agent's address.'

As she sprang to her feet, he said, 'Angelica will be nearby. If we are there, will you tell her?'

She smiled. 'Perhaps.'

Later, she said to him: 'I did mean it, when I talked about finding you someone. Someone who will understand.'

*

At ten o'clock on Tuesday, two days before the trial, Henry and Edith boarded a train to Norfolk. Higgs had written to say that he'd instructed his lawyer to enter a guilty plea, in return for no imprisonment – the Free Press Defence Committee had agreed to pay the fine. There had been nothing at all from Addington. The train burned on and on, devouring the landscape, opening up great distances behind.

XXXVII

They were waiting, sitting on a bench in a small bleak room at the Old Bailey. Frank offered John a cigarette but he shook his head. Shortly, Frank's smoke layered up towards the ceiling. Vague conversation and hard, articulate footsteps could be heard outside on the hallway. Shadows bobbed past the squares of blurred glass in the door. The courtroom was close by. John uncrossed and recrossed his legs: the one that had been suspended was clotted with feeling, or absence of feeling. Frank finished his cigarette. His hair was fallen slightly out of its style, a few strands loose on his forehead. He pried them back with a finger. 'Can't be long,' he said.

It was possible, merely possible, merely, that at the last moment Higgs might change his mind and plead innocent. Or that the judge might decide to have the trial regardless of a guilty plea. That was why they were sitting here. The merest possibility, like the wink of light on the pavement that for a second promises treasure, which you know, more surely with each advancing step, is just some sorry fragment – but still, you must stoop and look. John was no longer allowing himself to think. He was tensed in the pure present, existing only in the waiting, the advance. When Frank started another cigarette, this time he

362

accepted the one that was offered. Their smoke slowly layered. After another twenty minutes, footsteps stuttered and stopped at the door, a shadow strengthening against the glass. Mr Haslam, John's lawyer, came in, wearing a look that reminded John of his father greeting patients. They stood.

'Gentlemen,' he said, and then, turning to John, 'It has gone as expected. The judge accepted Mr Higgs's plea, and set a £100 fine, with some conditions. As you know, the result is that the book has been found obscene and will be everywhere destroyed.' He folded his top lip over his bottom. 'My clerk took down the judge's summation, if you would like to hear it.'

'No, thank you,' John said.

'Very well.' He looked between them. 'You are of course free to leave. I can escort you—'

'No, thank you.'

'Of course.'

Haslam left.

'That's that then,' Frank said. His nose twitched.

John held out a hand to him.

Frank's eyes flicked to the door and he touched his moustache. 'Let's get home,' he said. 'Let's not be here another minute.'

They were collecting their things when Miss Britell thrust into the room, dressed in dark orange, looking like Italy. 'I hoped I would still find you,' she said relievedly. 'You must be Mr Feaver. Mr Addington, I'm so sorry.'

'This is Miss Britell,' he said to Frank. 'She is a friend of Mr and Mrs Ellis.'

'More's the pity,' she said. 'I was in the public gallery. I wanted to see it, though at first they were refusing to admit women on grounds of decency – we had to make a fuss before they did. And after all, it was hardly anything. What there was, I wish I hadn't seen. Higgs looking stupid. The judge was hideous. He said to Higgs, "You may have been gulled into thinking this was a scientific book, but anyone with a head on his shoulders could see it was a sham, entered into to sell a filthy publication." He made him swear to resign from the Legitimation League and give up his magazine.'

'I did not want to know,' John said.

'You'd have found out soon enough,' Frank said.

'I'm sorry,' said Miss Britell. 'It made me so angry, I didn't think.'

'It's all right,' Frank said.

She lit a cigarette. 'I wanted to tell you, Mr Addington, that I shall never forget the speech you made. Never in my life, I promise you. I've always thought yours and Henry's book the most wonderful thing. Whatever you decide to do now, I would like to help in any way that I can. I could translate – I know German. Or I could – I know I said this before – I could gather cases of woman inverts, my own included. I do think it is needed.' She breathed out smoke uncertainly. 'Perhaps you have a new plan. Perhaps you have not made up your mind yet.'

'Where is Henry?' John said.

'In Brixton, I assume. Hiding away. Please know that I am furious with them, him and his wife.'

'What did Mrs Ellis do?'

'She took his side.'

'She is his wife.'

'That shouldn't matter.'

'Not when he is wrong?'

She nodded. 'Could I write to you? Not immediately.'

'I shall have a new address soon,' he said. 'So I should have yours.'

'I am going to Norfolk today,' she said, taking out a card. 'That is the address there. And I will write mine and Mrs Ellis's on the back.' She handed it to him. 'Thank you. I will hope to see you again. Goodbye, Mr Feaver. Goodbye.'

'Come on,' Frank said uneasily, once they could no longer hear her boots on the hallway. 'I thought she'd never stop. I don't like hanging about here.'

It was even worse, leaving, than it had been to enter. John felt that they must advertise on themselves some taint or sign of criminality, that someone would surely stop them and ascertain what trial they had to do with – a man did drift near them, and John took a great stride out of his way. They both walked quickly, Frank with his hands driven into his pockets and his head bowed, as though he were trying to get out of bad weather.

Outside, the weather was bad. Once they were some distance down the street Frank stopped and took off his hat, tilting his forehead to the threatening sky, blinking rapidly.

'What is it?' John said impatiently. He had an unreasoning desire to walk faster, to get further away.

'Relief,' Frank said, blinking still.

John set off walking again. Frank jogged to catch him up, his hat resistant in his hand and his hair flopping. Spots of rain were beginning to fall. 'Don't be like that,' Frank said, water appearing on his chin. 'You're relieved. Doesn't mean it's what you wanted, you're just relieved.'

John made no reply. They walked, fitting in the cracks and gaps that opened between the men and women on the street. Beneath buildings black as slate, unblemished stone showing like rubbings of chalk. With the traffic, that surged and stalled, slipped and rushed; that strained and rolled and chanted and drummed, that clapped and dashed its rhythms on the road. The spots of rain became bigger, ungainly and splashing, and then steepened into a downpour, that sent the men and women hastening over the pavement, umbrellas rising moistly like toadstools; that shined the traffic; that stained shopfronts and stirred the mud and raced it into the gutter; that poured from the awning under which they stood for shelter, crowded by wet rueful faces. John tried to distinguish the smell of Frank among the others – he was aware of the side of his ear, of the line where his wrist disappeared into his pocket. He slipped secretly into these places. At last the rain spent itself and lay quivering on the road, broken and scattered by the travelling wheels.

They began to walk again, to the house in Paddington, through the black streets, under the splitting sky, with the march of the traffic – in their freedom. For this was the element in which they moved; Frank eagerly, John with uneager acceptance. It was palpable, what Frank called relief: the flattening of the great thick walls, jagged with glass, that had forced them to the Old Bailey, the spaciousness opened up. But it was a featureless landscape, disturbingly empty. There were lonely figures picked out on it – Catherine, his children, Frank – and a pressure, a pulse of threat, like a shadow moving behind glass. It was a travesty of freedom, laid out as a trap.

'That woman, Miss Britell – she mentioned a speech,' Frank said.

'I spoke at the dinner for Higgs.'

Frank slowly shook his head. 'You gave yourself away, didn't you?'

John looked ahead of him, at the jumble of persons and wants. 'I have given it all away. There is nothing to show for any of it.'

'You aren't going back to how it was before,' Frank said.

They walked. The fallen rain took on shapes, burbled and crept. Frank whistled softly, his hands in his pockets. The sky was still split, the great mass of cloud slowly tearing, so that the day had a suppressed brightness. They turned onto their street, walked to the street lamp opposite the house. The house rose tall and stark and empty; they stopped at the gate and looked up at its frightening familiar ghost.

'What must I do now?' John said.

'I'd like you to meet my mother,' Frank replied.

XXXVIII

Henry was in the garden.

It was too cold to be sitting outside. He was shaking in his jacket. The ground was soft and damp beneath him; fresh mud was easing onto the heels of his boots. There were grass marks hatched widely on his palms. The tree leaned in the wind to touch the wall, returned to itself. He had been sitting here yesterday when the telegram arrived, telling what had happened in the court. It had been a long day.

Edith came out now. He watched her cross the grass.

They took the measure of each other, him holding tightly to his knees. The tree scraped on the wall and Edith turned to look at it, the wind sending a ripple over her hair. She turned back and said, 'Shall we go for a walk?'

They walked out across the salt marshes, on the raised winding paths, striped green, tawny yellow, brown. The sky everywhere extended, seemed to travel out, far beyond the clean, flat edge of the land. Clouds rode in it like waves, black-bellied, curved, rising and thinning to spray. Birds beat against the wind and were deadened by it, suspended on its crest, before falling back into life, beating on. The reeds whispered of the sea. The sea, when they reached it, was flat, conquered by the advance of the sky.

'Do you regret it?' Edith asked, as they looked.

'Which part?'

'Not going to court, I meant. Which part do you regret? Do you wish you had never written it?'

He had been considering. 'It was bad luck – Wilde, Owen, Higgs. Wilde especially. It might none of it have happened.'

'And then?'

'And then the book would have been free to do its work in the world.' The sea crackled in doubt. 'I cannot regret writing it, and I cannot regret not going to court, for the same reason. The work alone matters. I must go on writing about sex. It is the secret. But I do not think I can publish in England again.'

Edith's face wrinkled. 'It is a stupid old country.' A flock of birds struggled overhead, dabbing the beach with shadow. 'You are brave, Henry.'

His lips inclined in a smile. 'I do not think so.'

'What else is it then?'

'It is simply necessary to ignore the present, and its obstacles.'

She stared at the sea. 'What a pity we cannot all join you there, in the future.'

'We are there already,' he said. 'The New Life.'

The sea crackled. And then they noticed – who was it that noticed first? – a figure, wind-blown, arm raised, fabric flapping. Angelica, in a dress of sheerest blue, approaching across the sands.

Afterword

The New Life is a fiction, but some of its characters and events have historical analogues. John and Henry are loosely based, respectively, on John Addington Symonds (1840–1893) and Havelock Ellis (1859–1939), who in the early 1890s wrote a book together called *Sexual Inversion*. This book did indeed run into trouble with the law in the wake of Oscar Wilde's imprisonment, though in reality its two authors never met, and the book was published only in 1897, four years after Symonds's death. Symonds was married to a woman called Catherine (1837–1913); Ellis was married to a writer called Edith (1861–1916), who was attracted to other women. Those familiar with these two men and their biographies will recognise certain other details in this book, but, if they are expecting any significant fidelity to the facts, much of it will surprise them. Readers can get an easy sense of the scale of my departures if they recall that Symonds died in 1893, and that this novel begins in 1894.

With the iconoclastic enthusiasm of the ex-historian, I have ruthlessly exploited and adapted materials from the past in the service of the story I wished to tell. Some of the letters between John and Henry, those that are interspersed between the chapters and which discuss the proposed book as well as contemporary theories of homosexuality, contain genuine phrases and bits of sentences belonging mainly to Symonds but once or twice to Ellis, alongside those of my own invention (all other letters in the book are entirely fictional). John's speech in Chapter 34 draws on a letter Symonds wrote to the German sexologist Richard von Krafft-Ebing in the 1880s. Several of Jack's answers to the questionnaire in Chapter 16, and all the case studies read aloud at Bow Street Magistrates' Court in Chapter 31, are adapted from the thrillingly intimate self-descriptions published in *Sexual Inversion* (John's case study is Symonds's). The quoted commentary on the Higgs case in Chapter 33 is adapted from commentary on the trial of the man known to history as George Bedborough (real name George Higgs) in 1898. All of the questions recurring through Chapter 21, with two exceptions, were posed to Oscar Wilde during his three trials in 1895, though they are here presented non-sequentially, and in a new relation to one another. The very last questions were addressed to the judge by Wilde himself immediately after he was sentenced.

Anyone who is interested in seeing these materials in their original form, and in learning more about this remarkable historical moment, is encouraged to consult the following works, which, along with others, have allowed mine to be written: *The Memoirs of John Addington Symonds: A Critical Edition* (2016), edited by Amber K. Regis; *My Life* (1939) by Havelock Ellis; *John Addington Symonds: A Biography* (1964) and *Havelock Ellis: A Biography* (1980), both by Phyllis Grosskurth; *Sexual Inversion: A Critical Edition* (2008), edited by Ivan Crozier; *John Addington Symonds and Homosexuality: A Critical Edition of Sources* (2012), edited by Sean Brady; *John Addington Symonds: Culture and the Demon Desire* (2000), edited by John Pemble; *The Pursuit of Serenity: Havelock Ellis and the New Politics* (1999) by Chris Nottingham; 'The Superwoman: Theories of Gender and Genius in Edwardian Britain' by Lucy Delap, published in the *Historical Journal*

(2004); *The Eighteen Nineties* (1913) by Holbrook Jackson; *Edward Carpenter: A Life of Liberty and Love* (2008) by Sheila Rowbotham; *Henry Sidgwick: Eye of the Universe* (2004) by Bart Schultz; *Women at Cambridge: A Men's University – Though of a Mixed Type* (1975) by Rita McWilliams-Tullberg; *Coming Out: The Emergence of LGBT Identities in Britain from the 19th Century to the Present* (2016) by Jeffrey Weeks; *Hellenism and Homosexuality in Victorian Oxford* (1994) by Linda Dowling; *London and the Culture of Homosexuality, 1885–1914* (2003) by Matt Cook; *Strangers: Homosexual Love in the Nineteenth Century* (2003) by Graham Robb; *Nameless Offences: Homosexual Desire in the 19th Century* (2003) by H. G. Cocks; *1900: A Fin-de-Siècle Reader* (1999), edited by Mike Jay and Michael Neve; *Who Was That Man? A Present for Mr Oscar Wilde* (1988) by Neil Bartlett; *The Trials of Oscar Wilde* (1962) by H. Montgomery Hyde; *Irish Peacock and Scarlet Marquess: The Real Trial of Oscar Wilde* (2003), edited by Merlin Holland.

Notwithstanding that I have written a novel, purely with a novelist's intentions, I would be pleased if I have managed to contribute something to our store of understanding. Truths needn't always depend on facts for their expression.

Acknowledgements

I am extremely grateful to Clara Farmer at Chatto & Windus, and to Sally Howe and Nan Graham at Scribner, for believing in this novel so passionately, and for improving it in many significant ways. It is a privilege to be published by them. I would also like to thank Amanda Waters, Stephen Parker, Priya Roy, Isobel Turton, Sophie Painter, Carmella Lowkis, Jen Acton and Natalie Ramm at Chatto; and Kyle Kabel, Jaya Miceli, Dan Cuddy, Zoey Cole and Abigail Novak at Scribner. Thank you to Mary Chamberlain and Eugenie Woodhouse.

The day I first visited the offices at Rogers, Coleridge and White was the day I gave up the excuses and started to write this book. Jenny Hewson was a great encouragement at the beginning. Later, Peter Straus assumed responsibility for me. His support has been invaluable, and I am lucky in his friendship. Many thanks also to Tristan Kendrick and Sam Coates.

In early 2017, Andrew O'Hagan took me out for lunch and gave me a fizzing pep talk, which was exactly what I needed. Nicholas Spice very generously read part of an early draft, and provided excellent comments. Mary-Kay Wilmers, as the brilliant editor of the *London Review of Books*, gave me the opportunities that made me feel like a writer; most importantly, she made me a much better one. My other colleagues at the *LRB* have improved me in just about every way.

Writing is fun some of the time, but my friends are fun all of the time. I cherish you.

My school English teacher, Angela Baker, saw something in me that I was too young to see for myself. When she retired (I was twelve), I gave her a letter promising that if I ever wrote a book, I would dedicate it to her. I so wish she could have seen it.

My surpassing debt to my parents is not at all repaid with a dedication, but it'll have to do for now. They, and my siblings Paddy and Olivia, have made existence very enjoyable for me.

I have not yet found out all the ways to say I love you to Duncan Wilkins, but this book is one of them.